Sisters

of the

Veil

The
Jared Russell Series

Sisters

of the

Veil

To Robert

Happy Vacation, have
a great time.

Bryan M. Powell

Sisters of the Veil
Copyright © 2012 by Bryan Powell. All rights reserved.

Cover design by Bryan M. Powell
Interior design by Bryan M. Powell

Published in the United States of America

Political - Fiction, Adventure – Fiction, Contemporary – Fiction, Romance – Fiction, Christian – Fiction, Suspense – Fiction, Father and Son – Fiction, Women's – Fiction, CIA - Fiction
12.09.29

Endorsements

Great premise and a very timely story. Americans are concerned about the potential collision course similar to what you describe in the book. It is very obvious that you've researched the topic well. This gives credibility to the work so the reader doesn't question the viability of your book. You give the reader characters that are sympathetic, and some we don't want to like but end up caring about. A strong message of forgiveness and community comes through. I think the story helps reveal the reader's possible hidden prejudices. Overall, it's an ambitious book, and I am in awe of your work.

Well done!
Cindy Prince

It is a very relevant issue, one which probably every American feels very strongly about. I thought it was a very interesting idea to have American builders working on a mosque. And your main character has a lot of challenges to face.

In Christ,
Diane Grabau

Dedications

To my patient and supportive wife, Patty, who has traveled this journey with me and read, and re-read my stories numerous times. Who also waited up for me more nights than I can count. To my granddaughters, Reagan and Madison, who kept asking for the next book in the series.

Special Thanks

To my friends: Blake Turner and Cathy Hansard, my critic group: Azalea Dabill, Diana Grabau, Cindy Prince, Tracy Wainwright, Nancy Bolton who spent their 2012 summer reading and critiquing my manuscript.

And especially to the Lord; without Him, I could do nothing. We are indeed co-laborers in the task of spreading the gospel through stories. He is the author and finisher of my faith; I am His ready scribe.

Bryan M. Powell
February, 2013

Cast of Characters

Sheik Ibrahim El Bashera, a moderate Islamic evangelist from Lebanon – his preaching violated political thought.

Imam Ahem Mohamed Fahad, a radical Shi'ite cleric bent on carrying out a blood curse.

Sirus Rashad Hassani, a Good Samaritan who helped the wrong person.

Aisha Hassani, Sirus' wife – were it not for her quick thinking, her family would have been slaughtered.

Shirin and Ahmad Hassani, Sirus' young adult children – their hatred for America did not absolve them of the blood curse.

Jared Russell, a former marine turned architect – his mission was to build the second largest Mosque in Michigan, but God had other plans.

James Osborne, AKA Jimbo, as superintendent of construction, he was right where his superiors wanted him.

Fatemah Bashera, the daughter of Sheik Ibrahim El Bashera, having escaped to America years earlier, she embraced both cultures, but there was something which set her apart . . . it was her faith.

Prologue

Tehran, Iran

It was 2005 and Tehran was not a safe place.

What started as a small demonstration in Shahr Park soon grew to thousands of chanting protesters demonstrating against the newly elected president. Clouds of acrid smoke from tear-gas canisters wafted across the open space between police in full riot gear and the unruly mob of protesters.

"Fire!"

Government troops opened fire, and eight people fell to the pavement—dead. They were among a group of protesters demonstrating against the rigged election.

Imam Ahem Mohamed Fahad, a Shi'ite cleric, stood alongside the president and watched the scene as it unfolded from the safety of the presidential palace. He flicked off the large-screen television and sneered. "I hope that is the last we'll see of those protesters."

The president rocked back on his heels. "I doubt it."

Fahad turned and raised an eyebrow. "Oh? And why do you say that?"

The leader of Iran knit his fingers behind his back and paced. "Because I understand the nature of the protesters. Are you forgetting how we got here in the first place? They are useful idiots."

Fahad, having grown up in the same city as the president, was a staunch supporter of the new regime's president and an avid twelver. His view of the coming Al Mahdi drove him to desperate and wild conclusions. He was a dangerous man. Now he stood in the unenviable position of spiritual counselor and guide to a man with a growing arsenal of nuclear warheads at his fingertips.

"I urge you to remove all vestiges of western culture from our country, only then will the Al Mahdi come and rid this world of the Great Satan and her harlot sister the Zionists. We must free ourselves of the secular, westernized influences of the US government as well."

"Patience, my friend, first we need to solidify the opposition. If they don't fall in line, they will soon fall under the wheels of Islamic justice." The president's eyes bored a hole through his mentor.

Fahad shifted uncomfortably under his malevolent gaze. "Then we need to address the problem of dissident voices."

"Yes, that, and the infecting poison pouring into our country through the internet. We need to find ways to shut that down."

"How do you propose doing such a monumental task?" Fahad asked. He silently prayed to Allah that he would be given the Ministry of Culture and Islamic Guidance to run instead of the president's weak-willed nephew, Said el Rushdie.

"As we speak, my private police force is rounding up the opposition leaders of anti-government web sites. The problem is, when you shut one down, five more arise."

"It doesn't help that the president of the United States' latest speech sent a strong message of support for demonstrators. It has further fired-up criticism." Fahad said.

The president crossed his arms and stroked his chin staring through the window. "They should know that the nation of Iran will never kowtow to US demands, neither will we let our sovereign rights be trampled."

"Then there is the opposition from our own mullahs and clerics." Fahad paused and chose his next words carefully. "Would you authorize me to set up a commission to govern what is spoken in mosques and from the pulpits throughout Iran?"

The president stopped midstride. Though shorter than his mentor, his fiery eyes and unquenchable thirst for power made Imam Fahad's skin crawl.

"I am reluctant to make a martyr out of a Muslim cleric. Have you forgotten the lessons we've learned from the Ayatollah? The anti-Shah, anti-west messages by his supporters gained a foothold, and that is how we got here. I don't want history to repeat itself."

"But sir, it is already happening."

His leader looked up. "There is also a growing number of cults among our people. I have reports that Christianity is the fastest growing religious cult in *my* country, *your* country. I want you to arrest the adherents of Baha'i Faith, the Zionists, and Christianity. I want them tried for treason and executed."

Fahad straightened, "What about censorship of the loyal opposition?"

The president smiled. "Censorship of the *loyal opposition* as you call it, is being handled by Said el Rushdie and the Ministry of Culture and Islamic Guidance. No books or magazines which speak in opposition will be permitted to be published. No audiotapes, no movies or music which is pro-west or anti-government will be approved. Now if you have a problem with one particular cleric, then you have some latitude in pursuing him under these guidelines."

Fahad nodded, satisfied. He turned and bowed to the president. "Thank you, my friend. I believe that is all I needed to hear."

He stepped from the presidential palace and was ushered back to the dusty streets of Tehran and disappeared amidst a sea of humanity. He was a man on a mission.

Sheik Ibrahim El Bashera, a moderate Islamic evangelist from Lebanon, found eager audiences throughout Tehran. His messages of peace and cooperation drew crowds numbering in the tens of thousands, and he could see the tide turning away from the radical Muslim movement. However, he knew his messages didn't sit well with the current administration.

Knock! Knock! Knock!

Ibrahim jolted upright in bed. A knock on his hotel door at two o'clock in the morning meant one thing—death. Sensing danger by the heavy handed pounding, he quickly abandoned the idea of defending himself. He grabbed what few belongings he owned, climbed through the bathroom window and onto the roof. An instant later the door burst into splinters as someone kicked it open. Shots rang out. Fearing for his life, he leaped to the ground and dashed into the night as a hail of bullets dogged his footsteps.

His ministry in Tehran was over.

Knowing he had only seconds to spare, he ran across the alley into an abandoned building and pulled his phone from his pocket. Adrenaline raced through his veins causing his fingers to tremble. He fought to control his breathing as he waited for the call to go through to his wife in Beirut, Lebanon.

Her sleep tinged voice answered. "Hello?"

"Marla," he said between gulps of air, "sorry to wake you so early but someone just tried to kill me."

"Who?" she sputtered.

"I can't say for sure, but I have a feeling it came from someone high up in the administration."

"Why Ibrahim, why would you say that?"

He glanced over his shoulder and pushed deeper into the darkness of the building. "The government has recently enacted new laws in an attempt to silence opposing voices. I fear that if they can't capture or kill me, they might come after you in retribution. I want you to take the family and leave Lebanon. Go to the US embassy and seek asylum. Go quickly."

"Ibrahim, what are you going to do?"

Ibrahim heard footsteps, ducked behind a dumpster and lowered his voice. "Someone is coming, I must go. Get to America anyway you can. It's the only place you will be safe. I'll meet you there as soon as possible."

Five hours later Sheikh Bashera crept up to the gate of the US Embassy on Taleghani Avenue.

"Sir," Bashera spoke to one of the two armed Marines posted on either side of the iron gate. "I need to renew my visa, where do I go?"

"Follow the walk to that building. Go in and get in line." The Marine indicated with a nod. "They will take care of everything."

As Bashera walked along the well-maintained lawn, he couldn't help but notice the contrast between what was outside the gate and what was inside. Here, amidst concrete sidewalks lined with flowers and pristine water fountains, he could see the dusty streets of Tehran with its squalor and filth piling up. The eight-foot iron fence did little to keep out the stench of refuse left from weeks of neglect. He sighed deeply as the realization struck him, everything he held dear was about to be ripped from him.

He stepped up on the porch of the building dating back to the turn of the century and entered. To his surprise, there was already a long line of people all having different issues to resolve. He resigned himself to a lengthy wait and got in line. By the end of the day, he'd made his appeal. His long journey to America began. At the end of three weeks he stepped off an airplane at LaGuardia International Airport in New York. He was ready for a new beginning.

Chapter 1

Seven years later…

Crunch!

Ahem Fahad gripped the steering wheel. He had just passed the Takhti Sports Stadium, in his race to the hospital when a fuel truck struck him from behind. His car hit the guard rail with devastating force and spun. All at once his world turned upside down. The screams of his wife and daughter echoed in his ears as the car flipped on its side. Sparks from metal scraping on pavement flew through the air. The fuel tank ruptured. Within seconds, flames engulfed his car. Fahad looked over his shoulder. His ten-year-old daughter, Masala, writhed in pain in the backseat, blood soaking through her burqa. At any moment, they would all be dead.

The skidding car came to rest along the side of the highway and flopped on its ruptured tires. The face of a man appeared at the window.

Sirus Rashad Hassani watched the accident unfold and stopped to help. He leaped from his car and ran to the side of the burning vehicle. The flames licked around him like some hungry beast. He could smell the fuel burning, see the paint bubbling up on the hood and knew he had only moments to spare. He smashed the side window with his elbow and pulled Masala to safety, then returned to the driver's side. Smoke filled the driver's compartment where Fahad and his wife appeared to be unconscious. Kicking in the window, Sirus reached in and yanked open the door. He dragged Fahad to safety, then returned and freed his wife from the wreckage. A moment later the car exploded, sending a huge ball of flame into the sky.

Seeing the blood oozing through the little girl's clothes, Sirus grabbed her and rushed her to his car. He placed her in the back seat and raced in the direction of the nearest hospital. He headed northwest on Mahallah Street, slammed on his brakes as he approached the round-about. As he came out of the curve, he again cut to the right and on to Hejrat highway.

"Hold on little girl, the hospital is just a few blocks away."

She moaned.

Slowing his speed, he turned sharply and raced to the emergency ramp at Besat Hospital. He honked the horn three times, and a trauma team rushed out with a gurney.

"Poppa did—" her voice faded.

Sirus could see the back seat of his car was soaked with the little girl's blood, and the color of her face was ashen gray.

"She isn't breathing," the emergency-room nurse cried.

"Get the respirator," the trauma doctor hollered.

As the emergency team fought to save the little girl's life, a nurse pulled Sirus aside. "Sir what's your daughter's name, she is not responding." Urgency filled her voice.

Sirus stepped back and rubbed his forehead. In his haste to save her life, he had failed to ask what her name was.

"I, I don't know. Her family was involved in a terrible accident. She was bleeding badly, and I brought her here as fast as I could. She was losing so much blood."

The nurse listened, pen in hand. "What is your name and phone number? The police will need to contact you for more information," she said and handed him the clipboard.

Sirus wiped his bloody hand on his pants. It was only then he realized his fingers were shaking uncontrollably. "My name is Sirus Hassani," he said, as he scribbled his phone number on the chart.

As he handed it back, he heard the lead trauma doctor scream, "We're losing her, we need to shock her."

There was a flurry of activity and as quickly as it started, it ended.

A nurse stepped to the doctor's side and spoke softly in his ear. He turned and looked at Sirus and nodded. Pulling off his gloves, he wadded them up and stepped from the circle.

A lump formed in Sirus' throat, and though he didn't know the little girl, yet his heart ached for the pain he knew her parents would soon feel. He dreaded what he knew was coming. The look in the doctor's eyes told him all he needed to know. Then his thoughts turned to his own daughter, not much older than this little girl. It was all he could do to keep from losing control.

"Sir, I understand you don't know who that little girl is?" the doctor said.

He nodded. "Yes, that is correct. Her family was in an accident. I thought I could help by bringing her here." He looked around.

All at once the doctor became agitated. "Sir, I need you to come with me." He turned sharply and led Sirus deeper into the hospital. The doctor nodded and held out his hand directing him to a small waiting room.

"Please, step in."

Sirus followed the doctor's instruction and stepped into the room. He was immediately met by two fierce eyes, owned by the man he saved minutes ago. One look at Sirus and the man turned on him like a hungry beast. "Why did you take our daughter?" he screamed.

"Sir, I was just trying to help."

"Well you didn't, now look what you've done. I hold you responsible for her death. I curse you, curse you with a blood curse."

Sirus stood stunned, trying to make sense of it all. *Who was this man?* The sudden realization struck him like a kick in the gut. *He was Imam Ahem Fahad, spiritual councilor to the president. One of the most powerful and influential men in Iran, and he was angry with me.*

Sirus bolted and ran for his car before Fahad could call security. He slammed it in gear, leaving black, smoking tire marks as he sped from the scene. He wished this day had never started. Driving his bloodstained Fiat through the crowded streets of Tehran, he speed-dialed his home.

"Aisha, my dear, pack what clothes you can, tell Ahmad and Shirin to stuff what they can in a suitcase and come to the lobby. Oh, and grab our passports," he demanded.

"Si, what's this all about?" His wife Aisha asked, fear in her voice.

"Don't ask any questions. Hurry!"

He closed his phone, tossed it in the empty seat next to him and cursed himself for being so stupid. As he raced through the city, he turned on the radio. He couldn't believe his ears as he listened to a public service announcement.

"Be on the lookout for a white Fiat, license plate XJK 349 driven by Sirus Hassani. He is wanted in connection with the brutal killing of Imam Ahem Fahad's daughter. If you see him, do not approach him, he is extremely dangerous."

Rounding the last corner, he brought his car to a halt a half a block away from his upper class high-rise. Pulling a hood over his head, he walked into a crowd of people who gathered along the police barricade. A signal was given, and the police swarmed the building.

"What's going on?" he asked one of bystanders.

The man turned, and paled. "You, you're the one they're looking for. Here he is!" The man screamed at the top of his lungs. "The child killer, he's over here!"

Sirus stood for a moment, stunned. "No, I didn't kill any child," he said, backing away.

"Yes you did, Imam Fahad said you killed his daughter," called the man.

Sirus turned and ran for his car. As he neared it, he saw his family across the street and waved wildly.

"Follow me."

Gulping for air, the four gathered by the side of his car. Sirus looked at the bloody backseat.

Driving this car to Qom was out of the question, he thought.

"Aisha, I want you and the children to take the next taxi to the bus station and buy four tickets to Qom."

"But Si, we haven't—"

He gripped her arms and leaned in close. "Go to Shaquille's, ask no questions."

As he spoke, a taxi passed by the intersection. Sirus hailed and the driver circled back.

"Jump in, you must go. Now!" he commanded.

"But Si," Aisha protested, "aren't you coming?"

Leaning heavily on the frame of the car door, "Yes of course, I'm coming. I just have one small detail to attend to and I'll meet you there," he said in an assuring tone, though he doubted every word. "If I'm not there in an hour go without me."

"But father, how will you get there?" his twenty-year-old daughter Shirin asked. She was clearly upset at the sudden urgency in his voice.

"Don't worry, I'll be along."

"Father," Ahmad said.

"Ahmad, you are twenty-three now. You are a man. Be strong for your mother and me. Now go." He slammed the door of the taxi, and tapped two times on its roof.

The driver gunned the engine and sped away.

Sirus looked at his clothes. They were covered in blood. He pivoted and ran down an alley looking for something to change into. On the backside of the apartment complex was a line of drying clothes. Glancing around for any unwanted eyes, he grabbed them and ducked behind a trash dumpster. Within a few minutes he emerged wearing a clean tunic. After making sure he had all his personal affects, he stashed his bloody garments underneath the dumpster and set out for the bus station.

Knowing the police would be watching for him, he made a desperate decision. He caught movement to his left as a city transit bus stopped across the street. Amid honking horns and squealing brakes, Sirus dodged across the busy highway and jumped in. No sooner had he found a seat, the driver closed the doors and pulled away. Sirus cocked his head and looked back to see additional police units converging at the intersection where he stood a moment before. He was safe, but for how long?

Hiding behind an old newspaper, he listened to the conversations going on around him. He prayed to Allah that no one would ask him a question or worse yet . . . recognize him. He froze as the elderly man sitting next to him, leaned forward and asked, "Did you hear about the Imam's daughter being killed? It's on all the news stations."

Sirus held his position, praying someone else would answer. Peering over the top edge of the paper, he watched the man next to him react. It must have been the same as his when he first heard the news, a look of utter disbelief.

"They say it was a crime of opportunity. Some man snatched the little girl off the street and brutally killed her."

With a knot in his stomach, Sirus knew he had to leave Tehran and get out of Iran. As of an hour ago . . . he was a hunted man. If the Imam ever found him, he would be dead. With trembling fingers, he thumbed through his wallet. *Two hundred fifty Rial, not much to make an escape, less after I pay the bus fare.*

All at once, his phone rang. *Who could be calling me, I don't recognize the number.* With reluctance, he pushed the button. "Hello?"

"Is this the man who brought the injured child to the hospital?" the voice inquired.

Sirus froze. His mind said hang up, but instead he answered it.

"Yes?"

"This is Doctor Mohan Dasht. I am the doctor who treated her."

Sirus' heart pounded in his chest. He held his breath. He'd forgotten he'd given them his name and phone number.

"How did you find me?"

"It doesn't matter. I need you to listen. You didn't kill that little girl," the doctor said without preamble.

"I know, all I did was try to save her."

"No, you're not listening. The wounds she suffered were not from the automobile accident. We found *Christian literature* in her possession and upon closer examination, it became apparent that the girl was beaten and stabbed before the accident ever occurred."

Sirus' mind raced. "Then why are they saying I killed her?" he asked.

After an uncomfortable pause, the doctor spoke in a low tone. "Don't quote me, but I think her father, the Imam, did it and is blaming it on you."

"But sir, how does that help me? I am being accused of murder."

The doctor sighed into the phone, "Look, I have to go, I've already said too much—"

"But doctor—" the line went dead.

The bus came to a stop along a busy outdoor market. Sirus took a deep breath and approached the driver. He handed him the fare without making eye contact and stepped off the bus.

As it pulled away, Sirus realized he was standing in the midst of people going about their everyday lives as if nothing was wrong. Fathers and mothers with their children in hand mixed with older men with canes. Women stood and argued with merchants over the price of a chicken. No one seemed to care that his world had been ripped apart. All at once, he felt helpless, alone.

Movement caught his eye as a pair of police officers pushed their way through the crowd. Adrenalin shot through him. Not knowing if they'd seen him, he pressed his way forward, keeping a close eye on the officers. They hadn't seen him, but he was taking no chances.

Across the road was a caravan of Kurds. Most were on foot, some on bicycles and a few guided ox carts. Knowing the police wouldn't bother with them, he climbed into one of the carts and covered himself with some Persian carpets. Within minutes, the caravan resumed its journey.

Chapter 2

The Bus Terminal in Tehran

"But mother, why was father covered in blood?" Ahmad demanded in a respectful but urgent tone.

Aisha shrugged her shoulders. "I have no idea, and I was too frightened to ask. I fear he has done something evil, though I can't imagine what." Her black burqa flapped in the breeze as she led her children into the terminal.

She stepped up to the ticket counter and placed her elbows on it and waited. It was cold and hard to touch. Funny, how such a thing made her think of her life, cold and hard. The words of her husband rang in her head. "Get four tickets, go to Qom."

Movement caught her eye as a television flashed the images of a man running from the hospital, blood on his clothes. It was Sirus. The ticker beneath the pictures said it all.

Paralyzed at the news, Aisha couldn't believe her eyes. She wouldn't believe. They were saying awful things, accusing him of killing the daughter of Imam Ahem Fahad, counselor to the President of Iran.

She made a snap decision. Looking at the ticket agent, she said, "Call a taxi. I need to get to the airport, as quickly as possible."

Hands outstretched, Ahmad faced her, "Mother, please, what are you doing? Why are you taking us to the airport?" he asked.

"I am saving your lives. That's what I am doing, now quickly."

The taxi came to a stop at the front door of the bus terminal. "Get in, we must hurry," her voice tensed as she pushed Shirin forward.

"But mother," she pleaded. "What about father?"

"Your father is a hunted man. If he makes it here alive, it will be a miracle. Plus the Imam will have his men everywhere watching for him. They are probably waiting for him at Shaquille's house as we speak. It's the logical place to look for him since they didn't find him at home." She looked over her shoulder, fear etching her eyes. "Driver, take us to the airport as fast as possible."

Exactly thirty minutes later, they exited the cab and entered the terminal of Tehran's busy International Airport.

Aisha walked up to the ticketing counter and placed her hands on the granite. It was smooth as glass, and reminded her of the posh kitchen counter she was leaving behind. She swallowed hard and spoke with a clear voice, "I'd like two tickets to the United States of America please," she stated keeping her voice level.

Every fiber of her body cried out in protest, yet her motherly instincts knew this was the only way. Her heart pounded in her chest. The palms of her hands grew slick as she handed the ticket agent their passports and visas. She would send her children into the one place they would never think of looking. At least Ahmad and Shirin would be safe and hopefully, with Allah's blessing, they'd live to see another day.

The ticket agent's eyes widened. He looked past Aisha at Ahmad and Shirin. "Any particular place in the United States?" he asked.

Aisha blinked. She knew little of her husband's plans, only that he and his brother Shaquille had won the contract to build a large mosque in America, and had talked about going there to oversee the project. At the time, she'd put little stock in his aspirations.

"Ahmad, do you remember where your father and Uncle Shaquille were going to build the mosque?"

"Mother, you can't send us to the United States, not without father." Ahmad protested.

The pupils of her eyes burned like coals, "Yes, I can, now tell me where it is going to be built."

The air between them scintillated with electricity as Ahmad's eyes burned with defiance.

He crossed his arms, and thought. "Somewhere outside of a city called Detroit in the state of Michigan."

"Stanford, it's in some little town called Stanford," Shirin said, though clearly displeased with the sudden turn of events.

"It's a good thing your father had the wisdom to have you learn English or this would be much more difficult. Now look, you two will go on ahead of us and as soon as your father arrives, we will follow you," she said though she doubted it.

"But what will we do in America? We don't know anyone, and we don't have a work permit to get a job—" Ahmad was cut off by the wave of his mother's hand.

"I will call your uncle. He will arrange everything."

She returned her attention to the ticket agent who had watched the verbal exchange. His expression was either one of impatience or suspicion, Aisha couldn't tell and wasted no time worrying about it. "Two connecting tickets, first to Detroit, and then to Stanford, Michigan."

The caravan snaked its way through Tehran and turned southwest onto the Persian Gulf Freeway. Progress was slow, but Sirus knew it was safer than traveling in public, with his face on every television.

Buried beneath a mound of Persian rugs was not his idea of traveling in style. As the co-owner of Hassani construction, he enjoyed luxuries known only to the wealthiest few. He and his brother, Shaquille, built many of the largest mosques in Iran, Syria and Lebanon, with the latest being built in America. Since it was going to be the second largest mosque in the state of Michigan, Sirus had even planned to move to the United States to oversee its construction. That was then. Now, all that mattered to him was living long enough to see another day.

He peered through the slats of the ox cart and realized they had passed through Kashan and were nearing Qom. He thanked Allah, the merciful, for his help.

The caravan came to a halt amidst a cloud of dust. "We will camp here for the night before pushing on to Qom," the caravan leader said to the ox cart driver.

Sirus lay awake smelling the aroma of roasted mutton over an open fire and wished he could slice a piece of meat from it and eat it.

That night, while everyone slept, Sirus pushed his way out from under the carpets. *This must be what it's like for a young butterfly to emerge from its cocoon,* he thought. He stood for the first time in a day and a half and stretched. Every muscle in his body ached.

He crept past the fire pit where they had roasted dinner. The aroma of the freshly cooked meat made his mouth salivate. Desperate for something to eat, he pulled off a chuck of meat and chewed it like a ravenous animal. It wasn't much to stave off his hunger, but it would have to do. With many miles to go before reaching the safety of Shaquille's house, he knew he needed to hurry. Seeing a bicycle, he decided to borrow it and return it to its owner the next day.

As he peddled past a tent, a man with a gun stepped out and took aim.

"You there, what are you doing stealing our bicycle?"

Sirus knew it would be stupid to try and out run a bullet. He stopped and walked back to the man holding the gun, then shrugged.

"I wasn't actually stealing it. I was going to use it to get home and return it tomorrow." Sirus said and lowered his eyes to the ground.

A moment passed in which the only thing he heard was his own heart crashing against the wall of his chest. It was all he could do to control his breathing. After a tense moment, he heard a snicker. He raised his eyes and saw that three other men had joined him.

"You think fast for a city boy," the elderly man said. "Stealing is as much a crime among the Kurds as it is among the Muslims, but since you weren't actually stealing it, I forgive you."

Sirus untangled the riddle and smiled, "Thank you—I think."

The twinkle in the man's eye told him he had nothing to fear.

"So why were you not stealing my bicycle?"

Sirus put his hands in his pockets and scuffed the ground. A small puff of dirt swirled in the light wind as he thought about his options. He was desperate to see his wife, his daughter, his son. But for the moment, all he wanted was to stay alive. It was obvious that he was not going anywhere without telling the man the truth.

After his long and detailed explanation, the four men standing around him gathered a short distance away. A heated conversation ensued involving a lot of hand waving and finger poking.

The older men returned. "We have decided that you are no murderer," said the leader of the caravan.

"We heard about the little girl. We also know that you cannot believe the word of a Shi'ite Imam."

Sirus began breathing again.

"You may use the bicycle as long as you like. God be with you."

"Thank you my friends, Allah blesses you," Sirus said, then he climbed on the bicycle and with a nod, began peddling toward Qom.

The night closed in around him sending a chill through his thin covering. Not being accustomed to riding a bicycle for any amount of time, his legs burned like fire after fifteen minutes yet he pressed on. By midnight, he'd passed the city limits and entered the city. Imam Khomeini Boulevard, usually a crowded thoroughfare, was deserted. As he expected, all the shops were closed and the few restaurants that were open held little interest. The thought of seeing his wife out-weighed any other desire he may have had.

He crossed Kargar Beheshti Highway and saw a shadow move. His breath caught as two men stepped out of a doorway and out into the street. He couldn't tell if they were following him, or if they were looking for another bar. Driven by fear and the yearning to be reunited with his wife, he pushed his legs to the limit. After peddling for another ten minutes, he paused long enough at an intersection to catch his breath. He swiped his face with his sleeve to keep the sweat from running into his eyes. There, in the distance, was the bus terminal. He gritted his teeth and willed himself forward. A woman stepped out of the terminal and waved. After a long held breath, Sirus exhaled, *Aisha!* He dropped the bicycle and the two met in a warm embrace.

"What took you so long? I've waited here all day and into the night," Aisha asked as she clutched her husband.

"It's a long story, but let me say, I'll never want to see another Persian rug for the rest of my life." A weak smile parted his lips.

Pulling back, Aisha sniffed, "You smell like a goat."

Sirus bent down and picked up the bicycle and leaned it against the wall. "I feel like one too. I'll tell you about it, but since it's so late, let's grab a bite to eat and find a hotel to spend the night, and I'll call Shaquille in the morning," he said.

"The way you smell, don't you think you should get a room, take a shower and then go eat?"

"Not funny, I'm starved." It was then, he realized she was alone. "Where are Ahmad and Shirin? He asked, looking around.

Aisha's eyes searched the ground. The joy of reuniting with her husband mingled with the fear of dishonoring him. "I, I sent them to America."

The words stunned Sirus and he stood staring into the darkness. "Why would you do such a thing without consulting me?" His voice rose.

Movement caught Aisha's attention. She turned and the shadow of a man receded around a corner.

"We are being watched. We must leave." Urgency colored her voice.

A taxi came to a stop, and they got in. As the taxi pulled away from the curb, Sirus glanced over his shoulder. His heart leaped as he saw a man emerge from around the building. He knew his wife had made the right decision.

A few minutes later, the battered taxi stopped in front of a dingy restaurant in a seedy part of Qom, one of the few still open for business. Sirus thanked the driver, paid him and got out. Taking a breath of fresh air, Aisha sighed and followed him into the dimly lit restaurant.

After a Spartan dinner spent with Sirus retelling the events of the day, they stepped out of the restaurant and stood a moment under a single streetlight. By then, a light rain had drifted in and Aisha held her husband close.

All at once, a car appeared out of the shadows. A gun extended from an open window spraying bullets across the front of the building. A moment later, Sirus and Aisha dropped to the rain-soaked sidewalk, dead. A pool of crimson gathered around their bodies and mixed with the falling rain forming a river of blood. To the police, it was a case of someone being in the wrong place at the wrong time. But in reality, it was a well planned—well timed—well executed murder. Sirus and Aisha Hassani were the first to fall victim to the blood curse, but they would not the last.

Chapter 3

Seattle -Tacoma International Airport

DELAYED

Jared Russell stared at the monitor in disbelief. The word blinked back at him, mocked him like a playground bully, taunting him as if to say, "you failed."

Why God? After all I've gone through to get here just to be delayed by a lousy storm.

You know how important this appointment is. If I miss it, it could mean my job. How could I face my father? How could I face myself?

I don't understand.

Jared paced across the seating area of the Seattle-Tacoma International Airport, his movements akin to a caged panther. He stopped and looked up at the bank of monitors for the tenth time in as many minutes. An impatient sigh escaped him, frustration spilling out like lava.

"Hurry up and wait, just like the military," he muttered.

Movement caught his eye as a prim gate attendant picked up a microphone, cleared her throat and addressed the stranded travelers. "Ladies and gentlemen, we are sorry to announce that American Flight 601 departing from Seattle to Stanford, Michigan, has been delayed due to weather. Please be patient. We will update you as soon as we get more information."

Jared turned and stared through the glass wall. It was the only thing that stood between him and the violent storm. With every clap of thunder the window vibrated like the top of a drum, with every bolt of lightning it threatened to come crashing in.

"Again."

The stocky man standing next to him looked up. "What did you say?"

Jared cocked his head and cast his eyes to his right. "I said 'again.' She should have added *again* to her announcement. We've been delayed three hours, and if we don't get a flight soon the airline will need to roll out bunk beds."

"No, before that, you said something about the military. Did you serve in the armed forces?"

It was obvious to Jared the man was as bored as he was and wanted to talk. "Yes, sir, I did."

"I'm guessing you were in the Army."

Jared shook his head. "No. Why do you say that?"

The shorter man stepped back and shrugged. "Oh, I don't know, maybe your size. You're what six' three"? Six' four"? Either way, you're too big for a sub-mariner."

Jared crossed his arms and bit back a smile. "I'm six' two" and you're right. I'm too big for a sub. I couldn't stand the confined space anyhow. No, sir, I was a Marine and proud of it."

The man stuck his hands in his pockets. "Oh, a jar-head," his voice rose with interest.

Jared squared himself in front of him and put his hands on his hips. "There were times in the past when that comment would have landed you in the hospital."

The man swallowed hard. "Sorry. No offense intended."

Jared relaxed and let out a chuckle. "None taken. What I

meant to say was that some of my old friends would have jumped at the chance to get into a brawl over being called a jar-head."

"Well, all the same, I want to thank you for your service to our country." He stuck out a burly hand.

Jared straightened, towering over the shorter man with his hand outstretched. He smiled. "It was an honor to serve."

The two shook hands warmly. "The name's James Osborne, but you can call me Jimbo." His southern accent stood in stark contrast to the mid-western twang Jared had grown up hearing. "I never served in the military," he continued, "but I admire those who do. How long did you serve?"

As he spoke, a man and woman dressed in middle-eastern clothing rushed up and stared at the monitor. Their flight had been diverted, then canceled sending them and a lot of weary travelers scurrying through the concourse. Still breathing hard, the man pointed to the blinking word 'DELAYED' and relaxed. He spoke softly to the woman next to him and went and found a seat.

Jared grabbed the handle of his roll-on luggage, eased over to the seating area, and dropped into a seat next to them. The form fitting plastic chair barely able to contain his frame was cold and hard.

"I served my country for eight years," Jared replied. Not wanting to say too much.

Is it my size, my color, my military background or my imagination? . . . Why do I get the distinct feeling these people next to me don't like me sitting next to them?

All of a sudden, the wiry, dark-skinned man to his right bristled, stood, and gathered his luggage. "Come Shirin, let's get out of here," he said with a sneer.

The younger woman looked at Jared. Her eyes held pain and spoke of embarrassment, of apology. She pulled her shawl over her head and followed the man to another seat.

"I hate America and I hate Americans," seethed Ahmad. "Why did mother send us to this God-forsaken place?"

"Ahmad, we have been over and over this ground. Mother believed our lives were in danger."

"In danger of what?"

Shirin laid her hand on his. "I don't know Ahmad. All I know is that we're here now, so we might as well make the best of it. This must be Allah's will, or it wouldn't have happened."

Jared watched them from across the room. *I wonder what secrets cower behind her veil.* He returned his gaze to Jimbo. "Did I say something wrong?"

Jimbo leaned in. "No, forget them. They're just a couple of," he lowered his voice, "furin'ers, come to stir up trouble if you ask me."

Being a black man, raised in a white society, Jared was sensitive to racial innuendo. He narrowed his eyes and spoke through clenched teeth. "Look Jim, Jimbo, I served six tours of duty, Iraq and Afghanistan fighting to help those 'furin'ers' as you called them." He nodded in their direction. "They deserve freedom like you and me, and if you think about it, unless you are a Native American, we are all *furin'ers.*"

Jimbo's face reddened. "Yeah, I suppose you're right. I just hope they don't cause no trouble while they're here."

Jimbo was a no-nonsense man, a true son of the South. He came complete with all the usual prejudices and bad grammar that some might expect. His speech was peppered with double negatives but everyone he spoke with seemed to understand what he meant.

Jimbo wasn't happy with being corrected, but Jared was no stranger to taking a stand. Prejudice was nothing new to him. He grew up with it and learned how to deal with it. His faith in the Lord, and his love for the country gave him a deep appreciation for the freedom he enjoyed.

Jimbo crossed his arms over his robust chest, resting them on his belly. "How did you get interested in the Marines anyway?" attempting to restart the stalled conversation.

Taking in a relaxed breath, Jared leaned back. "I don't know. I suppose I always liked the regimented lifestyle. My momma and daddy are Christian people. Dad guided our home with a firm grip. He encouraged me to get into the ROTC in high school. After I graduated, I continued with the program in college and entered the Marines as a lieutenant." He eyed the gate. *Any movement? None.*

"How about you, Jimbo, where you from?" He attempted to guide the conversation away from himself.

"Me? I'm from Daphne, Alabama, a little town on the east side of the Mobile Bay, 'bout eleven miles from Mobile. The best shrimp in the world come from right in my own backyard," He looked around. No one was listening.

"Oh? What did you do in Mobile?" Jared probed with growing interest.

A distant look filled Jimbo's eyes and he muttered. "Uh . . . well there wasn't much going on in the building industry in Daphne, so I got on with a big company in Mobile. They move me around a lot . . . don't get no time to go back much no more."

Jared nodded as he tried to untie the knot of double negatives thrown at him.

"Is that so? Maybe I should come down and check it out. I sure do love to hunt and fish." Jared felt a common link with a fellow angler.

He started to ask another question when the gate attendant toggled the microphone, "Ladies and gentlemen, American Flight 601 has now arrived. We will begin boarding within a few minutes. Please have your tickets ready as I call out your sections."

The anxious travelers rose and began shuffling toward the gate. Even though the gate attendant tried to maintain order, the mass of people surged forward as if driven by panic or fear. Jared grabbed his military issue backpack, camouflaged wheel-on luggage, and followed the crowd. In the confusion, he noticed the young middle-eastern lady had gotten separated from the man she was with. Assuming they were married, Jared stopped and held the line in order to let the woman in. "Ma'am, go ahead and get in."

As she did so, the young man came back to where she stood. The veins of his neck strained. Jared caught the woman's eyes. She smiled briefly and her cheeks pinked.

"Shirin, this way." He grabbed her firmly by the arm and shoved her toward the gate.

A flash of anger swept over Jared like a heat wave and every muscle in his body tensed.

He reached for him, but a firm hand landed on his shoulder. "Hold on now, friend. Don't go getting involved in a domestic dispute."

Jared turned.

It was Jimbo's hand. His jaw was set, his intense gaze boring into Jared's eyes, white as lightning. Jared ground his teeth. "I can't stand to see a man mistreat a lady, that's all."

"Yeah, well, this ain't no time to be giving lessons on chivalry, buddy."

Jared stepped out of line. His breathing shallowed, the palms of his hands grew slick and the surface of his skin scintillated with a thousand pin-pricks, the result of Post-Traumatic Stress Disorder. One of the side benefits of war.

"Hey man, where are you going?" Jimbo called out after him.

"I need a break. Leave me alone."

He turned the corner and disappeared. His footsteps echoed off the cold, hard walls of the men's room as he stepped up to one of the sinks. He twisted the knob, letting the cold water splash into his cupped hands and flipping it into his face. The man looking back at him in the mirror was not the same one who left college and volunteered to serve his country. He'd left part of himself on those blood soaked streets of Iraq and Afghanistan. Sometimes he wished he had died and not his friends.

"I am going to try one more time to reach father before we take off," Ahmad said, and he pushed the redial button.

His face clouded.

"Busy?" Shirin asked.

He nodded. "I can't believe he'd be on the phone that long."

"Try calling mother or Uncle Shaquille."

Ahmad scrolled through the index file until he found the number and pushed okay. It rang.

"Hello, Uncle Shaquille? This is Ahmad." He waited.

"Yes, we are safe. Where is my father? Did mother get there yet?"

The color drained from his face and the phone slid from his hand and landed on the floor.

"What is it Ahmad? What happened?" Shirin asked, and she picked up the phone. The line went dead.

Ahmad just sat staring out the window, stone faced. He bit back tears. Shirin struggled to make sense of it. Finally he turned but the words barely squeaked out.

"Father and mother are dead."

Jared dried his face with a paper towel and walked out of the men's room. He looked at his watch, "Uh, oh, I'd better double time it or I'll miss my flight," he said to no one in particular. By the time he got in the gate, most of the passengers had already boarded. The gate attendant stood by the door; hand on her hip, looking at her watch. He pushed past her, and stepped through the first class section into the narrow passage way looking for 24A. After stuffing his carry-on luggage in the overhead bin he peered under it.

Great, exactly what I needed.

The young middle-eastern couple was sitting in seats 24B and C and they were weeping.

"What? How?" Shirin sputtered, her hand covering her gaping mouth.

Between sobs Ahmad detailed what he knew. "Father and mother met in Qom as planned but apparently he was followed . . . They never made it to Uncle Shaquille's house . . . " he gulped back his tears. "They went into a restaurant for a meal. Witnesses say as they came out a car with its windows darkened drove by and gunned them down." His words came in short jerky phrases.

Shirin buried her face in her hands, sobbing. "It is as mother feared. It's the blood curse."

"It can't be. The officials say it was a case of mistaken identity. That it has happened before at that same restaurant." Ahmad's voice came out husky, thick with emotion.

Taking a halting breath, Shirin jutted her chin out. "I don't believe it."

Jared held his position, not sure if he should intrude. Hearing the flight attendant's warning to take a seat, he reluctantly slid in next to them and fastened his seatbelt.

In an attempt to strike up a conversation, Jared leaned over and smiled. "Well, we're finally going to get out of here."

The man shrugged his shoulders and started to say something when a gentle hand lighted on his arm. "Ahmad, don't be rude."

His black eyes flashed, and he turned and said in Farsi. "Woman, if I need counsel from you, I will ask. Until then, hold your tongue."

The smoldering anger Jared had quenched in the men's room flashed to life again and burned in the pit of his stomach. His breathing grew shallow yet he spoke with a controlled tone to the woman called Shirin. "As-Salamu Alaykum."

She adjusted the shawl, wiped the tears from her eyes and returned his smile. "Peace be upon you as well."

Ahmad's gaze whipped between them and Jared sat back and smiled.

This is going to be an interesting flight.

He again tried to talk to the man she called Ahmad but he sat stone faced, cold and aloof. It was clear to Jared he wasn't interested.

Hmm, I wonder if all Muslim-Americans are as prejudiced as some non-Muslim-Americans I know.

The seat across the aisle was empty, and Jared thought about taking it, but Jimbo slid in beside him. "Well, buddy, we're finally getting' outta here." he said, after making one last trip to the sky bar.

Jared suppressed a grin. "Yes, sir, and it appears that we're heading in the same direction, too."

Jimbo stretched the seatbelt as far as it would go over his belly, snapped it in place, and let out his breath. "Is it my imagination, or are they making these things shorter?"

The flight attendant in the aisle gazed at them, turned and pushed through past Jimbo's elbow.

"Let's just say that the refreshment cart stops here," said Jared, with a wide smile.

Jimbo pulled his elbow in and leaned toward Jared. "Do you live in Stanford or do you have business there?"

Lowering his voice, Jared was reluctant to say too much, knowing the reaction he'd get. "My boss is sending me to oversee a building project."

Jimbo's expression went blank for a moment. He whispered, "That project wouldn't involve building a . . . mosque, would it?"

Jared stiffened. "As a matter of fact, yes, but how did you know?"

Before he could answer, the flight attendant demanded their attention for the usual evacuation procedures. Within minutes the engines wound up and the airplane surged forward, thrusting them back into their seats.

Chapter 4

American Flight 601

The seatbelt light blinked out, and the pilot announced that passengers could begin moving about the cabin. The flight attendant looked at the narrow gap in the aisle between Jared's and Jimbo's shoulders and cleared her throat.

Shifting to let her through, Jared gave her an apologetic look. "Sorry, ma'am, I didn't have anything to do with this seating arrangement." Glancing at Jimbo and then at the man next to him.

Ahmad's eyes tracked upward from the *Sky Mall* magazine and stared back at Jared with an icy gaze.

If looks could kill, I would be dead.

Jared turned back to Jimbo who was snoring soundly. He knuckled him on the shoulder to wake him. Jimbo's eyes widened. He yawned, and the air between them rippled with alcohol.

Good thing there was no open flame nearby.

"How'd you know about, uh, the Mosque," Jared whispered.

The moon-faced man next to him reminded Jared of his fifth-grade teacher. The man's forehead wrinkled as he thought a moment. "Well, that's why I'm going to Stanford. I'm the superintendent over the project."

Jared nearly left his seat. "You're what?"

"I'm the superintendent of the building project. And you are?"

"I'm Jared Russell, the junior partner with the Architectural Design Group of Xavier and Wright. I'm overseeing the project and they never told me about no superintendent."

How quickly he'd picked up on the man's poor grammar. Jared grimaced.

"Well Jared that was a last-minute decision. I'm sure your boss, what's his name, Xavier? He will tell you all about it."

Jared sat back and rubbed his neck. *As the project manager, whoever hired Jimbo should have informed me of the decision.* Part of his duties were to communicate with the designers and contractors, answer Requests For Information, and constantly review the blueprints as the project progressed. It was an intimidating assignment, the more he thought about it, the more he liked the idea of having someone come along side to help.

"Well, in a way, I guess I'm glad to have you aboard." Jared said. "With this being my first big project, I'll need all the help I can get."

Lowering his voice, Jimbo continued, "I understand this thing is big. I mean *really* big."

Jared let out a low whistle. "Yeah, eighty-five thousand-square-foot facility big. Between the auditorium, a library, community center and academy, it will be one of the largest of its kind in Michigan."

The lines in Jimbo's forehead deepened. "I understand it's gonna cost around ten million, and take two years to complete."

"It will be interesting to see how the community reacts to having Michigan's second largest you—know—what being built right in their back yard," Jared admitted.

"From what I gather, the city fathers of Stanford made the Organization for Islamic Development a sweet deal."

Jared's head was swimming. For this guy to be a last-minute hire, he sure knew an awful lot. The first thing he was going to do was to find out more about Jimbo, his background, his experience and why they didn't warn him about his drinking problem. He certainly couldn't have a drunk on the work site. Despite his misgivings about the Islamic Training Center's religious influences throughout the region, he was more concerned with having to build it to the correct specifications, on schedule and under budget. Now he had two more concerns—Jimbo Osborne and his drinking.

The dim lights in the coach section gave Ahmad's face an even more ominous look. After much deliberation, he said, "Just as soon as we land, we need to turn around and fly back to Iran." His parents had been murdered, he and his sister were on an aircraft headed to a strange city in a foreign and hostile country, and they knew no one. In his anger and pain, he wanted to lash out at someone, anyone.

After a pause, Shirin had gained control of her emotions and turned her chocolate eyes in his direction. "And do what? Kill the Imam?" she whispered. "You don't even know what he looks like, let alone where to find him. All you'll do is get Uncle Shaq, me and yourself killed in the process." Her words sliced the air like a hot sabre through butter.

Ahmad's hands formed into two fists. His voice grew husky. "I will hunt down the man who is responsible and kill him with my bare hands."

Jared's fitful sleep was interrupted when the aircraft touched down and rapidly decreased speed. He glanced at his watch. The illuminated hands pointed to twelve fifty-two, and he felt fatigue setting in. The halogen lights outside glowed orange in the falling rain, giving the airport a ghostly appearance. As the aircraft taxied to its gate, he glimpsed a row of Apache helicopters, part of the Southern Michigan Army Air National Guard Unit, the 185th Apache Helicopter Attack Battalion. Ahmad and Shirin appeared to be asleep and Jared craned to see around them.

"Those Apache Attack helicopters sure bring back some bad memories," Jared said, as he gazed out of the small window.

Jimbo, who'd been asleep, jolted conscious, and strained to look past him. "You say you were in Iraq and Afghanistan, did you see much action over there?"

Without hesitation, Jared faced Jimbo. "Yes sir, more than you know." He pinched his eyes closed and tried to shut out the memory, it didn't work. He lifted a sweaty hand, ran it across his face and breathed heavily. "If I could just . . . " His voice grew thick with emotion.

Ahmad roused and opened his eyes.

"Sorry if I woke you," Jared raised his hand in a placating gesture.

The young man turned, leaned close to Shirin and said something. Jared couldn't tell what but she looked over Ahmad's shoulder and scowled.

The aircraft made a gentle stop, and the seatbelt light blinked off.

Standing, Jared grappled with memories. *Could I have done something to prevent their deaths? Why did they die, and not me? Why did I live? I wasn't any better than they were.*

He spoke over his shoulder as he grabbed his carry-on luggage from the overhead storage compartment. "I left a lot of friends on the field of battle, and it still haunts me."

Jimbo's rugged face grew somber. "Man, that's some pretty heavy baggage, and I'm not referring to your carry-ons. I wish I could help you carry it, but I got no clue as to how."

Nodding, Jared added. "That's okay. My Lord Jesus gives me grace to make it through each day."

At the mention of Jesus, Ahmad bristled, released his seatbelt, and squirmed out of his seat. He pushed passed Jared, his face twisted in disgust.

What did I say this time to get him so upset? He wondered.

"Come, Shirin, let's get as far away from these infidels as possible. I hope we never cross their paths again," he glared over his shoulder and pushed past the other weary travelers.

Shirin tugged her carry-on luggage down the aisle and off the plane. Jared emerged behind them into the concourse. He could hear them bickering.

"Ahmad," Shirin called, her words coming in short bursts, "would you slow down and help me with this big one. I keep dropping everything." Her voice was drowned out by a public service announcement.

He slowed his pace long enough for her to catch up, then grabbed one of her suitcases

"Let's get to ground transportation and the car rentals and see if we can rent a vehicle," he said and set off in a half run.

Breathing hard Ahmad and Shirin arrived at the car rental counter, as a young man from India greeted them.

"Hello, how may I help you?" His buoyant voice carried an upward swing.

"We need to rent a car for a few days." Ahmad fingered his credit card.

"Will you be staying local or going across the state line?"

"What difference does that make? We need a car now."

Shirin nudged him in the ribs. "Ahmad, calm down. You won't get out of here any faster by being rude."

He glanced at her in silence, anger written on his face.

Ahmad wasted no time and completed the paperwork, and they disappeared into the night.

Chapter 5

Stanford, Michigan

The storm that pummeled the west coast targeted Michigan and swept across the nation's midsection. With the arrival of flight 601, the residents of Stanford already felt the winds of change, which not only affected the weather, but the culture.

Jimbo pushed through the narrow aisle and exited the plane. He found Jared standing, watching the young Middle-Eastern couple disappear in the crowd of travelers.

"Don't wait on me, Jared, I'm moving a bit slow," Jimbo said between breaths.

Jared shifted his backpack and yawned. "You're not getting rid of me that easily. Since you and I are partners for the next two years, you might as well get used to it."

Ten minutes later they arrived at the ground transportation counter. Jared looked at his watch. *Definitely not marine speed.*

"Do you have a vehicle that Xavier and Wright reserved for Jared Russell?"

The agent scrolled through the screen.

"Yes, we have two, one for Jared Russell and one for James Osborne."

Jared looked at Jimbo and rubbed his chin. *They certainly moved fast for him being a last-minute hire.*

"What type of car did my company lease for me?" craning his neck to see the monitor.

"A Land Rover. Is that the one you want?"

Jared nodded wearily. "Yes, I'll take it. How about the other one?"

"That's a Ford F150. Is that acceptable?" Jared knew he had the better deal, and smiled. "That's okay with me if it is with Jimbo."

With a shrug, Jimbo extended his hand. "Hand me the paper-work and let's get this show on the road."

Walking to the parking lot, Jared glanced over his shoulder. "Say Jimbo, why not save the company a few bucks and you and I share a two bedroom apartment until we can find our own places?"

His superintendent slowed his pace as he approached his vehicle. "That sounds fine with me, if you don't mind living with a slob." His face relaxed into a wry smile.

Jared rubbed the back of his muscular neck. "I know what it's like to live with slobs, I'm a former marine, remember?" He popped open the trunk and tossed in his luggage. "But first, let's find a motel and get a good night's sleep. We can start fresh in the morning and check out a few apartments."

The next day started like the previous one ended. The weather was as nasty as it had been in Seattle.

Jared thought about wearing a golf shirt and khaki slacks. When he looked out the window and saw the sky, he decided to wear a sweater and blue jeans. The advertisement for the continental breakfast bar far exceeded the reality, and Jared settled for a bowl of oatmeal and a cup of over-ripe coffee. *At least they have Wi-Fi,* he thought. He began to scan the internet for apartments. Hearing movement, he glanced up from his computer. It was Jimbo, wearing the same rumpled clothes from the day before. He came bustling through the door and headed straight for the coffee pot.

Jared gulped the last of his cup, "Morning!"

"What's so good about it?" he said, in a gravelly voice.

Jared leaned forward, poured two mugs of coffee and offered one to Jimbo. "I didn't say 'good morning.' I just said 'morning.'" He looked at his watch, "At least for another half-hour."

Jimbo stared blankly. "I swear the clock said seven-thirty when I looked at it."

"Yeah well, it may have but that was before you decided to sleep for another four hours."

"Three and a half."

Jared shook his head and resigned himself to the fact that Jimbo lived on Alabama time.

"I found a couple of two-bedroom efficiency units in an Extended-Stay Lodge not too far from the job site. How about you and I check them out first, then go to the construction site."

Jimbo took a seat across from Jared. His bleary eyes stared vacantly back at Jared. He had not slept well, Jared noted. Finally, after several swigs of the black brew, he peered over the rim of the mug at Jared. "Yeah sure, maybe by then the ground will have dried out a little."

Jared cocked his head. "Maybe by then you'll have dried out, my friend."

His superintendent leaned back, gulped the last of his coffee and eyed him. "There was a time when saying that would have landed you in the hospital."

Jared slapped his knee and laughed. "Very funny, Jimbo."

He raised his eyebrows. "It wasn't meant to be."

Jared's smile evaporated like the morning dew.

Then the lines in Jimbo's face slowly crinkled into a broad grin.

Jared let out his breath. "Well, you got me that time. Seriously, I doubt this Michigan mud will dry soon. We may need to wait until tomorrow."

"That suits me fine."

After breakfast, the two men stepped outside and headed to their vehicles. The pavement was wet, and the droplets on Jared's windshield made it look like it was weeping. He wondered if they would ever break ground.

They found a two-bedroom apartment without trouble and put down money for six months. By the time they got their luggage moved in, the day was spent.

"Hey boss, how about I go out and pick up a pizza and a six pack?"

Jared's stomach growled. It would have been easy to say yes, but he was concerned that it might destroy his testimony. "The pizza sounds good, not the beer."

"What? No beer?" Jimbo held his hands out, "I thought all marines drank."

Jared shoved his hands in his pockets and looked straight at Jimbo. "Not this one."

The two stared at each other for a moment. Jared wondered what Jimbo would say or do next.

Jimbo let out a tense breath and shook his head. "A tea-totaler, I'm living with a tea-totaler."

Jared left to find a local church to attend the coming Sunday, and Jimbo headed for the nearest bar.

Chapter 6

The Construction Shack

The annoying sound of his alarm brought Jared to an upright position. It was seven o'clock in the morning, and he was anxious to get started. It was his favorite time of the day. After a scant breakfast, Jared found his tattered Bible and opened it to Mark 10:45 and read, "For even the Son of Man did not come to be served, but to serve, and to give his life a ransom for many." The import of that passage caused him to reassess his values and goals. *Lord, help me to have the mind of Christ today and to seek ways to serve the people you place under me.* After praying over his to-do list, he finished his cold cup of coffee and slipped out of the apartment, hoping Jimbo would soon follow. He didn't.

The early morning breeze sent a chill through Jared's flannel shirt. Rubbing his arms to chase away the goose bumps, he wished he had a coat. *Another cool start, at least it's dry.* A column of condensation followed him, then disappeared in the thin air, as he walked to the Land Rover. He got in and inhaled.

The Rover was a far cry better than the clunker he left with his mom and dad back in Seattle. He loved the new-car smell.

Unfortunately, it won't stay that way coming in and out of the job site. I'll have to wash it every week. Even that won't help much.

The steering wheel was cold as ice sending a chill up his arm as he drove through Stanford. He wished he'd worn his gloves. By the time he arrived at the job site, the heater hadn't knocked out the chill, and he could still see the condensation each time he exhaled.

The newly graveled road that led to the parking lot crunched under his wheels. It was Friday and the day held much more promise than the previous. He stopped in front of the construction office, got out and began walking toward the door.

He had expected it to be a new pre-fab modular unit, but it was an older brick-ranch. Disappointed, he fished the key out of his pocket, shoved it in the lock.

Nothing.

The key wouldn't turn. Jared placed his shoulder against the door and pushed.

Crack.

He looked at the splintered door. "Well, I guess Mr. Xavier will be buying a new door for the office," he muttered, noting the absence of a security system. "We'll need that too."

After being closed up, the house smelled dank and musty. Jared opened the windows to let fresh air in and began to inspect the rooms. The main construction office which he named *The Shack,* after a book he had read, consisted of three-bedrooms, one-bath and a basement. It was far from the up-scale offices of Xavier and Wright back in Seattle. Although he was a junior partner, at least in Seattle, he had a private bathroom. *This place has only the one, and we'll all have to share it. Great!*

It was obvious to Jared that the last residents took little care of the house. It needed new carpet and a fresh coat of paint, but he needed authorization. A matter he planned to resolve the next time he called his boss.

He decided to make the living room and kitchen into the front office and waiting area. The master bedroom would be his office. The second bedroom would be the blueprint room, and the smallest bedroom would be for the filing cabinets. He took out a note pad and began writing down questions and requests to make when he called Mr. Xavier.

I've got to check on the equipment and furniture delivery. They should have been here by now.

Jared started down the rickety stairs that led to the basement. They groaned. The railing wobbled. *It looks like Jimbo and I will have to do some shoring up before someone breaks their neck. In the meantime, we'll have to use the outside entrance to get in and out.*

Upstairs, Jared took a seat on a rickety metal chair and dialed the home-office. "Mr. Xavier, please," he said to the receptionist. In a moment, he heard a click, followed by the familiar voice of his senior executive.

"Hello Jared, how was your flight?"

"It was interesting, but good. It was delayed by three hours, and I missed my appointment with the surveyors. Other than that the flight went well."

He heard Mr. Xavier shuffling some papers. "Yes, they called me and said as much. I told them to get started, and they could fill you in on the details when you got there."

Jared felt a twinge of frustration. The surveyors called his boss? They had his cell number, why didn't they call him? Jared swallowed hard and began reading off his office needs.

"Sir, the office is a small three-bedroom house with one rest room. Do you think we could get a modular unit out here? I believe we need a lot more space to conduct business. And the equipment hasn't arrived."

Mr. Xavier let out a long sigh. "Now Jared, I know about the condition of the house. It will have to do for now. I want you to focus on getting your secretaries hired, and the work-crew filled. Once those things are accomplished, maybe we can talk about these minor items. As far as the office equipment is concerned, I'll make a few phone calls."

Jared felt the implications of 'junior partner' weighing in on him like the whole ramshackled house. *It wouldn't do if* . . . He started to respond when the words, 'don't be rude,' wafted across his mind. He took a deep breath, held it and let it out.

"Oh, by the way, I met a guy on the flight who claims to be my supervisor, Jimbo Osborne, is that so?"

Jared waited for an answer . . . none came.

"Mr. Xavier? Are you there?"

"Why yes," Xavier answered. "It was a last-minute decision. It's not that we didn't think you could handle things down there." His voice sounded hollow, insincere, distant. "We just felt you might be a bit overwhelmed, this being your first big job and all. So we called our branch office in Alabama. They assured us that ol' Jimbo would be the man for the job. What do you think of him?"

Jared shifted in the aluminum chair. It squeaked. He felt the spotlight of scrutiny and bit his tongue.

"Well you know how first impressions are. I'm sure he'll work out in time. You were aware of his drinking problem?"

There was another long pause. Jared felt like a jerk for bringing it up.

"Now not all of us share the same tee-totaling, *Christian*, view as you, Jared. Give the man a chance!"

His list of other questions wadded as his fist closed. He sighed deeply and thanked his boss. He hung up just as Jimbo stepped through the open door.

Earlier that morning, Jimbo listened to Jared moving around the apartment and decided not to get in his way. He had his own routine, and it didn't involve reading the Bible. After Jared left, Jimbo fixed himself a pot of coffee and read the local newspaper, then logged onto his computer. He had a job to do, and he needed information...a lot of information. He found what he was looking for, smiled, shut his computer down and drove to the job-site.

Unfolding himself from behind the wheel of his truck, Jimbo got out and stretched. The cold air cut his throat when he inhaled causing him to cough uncontrollably. After a few minutes, he straightened and leaned against the truck. *I gotta do something about this weight.* Then he set off with measured steps and began pacing the perimeter of the property. In less than five minutes, he was breathing hard. Despite the cold, half-moons of sweat formed around his armpits. He stopped and pulled a handkerchief from his pocket and mopped his brow.

Shielding his eyes against the sun he scanned the property from side to side. Overwhelmed by the enormity of the task ahead he let out a weary sigh. Already he could see many potential pitfalls, and this was only phase one. By the time he finished walking the property, the sun had moved from low on the horizon to straight up. He needed a break. He needed a drink. His parched lips required more than Chap-Stick, but the ruse he was playing could only go so far. No booze today.

A rocky knoll occupied the center of the job site, well-marked with wooden stakes and red flags. There the assault against the Michigan landscape would begin.

It's going to be a lot of blasting. Dynamite . . . Muslims . . . that makes for an interesting combination.

Jimbo counted the paces from the frontage road to the construction shack and to the center of where the mosque would be built. *Should be enough.*

He pulled out his cell phone and dialed a number he'd committed to memory.

"Yes sir, I made it here just fine." He waited. "Yes, I understand. Keep my distance and watch." He listened to what he already knew.

"You know as big as this thing is, it's going to get messy. Someone's liable to get hurt."

His boss read off a long list of do's and don'ts.

"Yes, but who's going to watch my back?"

He nodded as his boss reiterated his instructions.

Jimbo snapped his phone shut and let out a few choice words and kept walking. He would begin as soon as the Michigan permafrost gave its permission.

He didn't like the role he would play, but he was committed to seeing it through. So what if he had to lie. As long as his boss was happy with the results, it didn't really matter whose feelings got hurt. *This is going to be a long two years.*

He stopped outside the open door of the construction office and listened.

Chapter 7

The First Church downtown Stanford, Michigan

The familiar sound of church bells rang out the hour as Jared pulled into the parking lot of the 'First Church.' He parked his Land Rover in one of the well-marked visitor parking slots, picked up his Bible and walked to the front of the church. Pulling the handle of the large wooden door he stepped in. He let his eyes adjust to the defused lighting.

"Good morning." A greeter approached and extended a warm hand. "First time here?"

"Why yes, I'm new to the city, and I thought I'd check out your church."

"Wonderful, today we have a guest speaker. We currently are between pastors. I hope you enjoy the service."

The greeter guided Jared past the welcome center and into the spacious and well-appointed sanctuary. Soft music played in the background and it was obvious that the membership took great pride in their facility. The elderly gentleman handed Jared a bulletin. "Again, it's nice to have you with us."

"Thank you," Jared sat and the man left him alone. For a moment, his thoughts wandered back to the young couple who sat next to him on the plane. They didn't seem happy. The man was abusive and angry. The woman . . . Jared couldn't forget the pained look on her face as she struggled with the luggage. He sent up a brief prayer for them with the hope that they would come to the Lord.

The organ began to play, interrupting his reverie. The robed choir assembled and began by singing the Doxology, soon the congregants scattered throughout the auditorium joined in. After a few anthems, one of the church leaders introduced the morning's speaker.

A well-dressed stately man with a slight tinge of gray at the temples rose to his feet and strode to the pulpit. He drew his message from the Beatitudes and gave an interesting commentary. His comments on loving one's enemies caused Jared to question why he was in Stanford in the first place. During the invitation, Jared wrestled with his own emotions. His mind refused to accept what his heart yearned to believe. The message was all too simple, love those who hate you. Do good to those who would kill you. It didn't make sense yet that's what the Good Book said. Jared stood, eyes pinched tight, as he argued with the Lord. All at once he felt a tug on his shirtsleeve. It was the older man who first met him.

"Sir, are you all right?" he asked in a low tone.

Jared opened his eyes and looked at the older gentleman.

"I guess I just lost track of time," he said with a weak smile.

He left the service with more questions than answers, more doubts than promises, and more uncertainty than ever before. Issues he thought he'd settled confronted him again. He needed time to think, to clear his mind, to pray.

After church, Jared spent the rest of the day painting, cleaning the carpet, and mulling over the pastor's message.

Why would God call me to build a Mosque? Doesn't He know what they teach? Their radical beliefs are already having a devastating effect around the world, and now they're taking over our country. Jared wrestled with the Lord, agonized and pleaded with Him throughout the day.

"Lord, I know You have a purpose for my life. You saved me and protected me in battle, now I'm facing an even bigger challenge. You gave me this job, but I don't understand why. Please give me wisdom and an understanding on how I'm to serve You in this situation. This isn't easy, yet despite my misgivings, this is Your will for me at this time. Give me grace to follow You and to love those who don't love You and Your ways. In Jesus' name, amen.

By the time he finished painting and praying, he was determined to live out his faith.

A distant crow greeted the morning with an ominous call as Jared cut across the parking lot in front of the construction shack. It was the start of a new week, and he took in a breath of fresh cool air and savored the moment.

He stepped into the office. The smell of new paint greeted him. It was a welcome relief to the musty odor that hit him when he first entered the house a few days ago.

He was ready to start, or so he thought.

The sound of a heavy motor laboring up the gravel driveway brought him back to the door. A large panel truck pulled up and began backing toward the steps. The driver jumped out, dropped its lift, and cocked his head.

"Here, mister." He thrust a clipboard at Jared. "Sign on the bottom, acknowledging receipt, and my guys will unload your office furniture." His shirt stretched across his belly, oscillating when he spoke.

Jared complied and handed it back. The driver gave a sharp whistle, and three unsavory men jumped out of the cab and climbed into the back of the truck. Jared was amazed at how quickly they unloaded a new copier, desks, and an assortment of office furniture.

"So much for my to-do-list," Jared said and patted the driver on his rounded shoulder. "You sure you guys won't stay and help me unpack all this?"

The burly man mopped the sweat from his brow with a dirty rag and wheezed. "Not on your life, mister. We have three other deliveries to make before day's end. You're on your own from here. Good luck."

Jared stepped back inside and plopped down on the aluminum chair.

Jimbo should be here by now, I wonder where he is. He picked up his cell phone and dialed his number.

A groggy voice answered, "Hullo?"

"Jimbo, are you still in bed, I need you down here now! We have a job to do, and I can't have you sleeping off a drunk or something."

"Is that so?"

Jared whipped around and saw Jimbo standing in the open door. A wide grin stretched over his face.

"You don't think I'd miss all this excitement by sleeping off a drunk, now do ya?"

Out foxed, Jared let the phone slide from his hand down into his lap.

"How long have you been standing out there?"

Jimbo shrugged his rounded shoulders. "Oh about long enough to hear you fussin' about your list not getting' done. Look man, we've a long road ahead of us. You gotta pace yourself or you'll burn out."

Jared couldn't help but return his partner's wide grin.

"Yeah, I guess you're right. Maybe I'm a bit too regimented. I got that from my dad."

"Well I'm sure your dad's a fine man and taught you right, but you made a good point. You're too uptight. Now relax and let's knock this job out of the way by lunch." He started ripping off the padding from the love seat.

Jared eyed his superintendent. *I think I'm going to like this guy after all.*

By mid-afternoon, they nearly completed setting up the office. They pushed through lunch and though the temperature was cool outside, both men worked up a sweat and an appetite.

"Okay, boss, why don't we get us something to eat and call it a day?" Jimbo asked.

Pushing back in his chair, Jared considered him for a moment. "I don't know. I have a ton of paperwork to prepare for tomorrow."

"What's tomorrow?"

Jared arched an eyebrow. "The day we begin hiring people to build this monstrosity. I want you here bright, early, and sober. You got that?" The silence in the room became intense . . . neither spoke . . . no one needed to.

Finally, Jimbo lifted his girth from the couch and cast a jaundiced eye in Jared's direction. In his best Irish, he said, "I'll be here as sober as a priest." Then he winked and left.

Chapter 8

The Construction Shack

The sun rose over the meadow, and the dew glistened like a field of diamonds. A hushed fog drifted across the valley, stirred by a light breeze. By Michigan's standards, it was a typical spring day. The sacred silence was broken as the wheels of Jared's vehicle crunched over the gravel road leading to the construction shack. Anxious to get started taking job applications, he thought of the first time he stood in front of his squad as a young lieutenant fresh out of college. So full of theories . . . so full of himself. It only took one firefight before reality struck him like a bullet. Having men look up to him for whom he was responsible was a sobering experience, but it prepared him for what lay ahead.

A wave of tension, exhilaration, and dread washed over him as he stepped out of his truck. He ran his hand over his face. *Lord, give me grace and send in the right people to fill these jobs.*

A few short strides across the uneven parking lot and he entered the construction shack. Knowing it would be cool that morning, he'd left the heater running. The friendly atmosphere of the office engulfed him and welcomed him in. He took a seat behind the new desk and began to review his to-do list. The front door opened and closed. He hoped it was Jimbo.

It wasn't.

Jared stepped into the waiting area. He did a double take and stared at the young Middle-eastern couple he'd encountered in the airport. Their faces spoke volumes. Jared didn't know who was more surprised.

"Uh, hello, Mr. Ahmad, is it?"

A flash of color grazed Ahmad's face. Jared thought he would bolt, but instead he stood, rigid, intransigent.

"No, Ahmad is my first name. I am Ahmad Hassani." His voice was cold and hard. He clearly was not pleased to see Jared again.

"I have been sent here to help build this Mosque to Allah."

Jared stood and sized up the smaller man. He guessed he was no more than four foot-ten and a hundred-twenty pounds at best. But from the way he said, "Allah," he knew he as a man of passion, of zeal for Islam, someone he would not want to trifle with.

"My sister Shirin also has been sent to work here, this is the will of our parents and Allah."

Jared glanced past Ahmad. Shirin stood quietly, her colorful head covering pulled tightly around her face revealing only her almond-shaped eyes; eyes that spoke of intelligence . . . and interest, and his heart skipped a beat. "This is your sister, not your wife?"

Ahmad didn't miss a beat, "Yes. That is correct, and we are here to apply for a job."

"You said your last name is Hassani. Are you related to the owner of the construction company?"

"That is correct. I am Shaquille Hassani's nephew." He was proud of that name.

"So you're Shaquille's nephew? Mr. Xavier told me that Sirus and his family were coming to oversee the construction of the project, but I had no idea . . . " Jared's voice trailed off.

"Yes sir," Ahmad answered, his tone cold as ice. "But my father will not be coming. I am coming to represent my father's interests."

Jared stood for a moment not sure how to proceed. "I guess we got off to a bad start a few days ago. What do you say we start all over again?"

Nodding, Ahmad continued, "Fine, as long as you understand we are Muslims and we are not interested in hearing about . . . "

Shirin's gentle hand touched his shoulder.

Ahmad's fiery black eyes flashed, but she stood her ground.

Jared cleared his throat. "So I suppose Mr. Hassani wants you to act as the representative for the unskilled labor force, sort of a go-between. Is that right?"

"Yes, that is correct."

"What kind of experience do you have?"

He shrugged his shoulders. "I've been working for Uncle Shaq for several years. My father wanted me to take over the company when he retired, but . . . " his voice thickened with emotion.

Jared looked up from his notepad and saw Ahmad's eyes filling with tears. He swiped his face with his sleeve.

"Is there something wrong?" Jared asked.

Ahmad stiffened. "Yes, we recently were told that our parents were gunned down as they came out of a restaurant last week-end," he said biting back the rage that burned inside of him.

"They say it was a random act of violence, but we have our doubts." The corners of Shirin's lips trembled.

"I'm truly sorry for your loss, but what makes you say you have your suspicions?" Jared said in a softer tone.

Ahmad took in a ragged breath. Shirin leaned up and whispered something in his ear.

He nodded to her and said to Jared. "There are some things better left unsaid."

The telephone rang, but Jared ignored it. "So you are here to carry on the work of your father," he said with tenderness. "That is a very honorable thing to do."

Ahmad nodded and let a moment pass before continuing. "I've been learning the building trade from the bottom up. My sister Shirin," he glanced at her, "has been working for Uncle Shaq as well. She has good computer skills and is detail oriented. She is also applying for one of the secretary positions," Ahmad said with pride.

The color of Shirin's cheeks darkened at her brother's comments.

"Let me give you both an application and let's go from there. Would that be acceptable?"

They nodded.

Jared had placed an eight-foot table and some chairs in the center of the room where applicants could sit to fill out their paperwork.

"Please, take a seat. Could I get you a cup of coffee while you fill out the applications?" He handed them a stack of papers.

"No, we are fine." Ahmad said as he picked up a pencil.

Jared couldn't help but notice the slight movement when Shirin nudged him in the ribs.

"On second thought, we will accept your kind offer, black, please."

"I'll take mine with cream and sugar," said Shirin. Ahmad's eyes widened, but he held his tongue.

Jared watched the two exchange glances and smiled to himself. He turned and filled two mugs. "I hope it's not too strong. I make it according to Marine standards."

Shirin took hers and sipped. "It's perfect." Her eyes pierced his with an interesting glint.

Thirty minutes later Shirin crossed the space between the table and Jared, holding out her application.

He took the pages from her. "Very impressive." He looked up. A pair of eyes filled with anticipation bore into his.

"Why don't you report to work tomorrow morning at eight o'clock? We'll deal with your work permits later."

Relieved, Shirin turned to her brother. "Hurry up Ahmad." Her voice rang with excitement.

He finished scribbling the answers, signed it, and pushed the application across the table. Shirin snatched it and passed it to Jared.

The handwriting was less than stellar but legible. Jared did a quick review and looked up. "I'll begin your training tomorrow at eight o'clock, is that acceptable?"

Shirin clapped her hands with excitement. "Yes, that is acceptable."

Jared offered to shake Ahmad's hand. The air crackled with tension. Ahmad stood rigid, his arms locked by his side, fists clenched.

Have I offended Ahmad again by offering my hand of friendship? Why does he just stand there staring at my hand?

A nudge from Shirin brought Ahmad's arm up mechanically. The two men shook hands, but Jared felt the heat of Ahmad's eyes. He did an about-face and nearly pushed his sister into the cold of the morning, leaving Jared to wonder if he did the right thing.

Word traveled throughout the Muslim community in Stanford. They were hiring general laborers for the mosque project. By mid-afternoon, a long line of people waited to fill out job applications. Jared let Jimbo handle the hiring of the unskilled workers while he focused on filling the secretary position.

Jared finished looking over yet another applicant's paperwork. It was poorly written, with incomplete references. Letting out a long sigh, he thought, *How many more of these will I get?*

"Thank you Miss. We'll be in touch." He dismissed her with a weak smile and waited for the next prospect.

Glancing up from a stack of papers, Jared watched another candidate lay aside her pen and stand. She approached his table with movement as graceful as a swan, took a seat, and handed him her application. The slight smile on her face did not pass his notice though she did not allow her eyes to make contact with his.

Impressed by her beautiful handwriting, Jared sat up straight read the application with interest. From her background information and experience he knew she was well educated. His pulse quickened.

"Your application looks great, Miss, uh, Miss Bashera," he said, lifting his gaze. For the first time their eyes met. Instantly, Jared knew there was something different about her. He couldn't tell what, but in those dark, olive-shaped eyes, was a light that illuminated her whole body.

Jared's heart did a double step, and his breath caught in his throat. He swallowed hard before finding his voice and even then it sounded thin, raspy. *Why? After all, he was just hiring her, not asking for a life commitment.*

"You will work well as our receptionist, Miss Bashera. Could you come back tomorrow at eight o'clock? That's when I will begin your in-service training"

Although most of her face was covered with a sheer veil that flowed down over her burqa, her countenance brightened and her eyes widened.

"Oh absolutely, I'd be honored to work on—" she paused. Her chocolate eyes scanned the room of other applicants, "—on such a noble project."

Jared's head snapped up. Something in her voice struck him as odd.

"Very good, I'll see you in the morning."

She daftly stepped from the office and disappeared.

Jared stood and came around to the front of the desk. "Excuse me, ladies, but it seems we have filled all the positions. You may finish filling out your paperwork, and we will keep them on file if you like."

A slight murmur wafted across the room as the disappointed women rose to their feet and filed out. Jared felt a twinge of guilt, glad that phase was over, and anxious to begin the next.

The next morning Jared began training both the new secretaries in company policy.

Jimbo filled his labor force and by the end of the week, they were ready to break ground . . . if the weather permitted. Jared prayed the Lord would give Michigan clear and dry conditions. But that started a new kind of complications.

The virgin soil fought every attempt to penetrate it. Even Mother Nature threw everything she had at the project as if to say, "I don't want you here." The unrelenting rains and impenetrable mud made each step a miserable job. The first couple of months tested the resolve of the whole construction team.

Chapter 9

Jared's Apartment

The lead tank rolled forward, and the sky lit up with the explosion of an IED. The impact was so massive it flipped the tank upside down, killing the team of soldiers inside. Without warning, the air was filled with a thousand scalding bullets like a swarm of killer bees. The sound of rocket-propelled grenades exploding reverberated. Machine-gun fire laced the caravan like a cat-of-nine- tails. AK-47 bullets ricocheted all around Jared's vehicle as his convoy came to a halt along the narrow streets of Kandahar. If he didn't get out of his Humvee, he was a dead man.

Out of the corner of his eye, he saw an RPG screaming toward his vehicle. It struck with deadly accuracy, killing his driver instantly. Dazed but alive Jared rolled to his right and fell to the ground. The stench of sulfur, gun powder and his own sweat quickened his senses. Adrenalin surged through his veins. Without thinking, he grabbed the unconscious staff sergeant sitting behind him and pulled him to safety. Again, the earth shook, as the blasting continued.

He covered his face. Rocks and debris rained down upon him. He attempted to lift his head, but the weight of his fallen comrade pressed him into the hot sand. He struggled to breathe as grit and dirt invaded his mouth and lungs.

Jared woke with a jolt, covered with sweat, and gasping for air. He rolled over and squinted at the clock. Three o'clock in the morning. He was in his own bed. It was another dream. The same nightmare that played over and over in his subconscious, plagued his mind, haunted his soul. *Could I have saved my driver? Why didn't I check to see if he was alive? I just left him.* Guilt dogged his heels like the Hound of the Baskervilles.

When the blasting at the job site started, so did Jared's nightmares. Every time a charge exploded, he jumped as flashbacks of combat flooded his mind. His PTSD, returned with a vengeance.

After a week, exhausted, and bleary eyed, Jared leaned against Jimbo's truck. The gaping hole created by the dynamite resembled the Grand Canyon.

"Nightmares?" Jimbo asked.

Jared shrugged.

"You taking any meds?"

He squinted in the bright sunlight. His shoulders rose and fell. "I have them but they make me feel worse."

"Can't be any worse than what you look like now."

"Maybe now that the blasting is finished, I can get a decent night's sleep."

Jimbo gave him with a crooked smile. "You look pretty bad. Why don't you call it a day? I'll handle it from here."

Pushing himself away from the truck, Jared continued, "No, I'll be all right in a few days. By the way, how's Ahmad working out? Is he keeping the men in line?"

Jimbo rubbed the stubble on his face. "Yeah, he's good. He's a real hands-on sort of guy . . . works circles around me. The only thing as I see it is that he doesn't follow OSHA rules too closely."

"That's a problem. We can't afford accidents on the job site. I don't want negative press reports or have to call Mr. Xavier with bad news. So stay on him about that. Clear?"

"Clear, boss."

Jared wanted to say more but decided not to get Jimbo riled up. Jimbo didn't like the idea of having to deal with Ahmad any more than he had to. Jared watched his superintendent trudge off in the direction of an earth-moving machine. *I sure hope he doesn't cross swords with Ahmad, no telling what will happen.*

He hiked back to the construction shack.

Fatemah's friendly smile welcomed him as he stepped into the office.

"Mr. Russell, while you were out, several people called." She handed him a stack of pink memos. His outstretched fingers inadvertently brushed the back of her hand. He expected her to recoil. She didn't.

Although Fatemah's face and delicate hands were the only things visible, her deep brown eyes captivated him. He caught himself staring.

"Uh, yes, thank you Fatemah," he stammered and strode into his office.

As the door closed, Fatemah loosened her hijab and let it fall around the back of her head. Even though she'd spent the last seven years in America and learned to appreciate much of its history and culture, she never laid aside her Islamic heritage. Whenever she stepped outside she made sure her head and face were covered. She looked over at Shirin's empty desk. I *wish she was as conscientious.*

The door swung open and Shirin returned from delivering a message to Jimbo. Her face was flushed, and she was out of breath from running.

"Why the hurry?"

"Oh," she paused and bit her thumb nail. "I forgot to put my shawl on, and I think Ahmad saw me."

Fatemah's eyes widened. "That's not good. You know how angry he gets."

A moment later, Ahmad stomped in. His heavy footfalls vibrated the hardwood floor. His face was taut with anger as he took Shirin by the arm and spun her around.

"How dare you step outside and walk on the holy ground of Allah with your head uncovered, you adulteress!" He smacked her across the face, abusive language spilled from his lips like an open sewer, his eyes wild with rage. Shirin's screams only infuriated him. "You disgraced our family and brought the wrath of Allah upon us. I should stone you myself," he swore through clenched teeth. A welt rose on her cheek.

Fatemah stood and took a step toward Shirin.

"Stay out of this," Ahmad barked, his eyes two smoldering embers.

Jared, who was on the phone, ended his conversation and came out just as Ahmad backhanded his sister. He caught Ahmad's wrist when he prepared to swing and stepped in between them.

"What are you doing? Get your hands off of her or I'll have you arrested." Jared felt the veins of his neck stand out, and his fists closed into boxing gloves.

Ahmad stepped back and glared. For a moment, Jared thought he might lunge but Jared's imposing figure loomed over him like a dark shadow.

"This was a family matter, and you have no right to interfere," Ahmad seethed.

"You have no right to strike a woman, even if she is your sister. Now back off or you'll have to deal with me." Jared's voice boomed, his chest heaved.

"I found Shirin with her head uncovered. She needed to be punished," Ahmad said in breathless defense.

Jared inhaled and let it out. He spoke slowly to make his message clear to Ahmad and anyone else who might be listening.

"This is a workplace, not your home, and I'll not tolerate your abusing Shirin or any other woman. As long as she is here, she is my employee, and you will treat her as a co-worker and give her the respect, she is due. Do I make myself clear?"

Ahmad's face darkened. His eyes shot daggers. It was clear to Jared that Ahmad was not used to being reprimanded for following his Muslim faith. The smaller man crossed his arms and said with passion. "I demand reconciliation according to Shari'ah civil law."

Jared crossed his powerful arms and stood his ground. "I know nothing of this custom, and I won't change my position because of some foreign custom. I need you to get back to work," he growled.

They stood staring at each other. Two bull rams locked in a battle of wills. After what seemed an eternity, Ahmad blinked and Jared knew he'd won this round. Ahmad let out a frustrated sigh and looked at Shirin.

"I will deal with you later." His jaw locked, and he stomped out of the construction shack.

Jared narrowed his eyes and watched Ahmad leave. In the back of Jared's mind, he knew one day he and feisty little Ahmad would have a serious falling out.

An hour later, the phone rang. Fatemah answered it. "Hello?" she paused. "Yes I'll connect him." She pushed the hold button and buzzed Jared. "Mr. Jared, I have Mr. Xavier on line one."

It was time for their weekly briefing, and Jared picked up his note pad. After a few minutes of small talk, he read his list of questions. "Sir, do you know why they needed those rooms in the lower level of the mosque? With halls and corridors going all over the place, it's like walking around in a maze at Coney Island."

"No, that's what they wanted from the get-go. We simply drew up the plans to their specifications. As I understand it, it's probably for future expansion. According to the OID, all of their religious training centers are built in a similar fashion."

Jared checked off the question. "Interesting." He paused and let out a slow breath. "Well anyway, the building is coming along on schedule. By August they will be ready to put the sub-flooring down for the upper level buildings. The skilled craftsmen can finish the lower level out as the colder weather sets in. Mosaic tile setters and Islamic art designers will start their work as soon as the concrete is cured."

"I'm pleased to hear that, Son. Now you keep up the good work and keep me posted if you need anything. Talk to you later."

"One other..." The phone cut out mid-sentence, negating his accident report. The list was growing and so was his frustration.

Jared stood and rubbed the back of his neck. He understood the term 'Son' was a term of endearment, but it still irritated him, but he let it pass. With tensions mounting between him and Ahmad, he didn't need to add his boss to the list. The pressure made every muscle of his neck, and shoulders ache. It was only three months into the project, and already he needed a break.

He got none.

Chapter 10

Jared's Apartment

A set of headlights blazed through the sheer curtains announcing the arrival of Jared's guests and they were early. After reading their websites and visiting several larger churches, he decided to visit Canaan Baptist Church, a small startup church in the heart of downtown Stanford.

A knock on the front door got Jared's attention. He made one last run through the apartment looking for any discarded garments left behind by Jimbo. For the first time, he was glad Jimbo had chosen to go out on the town.

He swung the door open, allowing the aroma of freshly brewed coffee and warm pound cake to invite the pastor and his wife inside.

"Good evening Mr. Russell." The pastor's eyes danced in the light of the open door.

"Good evening. Come in and make yourselves comfortable. Can I get you something to drink, coffee or pop?"

"We're fine, but thank you," Cynthia said and eyed her husband. He returned a sheepish grin and followed Jared into his living room and took a seat.

The pastor let his eyes wander about the apartment. "Nice place you have here, Mr. Russell."

"Please, call me Jared. It sounds like you're talking to my dad."

"Oh, sorry Jared, is your father still alive?"

He nodded, "Yes, mom is too. They live in Seattle. I hope to visit them over Thanksgiving holiday."

The pastor crossed his legs and straightened his pant cuff. "Do you and your parents stay in touch?"

Jared leaned forward, elbows on his knees. "Oh yes, we talk at least once a week."

"That's so nice of you to honor your parents like that, Jared." Mrs. Carlson observed.

"Yes, both of Cynthia's parents have passed away, and it's hard when you want to talk to them and can't." The pastor patted her knee.

Jared nodded and allowed a moment to pass.

The pastor sniffed the air and looked at Jared. "Have you been baking?"

Cynthia caught her breath, "Oh James. We just got up from the dinner table."

The pastor held his hands up in mock surrender.

"That's fine. I was expecting you, and I thought I'd try to bake a cake. I hope you don't mind being my Guinea pigs," Jared chuckled. "Relax a minute while I cut the cake. I'd like to know how it turned out."

"Well if it tastes as good as it smells, I think you have a winner."

Jared reentered the living room carrying a tray of hot coffee and pound cake. "Here it is, straight out of the oven."

He took his seat across from them and studied the pastor's face as they enjoyed the dessert. He reminded Jared of a chaplain attached to his unit in Afghanistan, a middle-aged man with a dignified air, yet he moved with the energy of a younger man.

Cynthia radiated the joy of the Lord. Her laughter reminded Jared of his momma.

"Can I get you another cup of coffee, Pastor?"

He swallowed a bite of warm pound cake and nodded."

"How about you, Mrs. Carlson?"

"No thanks. I want to sleep tonight."

Jared filled the pastor's cup and retook his seat. For the next thirty minutes, Jared enjoyed the pastor's home-spun humor before settling down to more serious issues.

"Tell us Jared, about how you came to know the Lord."

For Jared, it was refreshing to share how as a young boy, his father opened the Bible and ran his finger along the well-worn verses. To this day, Jared still could hear his momma's 'hallelujahs,' and his dad's shouts of praise when he finished praying the sinner's prayer.

He wiped his eyes with a napkin, which the pastor's wife offered. "That sentinel event changed my life, my future. I don't know where I'd be without the Lord." His voice cracked.

"That's true of all of us, my friend. Only God knows what He saved us from."

The pastor and his wife sat in silence holding hands as Jared regained his composure.

"So how did you hear about our little congregation, Jared?" Pastor Carlson asked.

"I found you online. Your website looked great. I became even more impressed as I read your doctrinal position and standards.

"Well, I had a good friend of mine build our website. If not, I'd still be back in the stone age using the newspaper to advertise."

"The people I met at church last Sunday were warm and friendly."

"I teach our folks to welcome all who the Lord brings through the doors. You never know what pain lies beneath the surface."

Jared felt the pastor's gentle gaze and wondered if the man was clairvoyant. How could he know the wounds he bore on his heart from war, from discrimination…from rejection? He took a deep breath and released it slowly.

"Brother Carlson, in the short time I've known you, I get the sense that you are a man of wisdom, the wisdom that can only come from experience."

The pastor shifted in his chair. "Yes, well, I've been in the ministry long enough to have learned to trust God's sovereignty. He knows a whole lot more than I do when it comes to leading His people. My advice to you is to obey the Lord whenever He gives you direction."

"I believe your church is a group of believers from whom I can draw strength. If you don't mind, I'd like to join this Sunday."

The pastor's face brightened. "Jared, we I—would count it a privilege to be your pastor.

Jared sat in his office reflecting on the past several months since coming to Stanford. He'd settled into a routine of being invited to someone's home for Sunday dinner nearly every week. He found he had a family away from home. The only thing that bugged him was the repeated questions as to why he was helping the Muslims take over America. A question he often asked the Lord. A question he even asked himself. At times, he wondered where all of this multiculturalism would lead.

Is it Your will for me to stay in the construction trade for the rest of my life? Is there more, something greater, something lasting You have for me to do?

He heard the telephone ring and Fatemah's professional voice. A moment later she buzzed Jared.

"Mr. Jared, you have a call on line one."

He looked at the blinking light and wished it was his dad. "Hello?"

"Hello Jared, how's it going?" The radio voice of his pastor was a welcome relief to what he'd expected.

"Oh, hi, Pastor."

"You sound stressed, anything I can do for you?"

Jared bit his lip and wished he could tell him. He wasn't having a good week—again.

"No sir. It's just another one of *those* weeks. What can I do for you?" in an attempt to change the subject.

"Jared, I know you're a busy man and this might not work for you, but we're starting a unique out-reach program called, Open Hearts, Open Hands this Saturday. Could you come out and help us?"

Jared laid his pencil down. "I'm listening. What does it involve?"

"Well, we'll set up a literature table on the sidewalk in front of our church. Offer hot coffee or cider in the colder months and bottles of cold water during the summer. Because of the crowds of shoppers that the Islamic community is drawing downtown, I am confident we will hand out a bunch of literature."

Jared looked at his calendar and circled the date of the following Saturday. "Sounds interesting. Do you think the city will mind if you do this?"

"I asked myself the same question and checked with city hall. They issued me a license signed by the mayor, giving us permission to do this, as long as we stay directly in front of our building and don't impede pedestrians."

"Pastor, I can't make it this Saturday, but maybe I can come next week."

Jared parked his Land Rover along the curb. It was a cool morning, and the sun was pushing the shadows down the street away from the church. He walked down and met the pastor.

"Good morning, Pastor. It's a beautiful day to be doing this, isn't it?"

The pastor looked up from a stack of literature he was arranging. "Good morning Jared.

Yes it is."

"How did it go your first week?"

The pastor reflected a moment and shook his head. The last seven days had been so busy. "We made many good contacts and gave the gospel several times. All of them were of the non-Muslim sort, but there were a lot of interesting conversations."

"Well, I can't wait to get started," Jared said as he helped set up the table.

As Jared met people and handed out literature, he saw the need to get the gospel to the Muslims. There were so many who walked past without stopping. His heart yearned to see his co-workers show an interest in the literature he offered.

"Pastor, do you remember my secretary, Shirin, and her brother, Ahmad, I've mentioned to you? That's them coming our direction."

The pastor finished talking with a disinterested couple.

"Good afternoon Ahmad, Shirin." Jared said cordially, and offered them a drink. They both took one, and the pastor engaged Ahmad in casual conversation.

Ahmad interrupted him mid-sentence and held up three fingers. "There are only three religions, which worship one God. Judaism, Christianity and Islam," he began.

Jared stood back and waited. He knew what was coming. On one other occasion, he'd heard Ahmad tell his co-workers this message.

"But only Allah the merciful is to be worshiped as all-supreme."

The pastor stepped back and put his hands in his pockets. "It is true. There is one God, the Bible says there is one God and one mediator between God and man, the man Christ Jesus."

Ahmad's face darkened, and he backed away. His words sputtered out like machine-gun fire. "This conversation is over."

The pastor picked up some literature and offered it to him, but Ahmad pushed the flyers back.

"How dare you try to proselytize me?" His eyes burned with passion. "That's what's wrong with you people. You are always trying to push your religion down other people's throats. I spit on your religion, on your blasphemous literature."

The pastor's eyebrows rose. He hadn't expected such a violent reaction.

In the midst of the confusion, Jared watched Shirin pick up a few pieces of literature and casually slip them under her burqa. She looked around to see if her brother noticed. He didn't, and Jared was not about to say a word.

Ahmad muttered something in Farsi and pivoted on his heels. "Come Shirin. Let's get out of here," he said, teeth clenched.

The pastor shook his head as Ahmad walked away stiff-legged.

"It's going to be a real challenge for us to win that Muslim to the Lord. He must reject years of ingrained hatred and false teaching before he can turn from darkness to light."

Jared looked at his pastor. There was deep sadness in his eyes, a grief he too bore. He knew he needed to share the gospel with his workers, but it would be an uphill battle, one that could cost him his job, possibly his life.

"When you quote the Bible, they summarily dismiss its teachings, saying the Jews have corrupted the original words of God, and only the Qur'an can be trusted."

Jared watched as another Middle-Eastern couple approached.

"Usually when a Muslim gets into one of these exchanges the next time he walks by he will avoid eye contact and ignore us. We'll have to spend a lot of our prayer on Wednesday nights interceding for our Muslim friends. There will be a real celebration when the first Muslim is courageous enough to turn from Islam to Christ." His face brightened. "Love them to Jesus, that's the only way to win anyone, really."

Jared's chest tightened as he thought of the countless numbers of people who were blinded by Islam dying and going to Hell. Tears scalded his cheeks. He turned and rubbed his face with his sleeve.

Chapter 11

Ahmad's Home

Ahmad walked into the kitchen. Shirin sat reading, and the quiet atmosphere of the Hassani home shattered with the sound of angry voices. Nosy neighbors turned down their radios and televisions. Children stopped giggling, and everyone held their breath.

"What are you doing?" Ahmad's eyes burned.

Shirin looked up from the glossy pamphlet, eyes wide. She knew her brother's temper and hatred for Christianity. She'd been on the receiving end of his rants before and feared what he might do next. Swallowing hard, she took a deep breath and rose to her feet. She'd endured enough of his abuse, of his old country thinking that Islamic women existed to serve men's passions. Even though she'd gone to a small junior college in Tehran, she'd learned to think for herself. With every ounce of courage, she glared back at him.

"You don't have any right to control what I think or read Ahmad, you're so stuck on the old ways that you—" her defense was interrupted by the back of his hand across her face.

Her head jerked to the left, and she held her palm against her cheek; it burned like coals. Blood trickled from her lip. She licked it. It tasted like iron.

"Is this your way of responding when someone disagrees with you? Are you going to lash out in violence every time you don't like what someone says?"

Her questions infuriated Ahmad. He pulled back his hand, but she caught his wrist.

"This is America," she continued. "You can't do this." She spoke in a soft voice, but her words had an edge to them.

Ahmad broke her grip and began pacing, hands on his hips. "I hate America. They are so decadent, so worldly, and now they are trying to corrupt us with their religion."

"So what's so bad about reading what other religions say? In college, they even taught a course on opposing religions."

"Woman, what has gotten into you? You're driving me crazy with this, this attitude. What would Uncle Shaquille say if he found out you were reading this trash?"

He snatched the papers from her trembling fingers and tore them into pieces. His raven eyes pierced her soul. He stood with clenched fists. "The Qur'an does not allow the freedom of thought. Allah is great, and we must obey without question. It is our responsibility to defend his honor in the face of this evil society."

Tears welled in Shirin's eyes. "What? Are you going on your own Jihad? Are you going to make a bomb and blow some innocent person to kingdom come because they are not Muslim? Is that your way of spreading Islam?"

Ahmad's jaw jutted out, breath coming in short bursts.

Shirin feared he would grab her tongue and rip it from her mouth. But she had to know, the yearning deep within her cried out for answers, for something more. And she was willing to risk it to find out what was missing from her life, from her soul. She knelt down and began to pick up the scraps of paper Ahmad threw down. Tears scalded her cheeks and fell to the floor.

"Jihad should not be spoken of lightly, woman. It means to struggle, to spread Islam either by the pen, the spoken word or by the sword. I pray five times a day that in my lifetime I will see the whole world embrace Allah and his prophet Muhammad. I forbid you to read the infidel's literature again, or you will feel the wrath of Allah at my hand. Do you understand?"

Shirin cringed knowing that to continue to resist him could endanger her life. She nodded. Fingers crossed.

It was clear which approach Ahmad had decided to take, and she feared.

Chapter 12

The Construction Shack

After a long, hot summer, the cooler weather brought a welcome relief to Jared and the sunbaked workers. He watched the men assemble for their morning briefing.

He whispered under his breath, "Look at this, Jimbo. It's like standing in Mecca in the middle of Ramadan. There are bearded Saudis, clean shaven Egyptians, Pakistanis and Afghans from every stripe. Where did they all come from?"

Jimbo crossed his arms, stroking his chin. "Ahmad told me he was putting out the word over the Internet. He invited his brothers from all over the globe to come and to pay homage to Allah."

Jared suppressed a chuckle at the irony. "As long as they are *volunteering* to pay homage to Allah, we won't have to *pay* them, right?"

"Nice try boss, but I doubt it."

"Great, I'm struggling to keep up the inventory of the building supplies flooding in. I've had to rent a warehouse just to hold all the hand-carved doors from Turkey, the bamboo flooring from the Philippines and granite from India. Now this? I want you to handle how the men get paid, to pay homage, Jimbo."

One of the volunteers caught Jared's attention. "This is a labor of love," Abdulla said, a tile setter from Lebanon. The little man's eyes glistened. His chest swelled. "I am most happy to serve Allah and to help spread Islam here in America."

Jared ground his teeth at hearing the little man talk about spreading Islam. He lowered his eyes and sighed. *Lord, help me be an effective witness to these people. They are so blinded.*

Jimbo, who was nearby, shook his head. "This ain't no labor of love, this is a job; that's all and nothin' more. Now, if you will excuse me, I got work to do." He trudged in the direction of the construction shack and the coffee.

Jared's mouth gaped open as he watched Jimbo disappear around a large earth-mover. He shoved his hands into his pockets and walked into the lower level of the mosque. He let his eyes adjust to the interior light and began his weekly inspection. The artisans were hard at work finishing the tile, custom designers making the final changes on the Middle-Eastern art decor. Persian rugs lined the walls and the bamboo floor shone. It looked more like a palace than a basement.

"Ramadan?" Mr. Xavier repeated. It was their weekly update. His boss had Jared on speaker phone. It vibrated as he spoke in rising volume. "What's that got to do with anything? They were hired to do a job. They are non-union, general laborers. They have no right to call a halt because of some foreign religious holiday."

Jared sat ram-rod straight in his chair and looked at the closed door. *I'm sure glad it's shut. I'd hate to think what Ahmad would do if he overheard Xavier's rant.*

"Sir, that may be so, but I gotta tell you, for the next ten days in September, it's the Fast of Ramadan, and the work on the mosque will come to a stand-still."

Jimbo leaned back in his seat and shook his head. "Mr. Xavier, Jimbo here. Sir, ain't nothin' I'd like better than to order the men back to work but even if I did, they might not come. They are too committed to their religious code."

"What do you mean 'religious code,' Jimbo?"

A half smile crinkled one side of Jimbo's mouth. His eyebrows lowered. "Just what it sounds like, they spend the day praying and fasting, and then at sun-down they start eating again."

"That doesn't sound like much of a commitment to me." Xavier said flatly.

"Yes, sir, and I've even heard that some of the more liberal Muslims indulge in a night-cap, if you know what I mean."

"Well we certainly can't have them coming to work drunk, now can we?" Xavier said.

Jared picked up the phone. "Sir, from what I understand they don't. The Qur'an forbids drinking alcohol. But if we force them to work on their holiday, then we might have a riot on our hands. Personally, I'd rather they didn't set foot on the job-site in order to prevent that from happening." Jared sat back and stared at Jimbo. *You have a lot of nerve to talk about drinking.*

Following Ramadan, the weather turned nasty. It rained for two weeks. Then an Arctic blast came through like a locomotive. The ground turned into soup, making it impossible for the delivery trucks to get close enough to deliver their pay-loads. One truck loaded with plumbing supplies strayed from the gravel road, and sank up to its axle.

Jimbo came out to assess the situation, took one look at the driver, and let out a few choice words about his ancestry. He called a heavy-duty wrecker to haul out the embedded truck.

"At this rate," Jimbo said relating the incident to Jared, "we won't be on schedule, unless I get permission to work these guys over-time."

"Do what you have to. I'm getting all kinds of pressure from the suits back in Seattle for falling behind."

Jimbo shrugged his shoulders. "By Thanksgiving I'll have this project back on schedule and all the loose ends tied up tighter than a turkey." He picked up his hard-hat and gloves and headed back out to the work-site.

If I know Jimbo, he'll work the guys right through Thanksgiving and not pay them time and a half.

The next day, Jared leaned over the blueprint table when someone stormed into the construction shack, their heavy boots vibrating the floor. By the sound of the abusive language he was using, Jared had no doubt who it was.

"Those good-for-nothing rag-heads." Jimbo muttered.

Jared stepped into the front office. Shirin and Fatemah's faces blanched.

Jared's eyes narrowed. His breath came fast. He stepped so close to Jimbo, he felt Jimbo's chest heaving. It didn't matter who he was or who hired him.

"How dare you talk that way. I ought to fire you on the spot."

Jimbo stepped back, teeth clenched. "You can't fire me. I work for the C, uh, Mr. Xavier hired me." He made for the door.

"I don't care who hired you. As long as you are working here you are answerable to me, and you are never to talk like that in front of these ladies again."

Jimbo lowered his eyes and scuffed the floor with his grungy boot. "My apology ladies, I didn't mean no disrespect."

He spun on his heels and stormed to his truck. Jared watched as a rooster tail of rocks and dirt followed Jimbo out of the lot.

That evening Jared returned to the apartment, dreading another confrontation. Instead, he found Jimbo's room empty, all of his belongings gone. Relief swept over Jared like a cool breeze.

He liked him, and wanted to help him, but wouldn't stand for any racism, not on his watch.

Clusters of men gathered around a concession truck to discuss the preceding day. Word spread among the work crew, Jared was a man of honor. When he approached, older men nodded and greeted him with, 'Assalamu alaikum.' Younger men smiled, and held up two fingers in a V, 'peace be to you.'

Jared's face brightened, "Wa 'alaykum assalam, and upon you be peace."

At the office, the mood appeared lighter. He took his seat and reached for the phone. Fatemah breezed in with a cup of coffee.

He nodded and took a breath. *What is that?* He sniffed again. *Hmm, I've never known her to wear perfume before.*

He dialed home.

"I know it must have been hard for you to do that Jared, but you did the right thing," his dad encouraged. Jared usually called his folks Tuesday evening, but last night, they weren't home.

"How's Jimbo this morning?" his dad asked.

"I don't know. I haven't seen him. I'm not looking forward to it."

"Well, just treat him as if nothing happened and things will blow over."

"That's easy for you to say. Ahmad still acts like he could kill me."

"I understand Son, and now you have two."

"What do you mean?"

"Now you have two people who don't like you."

The next day when Jared left work, he opened the door of his Land Rover. A piece of cardboard fell to the ground. He leaned over, picked it up.

Every muscle tensed when he read . . . "One Day."

The electrical tape used to spell the letters was generic but the blood smeared across the letters left no doubt of its intent.

Jared saw no one around, but then, he didn't expect to. *Whoever left this, made their point.* He had his suspicions.

A day later he found another note on his windshield. "Watch your back."

Jared's hands shook. He let the cardboard slip from his fingers and caught himself on the fender. The stress of dealing with the city's constant demands for paperwork, building material shortages, personal conflicts, and weather-related delays sparked his PTSD, and now this!

Chapter 13

The Presidential Palace, Tehran

The soles of Imam Fahad's sandals squeaked as he strutted across the granite floor of the presidential palace. Passing through the wide corridors, he couldn't help but notice the ornate murals on the ceiling. Looking up, he admired the portrait of Muhammad with his foot on the neck of a mighty serpent, sword drawn ready to strike off its head. Other portraits lined the walls, pictures of the Al Mahdi leading the armies of the Persians into battle against the mongrels to their west. He took pride in his ancient heritage and longed for those days to return, days when Shari'ah law spanned the known world.

A gentle breeze wafted through the open windows. The sheer curtains undulated with a rhythm known only to nature. The Imam was guided to the office of the president, flanked by two guards dressed in the ancient regalia of Persia. They saluted the two armed guards on either side of the presidential suite door. A soft knock gained him entry.

He stepped in, and the door behind him closed with a soft thud.

Behind an ornate, desk sat the President of Iran.

"I see you have been busy, my Father," the President rose to greet him.

He nodded slowly, his hands hanging loosely to his side "Yes, Allah, the merciful, has been with me."

"I have you to thank for reducing my *loyal opposition* to a mere rabble."

Fahad rocked back on his heels, and locked his hands behind his back. "Your creation of the Commission for Cultural Reform was a stroke of genius my Son. We have driven Christianity underground and closed nearly all the synagogues in Tehran."

The leader of Iran motioned to him, "Please sit, my Father."

Fahad obeyed.

"Just so you know. I didn't call you in here to revel in the past. I have an aggressive vision for the future."

The Imam sat up straight. "I'm listening."

The President stood and began to pace. "The Internet is still pouring into our nation. Despite our best efforts to stop it, it keeps seeping in like an open sewer," he paused to allow Fahad time to absorb his last statement.

"Our Supreme Leader, the Ayatollah Khamenei set up the Supreme Council of Virtual Space in March, 2012, to oversee the Internet. I have authorized the ministry of culture and information minister, the police and the Revolutionary Guard to find new ways of shutting down the Internet."

"And yet it continues to pour into our nation." The Imam observed.

"Yes, and that is where you come in, my Father."

"Oh? How so?"

The President stopped in front of Fahad, and fixed his gaze upon him. "I want you to go to America and spread Islam until Shari'ah law becomes the law of the land."

Fahad rubbed his chin, deep in thought. "As I understand it, Islam is the second largest religion in the United Kingdom, and you want me to spread it to the United States. How?"

"Mosques are popping up all over England. And we are close to getting Islamic law instituted by Parliament throughout the United Kingdom."

"But the United States is a much larger nation, with fifty states and many laws supporting Christianity."

His leader stopped pacing. "I have taken quite an interest in the spread of Islam world-wide, and we have been rather successful in taking it from Africa to Asia, from Europe to South America."

"That is true, with the exception of the United States, sir. We have not done too well there"

"That is where you come in, my Father. I want you to go to the heart of the beast and begin building a base for spreading Shari'ah Law. You should know one of the largest populations of Muslims is located in the state of Michigan. And I have it on good information that Hassani Construction has won the contract to build the second biggest mosque in an insignificant city called Stanford."

Fahad jolted up in his chair as if he had been electrocuted. "Did I hear you correctly? Did you say Hassani Construction is building the mosque?"

"Why yes. Are you familiar with the Hassani brothers?"

Fahad's eyes narrowed. "Yes, or at least I think I am. If you will remember, my daughter was murdered by a man with that same last name. His name was Sirus Hassani."

"You said *was,* did something happen to Mr. Hassani?"

He nodded. "Let's just say that Mr. Hassani won't be murdering anyone else's daughter."

The President paused and contemplated the floor. "Will it be a problem for you to go solidify our efforts to spread Islam from Stanford?"

Imam Fahad stood and faced his leader. "I would count it a privilege to spread Islam and to cause many to worship Allah, the merciful. I also have unfinished business with the Hassani family."

The President crossed his arms and looked up at him. "You know we can't just send you to America through the front door. You have been so involved in the, uh," he paused and smiled, "the elimination of our *loyal opposition*. The Masad, Interpol, the CIA and who knows who else will be watching for you."

Fahad stepped to the window and stared out. "How do you propose I go forward from here?"

The President stepped next to the Imam and gazed through the window. "Good question. We have arranged for you to travel through the United Emirates to Brazil and then up through South America and across the border into San Antonio. We have contacts who will take you to Michigan."

The Imam turned to him. "When would you like me to leave?"

"Immediately, this will be a four-month process so as to not draw attention to your movements. There is one other thing."

"Yes, my Son?"

"We will expect you to stay in constant contact with our STAVA unit and keep them apprised of your progress."

"Most certainly, I will prepare to leave now," Fahad said.

The President walked his old friend to the door. "No need to prepare, I have made all the arrangements. You leave within the hour."

Chapter 14

Ronnie's Bistro

A swirl of crispy leaves skittered across an empty parking lot as the sun warmed the thin autumn air. The sound of a lawn mower gave way to the high-pitched scream of a leaf blower. Anticipation of another winning football season grew in the hearts of the die-hards. Fall arrived in Stanford, Michigan.

"I love this weather," Fatemah said as they drove to Ronnie's Bistro. With the windows down, her colorful burqa flapped gently in the wind.

Shirin let her shawl drop to her shoulders. Her hair blew wildly.

"Aren't you concerned? Ahmad might hear about you going out with no head covering?" Fatemah asked her eyes widening.

Shirin smiled and ran her fingers through her black hair. "No, I'm not worried. These days Ahmad is angry about everything. This is nothing compared to the time he caught me reading some forbidden literature."

The lines in Fatemah's face stretched. "What kind of literature?"

Shirin turned, an impish grin on her lips, her voice barely above a whisper. "Christian Literature."

Hand to her mouth Fatemah's heart skipped a beat. "It's such a delightful day, let's eat our lunch outside on the veranda, and you can tell me all about it."

She cleared the serving line, paid the cashier and found a table for two. Shirin approached as she lifted her bowed head. She smiled to see Shirin following, balancing a cup of iced tea on top of a plastic box containing chicken salad on a croissant.

"Here, let me help you before you spill your tea all over the place."

Giving her a slight shrug, she took a seat. "Thanks, I was about to lose the whole thing." She opened the container and began eating.

Fatemah leaned in close, her elbows on the table. "Now tell me what happened. Ahmad saw you reading. Then what?" Her heart pounded with dread and expectation.

Shirin brushed a few strands of hair from the corner of her mouth, inhaled and let it out slowly. "I told him he had no right to tell me what I could or couldn't read."

Hand on her chest, Fatemah sat wide eyed. "I would like to have been a fly on the wall when you said that."

Shirin sputtered in the middle of a sip of Raspberry tea. "It may be funny now, but it wasn't then. How's your sandwich?"

"Mmm, it's out of this world. Yours?'

Shirin picked at it. "Uh, I've had better. It has too much mayonnaise."

"Here, try mine, I don't think I can finish it all anyway. So what happened next?"

A passing car went by and tooted its horn. Neither looked.

"He got rough with me . . . again." Her throat closed with emotion. "For a moment, I thought he would follow through with his threats. You have no idea how scary it is to stand up to him."

"I've seen it, remember?" Fatemah's face clouded. Tears welled in her eyes. Memories long banished to the past roared forward.

Shirin raised a quizzical eyebrow as Fatemah rooted in her purse for a tissue.

"Fatemah, what's wrong?"

She blew her nose and dabbed her eyes. "Oh Shirin, I understand all too well what you're going through. I grew up in a strict Shi'a home. Father uprooted us from Lebanon and brought us here. Even though we were living in America, he insisted that my brother and I adhere to a very narrow interpretation of Shi'a theology. He demanded complete obedience to the teachings of the Qur'an. My life was a living hell."

Shirin reached out and took her by the hand. "Oh Fatemah, I'm so sorry. I had no idea."

Taking a ragged breath, Fatemah continued, "To make matters worse, or better, depending on your perspective, when I was still in my teens, I met a girl in high school, and we became best friends. We were inseparable. There was just one problem." She paused and took another sip of tea. She lowered her voice and looked around. "She was a believer."

Shirin covered her open mouth and stifled a giggle. "A believer? In what?" Her eyes danced.

"She was a Christian. I mean a real one. She read her Bible every day, prayed and lived what she believed."

Shirin folded her hands under her chin and leaned forward. "What was it like knowing a Christian person? Was she always pushing her religion all the time?"

Fatemah smiled gently and rocked back. "No, as a matter of fact, it was me who kept bugging her. I had so many questions about her faith, about the Bible, what it was like to be raised a Christian. I even asked for a Bible and started reading it."

Shirin's fork fell from her fingers and rattled on the concrete floor. "To read the Bible is strictly forbidden. It carries a serious penalty if you get caught. Why did you do it?"

Leaning forward, she took her hand. "I had to know, Shirin. I needed to find out what the Bible said."

"Did your father catch you? What did he say? What did he do?" Shirin's voice rose an octave.

Fatemah's heart sank to the bottom of her stomach. She still remembered the pain in her father's face the day she told him she'd become a believer in Jesus.

"When I told father that I trusted Jesus as my Lord and Savior," she paused and choked back her emotions. "He nearly killed me. The beating I endured left me unable to walk for weeks."

The color drained from Shirin's face.

"Once he tried to electrocute me by throwing a radio into the swimming pool where I was swimming, but the cord came unplugged. Another time he pushed me in front of an oncoming car but the driver swerved, missing me by inches."

"Oh Fatemah, I'm so sorry. I don't know what to say. Ahmad tells me that Allah is merciful but from what I've seen, Islam is the most intolerant religion. How did you survive?"

Fatemah swallowed the last bite of her sandwich and washed it down with a swig of tea. "I ran away from home."

"Where did you go?" Shirin asked, eyes wide.

"Fortunately my friend's pastor and his wife took me in until I turned eighteen. I stayed with them until I graduated. The next fall I enrolled in Junior College, that's where I learned my secretary skills."

Shirin covered her mouth with her hand. She had not expected to learn her secret. "But why do you wear the burqa and cover your head if you are not a true Muslim any longer?"

Fidgeting with her garment, Fatemah stared at the bright-red colors. "Don't get me wrong, I love my people. I know the blindness, the emptiness, the yearning to be free that burns in so many of them. My heart goes out to them because their mullahs keep them believing that if they die a martyr, they might go to paradise. The rest of them have no sure hope…" her voice cracked.

A tear scalded her cheek. Her fingers trembled slightly as she dabbed her eyes with a napkin.

"But why not dress like these people." Shirin waved her hand in a small circle.

"Shirin, I wear a burqa out of respect for my heritage. It's how I was brought up, no matter how abusive my father was." She smiled shakily, sat back and ran her finger around the rim of her glass of tea. "Plus I have a wardrobe of the most beautiful burqas, and I hate to see them go to waste."

Shirin shook her head and let out a tense giggle. There were no more words. The space between them prickled with energy.

A cool breeze blew Fatemah's napkin like a fluttering moth to the concrete. She drew a ragged breath to relieve her nervous tension. She wanted to tell Shirin that Jesus loved her but didn't want to push. She was interested, by the eagerness in her face, her questions, and the fact that she didn't run when she mentioned the name of Jesus. Oh yes, she was interested, but something held her back.

Fatemah wondered. *Was it fear of what her brother would say? Or fear of what he would do?*

Chapter 15

Canaan Baptist Church

Jared got out of his truck and walked toward the church for the evening service. He neared the front door, and couldn't help but notice the tight circle of men around Brother Dunlop. Fred Dunlop, a tightly wound man in his fifties, was one of the more outspoken men of the church, he often complained in Sunday school about the community being taken over by the, '*moslums,*' as he called them. Jared remembered seeing the same guys on the front porch of the local hardware store swapping fishin' stories.

He caught Fred's eye as he approached and said, "Evening, Fred…gentlemen." His attempt to be cordial fell on hard ground.

The men looked around their circle and exchanged glances but said nothing. Jared passed the group, followed by Fred Dunlop's malevolent glare.

He let the moment go and stepped into the foyer. He was met with the sound of laughter, a stark difference from what he'd heard behind him. "I gotta bad feeling about him," and "he could be one of them," still echoed in his ears.

"Good evening, Jared," an elderly woman said as he strode into the lobby.

"Good evening, Miss Annabelle." Shook hands, he greeted the other women then pushed further into the auditorium.

"He's such a nice young man. I wonder why he's not married." Annabelle's friend whispered under her breath, not so softly he couldn't hear. The two women exchanged glances and followed his every move.

He turned and smiled. "I heard that."

Hand cupped over her mouth, Annabelle restrained a giggle.

With a shrug, Jared found his seat and settled in for the message.

By the time Pastor Carlson finished peeling back the shroud of secrecy surrounding Islam, Jared's fingers ached from writing notes.

Fred stood to his feet interrupting the pastor' train of thought.

"Why do we need to know all about Islam anyway? I don't care what they believe so long as they don't bother me." His voice echoed cold and harsh over the gathering.

Pastor Carlson crossed his arms. He waited until the low murmur subsided before speaking.

"Well, if we are ever going to win them to Christ, we should know about what they teach. Don't you think?"

Heads nodded. Jared waited . . . no one said a word.

The pastor returned to his notes.

"It's amazing how far Islam has spread from just a few followers. Of course, it helps if you have the added advantage of holding a sword to your enemy's throat." Laughter rippled across the room.

"Seriously folks, Muhammad was a bloodthirsty warmonger, who attacked the surrounding villages and took captive the women and children. As his power grew, so did his influence."

"Let them try that here," blurted Mr. Dunlop. "They're in America and we won't put up with that kind of insanity, will we?" He turned to see if anyone else agreed with him. A few heads nodded.

"Actually Brother Dunlop, if you let me finish. I think we will all appreciate and understand our Muslim friends better."

The man gripped the chair in front of him. His white knuckles dug into the fabric.

"I don't want to understand them; I just want them to go on back to wherever they came from." His crooked finger jabbed the air like the horn of a rhino.

Jared screwed himself around in his seat and caught his eye. One look, and Fred knew it was time for him to sit back down and did.

The pastor cleared his throat and continued. "The debate is growing as to whether Shari'ah can coexist with democracy. In essence, Shari'ah law boils down to this. It's an eye for an eye, a tooth for a tooth and a life for a life religion." He paused to take a drink of his cold coffee.

A hand shot up. "Pastor, didn't the Old Testament teach the same thing, you know an eye for an eye and all that?" Jared looked. The question came from a new believer, a former Catholic.

The pastor lifted his Bible, turned to the Beatitudes, and read. "'You have heard it said an eye for an eye, a tooth for a tooth, but I say unto you, do not resist an evil person. But whoever slaps you on your right cheek, turn the other to him also.'" He closed his Bible and laid it aside. "You see, Jesus showed us a better way. He called it the Law of Christ or the Law of Love, and it's the only way to live in a world that's gone mad with hatred and prejudice."

He let a moment pass for the people to absorb the power of the Word of God. "The important thing to know about Islam is that it is a religion of works. Outside of martyrdom, they have no confidence that they will go to paradise. Even then, they have no assurance. We have the good news that sets men free from the bondage of works. God's Word assures those who come to Him, He will not cast them out."

An elderly hand rose. "What about Shari'ah law? Do we need to be concerned about it coming here? Possibly becoming a part of our law?"

The pastor listened patiently and considered his answer. "According to the Shari'ah, it is offensive for a Muslim to have to live under democratic constitutional law. This is the reason why Muslims want to replace our laws with Shari'ah law. Islam demands that Muslims form their own political system. As far as it coming to America, folks, it is already here. Scores of Muslims are flooding into our country. The mission field is coming to us, and we need to be able to give an answer of the hope that is in us with meekness and fear." Pastor Carlson clicked out of the program and shut down his laptop.

"As I understand the Bible, God's Word is His revelation of Himself to us. He wants us to know Him and have a growing, loving relationship with Him. Not so with Allah, he needs to remain obscure, elusive and impersonal. I'm glad we can know our God and be known by Him. Friends, these people have been blinded, and must be shown God's love if they are ever going to see the truth about our God."

The pastor's eyes glistened as tears ran down his cheeks.

"The Lord is not slack concerning his promise, as some men count slackness; but is long suffering to us-ward, not willing that any should perish, but that all should come to repentance.'"

A few 'amens' bounced around like exuberant children.

He closed his Bible and stepped in front of the podium. "That will be all for this week, but let's continue our study a week from now. Until then, pray for your Muslim neighbors. Show them kindness. Take them a meal or bake them a plate of chocolate-chip cookies. Do something to reach out and show them the love of God. You can make a world of difference in their lives by being there when one of them falls on hard times. Ask them how you can pray for them and let them know when God has answered your prayers. You can be a powerful testimony of the power of the risen Christ and who knows what doors may open for you. God bless, you are dismissed."

"What you said sure was an eye opener, Pastor Carlson," Jared said as they gathered around a table of refreshments. "What did you think about Brother Dunlop and his buddies sitting there, trying to intimidate you?" Jared poured a cup of hot coffee.

The pastor held his breath for a moment.

"There are a lot of people who think the Gospel is exclusive to them. That is one of the major impediments to the spread of the gospel," he said between bites of his favorite, a large chocolate-chip cookie. "Let's you and I make a covenant together to pray for God to lead a Muslim across our paths. And for courage to share the gospel with them."

Jared felt his ears ringing. Sweat beaded on his upper lip. He knew God was pushing him out of his comfort zone. He feared the unknown.

What would they think of me proselytizing them on Allah's sacred ground? Would they all quit? Go on strike? Or worse...attack me?

Chapter 16

Jared's Apartment

"Dad, it's either Ahmad or Jimbo. It's gotta be. If not them, who? I have no idea who else it could be," Jared said, holding the phone close to his ear. "Somebody wanted to get a message across in no uncertain terms. Maybe I need to take some precautions."

A moment of silence filled the air between Stanford and Seattle. "We'll be praying for your safety, Son, until you get home. Over the Thanksgiving holiday, we can do a little gun shopping."

His father's rich voice was a source of strength and encouragement to Jared. He inhaled and let his breath out slowly.

"I'd like that very much, and I've got just the kind of hand gun in mind. I also have an idea that I want to discuss with you, but not over the phone."

"Okay Son, we'll see you soon."

Jared flew to Seattle for Thanksgiving break. Along with eating his momma's cooking, he wanted to go hunting.

Thanksgiving morning Jared and his father left before dawn anxious to get a deer in their sights. The mountain air cut through

Jared's hunting coat and chilled him to the bone. He had forgotten how cold the mountains could get and wished he had worn something heavier. However, he refused to complain. He was glad to be out in the wild, away from the pressure of work and with his father. He cherished his years at home and longed for the day when he would return. But between his dad's deteriorating health and his job, he feared that would not be happening too soon.

By the time the sun broke over the horizon, Jared was perched with his father in a deer stand drinking coffee and keeping watch for any movement down below. Conversation remained light as each scouted his side of the forest. Three hours later they emerged from the woods each lugging a buck. After field dressing them, they headed home, tired and hungry.

"That was some great shooting Dad, one shot . . . one kill." Jared said and pulled off his boots and hunting gear.

Raymond Russell, was an avid hunter and proud of it. He turned, barely able to keep a straight face.

"Yeah, well, you gotta get up pretty early in the mornin' to out shoot your ole' man. How many shots did you fire before that buck dropped, anyway?

Their banter continued all the way to the butcher shop, where they delivered their prizes. They didn't return home until nearly two o'clock.

The aroma of turkey, pumpkin pie and coffee greeted Jared. His appetite went into overdrive.

"Mmm, mmm, that's the best smell in the world. Mamma, if that food tastes half as good as it smells, I may have to abduct you and carry you back to Michigan."

"Over my dead body, Son, this here woman belongs to me," his Dad said and gave her a hug.

Flora eyed them warily. "You boys going to stand there chewing the fat? Or are y'all going to get cleaned up? Somebody's gotta cut the bird," she said, a smile in her voice.

Hearing his mother's humming in the kitchen brought Jared back to simpler days, days before the Marines, the war, and

PTSD. He looked forward to Sunday and hearing his mother sing in the choir.

"Jared, would you do the honor of cutting our Thanksgiving turkey?"

Reading his mom's question as more imperative than rhetorical, he said. "Oh absolutely. Yes ma'am, I'll get cleaned up right away. Be down in a minute."

"Momma, that must be the best turkey you've ever fixed." Jared reached for the last drumstick.

His mother stood to begin clearing the table. "Now Jared," she said, stifling a chuckle, "you say that every Thanksgiving."

"But it's true," he said, still gnawing on the end of the drumstick.

"Don't talk with your mouth full. Don't they feed you in Michigan?"

"Yes ma'am. I mean, no ma'am. I mean, I have to do my own cookin' or go out. Jimbo is even a worse cook than I am."

She eyed him suspiciously. "Don't you think it's time you found a wife?"

His father's laughter reverberated throughout the kitchen, and he slapped Jared on the back. "Here we go again, Son. Your momma wants grandchildren."

Jared hung his head. "Oh, please. Can't a guy even compliment his momma's cookin' without it turning into a plea for grandchildren? At least give me time to find Miss Right. I've only been in Stanford eight months."

Flora harrumphed and retreated. She returned for another load of dishes, studying him. "What about the sister of that Muslim guy, what's his name? Ahmad?"

Jared could feel a speech coming. "Yes, ma'am, that's his name. But he wouldn't let me anywhere close to Shirin."

His mother was not to be detoured. "Well what about the other one, the one whose name I keep forgetting?"

Raymond carried out a load of dishes and returned with two slices of pumpkin pie. He handed one to Jared.

Jared took a bite and thought about repeating his compliment, but decided to swallow and keep going.

"Fatemah is different, but I don't think she would be interested in dating her boss. She's got too much class."

With a wink, he dad continued to probe. "Come on, Son let's take up this discussion while we catch the second half of the football game."

They settled into the living room for an afternoon of football, napping, and leftovers. That night, Jared trudged up the squeaky stairs to his bedroom. Not much had changed.

The trophies, the picture of him and his coach, a plaque bearing his Eagle Scout badge. A thousand memories squeezed into a twelve by twelve space. He inhaled and let it out. *It sure is good to be home.*

Pop, pop, pop.

Three holes appeared in the center of a silhouette thirty meters away. Jared smiled. The smell of gun powder filled the air. It brought back memories both bitter and sweet.

"Man, this gun is smooth," Jared replaced the empty magazine. He squeezed off the remaining bullets in rapid succession, punching out a hole the size of a quarter. He handed the gun to his father, adjusted his eye protection and waited.

Raymond loaded, aimed and fired.

"What do you think, Dad?" Jared asked.

"That sure is a sweet gun. The only one they have in the shop, or I'd buy one too." His father's smile told him all he needed to know.

"It's exactly like the sidearm I carried in Afghanistan . . . a Beretta 9 millimeter. It fits nicely in the palm, perfectly balanced. I think I'll take it."

It was Black Friday and Jared and his father stepped out of the indoor shooting range and into the gun shop. On the way to the counter, Jared picked up a shoulder holster, an extra magazine and ammunition.

"I'll have the store ship the gun to my house. The airline would never let me take it on the plane, even in my luggage. When I get back to Michigan, I'll apply for a concealed weapon permit. It will take a few weeks before the permit goes through, but I'll feel a lot safer."

"I understand, Son, but never forget one very important thing."

"What's that?"

His father crossed his arms and stroked his chin. "Safety comes from the Lord."

"Absolutely, Dad. I know that first hand. There were just too many times I saw His hand protecting me when I should have been wounded or killed."

Jared paused. "Did I ever tell you about the time a round got me right in the chest?"

His father's eyes went wide. "No, Son. I didn't think you liked talking about the war."

Jared wiped a sweaty palm across his face. "I don't. But feeling that gun in my hand, well it . . . " Emotions coalesced in his throat like dry crackers. Refusing to either come up or go down. He swallowed hard.

"Dad, it's happening again. The dreams. The nightmares."

His father reached over and rubbed Jared's neck. "Have you been on your meds?"

"No, sir, I thought I was getting better," he said as they walked to the car.

"You won't, if you don't."

"I hate taking them. I feel so dependent, so empty. I hear some of the guys in my unit have gone to drinking and using marijuana to help them get through the day. That's not for me."

Raymond pulled the car door closed and turned to Jared. "I know, Son, but those nightmares could drive you over the brink just as badly as the booze."

Jared shifted nervously and fingered the steering wheel. "I have an idea."

His dad pushed his hat back. "Oh, and what's that?"

Jared wrinkled his forehead. "I've been looking into animal therapy."

"Animal what?"

"To put it simply, animal therapy is an alternative method of treatment to help people with nervous disorders like mine to calm down. Say, a dog. Some like horses, but I think a dog."

"What, you figure dog food is cheaper than meds?" His father grinned

"Very funny, Dad. I've got an appointment with Captain Kelly over at Fort Lawson in a half hour. He runs the K9 unit. I'm going to talk to him about getting the next military dog they rotate out of service. Remember, my job was leading a K9 unit. I sure miss having EJ at my side, she was a great dog."

"Yeah, I remember you talking about her. It's too bad about her."

Jared bit his lip not wanting to reopen an old wound. He looked out the window as the scenery changed from country to city and from city to the front gate of Fort Lawson. They neared the gate and Jared flashed his military ID. The guard saluted and waved them through. Jared wove along the road to the section designated K9 Unit.

"What do you think your work crew will do when they see you with a dog, Jared?"

He considered the question. "I hadn't thought much about it, I don't really know."

"What kind of dog do you think you'll get?"

Jared pulled a piece of paper from his pocket. "He's a German Shepherd named Raleigh, soon to retire from the bomb unit. Captain Kelly says he's a pretty big dog." Jared rubbed his head. "That could be a problem."

His father turned in his seat and looked at Jared. "How so?"

"Whoever wrote those messages might feel threatened and do something crazy."

Chapter 17

Eddy's Biscuits

Jimbo was late . . . as usual.

Since their falling-out, Jared chose to meet with his foreman away from the office in case of another outburst. He took a swig of coffee and glanced at his watch.

A shadow crossed the table, just as he picked up the phone.

"Who you gonna call? I hope not ghost busters," growled Jimbo. His mood markedly improved.

Jared squinted in the sunlight. "Is that you Jimbo or is it a *fragment* of my imagination?" A wry smile parted his lips.

"You better hope it's me, or I'm your worst nightmare." Jimbo kidded, and slid into his seat.

Jared grimaced. "Sorry ol' buddy, didn't mean to upset you. How'd your trip to Seattle go?"

Jared pushed a menu over to his partner. His face brightened. "Man, it went great. I stuffed myself with Momma's cooking, and went hunting with my Dad."

"Did you get anything?"

Jared nodded. "Yep, we both got one. Two shots, two bucks, field dressed, and delivered to the butcher before Thanksgiving dinner."

Jimbo sat staring ahead of him. "Man, I can hardly wait for my vacation. I have twenty more work days, and I'm outta here." He shifted in his chair and looked out the window.

Jared's Land Rover rumbled to a halt close to the construction shack. He got out and untied a Christmas tree that he'd bought the night before. He carried it in and set it in its stand. After several trips into the cold morning air, the floor was strewn with decorations and lights. He stood admiring his work and humming *Joy to the World.* Ahmad opened the door and came in.

"What is that ugly tree doing in here?" Ahmad's piercing voice jolted Jared to reality.

He stared back at Shirin and Ahmad. His hum faded.

"This is a violation of our law! It is an insult! We refuse to return to work until that abomination is removed."

Shirin stood in the doorway, her arms crossed. Face set in stone.

Jared leaned against the desk. His mind racing. *The more I say, the worse this situation will get.* He didn't expect such a violent reaction. *How dare these two Muslims stand here and tell him how to celebrate his American tradition. They've no right. It's only a Christmas tree, for crying out loud.* He tilted his head back and held his breath until his heart slowed. *If I keep distancing them, I'll never win their confidence.* "I understand your position. I spent years working with Islamic people in Iraq and Afghanistan, but—"

"That is of no concern of ours. We demand you remove this symbol immediately." Ahmad said, he words clipped and rapid.

The three glared at each other. Tensions mounted. Jared blinked and his shoulders slumped.

I can't let this tree stand between us, between Ahmad and Shirin and the Lord.

"You're right. The tree is a powerful symbol of the spirit of Christmas. But since it's only symbolic, I'll move it to my office."

Ahmad and Shirin looked at each other. "That will be acceptable but we refuse to set foot into your office as long as that tree is there."

A tentative truce began. Jared lifted the Christmas tree and carried it into his office. He shut the door and breathed a sigh of relief.

Fatemah stepped into the office and was nearly run over by Ahmad as he sulked away. He was still breathing hard. She turned and watched him for a moment. "What was that all about?"

Shirin perched on her desk and cocked her head toward Jared's office. "I know it was petty, but I had no idea Ahmad would over react like that. If I didn't support him," she paused, her throat constricted and her eyes filled with tears, "he would have taken it out on me when we got home."

"You can't let Ahmad run your life," Fatemah said holing her hand.

Shirin lowered her eyes. Her hand covered her mouth. "I'm just so scared of him. I love him, but he frightens me so much."

"I should have said something."

"No! That would have only made things worse. You did the right thing by keeping quiet."

Chapter 18

Four weeks later...

Jared sat behind his desk fingering the walkie-talkie, dreading what he had to do. With Jimbo on vacation, dealing with Ahmad became his responsibility. *This won't be easy.*

He squeezed the 'talk' button. "Ahmad, could you come to the construction shack?"

Static filled the air waves with an annoying crackle. A moment later, Ahmad responded, his voice barely audible over the sound of hammering and circular saws.

"Say again."

Jared repeated his request and waited.

"I'll be there in ten minutes."

Jared pushed back and stepped to the door of his office. The fragrance of the Christmas tree reached out, beckoning him to stay, but he didn't, he couldn't. A great sigh escaped his lungs.

The blueprint room offered no solace. He was going to have to face Ahmad and not lose his temper. He heard footsteps behind him and turned. "Ahmad, thanks for coming. Coffee?"

Ahmad leaned against the doorframe, arms crossed. Jared didn't like the look on his face but said nothing."

After an uncomfortable pause, Ahmad broke the silence. "Yeah sure."

Relieved, Jared slipped by him. "If I remember, you like it black with no sugar."

"What gives you that idea?"

Jared paused and reflected back to his interview.

"The day you applied for a job, I offered you a cup of coffee, and you refused but with Shirin's, uh, encouragement you accepted it." Jared shook his head and chuckled to himself. "You took it black, no sugar."

"Yeah well, the truth is, I like it with both sugar and cream and plenty of it." A weak smile cracked his hardened face.

Hmm, that's progress.

Jared stepped out of the room, returning a minute later with two mugs, and set them down on the table.

"Thanks. Now what's this about?" Ahmad cut to the heart of it.

Jared pinched the bridge of his nose and took a breath. "As you know, Jimbo left on Christmas vacation, and I am covering his job and mine this week. That's why I called you up here."

Ahmad fidgeted with his mug.

"You see, Christmas this year falls on Thursday. Under normal circumstances, I would have given the men the rest of the week off. But because you don't celebrate Christmas, I'll expect you and the men to show up for work as usual. With Jimbo gone, I am leaving you in charge, and I'll have a list of jobs for you to do. And since it isn't a holiday, you won't be getting paid extra."

Ahmad crossed his arms and glared.

Movement caught Jared's eye. Shirin stepped into the blueprint room with a message, her eyes darting from one to the other. "Mr. Jared, you have a call on line one. It's Mr. Xavier, should I put him on hold?"

"Tell him I'll be with him in a minute."

She nodded and started to back out, eyeing her brother.

He glanced back at her. It was obvious to Jared that Ahmad didn't like the idea of losing face in front of his sister. He waited until she stepped from the blueprint room.

He returned Jared's gaze. "It would be an honor to labor for Allah on his sacred ground under such conditions," he muttered.

"Good, I will leave the work order with Shirin at the end of the day." He glanced past Ahmad.

"Will that be all?" Ahmad asked, hands on his hips.

Jared peered over the rim of the coffee mug and nodded. He took a gulp and swallowed. "Yes Ahmad that will be all. Thank you."

With a smirk, Ahmad stomped from his office . . . Shirin, close at his heels.

"What was that all about?" She asked eyes wide with curiosity.

"I'll tell you later," he spat through clenched teeth.

Jared watched the animated conversation through his window, glad it was over, but concerned what might happen next.

He picked up the phone. "Hello?"

The phone line came to life. "Yes, Mr. Xavier, that's who I was with. I told him and as you guessed, he didn't like it."

Except for an occasional phone call, all was silent. Jared pushed papers around, unable to concentrate. He was such a Scrooge, forcing his men to work on Christmas and not paying them extra. Nevertheless, Ahmad forced his hand. He was just obstinate and stubborn. Had it not been for Ahmad making such a big deal over the Christmas tree, he wouldn't have had to bring it up. Finally, after several attempts, Jared scribbled a list of objectives for Ahmad, though he still felt bad.

"Shirin?"

"Yes sir." Her voice gave away nothing. "Could you come
. . . " Realizing the quarantine placed on his office, he paused.
"Never mind, I'll be right out."

Shirin looked up from a stack of papers.

Jared did a double take. *Why was Fatemah sitting at
Shirin's desk?* He suppressed the urge to pry.

"This is the list I mentioned to Ahmad. Please give it to
him when he comes in tomorrow. I'll be off until Monday."

She read the paper. Then their eyes met, and Jared couldn't
tell if he saw frustration or worry, but the task didn't set well with
her.

As he turned toward his office, he stopped. His mind
caught up to what his eyes had seen. There it was, still on
Fatemah's desk, a small branch from the Christmas tree. Or was it
Shirin's desk? The little twig formed the perfect shape of a cross. *It
must have fallen from the Christmas tree when he carried it to his
office, but no, that was weeks ago*. The sprig was fresh. And with
Shirin and Fatemah playing hop-scotch for the last week, he
couldn't tell who was sitting where. Neither woman looked up
from their work. Jared rubbed the back of his neck and continued
to his office.

*Maybe it fell off. Evergreens are evergreen after all, or
possibly someone placed it on the desk. Either way, I'm not going
to say anything. That would only make matters worse.*

By four o'clock, what started earlier as a pain in the back
of his neck, developed into a full-grown migraine. The stress from
the confrontation with Ahmad joined forces with his sleepless
nights.

"Ladies, I'm going to do one final walk-through before
heading home. This headache is killing me." A pained look crossed
Fatemah's features.

"Can I get you something for it?"

Their eyes met, and Jared's heart quickened. "No Fatemah, but thanks. Since it's so quiet this afternoon, if you and Shirin have all of your work finished, you can leave a little early."

Two sheepish grins appeared, followed by a couple of giggles.

Their suppressed laughter lightened the mood, and Jared couldn't help but laugh along with them. He grinned. "I take it you agree."

The late sun disappeared behind the distant tree-line, and the temperature dropped quickly. Cold air cut through Jared's light coat, sending a chill up his arms as he checked out the work-site. He enjoyed the interaction with the men, building relationships. By now, he knew most of them by first name, and the names of their wives and children. He passed a group of day laborers, and he thanked them for their diligent work.

By the time he returned from his rounds, the shack was empty and the lights out, except for his. He stepped in and noticed a small colorfully wrapped box on his desk. No note, no Christmas card, just a box. He shook it lightly. Something inside moved. His fingers ached to untie the ribbon but he willed himself to resist.

Someone took an extreme risk giving me this. I wonder who.

He slipped the box into his coat pocket and made for the door. Not until Christmas Day would he allow himself the pleasure of opening it. His excitement was palpable. He felt like a boy waiting for Santa to come down the chimney.

This Christmas will be one I'll remember for a long time!

Chapter 19

Jared's house

A truck door slammed outside. A moment later, the pounding of a heavy hand on his door brought Jared upright. He'd gotten home and crashed on the couch long enough to be sound asleep when a truck arrived . . . he staggered to the front door like a drunken sailor, and peeked through the peep hole hoping it wasn't Ahmad looking for trouble. It wasn't. Instead, it was a truck from Fort Lawson.

He swung the door open, and an MP saluted crisply.

"Sir, I have a delivery for you. Would you please sign here?" He produced a clipboard with a blank line at the bottom.

Bleary from the pain medication he'd taken, Jared screwed his knuckles into his eye sockets hoping to clear the cobwebs. He leaned against the door and scribbled his signature, "What am I getting?"

The MP stepped back and pulled a large German shepherd from the shadows. "I think you were expecting this." Raleigh's high-pitched signature bark pierced his clouded brain like a bullet. Jared rubbed his forehead.

Great, for once the Military is on time.

"You came all the way from Seattle just to bring me my dog?"

"How else did you expect us to get him to you, sir?"

Jared's mind was in no condition for reason. "I don't know, maybe in a military container or something."

The sergeant let out a controlled laugh. "No sir. Nothing but the best for this guy." He knelt down and rubbed his furry neck. "Plus the Captain wanted you to take delivery of Raleigh before Christmas."

Jared smiled, stuck out his hand and took the leash. "Thank you sergeant, and give my regards to Captain Kelly." He saluted.

The MP returned it, turned crisply, and strode to his vehicle.

"Well boy," Jared looked down into intelligent eyes, "looks like it's time for you and me to get better acquainted. But first, I need to crash." Raleigh cocked his head as if to say, "What? No food?"

The next morning, Jaed emerged from his bedroom in jogging clothes. Seeing the gift someone left on his desk, he was tempted to open it. *Who in the world would give me this? Not Fatemah and surely not Shirin or Ahmad. But who?* He resisted the urge and looked down at Raleigh, "What? Do you think you get a day off just because it's Christmas? Let's go."

He swung the door open, and Raleigh bounded out stretching the ten ten-foot strap tight. "Hold on, let me get the door locked," Jared said, and twisted the lock.

Raleigh, a highly trained and decorated bomb-sniffing dog, matched his every move, keeping one eye on his surroundings and the other on Jared. Five kilometers later, they returned sweating and panting. Jared filled a bowl with water and placed it on the floor for Raleigh. He pulled a bottle of water from the refrigerator for himself. Rolling the cool plastic across his forehead, he looked down and watched his new friend lap up the water. Raleigh finished, lifted his head as if to say, "got milk?" Jared smiled, twisted the lid, and chugged his water down.

"So you're hungry. Okay," and popped a couple of bagels into the toaster oven. He opened the refrigerator door and scanned its sparsely filled shelves. With a grudging sigh, he picked up the box containing his previous night's dinner.

"You're feasting now ol' buddy. This was a good pizza."

Raleigh pounced on it like a hungry tiger.

Thumbing through the stack of papers that had accompanied his dog, Jared glanced down.

"You're a regular Sergeant York, aren't you Raleigh." Raleigh's ears perked up, and he let out a whine.

It was not until after breakfast, that Jared's curiosity finally got the better of him. He could wait no longer. He had savored the moment as long as possible. He had to find out what was inside that small box wrapped in bright Christmas paper.

"Here Raleigh, make sure it isn't a bomb."

He eagerly sniffed it, looked back at Jared, and shook his head.

"All clear?" again, Raleigh signaled as he had.

"Good, because you don't want this to blow-up and ruin my handsome face, now do ya?"

Raleigh barked.

"Yeah, right." Carefully, he began unwrapping the box. His fingers twitched a little with the adrenaline rush. He took a deep breath and lifted the lid. Raleigh poked his nose in the way keeping Jared from seeing what was inside.

"Pardon me," he said, brushing the nose aside.

He removed the stuffing paper and peered down. Laying on a bed of cotton was a small two by three inch, hand-carved wooden cross.

Jared lifted the cross into the light. To his knowledge, the wood was not native to Michigan, nor could it have come from some other part to the US. It had the rich texture of some exotic wood, either Olive or Ebony, he guessed.

Wherever it came from, it is very rare and very expensive. Hand carved, from one piece of wood. A skilled craftsman created it.

"I will treasure this for the rest of my life," he said to Raleigh. The dog yawned and shook his head as if he agreed.

There was a small hole on the top of it through which he could run a thin chain, but the meantime, Jared decided to carry it in his pocket. Every time he touched it, he remembered the great sacrifice of two people . . . his Lord and Savior, and a secret admirer.

Chapter 20

The Construction Shack...

The slender form of Imam Ahem Mohammad Fahad appeared at the far end of the construction site. He tread carefully through the thick blanket of snow and approached the office. His domed head played host to a few white strands of stubborn hair, which he covered with a turban. He clutched his robe in bony fingers and gently lifted it picking his way to the door. Beneath his shabby, white beard, his squared jaw jutted with anger.

He entered the construction shack shortly after the secretaries and scanned the room with a jaundiced eye. His face reddened. Fatemah and Shirin stared at him wide eyed, heads uncovered.

"How dare you uncover your heads in my presence you witches!" he bellowed. "Leave this room or I will have you stoned!" He extended his scrawny finger and pointed to the exit.

More frightened than embarrassed, Fatemah and Shirin scampered to the safest place they could find, the restroom. They closed the door, panting.

"What should we do?" A quizzical look masked Shirin's features.

Leaning against the door with an ear to the wood, Fatemah held up a finger. "I don't know. Maybe we should call Mr. Jared."

Shirin frowned. "I left my cell phone in my purse." She nodded in the direction of the office.

"Me too, but it's too late anyway. I just heard someone pull up, and it's probably him."

The sun rose over the snow-covered building site. It glistened like diamonds. Icicles hung from the eves of the construction shack in a row of jagged teeth. Jared, excited to start a new week, jumped from his vehicle.

"Come on Raleigh, we have work to do."

Raleigh, always ready for a new adventure, piled out and sniffed the area. A gust of bitter wind whipped around them, sending shards of ice crystals swirling, temporarily blinding Jared. Shielding his face, he pushed through the drifting snow toward the door. Raleigh growled.

"What is it, Raleigh?"

His new friend lowered his head and crouched. "You smell trouble?"

Raleigh let out two sharp yips. Cautiously, Jared turned the doorknob and stepped inside.

Imam Fahad occupied the center of the room.

Agitated.

Jared stood rigid, letting his eyes wander from side to side. *Where are the ladies?*

"My name is Ahem Mohammad Fahad, the Imam of this mosque." His statement was curt, his voice without inflection.

"Heel, Raleigh." Jared said.

The shorter man's face repulsed at the sight of Raleigh. He stood, resolute, his hands behind his back. "With the completion of the lower level, the Center for Islamic Studies is now an active holy site under the direct authority of Allah, the merciful, and under my supervision." His eyes burned. "Every square foot of this property is now under my jurisdiction. I took the liberty to inspect your office, and I demand you immediately remove that detestable tree. Do you understand?"

Heat rose to Jared's face as he stared into two black eyes that burned like embers. *That pathetic Christmas tree is dried and brittle. Hum, your timing couldn't be better, I was just about to do that.* Jared nodded. Not willing to dignify his answer with a verbal assent.

The Imam began to pace with his hands knit behind his back.

"Furthermore, I invoke Shari'ah law to be adhered to in its strictest interpretation by all persons on this holy site, do I make myself clear? Mr. . . uh . . . Mr. Russell?"

Jared towered over the little man, his face grim. Jaw locked. "Sir, I mean no disrespect, but this is America, and I am under no obligation to adhere to your foreign law . . . "

The wave of the Imam's hand cut Jared off before he could build his argument.

"Laws that will soon be implemented, to which you will comply or be crushed." His voice grew tense.

Two powerful hands formed into fists, the muscles in Jared's neck knotted. "I will need to call my boss, but until then you are not in command here." The walls reverberated.

The Imam ignored him.

"All decisions must be approved by me before any action is taken. I have set up my office in the lower level, and have a direct line of communication between your office and mine. You will call me if there are any changes to the blueprint or building codes."

He strode past Jared and Raleigh to the front door. He'd won a great victory for Allah, and by his expression, he knew it.

"You might ask one of your *women* to provide you with a copy of the Qur'an and study it, as I expect you to follow its teachings so long as you are here." He said over his shoulder, and stepped out into the cold, leaving the door open.

Raleigh bolted after him. "Heel Raleigh!" He stopped short with an anxious yip.

"We'll deal with him later."

Fatemah and Shirin emerged from the bathroom with their hands over their mouths.

"Is he gone?" Fatemah asked, her eyes as wide as a stopwatch.

Jared nodded, "Yes, but not for good, I'm afraid."

"You'd better be afraid. He is a dangerous man," Fatemah looked through the curtain. "My father told me he was the reason we came to America. I grew up in Beirut, Lebanon, and for a while, my father was like your old-fashioned evangelists. He went around preaching a moderate view of Islam. His travels took him as far as Iran, preaching tolerance and unity."

Jared stepped to the window beside her and peered out. The man was nowhere to be seen.

"So what did he do that drove your father to come to America?" Shirin pressed.

"My father believed the Imam put out a 'blood curse,' on him. He called mother in the middle of the night and told her that someone tried to break into his hotel room. He barely escaped when he heard gun shots. That's when he told mother to grab what she could and take us to the airport and get out of the country, that he feared they might try to kill us." Her eyes welled with tears, and she swiped her sleeve across her face.

"Oh Fatemah, I had no idea!" Shirin clutched Fatemah's hand to her chest.

"You know, Uncle Shaquille believes Imam Fahad was responsible for the death of my parents." Shirin's statement spread a chill throughout the small room like the first offerings of winter.

Jared's jaw dropped. "Shirin, what makes your uncle think that?"

Shirin's eyes sought the floor, and she said softly. "Uncle Shaquille said that father was accused of killing the Imam's daughter. Father didn't. He couldn't have, but that's what the Imam told the police and the news service. He proclaimed a 'blood curse' upon him." Her voice trailed off.

"Is that why you came to America, to get away from the 'blood curse'?" Fatemah asked.

Jared's eyebrows rose, his forehead wrinkled. "A blood curse, why? Why? What is that?"

Shirin perched on the corner of the desk. "According to Shari'ah Law, under a blood curse my father could be killed by the Imam or someone representing him without consequences. The only thing he could do was run for his life. He tried to escape by going to Uncle Shaquille's house, but he never made it. He and mother were gunned down coming from a restaurant."

"I am so sorry to hear that."

"Do you remember the day you met us on the airplane coming to Stanford?"

"Yes, you and Ahmad were really upset. I thought it was something I said."

Shirin shook her head; a few strands of hair fell across her face. She lightly brushed them aside. "No, it wasn't anything about you. We'd been so worried about our parents since we left. Ahmad called Uncle Shaquille to see if he knew anything."

Jared rammed his hands in his pockets. "And that was when you learned about your parents?"

"Yes, he'd just gotten off the phone with him."

Jared pulled a hand out and ran it over his hair, pacing to the window. His voice remained calm, but his mind fluttered like a moth around a light bulb. "So, do *you* think he had your father killed?"

A tear coursed down her cheek. "I don't know. I didn't know who he was until he said his name, and I didn't know he'd come to America."

Jared looked at Shirin and then at Fatemah. "Do you think he recognized you?"

Fatemah's features spoke volumes. "I don't know. It was seven or eight years ago. I doubt he could associate me with my father's time in Iran."

"And you, Shirin?"

Shirin stood, her arms wrapped tightly around her slender waist. "If he ever finds out we are Sirus Hassani's children, I don't know what he'd do. Even so, I'm more concerned about what will happen when Ahmad learns Imam Fahad is here."

Jared felt his shoulders stiffened. "Why do you say that?"

A fire burned in Shirin eyes, her jaw set. "Ahmad swore he'd kill the man responsible for killing our parents."

Taking a hard swallowed, Jared tried to process the information. "That's what I was afraid of. He said something about invoking Saria Law. What is it?"

Fatemah spoke up. "They pronounce it Shari'ah, and it spells trouble."

"And it's coming to a theater near you." Jared said with sarcasm.

The corners of Fatemah's lips turned down. "Do not take him lightly. He is serious and dangerous."

Jared sighed and moved toward his desk. "We've got a major mess on our hands, and I hate it that you ladies are caught up in the middle of it."

If Mr. Xavier knew about this guy, he is either a good businessman and lousy politician, or a very good politician and a not so good businessman. Either way he has made it difficult for me to do my job . . . if I still have one.

He picked up the phone and dialed the home office.

"Good morning Jared, and Happy New Year!" Mr. Xavier said in a celebratory tone.

There was a pause as Mr. Xavier shifted gears, "I'm sure by now you've met Mr. Imam or whatever he calls himself. Is that why you are calling so early?" His voice was etched with concern.

Jared fingered the cross in his pocket. "Yes, Mr. Fahad just left. I got a bad feeling about this guy." He paused for a sip of hot coffee. "He tells me I am not the project manager, that he is, and that all decisions must be approved by him. Is that true?"

Jared heard his boss shifting the phone from one ear to the other. "He stopped by last week on Thursday and gave us the same spiel. We are in the process of checking his credentials and trying to find out who he is. We don't even know if he is legally in the U.S., but in the meantime, try to get along with him."

"Get along with him!" Jared was incredulous. "He said I am to comply with some Islamic code or something . . . he called it Shari'ah law."

Xavier laughed nervously, "Well, I don't know about that, but let me handle it from this side, and let's see if we can get rid of him quickly before—before it all hits the fan. Okay? Oh, and Happy New Year!"

"Ah, you too Sir." Click. Jared sat staring out of his window. Things just went from bad to worse.

Chapter 21

Beneath the Mosque...

"Allah—"

The mid-morning air crackled with the voice of Imam Fahad. He stood at the top of the stairs with a bullhorn, calling the faithful to assemble. The men laid aside their tools and jostled into the newly completed auditorium beneath the Mosque. The Imam called out the first of five daily prayers. The men knelt in tightly packed rows toward Mecca and began to recite.

Just returned from vacation, Jimbo heard the noise and followed the men. Not knowing what to expect, he stepped into the assembly. A gasp like a supersonic shock wave spread from the front to the back.

"Who are you and why have you caused the men to stop working?" Jimbo spun the little man with the bullhorn around.

The Imam paused and lowered his eyes in a malevolent gaze. "Who are you and why have you interrupted our prayers? You have violated the holy law of Allah, and you are worthy of death, infidel dog. Leave this place I will kill you myself." His words, coupled with spittle, flew at Jimbo like angry hornets.

Jimbo, not to be intimidated by an old man wearing bed sheets, turned the air blue with his profanity.

Fatemah burst into Jared's office. "Mr. Jared, Mr. Jared! The Imam and Mr. Jimbo are yelling down in the auditorium," she said, gulping for oxygen.

Jared, leaning over a blueprint, jerked up and bolted through the door, Raleigh at his heels. By the time he reached the lower level, he found the two staring at each other like pit-bulls. Fearing for his own safety, he forced himself between them. He must stop them from coming to blows.

"Jimbo, step back and let me handle this."

His superintendent glanced down at Raleigh, exhaled, and followed his command. Imam Fahad was like The Rock of Gibraltar.

"What are you doing with that bullhorn?"

Imam Fahad lifted his chin and stared into Jared's eyes, his teeth clenched, a slight tremble in his taught lips. "I am calling these men to prayer. It is Allah's will. Stand aside."

Jared's chest heaved; his hands ached to close around the little man's throat. *God, give me strength!*

The eyes of hundreds of men bore down on him like a thousand rays of darkness.

"Mr. Fahad, how long do your prayers last?"

The boney man raised his eyes to the heavens, "Our prayers to Allah, the Merciful, last five to ten minutes, and we pray five times a day."

His breath reeked and Jared resisted the urge to recoil. After some quick calculating, he continued, "Okay. That's fifty-minute max. We give the men a thirty-minute lunch break, and you use the two fifteen-minute breaks for your prayers. The remaining twenty minutes each day the men will make up by coming to work early. If not, it will take a year longer to finish your Mosque, and cost Allah another two million dollars. Do you think Allah would approve of that?" He didn't blink.

Raleigh showed his teeth and growled.

With his eyes shifting between Raleigh's teeth and Jared's firm gaze, he waited.

Jared took his momentary pause as acquiescence. "Good, then it's settled."

He grabbed the bullhorn from Fahad's hand and turned to the assembled crowd. "Men, show up to work tomorrow at six thirty. You will not be paid overtime and anyone who is late will be summarily fired. Mr. Jimbo will be checking your time cards, and you will be answerable to him. He will see to it that you get your last paycheck. Does everyone understand?"

A reluctant murmur rustled like windblown leaves through the assembly.

Imam Fahad narrowed his eyes. He was out-maneuvered. "Soon these Infidels will feel the wrath of Allah and be sorry for bringing dishonor on me, his humble servant," he muttered under his breath.

Scanning the crowd, Jared noticed Ammad. He stood to his left, the veins in his forehead bulging, his fists balled, breathing through teeth clenched with hatred. Hope of winning him to the Lord dimmed in Jared's soul.

"Jared, let's get out of here before these guys decide to go jihad on us," Jimbo whispered.

With a nod, they backed out of the basement and into the light of morning.

"I got a bad feeling about this guy, Jimbo." Jared said as he glanced over his shoulder.

Jimbo cocked his head. "Me too, I didn't recog . . . I mean, why didn't you warn me about him?"

Shrugging his shoulders, Jared bit back a smile. "I just met him myself, and since you didn't come to the office this morning for our weekly briefing, I figured you two would make your own introductions."

Jimbo stared at the ground, hands in his pocket. "Yeah well, I'm still steamed about you embarrassing me in front of those . . . those women a few months ago."

"You had it coming, now get over it and let's move on."

An uncomfortable moment passed. Jimbo responded pushed his hard hat back on his balding head, eyebrows raised.

"I suppose you're right," he said, wiping the sweat from his brow. "I have a way of shooting off my mouth before I think."

Jared's face softened.

"I see you got your dog." Jimbo said in a conciliatory tone.

"Yep, his name is Raleigh." The dog's ears perked up, and he lifted one paw.

Jimbo bent at the waist. "It's nice to meet you Raleigh."

Raleigh barked twice.

"I think he likes you, Jimbo. Let's get some hot coffee, and you can tell me all about your vacation."

His superintendent lingered. "I'll be along. I've got a phone call to make."

They parted, Jimbo fishing his cell phone from his pocket.

Jared, the cold breeze cutting through his flannel shirt, rubbed his sleeve and said over his shoulder. "Okay, I'll see you after you've finished. We've still got to have our briefing."

Chapter 22

Ahmad's Apartment

"Did he recognize you? Does he know who you are?" Ahmad paced the floor of their apartment, glancing out the window.

Shirin took a seat at the table. "I don't think so, he was so concerned with Mr. Jared that I doubt he was thinking about me or Fatemah."

Ahmad plopped down on the couch. "He's *got* to know we're here. With a large Hassani Construction sign planted on the curb, he'll put two and two together and come looking for us."

Shirin buried her face in her hands and began to sob softly. "Why would he want to kill us? I'm just so scared."

Ahmad looked at his calloused hands. "Uncle Shaq said it was the blood curse, that after father allegedly killed the Imam's daughter, he ran. The Imam wants to avenge his daughter's death by wiping out all Hassanis."

The ticking of the wall clock marked the passing of time. Time was running out for Ahmad and Shirin. Shirin looked up and saw her brother kneeling in front the window, facing east, deep in prayer. After a few minutes, he stood and his voice was cold as ice.

"It is the will of Allah that I avenge the blood of our mother. Imam Fahad may have thought he had justification for killing father, but he had no right to kill mother, nor does he have any right to come for us. Soon I will find him, and kill him."

Fatemah stepped from the construction shack into the brisk afternoon air. It was payday, and she carried a stack of pay checks for Jimbo. As she passed a cluster of men, Jamal, one of the day laborers, stepped out and began following her. Unaware that she was in any danger, Fatemah entered the auditorium looking, for Jimbo.

"Well, well. What have we here?" leered the man. His eyes filled with lust.

Fatemah, though physically fit, was no match for her aggressor. He grabbed her by the throat and shoved her against the wall. She squirmed, but felt his hand tighten.

"If you don't stop moving, I'll stick you with this." He produced a knife and held it close to her face. Fatemah's eyes widened. *Oh God, help!*

There was a flash of movement, and the man's face contorted. His grip loosened and he fell backward, a pool of blood forming around his limp body. Above him stood Imam Fahad, a bloody six-inch knife in his hand.

"Are you okay, miss?" the Imam's voice was kind and gentle, a sharp contrast to the ugly scene at her feet.

Fatemah blinked, hoping it was a dream. "I, I guess. What—why?"

In the scuffle, she'd dropped the stack of pay checks, and they lay scattered across the floor.

The Imam knelt began to pick them up. He paused at one, then handed the stack to Fatemah. "Here, young lady, go in peace and may Allah go with you."

Too frightened to respond, she nodded and scurried away. Walking past a hall she saw someone in the shadows. She backed away fearing another assailant, but Jimbo stuck his face into the light and motioned at her to come. She obeyed and found Ahmad's face buried beneath one of Jimbo's meaty hands.

"What's going on?" she whispered.

Jimbo peered around the corner at Fahad where he knelt over the dead man.

"Ahmad and I were just discussing the prudence of attacking an unarmed man." He released his grip on Ahmad's jaw, and he squirmed free.

"If you didn't interfere we would be looking at two dead men not one," Ahmad said through stretched lips.

Jimbo rocked back on his heels and said barely above a whisper. "Yeah, yours and Jamal's." He turned on his heel and walked out of the auditorium.

Chapter 23

The Center for Islamic Studies

"I'm surprised that nothing was said about Jamal's death." Jimbo said. It was the following day, and Fatemah shuttered at the memory.

"I'd never seen a man killed before, but I'm glad that Imam Fahad showed up when he did. Who knows what might have happened.

"I do."

Fatemah's eyes widened. "You do?"

"Yep, I happened to be coming down the hall when I saw Ahmad following Fahad. He was muttering something about avenging his mother. I grabbed him and discovered he had a knife under his shirt."

Fatemah's hand covered her mouth.

"If I didn't intervene, either Fahad or Ahmad would have been killed."

"It is as Shirin said. Ahmad has taken a blood curse to kill the Imam."

Jimbo listened. His face darkened.

"Do you think I should have called the police?" Fatemah asked.

Jimbo shook his head. "No, you did the right thing. Even so, we'll need to be careful from now on."

The following week, Jared and Raleigh stood in the blueprint room. A light knocking on his door broke the silence. Raleigh jumped to attention.

"Come in."

The door opened just wide enough for Shirin to slip in. Her face was clouded.

Raleigh came to her side and lifted his head. She backed up with her hand clutched to her chest.

"Raleigh." He slunk to his bed and curled in a ball.

"What is it, Shirin? You look, uh worried."

Shirin shifted and looked away. "That's just it," she said, eyeing Raleigh. "It's about your dog. Ahmad and the work crew are frightened. They heard he is a bomb sniffing dog."

Jared straightened and laid aside the ruler he was holding. "He was a bomb sniffing dog, but now he's my pet. Is that a problem?"

She twisted her lower lip with her fingers. "The men, they think you are spying on them, that you don't trust them because they are Muslims.

Jared's forehead wrinkled. *Why would they be concerned if they weren't hiding something?*

"Miss Shirin, I love big dogs, and got Raleigh because…I live alone and needed someone to talk to. I assure you, I am not spying on anyone."

She tugged on her ear. "We are not radical Muslims like those in the Middle East. We want a place to worship just like you, is that too much to ask?"

Jared looked at her, the lines about his eyes etched into a smile. "Tell your brother, he and the men don't have anything to worry about."

Shirin nodded and let out a long sigh. "I had a dog once... back in my home in Tehran." Her lower lip quivered. "Her name was Toto, you know, like the dog in the movie?"

Jared smiled. "Was it a terrier?"

Shirin paused, her eyes taking on a distant look. "Yes, I miss her and my parents so much." She shook her head and sighed again.

A moment passed as Jared thought of a thousand things to say. None would ease her sorrow.

"I'll tell the men not to be afraid of Raleigh," she promised, and slipped from the room.

Jared returned to his work. For the most part, what he said was true, but he had his doubts about some of the men. Those surrounding Imam Fahad made him wonder.

A knock on the door got his attention.

"Come in."

The door swung open and Jimbo pushed into the small room.

"Did you say something about a morning meeting?"

Jared leaned back in his chair. "Yes, though it's past noon." He couldn't help but enjoy the way Jimbo paid little attention to time.

"Well, I'm here now, so what do ya want to talk about, I'm busy."

"What, you have a hot lunch date?" Jared kidded.

"Yeah, I have a date with a hot lunch, want to join me?"

Jared smiled, "Why not. I'll go over the week's work goals over lunch. There is one thing I'd like to say before we go."

"What's that?"

"I'm doing my best to stay out of the Imam's way, and I'm asking you to do the same."

Jimbo chuckled. "There's nothing better I'd like to do than to stay away from him, but I have a feeling, we are going to lock horns one of these days."

Chapter 24

On the job-site . . .

The three-story scaffold leaned precariously and began to collapse. Jared watched in horror. Ahmad, unaware of the danger, talked with one of his men below. On impulse, Jared ran, and shoved him hard. Ahmad fell and rolled. With a screeching grumble, the scaffold hit the ground, crushing Jared's legs. He cried out, and Raleigh bounded to his side. The dog tugged on his shirt, tearing it and whining, as he tried desperately to pull Jared from the rubble.

The men gathered, shouting and pointing, and began to lift the tangled mess. A large platform hung over Jared's head, threatening to fall. The more the men struggled, the more unstable it became. Jimbo stepped to the middle of the crowd and yelled. Heads turned.

"You—get a forklift over here and raise it up as high as it will go! Hook on to that platform to keep it from falling."

Kaleel, an agile young Lebanese, leapt into action.

The forklift was in place.

"Okay men, on three, lift!" cried Jimbo over the growling of the forklift.

Their combined effort raised the twisted frame it enough for a few workers to drag Jared to safety.

"I think my leg is broken," Jared grimaced as he caught his breath against a rising tide of pain.

"Yeah buddy, it's pretty bad. Let's get an ambulance out here and get you to the hospital."

"What about Ahmad? Is he safe?"

Jimbo glanced over his shoulder with a whistle. "He'll live, but he ain't too happy about it."

"Ahmad, are you all right?" Jared asked.

Spring to his feet, Ahmad threw his hard hat down and kicked it, sending it tumbling across the uneven ground. He marched toward Jared with fire in his eyes. "Why did you do that?"

Propping himself on one elbow, Jared narrowed his eyes. "I was trying to save your life—*some thanks!*" He grimaced.

"If Allah wanted me to die today, I should have died."

Jared held his breath, trying to control his emotions. "Well maybe God didn't want you to die today, and sent me to save you. Have you ever thought about that?"

Ahmad stepped back, his raven eyes surveying the pile of twisted steel.

"Why would you do such a thing for me . . . I hate you. You are an infidel, a dog; I wouldn't have done it for you." His bitter words assaulted Jared in a withering barrage.

"Hey, now wait a minute, don't you go insulting my dog." He said, not realizing how serious Ahmad was. A moment later, he did.

"It would have been an act of kindness for Allah to have killed me." The malevolence in his voice made Jared's smile evaporate.

What can I say to this man to get through to him? They stared at each other, undying malice in one man's eyes, the love of Jesus in the other's.

~ 139 ~

A curious look spread across Ahmad's face. "But you did save my life. Why?"

Jesus' words percolated into Jared's mind.

"Because my God is a God of mercy. He is not willing that you should perish. So I should not let you die if I can help it. That's the difference between Allah and Jesus . . . Mercy."

The wail of the ambulance neared. "You should be grateful I was following the teachings of Jesus and not the Qur'an today."

Jimbo, who had been listening to the exchange, squinted at Ahmad, "Either way, you *are* alive, and you owe Jared a word of thanks."

Ahmad lowered his head and spoke softly in Farsi, then in English. "من همیشه درقرضتان هستم من مدیون به شمابرای کمکتان هستم" "I am indebted to you. Allah would not have asked me to save your life had the scaffolding fallen on you. But you have shown kindness to me. This is a most honorable act. The Qur'an commands me to place my life in your hands until I can repay you."

Then he bowed to the ground.

The look on Jimbo's face was priceless. With his mouth gaping open all he could do was shrug, speechless.

Jared, without taking his eyes from him, leaned forward, laid his hand on Ahmad's back and spoke softly.

"Well that may be so, but for now, let's just call it even. Okay?"

Ahmad blinked absently and nodded.

Jimbo cupped his hands and spoke to the men who had gathered around them. "All right everybody, show's over; let's get this mess cleaned up and get back to work."

The crowd dispersed, as the paramedics lifted Jared to a gurney and prepared to take him to the hospital.

The look on Ahmad's face told Jared he won this round.

The following day, Jared returned to work with his leg in a cast and hobbling on a pair of crutches.

Seeing him approach the office, Shirin dashed to the front door and swung it open.

"Please, allow me to help you get to your desk." Her soft voice sounded tender, inviting.

"That's okay, I gotta get used to these things. The doctors say I'll be on them for six more weeks."

"Oh, Mr. Jared, I am so sorry," she helped him out of his coat and hung it up.

She set his crutches to the side. "Why did you do such a thing? You know how my brother feels about you."

He thought for a moment, "Because my God tells me to love my neighbor as myself and to love my enemies, even those who treat me despitefully. It is a way of life that is opposed to the world's way."

"According to Imam Fahad, Shari'ah law governs everything on this property. Ahmad is no longer free. He is your servant until he repays his debt."

Jared nodded. "That's what Ahmad told me." He raised his eyebrows in question. "Are you saying your brother is like a bond-servant or something?"

"Yes, and also according to Shari'ah law, an eye for an eye, a tooth for a tooth, and a life for a life. And," she paused as if to gather her courage, "as Ahmad's younger sister, I too am your servant. We are obligated to serve you."

Then she bowed. Fatemah stepped to the door of his office. The two exchanged looks, she smiled and nodded.

"Well it seems like I have a couple of servants," Jared joked, trying to lighten the atmosphere. "What does that mean? Are you guys gonna be moving in with me?"

Shirin lifted her soft eyes to his, "If that is what you wish. We are here to serve you," she whispered in nearly an inaudible voice as she stood back up.

"Wow! That floors me. Tell ya what, why don't we simply keep the status quo, for the time being, and I will let you know if I need any serving done." The phone rang breaking the spell.

"Very well, if that is your wish."

"It is, but thank you anyway."

Ahmad sat in his apartment. It was Friday. He had just returned from a smaller mosque on the other side of town where Imam Fahad read from the Qur'an and delivered his weekly rant. It was in stark contrast to the act of kindness demonstrated by Jared. It was foreign to his thinking, to Islamic thinking, and it had made a big impression upon him. Many times he prayed to Allah for wisdom, for Allah to tell him why his life was spared. If it was Allah's will for him to die, he should have died.

He fingered the handgun he'd borrowed from an acquaintance. *Maybe I should end my life and fulfill the will of Allah.*

His repetitive daily prayers went unanswered. All he could hear was the name of Jesus, echoing in his ears. It was driving him crazy. Over and over he heard Jared's voice. *You should be grateful I was following the teachings of Jesus and not the Qur'an today.*

In the following weeks, Ahmad began to watch Jared. Impressed by the way his boss reacted whenever he faced a difficult situation. He began to realize how different he was from the Imam, Jimbo, and from anyone else he knew. He didn't know how he would repay his debt...but he prayed he would.

Chapter 25

City Hall, Stanford, Michigan

Imam Fahad stepped into Mayor Abdul Qadir el Talibani's office one late April afternoon. For the first time in months, he wore a smile on his weathered face. After seeing his people corrupted by the evil influences of the American Zionists, commercialism, and Christianity, he'd finally taken the steps necessary to correct the situation. His orders to the Mayor were simple and direct. "Enact Shari'ah Law over Stanford, Michigan."

Fahad stared over his rimless glasses at the newly elected mayor. He templed his fingers and assessed the man who claimed to be a moderate Muslim.

"Your narrow victory over that liberal politician brought in quite a few new councilmen didn't it Talibani?" The Imam said.

"Yes, but it helped that I promised to reduce both the size of city government and reign in its out of control spending."

"You spouted the same dribble all the other politicians do and the people swallowed it every time."

Talibani smiled. "With the influx of so many Middle-Eastern immigrants, it was never in doubt, but it was their vote that tipped the scale in our favor."

"Now it's time for you to earn your keep," Fahad said.

"My election is just the first step on a long journey."

The Imam touched the top of the mayor's desk. "This is just the beginning. I want anti-defamation laws enacted. I will not tolerate any criticism of Allah, Islamic law or the prophet Muhammad. That is blasphemy."

Talibani shifted his weight and he sat taking notes. "Yes my Father. Will there be anything else?" Sweat beaded on his upper lip, he pulled a handkerchief from his pocket and dabbed his brow.

"Yes, I want a press release to appear in next week's newspaper stating that it is a capital offence for any Muslim to convert to a non-Islam religion." Imam paced the floor, his fingers knit behind his back as if he were a professor giving a lecture.

"My Father, that will be difficult to enforce. This is America not Iran."

Fahad stopped and slammed his hand on the mayor's desk, making the paperclips dance. "I don't care what country we are in. I pray to Allah every day for Shari'ah Law to cover the earth as the ocean covers the sea."

"But sir—"

The Imam cut him off with a wave of his hand. He leaned over the desk and through clenched teeth, he said, "I, we have ways of controlling our people, but I want there to be no misunderstandings. I will not tolerate anyone proselytizing the faithful."

Talibani shrank back in his chair. "My Father, what should be done about the preacher who distributes literature in front of his church? Legally he has the right to do so under the US Constitution."

The Imam straightened and placed his hands on his hips. "Find a way to curtail his activities; littering, causing a public disturbance, inciting a riot. I don't care how, but stop that man. Do you understand?" His voice curdled with fury.

Talibani nodded, too frightened to respond.

"Furthermore, I want the name of Jesus Christ banished from society. I don't want to see it written or spoken publicly. I also demand that the local radio broadcasts of Sunday sermons be curtailed along with playing of Christian music."

The mayor's fingers twitched slightly as he wrote out the demands, then looked up.

"Since the election swept in a majority of city councilmen, all of whom are members of your congregation, I'm confident that we can enact these changes over time."

"Time?" he boomed. "Time is not on our side. I want these changes implemented as soon as possible."

"My Father, this still is America, democracy is the rule of law. We must go slowly or," he paused and looked in the direction of his secretary sitting at her desk. "or the people will revolt."

"Revolt," he sneered. "You've been corrupted like all the others. All you care about is getting re-elected."

"If re-election furthers our cause, then I'll do whatever I must to stay in power."

The Imam resumed his measured pace. A wicked smile parted his lips. "Then say what you must, do whatever you need to do. Remember, lying is not condemned by Allah if it spreads Islam."

"I know, you have taught me well, my Father." The mayor shifted in his chair.

Fahad came around the desk and lowered his voice. "Do you think the infidels will connect us?"

"No, I've been meticulous in hiding my birth certificate and reinventing my past. There is no way anyone will ever discover that you are my—"

The door burst open. "Mr. Talibani," said Miss Elaine Rakestraw, her arms loaded of legal papers.

She looked up, eyes flickering from one man to the other. "Oh, I'm sorry, Mr. Mayor, I didn't know you were with someone," she backed away.

"You were away from your desk when my spiritual leader, Imam Ahem Mohammad Fahad stopped by. Could you go and get our guest a cup of coffee?"

Miss Rakestraw blinked and looked at the papers in her arms.

"That's all right Miss Rakestraw, bring me the papers and run along."

She avoided eye contact with the mayor, laid the papers on his desk and scurried from the room.

"How much do you think she heard?"

The mayor fingered the hem of his sports coat.

"I'm not sure, she's a holdover from the last administration and I haven't had the chance to replace her. She is the only one who knows anything about running this office. But she has an annoying way of barging in here without knocking," the mayor said as he looked at the closed door.

"How soon can you get a replacement for her?" Fahad asked.

Talibani sighed and looked at his uncle. The two stared as Fahad stepped in front of the mayor's desk. An unspoken message passed between them.

Chapter 26

Canaan Baptist Church

Pastor Carlson finished his Sunday message and invited the unbelievers to come forward. Among the many who came to pray was the Benson family, recently moved to the community. After the formality of inducting them into the membership, the pastor took his place down front.

"Folks, please welcome Mr. and Mrs. Benson to our church." Then he closed in prayer.

Jared stood in line and greeted the newcomers. Glancing around, he saw Elaine Rakeshaw, a regular visitor in line behind him.

"Oh hello Miss, uh,"

"Rakestraw, Elaine Rakestraw. She pushed a smile across her lips.

"Yes, Elaine, haven't I seen you a couple times down at city hall?"

She nodded, tucked a few unruly hairs behind her ear. Her actions were quick and uneven. It was obvious to Jared that his attention made her nervous. She let her eyes search the floor. "Yeah, I work there, at least for a while longer. With the new mayor taking office, I figure it won't be long before they fire me and get a Muslim secretary." She laughed nervously.

Jared put his hands in his pockets and rocked back. Elaine was nearly as tall and dark complexioned as he. "Well I guess you could convert to Islam," he joked.

"Very funny, if the preacher heard you talking like that in church, you might find yourself on the outside looking in."

The line of greeters moved forward a step and before he could come back with a pithy comment, Pastor Carlson stuck his hand out. "Hello Elaine, it was nice to see you in services again. Let's see," he paused in mock reflection, "you've been coming long enough to have earned an honorary membership. Don't you think it's time to make it official?" His fatherly candor disarmed Elaine. She shrugged her shoulders.

"Yes, well uh, no. Actually, I do want to join but that's not why I came forward today." She looked from side to side. "Could we meet, I mean in private, you know for council?" She twisted her lip expecting rejection.

Mrs. Carlson stepped to her husband's side. "I would love to meet with you if you don't mind if my wife joins us."

Elaine sighed, hand to her chest. "Oh yes, I would be much more comfortable talking to both of you."

"What, may I ask, is the nature of your inquiry?"

She forced a smile and looked at Jared. He took his cue. "Oh I get it, please excuse me. I'll catch you later."

Jared stepped out of line and was met with a gaggle of elderly women who took great pleasure in engaging him in small talk. Usually their conversation revolved around his singleness.

"Now Jared, we mustn't miss the opportunity God puts in front of us." One lady let her eyes cut in the direction of Elaine.

Jared got the implication. "Yes ma'am, and I appreciate your advice."

He started to take another step when a gentle hand lighted on his arm and held him in place. He glanced down, it was Alice Nunnley, the widow. He groaned inside. *She always has advice for me that no one wants.* Jared tried to back away as she proceeded to give him a lesson on romance but her hand held him in place. He strained his ears, half listening to what the pastor and Elaine were saying. *What is Elaine saying? Something about the mayor?*

Elaine's voice was low but not so much that Jared couldn't hear it, if only in snatches. "It's about the mayor. I think he is—"

Mr. Dunlop stepped up and interrupted her before she could finish. Embarrassed, she slipped from the auditorium. Jared followed her with his eyes until she disappeared through the side entrance. Pastor Carlson caught Jared's attention with a quizzical look and shrugged his shoulders.

"Pastor," Fred Dunlop interrupted, "the men and I need to meet with you this afternoon about a matter most urgent. Could we meet, say, three o'clock?"

The pastor returned the man's gaze. A moment passed in which neither man spoke. A gentle nudge from Mrs. Carlson brought her husband back to his senses.

"Uh, yes, I think that can be arranged. What do you and the others want to talk about?"

Mr. Dunlop shifted his eyes and lowered his head. "It's better we wait until we can talk in your office before I say anymore." His eyes caught Jared's.

Chapter 27

The Church parking lot

By the time Jared extricated himself from his would-be romantic mentor, the auditorium was nearly empty. With the sun high overhead, he paused in the foyer to slip on a pair of shades before stepping outside. It was well past noon and his stomach growled, reminding him that it was time to do some serious thinking about where to eat. He fished the key from his pocket, and noticed one other car sitting nearby. Someone sat behind the wheel, looking down.

A light knock on the driver's side window brought Elaine's head up with a jerk. She'd been crying. Her eyes were red and puffy and her lower lip trembled. He couldn't help but empathize with her, he hated to see a woman cry.

"Sorry if I startled you, Elaine, I saw you sitting there and wondered. Is everything all right?"

She dabbed her eyes and took a ragged breath. "Yes, everything's fine, I just . . . " her voice caught in her throat like a ball of dough.

She pulled the handle and slipped out of the car as gracefully as a swan. Jared stepped back and gave her space.

"What is it that's got you so upset?"

She gulped back a sob. "Oh it's nothing really, I over react at everything," fanning herself. "I'm such a twit."

Jared pursed his lips and waited.

"You see, I was talking to the pastor when this man came up and interrupted me right in the middle of what I was saying. He was so rude." She threw a wadded Kleenex to the ground with all the force she could muster. "All I could do was come out here to cry."

He listened a moment longer. "Yeah, that was Mr. Dunlop. He's like that; rude and bigoted." His stomach growled again and he put his hand on it to muffle the sound.

Elaine chuckled with a catch-breath. "Sounds like you're hungry."

Jared rubbed his midsection. "More like famished. Are you interested in Sunday dinner at Mother's Finest?"

Her face brightened. "I've heard about it, but never eaten there."

"Good, let me be the first to introduce you to the best cooking this side of home. Do you mind following me? After we eat, I need to get home and check on Raleigh."

"Raleigh? Who's that?"

"My dog, hop in your car and follow me."

Mother's Finest

"You're right. This has got to be the best pot roast I've ever eaten." Elaine mopped the last of the gravy with a homemade biscuit.

"Glad you liked it." Jared said and dabbed the corners of his mouth. "I know this wasn't a date and all, but if you don't mind I'd like to pay for your meal, since it was my idea to order the most expensive thing on the menu."

She hesitated.

Jared couldn't tell if it was pride or worry.

Her chocolate brown eyes rose and met his. Jared read pain in them. "I appreciate your offer, really I do, but right now my life is too complicated to start a new relationship."

Jared was taken aback. Thanks to Alice Nunnley and her romantic advice, he'd considered the idea. The thought of this turning into something more passed through his mind as the casual conversation rolled along. Until that moment, she'd said nothing to cause him to doubt her stability. But her last statement caused him to sit up straight. He nodded and waited to see if there was more.

She fidgeted with her water glass and let out a frustrated sigh.

"Jared, I'm scared," she sputtered.

Jared's eyes widened. "Scared of what?" His mind raced. "You've got a good job. You told me you live in a nice neighborhood. What are you scared of?"

She lowered her voice. "That's just it. I have a good job but I've heard things, I've seen things and I know—"

As the server reached in with a challis of water and refilled her half empty glass she jumped and nearly knocked her water glass over.

Jared noticed a slight tremble in the woman's voice.

"What have you seen that's got you so rattled?" He pressed.

She forced a weak smile and hesitated. "Look, I think I've said too much. I can't get you involved any deeper than you are."

"What do you mean, any deeper? Deeper in what?"

She swallowed hard. "You're building that Mosque, aren't you? That's pretty deep. Look I gotta go." Her movements were quick and jerky as she grabbed her purse.

Jared reached out and took her by the wrist. She froze.

"Look Elaine, something's got you pretty shook up and I don't want to pry, but if you need someone to talk to, you can call me night or day."

He reached for a napkin and scribbled his cell number on it.

She glanced down at the number. Slowly and deliberately she picked it up, folded it and stuffed it in her purse.

"Thanks, I might do that. I gotta go." She turned and headed for the door, her heels clicking against the tile floor.

Jared sat, wondering what just happened.

Chapter 28

The Pastor's Study

Just past three o'clock a sharp knock sounded on the pastor's study door. His chair squeaked when he stood and welcomed in five grim-faced men.

"Welcome Fred," Pastor Carlson tried to act relaxed, but his stomach churned. He waited for the deacons to take their seats. The looks on their faces told him small talk would only forestall the inevitable. He decided to take the lead.

"Men, let's pray and ask for the Lord's leadership on our conversation." His prayer was peppered with scripture and warnings about speaking ill of brother. As he concluded, he felt the temperature in the room rise and wondered if the heater had come on or if that many men crammed into such a small office had anything to do with it.

He sat up straight in his chair and looked at Fred, "So what's this about?'

Fred licked his lips and looked from side to side. "Pastor, I, uh, we have been talking about our brother Jared Russell."

Pastor Carlson had heard it all before. Someone got a burr under their saddle and gathered a few weak-willed listeners to form a self-appointed committee.

"So I understand you're concerned about Brother Russell's job?"

"Not so much his job but the influence his job is bringing and the presumed support of the Islamic movement. I believe he is really a subversive, working for the *Moslims.*"

Heads nodded Dunlop was just getting started. If he didn't nip this in the bud, he'd be looking at a church split within a few weeks.

"Fred, you need to understand. Jared is an avid witness. He is constantly witnessing to the Muslim people. Have you even once been out to our Open Hands, Open Hearts outreach program on Saturday?"

Dunlop shifted. "Uh, no, not yet."

"Well you have missed a blessing. Jared has been at nearly every one since we started. He loves *Moslims—*"

"That's what I mean, he's one of them," Dunlop's voice rose.

The pastor thought. *This is getting serious.*

"I demand that we bring this to the church for a vote. If you don't, we may need to consider other options."

Pastor Carlson sat back and rubbed his chin.

"Have you gone to him on a one on one basis and talked with him?"

Fred's gaze dropped, "Uh, no, not really. I mean us guys did talk to him once but he got real defensive."

The pastor nodded, "Wouldn't you? He told me about that. It was more like being at the Little Big Horn according to Mr. Russell."

"Well, we were just trying to make a point," said Mitch, one of Fred's right-hand men.

Carlson bit his tongue to keep from saying what he was thinking. He looked at Fred. "You know you have no scriptural grounds for calling a vote, don't you? This is personal—isn't it?"

All eyes turned to Fred. He cleared his throat, shaken. "Of course it isn't personal. I care about our church, our community. We are losing it to those *Moslims*."

"Yet you haven't once tried to win one of them to the Lord. And you want to vote out the one man who is in a good position to be a big influence for Christ."

Dunlop stood followed by the others. "Will you call for a vote or won't you?"

"I'll call a vote but will you comply with the outcome if the vote goes in favor of Brother Russell?"

Fred stopped at the door and looked. "I'll pray about it."

Chapter 29

Open Hands, Open Hearts...

The sun had risen high enough to send a shaft of light straight down the street, a warm gentle breeze blew and many shoppers lined the sidewalks looking for bargains. It was another Saturday morning and Jared joined his friend and pastor for a day of track distribution. "Where's Raleigh?" The pastor looked around to see if he was curled up in a cool shady corner.

Jared grinned, "I left him at the house. I figured if he were here, he'd scare off any prospects. We have enough trouble getting people to talk with us, we don't need to give them another excuse to avoid us."

Pastor Carlson nodded, and the lines in his face deepened. "Jared, I met with some of the deacons last Sunday afternoon. They expressed concern over your involvement with the Mosque project."

"Oh really? Are you sure it's not me personally or is it the project?"

The pastor raised his hands. "No, no, it's not you. But ol' brother Dunlop has lodged a formal complaint. It sounds absurd but he claims you are working for the Islamic movement. And he's calling on the membership to vote you out if you don't stop working on it."

Jared froze. A thousand words crammed into his throat at the same time. Nothing came out.

"Don't get me wrong, I'm not for the idea, but he seems to have a sizable group of backers. It doesn't help for city hall to be coming out with new Shari'ah friendly laws either."

A man walked by the literature table and the pastor talked with him for a few minutes before getting back to Jared.

"These laws are affecting our community from the courtroom to the bedroom. Everyone from the highest level of society to the lowest is feeling the pinch. I'm wondering when they will tell us to stop distributing this literature."

Jared hung his head. He had been so focused on doing what he thought was God's will that he failed to take into consideration its effects.

"Pastor, I believe this is what God wants me to do at this time. I believe I'm being a testimony to the Muslim workers. Even Ahmad is acting civil and he might come around in time."

The pastor rubbed his forehead. "All I know is that our church is divided, this town is divided. The citizens of Stanford went to sleep one day under Michigan law and woke up the next under Shari'ah law. After letting the camel get its nose in the tent, they discovered the camel has taken over."

"Pastor, I can't quit my job and I don't want to leave the church."

The pastor stood a moment in thought. "Jared, I can't tell you what to do, but let's covenant together to pray that God will change their hearts or our circumstances."

"Do you think it's too late? I mean for this city to throw off Shari'ah law?"

"I don't know. But there is one thing I do know. I am not going to knuckle under to the Imam's demands."

A stone whizzed past the table followed by another and another. A group of Arab youths stood at the end of the street taunting the pastor and Jared.

"You infidels! Why don't you keep your religion to yourselves and stop trying to push it on us?"

The youths closed the distance and Pastor Carlson stepped in front of the table.

"Young man, can I offer you a—" the bottle of soda was ripped from his hand and thrown to the pavement. Before he could react, the leader squared himself and punched him in the face. Blood spurted from the pastor's lip and he fell back.

Jared caught him and they fell to the street with a thud. Gravel cut into Jared's palms leaving them raw and bloody. The jolt of the pastor's weight shocked him. His mind flashed back to a street in Kandahar, the smell of sulfur mixed with sweat and fear spawned a memory he'd long suppressed. The sensation was as palpable as the day it happened. Jared blinked hard. A moment later, the table flipped over, literature scattered and fists flew. Then all went silent.

A shadow passed between the sun and Jared's swollen face. He squinted and a distant voice pressed into his numb mind.

"Jared?" Jimbo touched his shoulder.

He had been returning from a movie, and stopped by to say hi when he saw Jared and his pastor in a street brawl. He tore one Arab youth off and tossed him against the wall. Another he dropkicked, and then turned to the leader. The lanky youth pulled a knife and slashed at Jimbo, barely missing his throat. Jimbo grabbed his knife hand and spun around until the youth's arm was wedged tightly at his back. Jimbo smiled when he heard something pop and the knife fell, clanking sharply on the asphalt. The young Arab cried out in pain and the others scattered like a bevy of quail. Jimbo reached down and picked up the knife as a police cruiser appeared and rolled to a stop in front of the scene. Two officers jumped from the cruiser, their weapons drawn.

"Drop the knife and raise your hands!" The lead officer demanded.

Jimbo knew most of the officers on the police force but not these men. Their skin was darker, their uniforms were crisp and new, and even the cruiser was different. He placed the knife on the road and kicked it gently toward the officers.

"Officer, I found this boy and a gang assaulting these two men. I came along and broke up the fight."

He released the young Arab and pushed him in the direction of the lead officer.

The two uniformed men stood, guns still pointed, silent.

The youth, still holding his shoulder, pointed at the preacher.

"That's not true, that man came out from behind the table and tried to push his religion down my throat. When I refused, he got violent. All I did was defend myself and then this fat guy came up and pulled a knife on me."

Jimbo's mouth dropped open and he felt his face getting red.

Jared pushed himself away from the earth and wobbled to his feet.

"Don't move!" The first officer commanded.

Every muscle in Jared's body tensed. He rubbed the knot on the back of his head. "That's *not* what happened. A bunch of these youths started throwing stones at us, and calling us names. The preacher offered them a drink, and they attacked us."

The police officer looked down at the pastor; his face badly beaten. He looked dazed, his hair was disheveled, blood trickled from his lip and nose.

Jared helped him to his feet. The pastor wobbled and leaned heavily on the edge of the upturned table.

"Sir, we are going to arrest you and your friends for disturbing the peace, impeding the flow of traffic, and," the officer pulled a notepad from his pocket, "and for attempting to spread religious material to a Muslim minor against his will."

Jimbo, still with his hands raised in the air, looked over at Jared. "What have you got me into?"

Jared said through swollen lips. "Me? I didn't even know you were in town."

The young Arab pivoted and scampered around the corner out of sight.

"Look officers, let me explain—" The officer cut Jimbo off with a look. The second had never said a word. Both officers holstered their weapons. One stepped closer to Pastor Carlson and put his hands on his hips.

"We're going to let you off with a warning this time, but let me give you some advice." He paused to scan the littered sidewalk. "Clean up this mess and keep your religion to yourself. Don't be pushing it on other people, especially us, uh, on the Muslims. They come down here to shop and have a good time and don't want to have to deal with your propaganda."

Pastor Carlson ran his sleeve across his cut lip. "Officer, with all due respect, I have written permission, signed by the former mayor, giving me permission to set up my table on the sidewalk in front of my church and offer cold drinks. I am free to talk to anyone who will talk with me."

The lead officer crossed his arms. "Look preacher, you're not listening. That signature isn't worth the paper it's written on. Take my advice. Shut it down."

Jimbo stuck his hands out. "Wait one minute here, buddy. The Constitution gives these guys the right to free speech and freedom of religion."

The officer turned on him. "We found *you* with a knife, holding a minor against his will. Is that what you call freedom of religion? You'd better keep your mouth shut, or we'll arrest *you.*"

Jimbo's mind raced but he said nothing. He watched the two officers back away, get into the cruiser, and pull away. By then, a crowd had gathered, pointing fingers and nodding animatedly. His pent-up frustration needed to be vented and the on-lookers were his unwitting targets. "What are you looking at!" He spat. "Move along and stop gawking."

The mix of shopkeepers, patrons, and pedestrians broke up and returned to their routine as if nothing had happened.

"Say Jared, where's Raleigh anyway?" Jimbo asked.

Jared touched the sore place on his cheek. "I left him at the house."

"I'll bet that's the last time you do that, ol' buddy."

Jared nodded, "You're right about that. From now on he'll be with me wherever I go."

The pastor pushed himself away from the table. "I sure appreciate you stopping by when you did, Jimbo. I just hate it that it involved you in a fist fight."

Jimbo snickered and rubbed his knuckles. "Ah well, it kinda felt good to punch the lights out of those, uh, well you know. I'm just glad I showed up when I did."

"From the looks of it, you were enjoying dislocating that kid's shoulder." Jared rubbed his jaw gently. He didn't think it was broken.

Jimbo shrugged. "I was just doing what I was taught..." he stopped. "By the way, I wonder what Xavier's going to say when he hears you're mixing it up with the citizens of Stanford?"

A wry smile creased Jared's face and it hurt like blazes. "Well how 'bout we conveniently overlook that little detail the next time we talk with him?"

Jimbo nodded. "Yeah, just as long as you don't talk to him using Skype. If he sees your face the way it looks now, he might think you and I got into it." He paused and looked at the literature blowing in the wind. "You'd better get this mess cleaned up before the police change their minds." He turned and strode off in the direction of the nearest bar.

Jared watched his friend disappear then turned to his pastor. "It looks like the new city ordinances have affected us after all."

Pastor Carlson leaned over slowly and began to gather the scattered tracts and literature. "As I read the Constitution, I have the right to religious freedom. And no city ordinance is going to stop me from speaking out."

Jared glanced up at him. His jaw was set, his eyebrows furrowed.

"Yeah, well, welcome to the new reality."

Chapter 30

Jared's House

Jared bolted out of bed as if he had been jabbed with a hot iron. He lifted his cell phone from the nightstand and looked at the caller ID. It was two a.m. His bleary eyes barely focused. He didn't recognize the number. Curiosity forced his finger to the green button.

"Hello?"

Silence.

He pressed the phone closer to his ear.

Breathing, he heard breathing. Someone was there but didn't speak, or couldn't speak.

"Hello, are you there?" He waited.

"Yes." It was a few decibels above audible.

"Could you speak up, I can barely hear you."

"I can't, they might hear me." Fear etched her soft voice.

It sounded strangely familiar.

"Elaine, is that you?"

"There's someone outside my house and they are trying to break in." Her voice was muffled and low.

"Have you called 9-1-1?"

"No, I can't. I don't trust them."

Jared understood. He was still sore from the beating he and the pastor received a week ago. His breathing went shallow, his heart pounded like a jackhammer.

"Jared, listen, I found documentation that Mayor Talabani and that Imam guy are related."

The words struck him like a kick to the gut and he grunted.

"Do you have the documentation with you?"

"No, I've hidden it someplace safe, but they know."

Jared's mind raced.

In the background, he heard glass breaking.

Voices, screams.

"They're coming for me. Heeeelp!"

Shots rang out.

Elaine groaned and Jared heard her collapse. The phone clattered to the floor. He stood listening helplessly as two more rapid shots were fired.

His heart fluttered, sweat slicked his phone.

Then someone picked up Elaine's phone. Someone on the other end breathed jerkily into the receiver. Then the line went dead.

Before he could dial the police, the phone rang in his hand. He almost dropped it. A voice in his head screamed, don't answer it!

If he let it go to his voice mail, the caller would know his name. If he answered they would have confirmation that Elaine talked before she died. He pushed the green button, then hung up.

The next day, the newspaper headlines read. 'Brutal Killing, Another Home Invasion.' The article quoted the police chief stating that, "It was an on-going investigation, but it appeared to be another home invasion, a robbery turned violent.

The soft clinking of glasses filled with iced-tea, carried deftly by waiters and waitresses was all part of the atmosphere within restaurant. The low conversations of dozens of patrons and the aroma of fresh-baked bread was a welcome relief from the hectic schedule Jared had been keeping. The maître d' led him through the maze of circular tables and guided him to a booth. He took a seat and placed his drink order as Jimbo arrived.

"Is it my imagination or is it getting hot already?" Jimbo fanned himself.

"You're sitting in the sun, buddy, that's why you're so hot. Not to mention the fact that you're about fifty pounds over-weight." Jared said, his voice somber.

"Fifty pounds? Is that all? Make it more like seventy five," he said as he scanned the dessert menu.

"Look Jimbo, we have a problem."

He let the menu flop to the table. "Are those Arab kids still bothering you?"

Jared shook his head. "They're not Arabs, as I understand it, but they are Muslims and no, Jimbo, it's worse than that."

He went on to rehearse Elaine's phone call.

"So where do you suppose those papers are?"

"I have no clue, but they probably weren't in her house."

"So you are saying she said something about the mayor and this Imam guy being related?"

"That's what she said and then they shot her."

Jimbo pursed his lips in a high-pitched teakettle whistle.

"That's a pretty hefty accusation."

"That's a pretty heavy price Elaine paid for making it."

They sat and stared at each other. Neither spoke. Only the ticking of the large wall clock spoke of the passing of time, of life, of opportunities offered and now gone. Such was the case of Miss Elaine Rakestraw. Jared was determined her passing would not be in vain.

"There's another thing that's got me bothered." Jared glared out the window.

"What's that?"

"The timing is all off. I distinctly remember getting the call from Elaine around two a.m. but the paper reported the killing took place at midnight. I wonder why they got the time so far off?"

Jimbo ran his hand across the back of his neck. "I don't know but something's not right. By skewing the time by two hours, it gave the perp time to ransack the house. Do you think they were looking for those papers or just ransacked the house as a cover up?"

"I was thinking they want to make it look like just another home invasion."

Jimbo poured another cup of coffee. "It's too bad about Elaine. From the few times I saw her, she seemed like a nice lady. For some reason I get the feeling that I we've met before, but I can't put my finger in it."

Jared watched a sparrow land on the ledge outside and begin to snatch at a line of ants. "Yeah, she was nice, a bit mixed up, but nice."

Jimbo narrowed his eyes. "What we're looking at is a police cover-up if you ask me."

"That's great, so now who do we trust?"

Jimbo leaned back. "I know at least two that I don't trust."

Jared crossed his arms. "I agree those two middle-eastern officers don't endow me with a lot of confidence."

"Well at least you have Raleigh to watch your back."

The statement struck Jared as odd. He'd forgotten about the two threats to his life. Now he wondered who else knew about the threatening notes. Did Jimbo? And who was the mysterious person that had been following him?

"Look Jimbo, now that this Shari'ah law is spreading like wildfire, we've got to be careful not to upset the Muslim work crew."

Jimbo rocked on two legs of his chair. "Let me make a few phone calls and see what I can find out about the new mayor." He laid a twenty dollar bill on the table, lifted his girth from the chair and strode to the door.

Jared eyed him as the door closed behind him.

Who is this guy and what connections does he have that he can inquire about the Mayor?

Chapter 31

Gibson, Tate and Sutterfield – Attorneys at Law

Pastor Carlson fidgeted with his watchband, waiting for his appointment. The plush couch absorbed his weight but offered no relief from the load on his slumping shoulders. The dark paneled walls were laden with English Fox and Hound pictures.

"Mr. Carlson?"

He snapped to reality. Attorney Donald Gibson a portly man with deep set blue eyes stood, hand outstretched. "I presume you are Pastor Carlson." The attorney's probing eyes had an interested glint.

"Yes, I am. Thank you for seeing me on such short notice."

"Come into my office, sir." He turned to his secretary, "Mrs. Goodson, would you get our guest a cup of coffee?"

He led the pastor into his office. The door closed with a soft, firm thud.

Mr. Gibson took his seat and folded his hands on a paperless desk. Its smooth, polished surface reflected the recessed light from above, giving Pastor the illusion it was made of glass.

"Have you heard the news about Mayor Talibani's secretary?" Gibson asked.

Pastor Carlson sat on a plush leather chair. It felt cold but soon warmed. Out of habit, he crossed his legs and straightened his cuff. "Yes, it's tragic.

"I understand she was attending your church." His statement was assumptive.

"Yes sir. But how would you have known that?"

Donald smiled. "I read the police report and it mentioned the fact that she had several of your church bulletins near her body. One with the church's mailing address circled.

Pastor Carlson hunched his shoulders. He'd not heard that. "Yes, you're right, as a matter of fact, she attended our services a few weeks but then missed the next two." His voice trailed off.

"Oh? Was that unusual? I mean for her to be hit and miss?"

The pastor tugged on his collar. "Yes. The last time we talked, she indicated she wanted to join. Then something unusual happened."

"Go on."

"I'd forgotten all about it until now. After the morning service, she met me down front and asked for an appointment. I thought she wanted council about a spiritual need, but instead she said it was about the mayor."

"The mayor?"

"Yes but then we were interrupted and I never got a chance to nail down a time. Now she is gone and we'll never know what it was about."

Gibson took out a notepad and began to scribble. "I'm making a note to myself to do some checking around. I've had my suspicions about the mayor. His campaign was financed from outside sources with uh, let's say, questionable legality."

The door opened and Mrs. Goodson carried in a tray with a coffee pot and two cups. The aroma of the fresh brew reached the pastor's nose before she set it down on the corner of her boss's desk.

"Will there be anything else?" her voice was warm and congenial.

"No, Mrs. Goodson, thank you, that will be all."

She receded out of sight.

"So Pastor Carlson," Donald said pouring the pastor a cup of coffee. "You didn't come here to discuss current affairs, what is it that brought you here?"

Pastor Carlson took a sip. Its warmth permeated throughout his body. *I wonder where he got this. It's better than Starbucks.*

"It's about last Saturday. We have permission to hand out literature on the sidewalk in front of our church as long as we don't interrupt the flow of foot traffic. But last Saturday a group of Muslim teenagers started throwing stones at us, and as you can see," he pointed to the shiner around his right eye, "I was on the receiving end of Shari'ah Law. The ringleader accused me of starting the fight."

"Yes, I read about it in the paper. The Press is saying you're not going to back down from your stand against the new city ordinance. That isn't a good match-up."

The pastor nodded. "Kind of like David and Goliath."

Donald tapped his fingers together. "That's about the ratio, as I recall the story."

"Yes, but do you remember the outcome? The little guy won and the big guy fell, hard."

Gibson chuckled. "Chalk one up for the underdog."

"Mr. Gibson, the city of Stanford has just enacted some anti-defamation laws prohibiting free speech and my right to preach the gospel. If I preach that Jesus is the Son of God and that He is the only way to Heaven, I could be arrested." After spending the night in prayer and fasting, he had called the offices of Gibson,

Tate and Sutterfield, attorneys at Law, and asked for an appointment. Now he questioned his sanity.

Donald peered at the pastor through rimless glasses. The pastor could see his mind already racing, as if he were playing a game of mental chess with an invisible opponent.

"As you know, my firm is well known for taking on social injustices and political hot potatoes. This case will surely test our mettle. But I think we have a pretty solid case against the city."

Pastor Carlson relaxed a little and took another sip of coffee. "It seems like the whole city has gone head-long after this Shari'ah law."

"Yes, I understand your concern. We have been watching the growth of Muslim influence in America, wondering when it would spill over into our American judicial system."

He reached into his brief case, drew out a newspaper, and slid it across his desk. The headlines said it all:

Fears of Shari'ah Law in America Grow Among Conservatives.

The article continued. "Threats of anti-Muslim sentiment in America have brought with it a wave of largely-unsubstantiated suggestions from conservative media commentators and politicians that America is at risk of falling under the sway of Shari'ah law."

The attorney watched every move his new client made. Assessing him, analyzing him, determining what type of metal he was made of.

"Actually we have been doing a lot of research and role playing in preparation for this day. We think we have a solid case here, and can sway the court to support the state constitution. If need be, we may have to appeal it, but that's a ways down the road."

Pastor Carlson nodded. "What about the restraining order on my preaching? Can you get that lifted?"

"Yes, for the time being, we will file an injunction against the city of Stanford requiring that the anti-defamation law be repealed. We also will request that the restraining order, placed upon you, be lifted so that you may continue you church ministry. That will give us time to get our ducks in a row and you can continue preaching without fear of being arrested."

The pastor's face brightened, "That sounds like a good plan to me, but how much is this going to cost?" His voice was edged with uncertainty.

Gibson stood, pushing back his plush seat. "Look pastor, don't worry about the costs. My firm has already discussed the matter and decided to take it on Pro-Bono. So what do you say we get started?"

Pastor Carlson leaned forward, elbows on his knees, head bent. "That's a big relief. For a moment, I thought we have to sell our property and go underground to have church."

"Well Pastor, I hope it doesn't come to that."

"I sure hope not. It gives me a greater appreciation of the freedom we have … had." His voice shook.

Attorney Gibson cleared his throat. "I don't want to paint too gloomy a picture, but this is going to be an uphill battle. We may lose a few skirmishes along the way. So don't get discouraged." His voice was flat and firm.

He paced the floor. "Already there is a Michigan Islamic Court of Appeals acting as a go-between for defendants and their plaintiffs involving Islamic disputes."

The pastor crossed his arms and pinched the bridge of his nose. "You know, we have been trying to get our church a tax-exempt status ever since we started but haven't been successful. On the other hand, as I understand it, this Mosque they're building here in town was given a tax-exempt status, calling it a nonprofit, tax-exempt group, a multipurpose, human service, charitable organization."

"See, that's what I'm saying. Depending on the judge and his interpretation of the law, the court may be stacked against us. So don't get your hopes too high. I think, in a way, we have sown the seeds of our own destruction."

"Oh? How so?" The pastor turned, a confused look filled his eyes.

"Well, think of it this way, by incorporating certain Jewish sectarian laws and honoring Christian-backed blue laws, limiting the sale of alcohol on Sundays, we have inadvertently opened the door to Shari'ah-friendly laws as well."

The pastor shifted his weight from one leg to the other. "You mean to say that it won't be long before shops and stores will be closed by sundown Thursday, and not reopen until sundown on Friday?"

Gibson shook his head. "That's right. I remember reading a newspaper recently stating that exact thing." He closed his eyes and read from the chalkboard of his mind. "Banks to begin closing on Fridays."

Pastor Carlson stuck his hands in his pockets and stared through the palladium window. The wind in the trees outside had shifted around from southwest to the north. "Looks like we have a storm brewing."

Gibson joined him. "Are you talking about the latest weather report or the latest political conditions?"

"Both. There's a storm brewing and it won't be long before Stanford will be embroiled in a huge mess. Citizens like Mr. Dunlop, who feel the Muslims have gone too far, will begin picketing City Hall, and protesters will protest against the protesters. It will be like the Race Riots of the sixties all over again."

Gibson sighed deeply.

"I'm afraid the city is already divided. Non-Muslim women are being treated as second-class citizens. They're ignored by Muslim shop owners and are made to wait until all the men are served. I've even heard that some non-Muslim women have been arrested for not wearing a head covering. Have you heard that?"

Pastor Carlson set his cup down, "Yes."

"This was not what the people thought they were getting when they voted to enact some of the Muslim laws. The Muslim politicians told them that this was the way of peace. But instead, it brought tension, turmoil and trouble. This is becoming a nightmare."

"Yes. An American nightmare."

Chapter 32

Woodbridge Memorial Cemetery

It was a sunny day and the few clouds, that passed overhead, offered little relief to the small group of mourners gathered around the graveside where they had laid Elaine Rakestraw to rest.

As Pastor Carlson closed the committal service in prayer, Jared caught movement to his right. Despite the spirit of the moment, he watched through his sunglasses. Raleigh, who had been leaning against his leg panting, scanned the perimeter. A low growl came from his throat and Jared cocked his head. There was the source of the movement, a small, dark skinned man in the shadow of a large willow tree. The prayer ended, Jared blinked, and the slender figure was gone.

All the way back to the construction site, Jared had the distinct feeling he was being followed. Raleigh paced the front seat, as if he sensed it too.

"You feel it too, boy?" Jared said in an even tone. Raleigh looked at his master and Jared reached up and stroked his neck. "Looks like we have company." He still saw no one but kept glancing in the rearview mirror.

A car ripped through the intersection in front of him, barely missing his front fender. He slammed on his brakes and skidded. Raleigh slid from the seat and landed hard against the dashboard. "Sorry ol' buddy, I didn't see that one coming."

Raleigh sneezed at the smell of burnt rubber. Jared's vehicle sat half way through the intersection for a full minute as he tried to control his breathing. A horn blaring behind him brought him to his senses. He eased the Land Rover across the road to the shoulder, got out and leaned over the hood with both hands on the hot metal.

Lord, this is getting bad, I'm seeing things, and feeling things that make me look behind every bush for the boogey man, like a kid afraid of his shadow. I know You say You have not given me a spirit of fear but of a sound mind, but right now I'm not there. Lord, I need You. Protect me, be with me, in Jesus' name, amen.

He got back in the Rover. When he arrived at the construction shack, he found a somber mood within. It seemed to him both Fatemah and Shirin had been crying.

"What's wrong?"

Shirin came to him, but stopped short of his personal space. She sniffed back a tear. "We were just talking about Elaine and how sad it is that she had no family to come to her funeral. We couldn't attend her funeral with your religion, but our hearts go out to you, and all those who knew her."

Fatemah came to Shirin's side, slid her arm around her slender waist, and gave her a gentle squeeze.

"With all the trips I've been making to City Hall, I got to know Elaine fairly well," Fatemah said with thick emotion. "She was a really nice person and I think we could have been good friends. I can't believe she's gone." Her voice broke.

Jared stood defenseless. A former marine wasn't used to dealing with this kind of emotional outpour. He lowered his head as a lump gathered in his throat.

"In the short time I knew her, she seemed like a really sweet person." He allowed a slight smile to push across his face. "A bit flighty, but really sweet."

Fatemah's head tilted, and her eyes met his with an intense look. "Oh really?"

Jared's pulse quickened. He'd said too much. He swallowed hard, thinking harder. After pawing the floor with his shoe for a moment, he sighed and looked up into Fatemah's brown eyes.

"I talked with Elaine a few weeks ago after church. I found her sitting in her car, she had been crying." He shook his head, a grin parting his lips. "My heart went out to her. I asked her if everything was all right and we ended up at Mother's Finest for Sunday dinner. She was all over the board emotionally and I got the feeling she had a lot of personal baggage. I wished I could have helped her more, that's all."

His answer seemed to comfort Fatemah, and the women returned to work but Jared felt he'd connected with Fatemah on an important level. Funny, he'd never noticed how beautiful her eyes were.

Chapter 33

The Auditorium of the Center for Islamic Training

Ahmad and Shirin arrived in time to hear Imam Fahad call the faithful to prayer. Shirin veiled in white walked slowly to the women's gallery, and Ahmad went to the men's section of the new facility. It was Friday. The Imam proclaimed this day a special holy day.

Ahmad's attitude toward Jared was changing. His study of history taught him the Crusaders were the aggressors who tried to drive them from their rightful land in the Holy Lands. He had looked at all Christians the way his ancestors did, before his dramatic rescue. But that was then. Jared was a caring person not the monster Islam and the Imam told him all Christians were. *If Mr. Jared was a Muslim hater, why was he heading up the construction of a Mosque? Why was he helping spread Islam? And why did he save my life?* Ahmad's question evaporated as the voice of the Imam rang through the intercom.

He joined his brothers when they prostrated themselves while Imam Fahad led in prayer.

"Praise belongs to Allah, the merciful. Let the whole earth be filled with the knowledge of his greatness." His voice carried over the loud speaker.

The prayer continued but Ahmad's mind wandered, not hearing what he'd heard a thousand times before. He blinked and saw the other men lifting themselves up. He too assumed a cross-legged position, hands folded, trying not to listen to that hated voice. As the message unfolded, it struck him that something wasn't right. Fahad was usually articulate. Today he appeared haggard, disheveled and confused. His quotes from the Qur'an were out of context. He mumbled and began to ramble.

"Slaves of Allah! We are living in very difficult and painful times; times filled with hardship, agonies, and calamity. Look at how the enemies of Islam have united against us. They never unite so well except when they are conspiring against Islam and the true faith."

Ahmad shifted his eyes from left and right. Men he'd worked with, men he'd spent hours with, sat mesmerized, drinking in every word. But he was not buying it, not this time. He looked at Fahad. *Murderer.* Ahmad's heart, like the tile floor, was cool and hard. Despite the occasional chants from his Muslim brothers sitting around him, the thought of his parent's deaths and his hatred for the Imam consumed him. If he could, he'd run to the platform and leap upon him and squeeze the life out of him. To do so would be suicide. But it would be worth it to avenge his mother's death.

"We must ask ourselves this: Why is it that they have the ability to inflict so much harm on us?"

Harm? He wondered. *What harm?*

"Are we not the slaves of Allah and the followers of His honorable Messenger? If yes, then why have they gathered against us to wipe us out?" The Imam shouted to the congregation.

Ahmad caught Shirin's eye across the room. She lowered her gaze and shifted. She had never completely bought into the whole Islamic thing, and now he was having his doubts.

"Slaves of Allah," the Imam continued, "how long will you allow the blanket of complacency to smother your zeal for Allah? You have allowed the Zionists, commercialism, materialism and Christianity to rob you of your zeal. Allah is a great God. He will not tolerate second place."

Bloody though his hands are, he has a point, Ahmad thought. All around him, was evidence of the influence of American culture on his Islamic brothers; a culture of affluence and opulence. It was the opposite from the life of simplicity and humility taught by his heritage. But it was America after all, and he had to admit, he enjoyed the same conveniences and luxuries Uncle Shaquille enjoyed back in Iran.

"When Allah said to defend Islam with the pen we obeyed. When Allah said to spread Islam with the spoken word, we submitted to His will. But Islam is not spreading; the Great Satan and the Little Satan resist us in every country. Already the Zionists seek to retake the Temple mount where one of our most holy sites, the Dome of the Rock, sits." Fahad's voice rose to fever pitch.

"Even now, the Great Satan is building her military bases in our very backyard. Soon they will threaten our most holy places, Mecca and Medina. The Great Satan and the Zionists are robbing us of our empire. Once the power and greatness of Allah was felt from Saudi Arabia to South Africa to China, but not anymore, my friends. Not anymore."

Ahmad's ears rang and his pulse quickened. This was getting out of hand. Did the man think he was back in Iran or wherever he claimed to be from?

"Not until the Great Satan and the Zionists are beaten into submission will we see the coming of Al-Mahdi, our savior. Then he will spread peace and justice throughout the world where once 'there was injustice and tyranny, and all will worship Allah, the merciful."

Ahmad followed the Imam when he led them to read aloud from the Qur'an.

"Among the Believers are men who have been true to their Covenant with Allah: of them some have completed their vow to the death, and among them some still wait: and they have never altered their determination in the least."

What is he talking about? Ahmad sat, confused, feeling out of place, wondering if anyone could tell he was beginning to question his religion. His hands slicked, his breathing shortened and he broke out in a sweat. If anyone knew the doubts in his heart, he'd be in deep trouble. It was a capital offense to question the Imam's teaching, and he was guilty.

"It is time for us, the most zealous, the most fervent, the most committed to defend the cause of Islam. I declare 'Jihad' on the infidels."

Fahad stood with his eyes lifted upward and quoted a verse Ahmad had been forced to commit to memory as a boy.

"And do not say about those who are killed in the way of Allah 'They are dead.' Rather, they are alive, they are alive, but you perceive it not. The United States will not protect you, nor are they able to release you from the oppression befalling you. Flee to Allah," his voice rose again. "There will be no might nor victory except from Allah, He alone is capable of everything, He is The Best Protector, and The Excellent Helper."

The frenzied masses rose to their feet and began shouting 'Abdul Akbar! Allah is great!' 'Abdul Akbar!' 'Allah is great!' They began to spill into the streets to let their message be heard. Ahmad grimaced. This time the Imam had gone too far. This was not Iran.

Shirin's face was ashen and she scurried to Ahmad's side. Under normal circumstances, he would be chanting with the rest of the crowd but he took her by the hand.

"Come Shirin, let's get out of here, I'm not feeling well."

Her eyes widened. He tugged her through the mass of shoving bodies. He needed some fresh air, and made a bee-line for the first exit he could find.

"Ahmad, what's come over you? You look like you're going to be ill." She began to fan him with her sleeve.

He leaned over, hands on his knees, panting after the struggle. "I don't know," he said between gulps of air. "I was sitting there and I got the feeling that everyone was staring at me, that they could read my mind, that they knew my thoughts." His words came, halting.

Shirin put her hand gently on his back. She hesitated, then asked, "What *are* your thoughts?"

He righted himself, wiped sweat from his brow, breathing heavily.

"You shouldn't ask such questions. It is dangerous to even think these things or Allah, the merciful, will know." The words were right but his voice rang hollow.

Imam Fahad stepped from the podium, his voice aimed toward his close followers. His bodyguards formed a tight circle around him. "I understand a ballot initiative circulating through the state legislature calling for the state to declare Shari'ah law unconstitutional. If it passes, it will be just the catalyst we need." The Imam's men pushed through the thinning crowd toward his inner sanctum. Fahad said to their backs. "We need to renew our personal war . . . the Jihad. I, as Caliph over this community, declare jihad and you are obligated to comply."

A few heads nodded and some men raised fists, pumping the air wildly.

"I don't care about the newly enacted state initiative. I am declaring a moratorium on the ringing of church bells; the recitation of the Torah or the Bible out loud or in public is prohibited. The cross is banned from being displayed at funerals and feast days, or on church buildings."

Ameer Abu el Telami, one of the Imam's trusted lieutenants leaned close. "My Father, I am here to do your bidding."

"Very good. This is the world I have dreamed of. Allah wills it, it will come to pass."

Chapter 34

Canaan Baptist Church

It was a hot, sultry Sunday evening in early September, when Pastor Carlson announced his decision, and that he was involved with a lawsuit. It came as no surprise to Jared. He'd felt the intrusion of the Shari'ah friendly laws.

He sat near the front and caught a glimpse of Fred Dunlop. The man stared at him with a steely expression, unblinking. Jared snorted. The vote to oust him from their membership had been close. It was Ms. Alice Nunnley's deciding vote that tipped the scales in favor, retaining him as a member in good standing. Now, this announcement, would profoundly affect him and the building project. What would Shirin and Fatemah think? What would Ahmad think? The fragile relationship between him and Ahmad could be jeopardized. And already he himself was at odds with some of the church family. He found himself caught between the American dream and burgeoning nightmare—an Islamic nightmare.

The pastor fingered his notes, on the smooth surface of the Plexiglas podium. His voice was low, somber. "Folks, we cannot stand by idly and let our freedoms be eroded," he said with passion and determination.

He stepped to the center of the auditorium, laced his fingers in front of him and looked from eye to eye.

"We have a command from God to preach the truth. If that runs against the grain of society, then so be it, but we must take a stand."

There were a few weak amens. The rest stared, wondering where this was leading.

"If saying Jesus is the only way to Heaven is against the law, then so be it. If our saying that salvation is by grace alone, through faith alone makes people mad, then that's the way it is. I'm not a Muslim hater, I'm a Bible lover." He held his Bible high above his head as he spoke.

"Folks, this will probably get real ugly before it's over and we need to be resolved to stay the course. Jesus said; 'These things I have spoken unto you, that in me ye might have peace. In the world ye shall have tribulation: but be of good cheer; I have overcome the world.' John 16:33."

He stepped back behind the podium.

Crack!

The front window exploded, sending shards of glass all over the floor and the nearest pews. People recoiled and scattered. Men yelled, a woman shrieked.

Jared ducked when another stone finished what the first one began and thudded to the floor.

Two masked men with clubs kicked in the front door and entered the sanctuary. "Death to the infidels! Death to the infidels!" One hooded men grabbed the pastor, shaking him

"We have heard enough of your hate speech! You are violating the law of Allah! Shut-up! You're coming with us!"

Pastor Carlson's face turned ashen.

To Jared's left, an elderly lady moaned. Mrs. Dunlop slumped over and fell, striking her head sharply on the floor. As if in slow motion, Jared returned to the action in front. The masked man dragged the pastor from the platform.

Adrenalin surged. Jared's training took over.

When the first intruder passed him, Jared stood, grabbed him by the arm, and twisted it behind his back making sure he dislocated his shoulder. The man screamed. Then Jared pulled his 9mm Beretta from his shoulder holster and pointed it at his head.

At the sound of the first stone smashing the front window, Raleigh had jumped to his feet. Ever since Jared's run in with the Arab gang, he'd been his constant companion, shadowing his every move. Now he stood just inside the backdoor, snarling, waiting his master's command.

"Attack!"

Raleigh leaped at the man holding Pastor Carlson. His teeth sank into his forearm and he dropped the club. It fell with the pastor and bounced across the floor. Raleigh sprang again, knocking the man down and the dog pounced on his chest, barring his teeth.

Within two minutes of the first stone, the two hooded men were writhing in pain on the floor in the center of the auditorium.

"Quick, someone dial 9-1-1," Jared hollered.

He stepped over to Mrs. Dunlop, where her husband hovered over her helplessly.

"Please, help us." Jared saw the pain in Fred's eyes. He knelt next to his wife, took her hand, and began to pray. It was a simple prayer, but it reached the ears of God before it was spoken.

Mrs. Dunlop's eyes fluttered and she took a deep breath.

"Oh Fred, I saw angels." A smile broke across her wrinkled face and her eyes focused on her husband. The encircling congregation breathed a corporate sigh of relief.

"Are you going to be all right, Mrs. Dunlop?" Jared lifted her head slightly.

She raised her hand to the knot on the side of her face and rubbed. "I'm a bit woozy."

"You just lie still and we'll get an ambulance out here as soon as possible." He stood.

After he finished the call, Mr. Dunlop eased up to his side. "I sure do appreciate what you did today. Not just for the preacher, but for my wife." He paused, and his face softened. He sighed. "I thought I lost her there for a moment."

Jared nodded. "I think you did, but God had other plans for her."

Fred Dunlop stuck out a weathered hand. "I've said some terrible things about you. I was so wrong. Will you forgive me?" His voice trembled.

Jared pushed down the lump in his throat. Despite the grief the elderly man had caused him, he'd prayed many times for the Lord to show him how to make peace with him. Jared squeezed his hand firmly. "I already have."

Five minutes later, two policemen arrived. They were the same two officers who the pastor and Jared met after they'd been beaten up.

The officers stepped through the broken door. Their boots crunched the shards of glass as they approached the shaken pastor. Neither spoke. One officer put his hands on his hips and surveyed the damage. The other crossed his arms and peered over his sunglasses. They were not happy to be in church on Sunday.

"Is there a problem, officers? We called you because these two thugs interrupted our worship service by throwing rocks through the window and entering our service yelling and screaming." Jared said with his hand outstretched.

The police sergeant uncrossed his arms and pulled a note pad from his pocket. "Are you in charge?" he looked at Jared.

"No sir, I'm not, but—"

"Then be quiet and step out of the way. Who is in charge here?" His voice cut through the low whispers.

Pastor Carlson, shaken, stood to his feet and approached the two police officers.

"I am, sir, I'm the pastor."

The officer straightened and looked the pastor in the eyes. "Weren't you the same guys who picked a fight with some teenagers a few weeks ago?"

Jared's muscles tensed.

"No officer, you must have me mixed up with someone else. We called you here today because these two thugs broke up our worship service. And before you let them slip through your fingers—again, please handcuff them. I wouldn't want Raleigh," he paused and looked at the German shepherd standing guard, "to chase them down in the street."

The police sergeant smirked, pulled a couple of fast-ties from a pouch, and cinched them on the two men's wrists. "There, are you happy now?"

The pastor smiled, and nodded. "Yes, I think that should hold them nicely until we get the paperwork filled out. I want to press formal charges."

"You will need to come down to the police station to do that. Are you willing to spend the rest of the day filling out the papers?"

Mr. Dunlop stepped up, caught the pastor's elbow, and leaned into his ear.

"Go for it, Pastor, Jared and I can hold things down here." A foxy smile crinkled his face.

The pastor's eyes widened. "What about your wife? Doesn't she need medical attention?"

"Yes, but she's a tough girl. I'll let the paramedics take care of her and check on her later. You need to take care of business on behalf of the congregation."

"Well, that settles it. I'll follow you boys to the police department. I wouldn't want you fellas to get lost."

"I think you're wasting your time, preacher." The other officer said.

Jared threw his hand in the air and rubbed his forehead.

"Look guys, you've got dozens of eye witnesses all saying the same thing. These two punks came in here and threatened us with clubs." He picked up one of the clubs. The officer's hands covered their holsters.

"A bit jumpy, aren't you?"

The first officer's face hardened. "You need to watch your mouth." They exchanged looks and started toward the door with the offenders in tow. The sergeant paused and looked at the bulging sports coat.

"Do you have a permit to carry that weapon?" he asked in a gruff voice.

Jared looked down at his coat and then back into the officer's raven eyes. "As a matter of fact, I do. Do you need to see my concealed weapon permit?"

"Yes, I think I do."

Jared reached into his back pocket, and the young Arab jutted his chin out. "Officer, he threatened me, said he'd like to shoot my head off."

Officer Mohan Amin, one of two new recruits, took the permit and scanned it. Before he handed it back, he narrowed his eyes and said to Jared, "Is that so. Maybe we ought to take you in for questioning."

Jared knew he was bluffing, trying to get him to make a mistake. "Sure officer, I'd be glad to make a statement. I'll just be sure to mention that you let the last perp get away."

The police sergeant's puffed out chest sagged and Jared stared him down.

"We'll be in touch." He handed Jared's permit to him.

Pastor Carlson looked at Jared, concern on his face. "Why do I get the distinct impression those officers think we initiated this mess?"

Jared watched the officers pull away. "I got that same impression. I think we know whose side they're on."

Chapter 35

Jared's Office

"Mr. Xavier, things are really getting out of hand." Jared said in his weekly update.

"Yes, I've been following the news. It doesn't help for you to be involved with a church that seems to be stirring up trouble," Mr. Xavier said, an edge of rebuke in his voice.

"Sir, I don't know where you're getting your information, but it's not the preacher who's causing all the trouble. With the mayor a Muslim and most of the city councilmen being Muslims and, I might add, members of a radical Mosque that I was hired to build, you should have known this was going to happen."

Mr. Xavier cleared his throat. "Uh, Mr. Russell, I think you're out of line."

"No disrespect, sir, just being straightforward."

"I can appreciate that, and we did consider the ramifications of building a mosque in that area. There are two things we didn't take into consideration; one is that radical Imam, and other, your preacher handing out hate literature, and inciting a riot."

Jared snapped a pencil in half. "Look, Mr. Xavier, you've got it all wrong. They attacked us, not the other way around. One thing's for sure. The fallout from the attack on the church last Sunday has the whole city shaken."

"Oh? How so?"

"Well, whatever goodwill the citizens of Stanford had, has evaporated. They're afraid, and angry. Even the moderate Muslims working on the mosque have been forced to choose between their civic duty of peaceful co-existence or Jihad."

"That spells delay and cost overruns in my book." Mr. Xavier observed.

Jared nodded and pulled another pencil from his drawer and scribbled a note. "With Ramadan in full swing, they are out on the parking lot of The Center for Islamic Studies chanting. It's been going on for hours. It's even dangerous to walk the streets during certain times of the day, especially on Fridays."

A knock on his door ended Jared's phone call.

"Come in."

It was Jimbo, his face was masked in worry.

"Was that Mr. Xavier you were on the phone with?"

Jared nodded. "Yes, why?"

"You might as well call Mr. Xavier back again." He plopped heavily on the couch.

"Uh-oh, what now?"

Jimbo leaned forward. "About half the work crew left early and are roaming the streets of Stanford. I was listening to the police scanner and heard there was a clash between some Islamic youth and non-Islamic. It left several Muslim shops with smashed windows and a car burning." He rubbed his forehead.

"Why is it I get the feeling there is more good news?"

Jimbo straightened. "You'll probably get a phone call any minute but don't be surprised if you hear from your pastor. Your church has been ransacked."

"Can't the mayor call in the State Patrol or declare a state of emergency?"

"That would make sense, but so far it hasn't happened."

Jared picked up the phone and dialed his pastor's number.

"Hello, Pastor? Jared here. Jimbo just informed me about the church. How bad is it?" he rubbed the back of his neck and he paced the floor in front of Jimbo.

He listened as Pastor Carlson gave him an update. "The damage is pretty extensive Jared, but I think it's going to have a unifying effect on the congregation."

"Oh really?"

"Yes, that's the way persecution works. It culls the casual follower from the truly committed believers." He interrupted himself. "Hold on a minute, Jared. Let's see if they are carrying it on the local news."

Jared pointed to the small TV in the corner. "Jimbo, turn on the television."

He responded with agility which surprised Jared.

The black screen came to life, a reporter microphone in hand talking, animatedly in front of the bus station.

"Who would have imagined the bomb Squad being activated in our sleepy town, but it is true. There have been two reports of bombs, one at the mall and the other at the bus station behind me. Thankfully neither was detonated or there would have been countless lives lost."

The cameraman widened his lens.

The reporter dipped the microphone closer to the man next to her. "I have with me, the chief of detectives, Mr. Eddy Marsh. Sir, do you have any idea who might have left those bombs? Or who might be behind these terrible attempts on innocent human beings?"

Eddy Marsh smiled, enjoying the lime-light. He adjusted his dark sunglasses and folded his arms.

"Yes, Miss Hensley, as a matter of fact, I've dispatched a couple of detectives to an apartment on Hill Street. We received a tip that a Jamaican born man, his wife, a Pakistani and their three teenagers were responsible for leaving the bombs."

The reporter spoke directly into the microphone, "Do you have any idea what type of bombs they were?"

Marsh paused to let the momentum build. "Yes, yes we do. They were homemade, organic, peroxide based devices, packed in rucksacks. The triggering mechanisms were two cell phones. If we hadn't jammed the frequency we might have had a bigger disaster on our hands. As it was it was pretty dicey."

The reporter took the microphone and pitched it back to the news anchor.

Jared leaned on the corner of his desk, shaking his head in disbelief. "Man, that's going to have a chilling effect on the whole community . . . Muslim and non-Muslim."

Jimbo flicked off the television, "The question on everyone's mind is, will the law step in, in time? What had happened to our government? This place should be crawling with FBI, CIA, SWAT, and you name it."

Jared shoved his hands in his pockets and fingered the cross. He let out his breath. "Only time will tell. From what I understand, Pastor Carlson's attorney started a ballot initiative to counter the anti-defamation suit against our church. If it fails to pass, we are in deep trouble. In the meantime, I think you and I need to make some plans."

Chapter 36

Jimbo's Apartment

It had been a long week for Jimbo. Covering for Jared when he went to Elaine's funeral, maintaining order on the work site, and keeping the men focused drained him. He was ready for a shower and a good meal. He walked up the sidewalk leading to his apartment, and noticed an envelope in the shrubbery next to the front door. He'd been coming home late for the last week, when it was dark and he hadn't noticed it. He picked it up and fingered the manila mail pouch. It was addressed to him but as he inspected the stamp, he noticed it was not canceled. *Hmm, someone hand delivered it.* He looked left and right. Seeing no one, he pulled the door key from his pocket and unlocked the door.

He closed and locked the door. Ignoring the same stack of bills on the table and the same pile of laundry near the washer, he pushed his way in and plopped on the thread-bare couch. Whatever was inside the envelope was thin enough not to give away any secrets. *Hmm, no return address either.*

He tore it open and its contents slid out on his lap. He sat staring at several sheets of paper, photocopies of a birth certificate and naturalization papers. The name printed on the lines meant nothing to him. Rashmond Fahad Mabarak. He kept reading until he reached the signature at the bottom of the naturalization papers. It was signed Abdul Qadir el Talibani. Jimbo's fingers trembled slightly. The signature across from Talibani's on the line reserved for the next of kin read, Imam Ahem Mohamed Fahad—uncle.

Jimbo snatched the phone from the coffee table. Not the one he used for personal calls to order pizza or Chinese, it had one number in its memory bank. He hit redial. "Sir, I think we have the connection we've been looking for."

Breathy static washed through the connection. "Look Jim, we've got to be careful going forward. Fahad can't know you're watching him, and we can't tip our hand to Talibani. You've got to keep a low profile. Bide your time."

"Can't I get a little help? I've got the Imam to watch, my boss is keeping me hopping, and the Muslims are ready to riot. As you said, I have my cover to maintain, not to mention this job."

"Jim, we gave you the assignment because you're the best. Keep your head down and your eyes open. This thing's about to break open any day now. I want you there when it does."

Jimbo took a hard swallow. His years of service, his training, his experience equipped him for this assignment. Yet he felt overwhelmed, "Yes Sir, thanks for the vote of confidence.

"Jim, do you have any idea who delivered this envelope?"

"Nope, not a clue, but there is the problem. Whoever it was figured out who I am working for and knew I needed actionable intelligence," Jimbo got up and pulled a bottle of water from the refrigerator.

"Well, we have it now, from an anonymous source."

"Great, we have a loose cannon running around Stanford who knows my identity."

"Like I said, you're the best. I know you can handle it. Send us the stuff you've collected and let us have a crack at it."

"Yes sir, I'll send it right out." Then the line went dead.

Jimbo sat and fingered the envelope. He turned it over. A stain on the front smeared his address. *Hmm, I wonder how long it's been sitting outside.*

Chapter 37

The Construction Site

"Somebody get me another box of blanks," hollered Abdulla, one of the skilled laborers. He had been shooting the anchors for the metal framing when he ran out of the 22 caliber rounds for his Hilti gun.

"That was the last box," another workman answered.

Abdulla stomped off looking for Jimbo or Ahmad, anyone who could solve his problem.

"Where is Jimbo, anyone seen him?" He demanded. He didn't see him anywhere.

Ahmad stopped what he was doing and lifted his walkie-talkie to call for him.

"I'm on the other side of the site with Curian. Whatcha' need?"

"We've run out of 22 blanks for the Hilti gun, do you know if there are anymore?"

"No, and I can't stop what I'm doing to get the blasted things. Get someone to run to the hardware store and get some."

"I'll go." Jared broke in over the static. "I don't need another delay. Because of Ramadan, we need to keep going."

Jared hiked to his vehicle, and saw a shadow behind, someone was following him. "Ahmad, what are you doing?"

"Mr. Jared, I am here to serve you, why not send me so you can concentrate on more important work." His dark eyes pled.

Jared hesitated, looked at his watch then back at his begging crew-chief. "Thank you, my friend, but really, I don't mind going. And frankly, it's dangerous to go into the city alone. You might run into some trouble, and then I would still have to leave work and bail you out."

Ahmad's face darkened. "All the more reason for both of us to go."

Jared shook his head dubiously. He smiled, opened the door and let Raleigh jump in first. "Well, if you insist, hop in."

"Ahmad, I need to pick up my dry cleaning, too. Why don't I drop you off here at the hardware store, and I'll go pick up my dry cleaning then come back for you. By then you should be finished."

"How should I pay for them?"

"Just have the store manager add it to our bill. I'll see you in a few minutes."

Raleigh looked from one side of the conversation to the other as if he understood what was being said.

"Yes sir! I am most happy to. Is there anything else you need me to do?"

Jared was taken back. The dramatic change in his former antagonist was blowing his mind. "No, my friend, it will only be a few minutes and I can handle it." Jared patted Ahmad's shoulder. He really liked Ahmad, especially his willingness to serve others.

As he rounded the street corner, he caught the movement of a group of men walking toward the hardware store and hoped it didn't spell trouble. By the time he returned, it was too late. Ahmad was on the ground encircled by the group of angry men.

Jared slammed on his brakes and came screeching to a halt. He jumped out, followed by Raleigh. The man holding Ahmad's feet felt Jared's fist crashing into his face. Jared tore him from Ahmad. Raleigh lunged at another attacker, his teeth ripped into his upheld arm. A knife he'd been holding clattered to the asphalt. The man screamed at the powerful dog. Jared grabbed another man and spun him around with a left hook to the jaw. He fell like a limp rag. That was the last of them. Jared knelt down and found Ahmad a bloody mess. His shirt was torn open, and blood ran from a gashed lip. His right eye was swelling and he had lacerations on his face and arms from being forced to the rough asphalt. Jared looked up at the row of hardware store employees. Some stood with their arms crossed, others with their hands in their pockets. Most wore a smirk.

Jared heard a siren approaching. He looked over his shoulder and saw a set of flashing lights. The police cruiser pulled to a stop, two officers stepped out and sauntered over to the front of the store. They were the same two officers who'd been called to his church a few weeks earlier. He couldn't believe it. Now they found him and Raleigh holding four bloody men at bay.

"Look Mr. Russell, you are going to have to stop inciting trouble. This is the third time we've been called into a situation involving you. So you need to watch yourself, buddy." Officer Mubarak's frustration spilled out. He knew he was building the Mosque, but he also knew he handed out literature to his Muslim brothers, now this. *Something had to be done with him.*

Jared took a sharp breath and held it a moment. "When I drove up, these guys attacked my friend."

The officer eyed Ahmad and smirked. "Your friend hum? That's not what we heard."

"You heard wrong." He snapped.

In front of the hardware store, several men glared back at him. One still holding a cell phone gave a toothless grin.

Jared bit back his anger, "Get these punks out of here."

Officer Mubarak shrugged his shoulders and looked at Ahmad. "You need to watch out who you hang around with, this guy is *not* your friend." Then he joined his partner and herded the youths to the car. Jared knew in his heart it wasn't over. He'd probably see them again on some dark night.

How long would it be before the police let the four men back out on the street? He turned his attention to Ahmad.

"You're pretty badly beaten up. I need to get you to the hospital."

"I appreciate your concern, Mr. Jared, but really, I'll be okay. I will have Shirin attend to me," he said through puffed lips. He turned his bruised face in Jared's direction. "Do you realize this is the second time you saved my life?"

Jared helped him to his feet. "Yeah, I guess it is." His heart skipped a beat.

Holding his side, Ahmad eased toward the Land Rover. He stopped by the hood, leaning heavily, and coughed. "I think they broke one of my ribs."

Jared opened the door and helped him in. "One? At the rate they were kicking you it would be more like half a dozen."

Ahmad wheezed a chuckle. "Don't make me laugh, it hurts."

"Are you sure I can't take you to the hospital or at least to an Immediate Care Clinic?"

"No, but thank you." He paused. "Mr. Jared, I've been watching you since you saved my life. What you said got me thinking...about a lot."

Jared started the engine and pulled out of the parking lot. Where was he and the conversation was going?

"You told me your God is merciful, not willing that any should perish. Although I don't understand what that means, I know your God must care what happens to me because He sent you to save my life a second time. I am doubly indebted to you." He paused and looked at his hands, calloused, bloody and thought about the difference in his life and Jared's. It was one of selfishness, anger and hatred. He felt dirty inside, ashamed. "I feel like I am on the edge of a cliff, about to step off, but I am ready to listen to your teachings. Your way is a higher way than the Qur'an,

your path is better. I want to know more about the God you serve."
His soft voice tugged at Jared's heart.

Jared breathed a silent prayer. *Lord, where do I start?* The
answer came . . . and Jared started at the beginning.

"Well, Ahmad, we need to get something on that cut lip
and swollen eye of yours. How 'bout we stop by a fast-food
restaurant and get a cup of ice for you."

Ahmad nodded in agreement, and they found a hamburger
joint. Jared pulled into the takeout lane, ordered a milkshake for
Ahmad and a number one combo for himself. The teenager at the
pick-up window peered in through the window.

"Looks like your buddy met with a boxing kangaroo."

Jared looked over at Ahmad, then back to the teen. He
handed him a twenty dollar bill.

"Could you add another cup of ice? It's for the kangaroo
we left lying in a back ally."

His eyes bulged. "Yes sir." It was all Ahmad could do to
keep from laughing. "I told you not to make me laugh." He said
with an arm wrapped around his chest.

"Keep the change." Jared put the vehicle in gear.

Jared rubbed his knuckles, flexing his fingers. He pulled
out into traffic. "Ahmad, I have an idea, let's drive over to the park
on Highlands Street and find a place where we can talk. Are you
okay with that?"

Ahmad nodded, "Thanks for the milkshake. I think I'll be
all right, but you must tell me about your God."

The park was bright and sunny, and green, the temperature
mild for late in September. Jared and Ahmad made their way to an
empty picnic table sat and ate their lunch. Jared finished, and took
a small Bible from his shirt pocket. He rubbed the camouflaged
cover. It was soiled and frayed at the edges, a gift from the
chaplain he carried since his days in the Marines. The impression
in the metal reinforced cover glinted, and he thought about how it
had gotten there.

Lord, where do I begin? He prayed as he opened the Bible.

Chapter 38

The Construction Shack

The grounds around the construction shack were quiet, except for an occasional delivery truck or the technician who came to fix the copy machine. In the office, Fatemah and Shirin filled out work orders and filed papers, unaware of the slender man approaching the front door. Stopping briefly, he glanced around to see if anyone was looking. No one was. He rounded the corner and came to the back of the house.

Confident that his movements were unobserved, he descended the stairs leading to the basement. He set his tool kit down and pulled out a small crowbar. Within a minute he'd jimmied the lock. "It's a good thing there is no alarm system." He muttered under his breath. The door creaked open and he gritted his teeth, hoping the occupants above him didn't hear. Carefully he eased the door shut and looked up. *No movement, that was good.*

The cool musty air invaded his nostrils. *Achew! This place must be a haven for mold down there*, he thought.

His heart pounded as a new surge of adrenaline coursed through his body. With palms slicked with sweat, he waited for his eyes to adjust. It was all he could do to control his breathing. He wasn't a thief, and he'd never even been arrested for speeding. All he wanted to do was serve the Imam and Allah. He wiped his hands on his pants. He had no idea his offer to do the Imam's bidding would lead to this, but what was he to do? This was the will of Allah. Just then, he caught movement to his left. It was a mouse. It was running along the top of a water line which extended from the far corner to above where he stood. The mouse paused long enough to eye the intruder before making an about face and heading back to the dark corner from where it came.

He stepped forward and his foot came down on a hoe, the handle flew up and cold-cocked him in the jaw. He stumbled backward seeing stars. Cursing under his breath, he stood back up and wondered if anyone heard the commotion. Once he got his breathing back under control, he went about his task. It only took a few minutes. Though it was cool in the basement, sweat beaded on his lip. He swiped it away with his sleeve. With great care, he twisted the bare wires around the posts of a small battery pack that connected to the detonator. He pushed the ends of the wires into the top of several sticks of dynamite. He inspected his work and smiled. *That ought to do it.* Confident that his work was done, he covered the wires with an empty burlap sack, stood, and looked around for any incriminating evidence. He turned to leave, and someone cracked open the door above the stairs. Every muscle in his body tensed. What should he do? If they saw him, should he run? Or squeeze the detonator trigger and die a martyr?

The sound of a telephone ringing broke the moment. The door closed and footsteps receded. He breathed a sigh of relief and looked at his watch. *Right on time. If that is who I think it is, Imam Fahad is setting up an appointment with Mr. Jared.*

He mopped his brow with the sleeve of his shirt. There was one more task to perform. Scanning the ceiling for a wire, he followed it until he was confident it was the right one. He reached into his tool kit, pulled out a pair of wire snips, and looked up. A moment later two wires hung down and his job was finished . . . for the time being. He retraced his steps and emerged from the basement enough to pop his head over the concrete ledge. He saw no signs of life. As he walked out of the stairwell, a shadow receded behind the metal shed.

Chapter 39

Stanford Municipal Park

Jared began, "In the beginning was the Word, and the Word was with God, and the Word was God."

"This book is the very thoughts and words of God. Holy men of God wrote it as the Spirit of God spoke to them. We can trust what His book says about God, and about how to get to Heaven."

"I've wondered about what the Bible says, but I never read it. What else does it say?"

Jared plunged in ahead. "It tells us about God's love for us; how He became a man in order to give us salvation. It says God was in Jesus, reconciling us to God."

"Does that mean the one you call," Ahmad forced out the word, ". . . Jesus, was possessed by Allah?"

This may be harder than I thought. "No Ahmad, that's not exactly what I was getting at. As He says, "in the beginning was the Word and all things were created by Him." Jared pointed to the next.

Ahmad cocked his head enough to see it.

"You see, the Creator, who spoke the universe into existence, took on flesh and became part of his creation, He lived among his people. Jesus is God."

Ahmad dabbed his cut lip with the make-do icepack meditatively. "I could be executed for listening to this teaching." Ahmad said, his face bore a look of concern.

"Yes, I know. Are you sure you want to continue?"

Ahmad breathed heavily, then nodded. "I must know how could God become a man?" His dark eyes probed Jared's face.

Jared turned over a few more pages. "The Word of God tells us how the Spirit of God hovered over Mary. It says in Luke 1:35 that the power of the Highest overshadowed, her and the holy child would be called the Son of God."

Jared pointed to the page, "Do you see where it said the 'Highest?' That is referring to God himself. God moved upon Mary and she conceived, even though she was a virgin, and so the child she bore had God as his Father and so he was the Son of God. This passage, fulfills another passage that was written hundreds of years earlier. In Isaiah 7:14, for example, it says, "the Lord himself will give us a sign, a virgin shall conceive, and bear a son, and his name will be called Immanuel, meaning God is with us."

Ahmad looked in silence with curiosity written on his face and listened to every word as Jared turned and read,

"There is another place in scripture that teaches us that being the Son of God was equal to God." Jared flipped a few pages and found Philippians 2:5-11. He ran his finger along the verses as he read them aloud.

"Christ Jesus, being in the form of God, didn't take any of God's glory from Him but was equal with God. But then, He made himself of no reputation, and took on flesh. He looked just like us, and lived among us in the form of a humble servant, a teacher of the Jewish law. Few followed him and one day, because of his teaching he was crucified on a Roman cross.

Because of that redemptive act, God the Father highly exalted him, and has given him a name which is above every name.

One day every knee will bow throughout all creation, in heaven, and in earth, and even under the earth, and they will confess that Jesus Christ is Lord." Ahmad digested the news he had just heard.

"But why?" he pressed. "Why would God care that much? Allah would never do that. Allah requires complete obedience. I know it is blasphemous, but Allah gives us nothing in return. What happens in this life is his will. This is the best we can hope for. If we live, it is his will; if we die, it is his will."

Jared looked at him thoughtfully. "You said that my God's way is higher than the way of Allah. Can I show you how it is higher?"

Eyes rounding, Ahmad nodded. "Yes please, I want to know."

Jared pressed on, his voice thick with joy. "Well, we already know Jesus is the Son of God, and that he humbled himself and died on the cross, but let me explain why. The first reason He died on Calvary was God's great love for us. One of the most notable verses in the Bible is John 3:16." His finger tracked the well-worn verse.

"For God so loved the world that he gave his only begotten Son, that whosoever believeth in him should not perish, but have everlasting life." Jared took a sip of his soda before pressing on.

"Are you feeling all right? You look like you're in a lot of pain."

"No, Mr. Jared, I'm fine. Please continue."

Jared nodded. "Okay, you see, God loved us even though we stand condemned because we have violated God's holy standard of righteousness. He knew there was nothing we could offer Him that would take away our wrong, so His Son died in our place." After another sip of soda, he swallowed the last bite of his cold hamburger.

"Do you remember the patriarch, Abraham?" he probed.

"Yes, Ibrahim, as we call him," Ahmad said.

"Do you remember the story of the sacrifice he made?"

"Yes, he sacrificed his son Ishmael, and Allah raised him from the dead, at least that is what we were taught from our earliest days."

Jared nodded thoughtfully. "So you accept the idea of the resurrection?"

"Well, yes, of course." He gave Jared an interested look.

"Well, let me tell you the story of that event in scripture."

"Abraham had two sons, Isaac and Ishmael. Ishmael was born as the result of Abraham's disobedience. But God promised him that he would have a son by Sarah, his wife, and he believed it. It was that act of faith, which God accounted for righteousness."

"So you see, Ishmael is blessed because he is Ibrahim's son, correct?"

Jared shook his head. "It's true that he was blessed. In fact, God made him the father of twelve princes. But along with that, God said he would be a wild man; his hand would be against every man, and every man's hand against him. No offense, but that sounds very much like the Islamic people."

Ahmad's eyes narrowed. "None taken, it is true. But what about Ishmael, didn't Ibrahim sacrifice him where the Dome of the Rock sits?"

A car slowed and passed them. Jared waited until it turned the corner before answering.

"Actually no, by the time Isaac was old enough for this to happen, Ishmael was probably in his late thirties or maybe forties. According to the biblical record, he'd moved out of Abraham's home.

"Hmm, I never thought about that."

"In the book of Genesis, in the twenty-second chapter, God tested Abraham's faith when He told him to take Isaac to the land of Moriah, and sacrifice him as a burnt offering on one of the mountains. It was Isaac who was on the altar when the angel of the LORD called unto Abraham out of heaven, and said, "lay not your hand upon the boy, for now I know that you fear me." Abraham looked, and saw a ram caught in a thicket by his horns. He offered the provided ram instead of Isaac. Abraham called the name of that place Jehovah Jireh: which means, 'in the mount of the LORD, He shall be seen.'"

Ahmad sat staring forward. "So Ibrahim didn't actually slay his son?"

"Nope, but God used that to teach us a powerful lesson."

"And that is?"

"The lesson of sacrifice. You see, God's ways are higher than our ways and He knew that animal sacrifices could not cleanse our sin. That's why Abraham called the place, Jehovah Jireh. It was on that very place, thousands of years later, that the Lamb of God, Jesus the Messiah, was crucified."

"I'm beginning to understand the meaning of sacrifice. Two times you risked your life to save me. Jesus did this."

Jared's pulse quickened. "That's right. John the Baptist called Jesus the Lamb of God who came to take away the sins of the world. My sins . . . and your sins, Ahmad."

Jared could see on his face his message was getting through.

"You asked me why I risked my life to save you. The answer is, God did it for me. How can I do less?"

Tears welled in Ahmad's dark eyes. "Allah would never do such a thing as die for men. He wants us to die for him, but not him for us. Your God is a kind and loving God."

"I have read the Qur'an Ahmad, and I've searched for forgiveness in it. I have not found any reference to it."

A cloud passed over Ahmad's bruised features, "That is because there is no provision for a Muslim for forgiveness. The best we can hope for is if we die a martyr, we get seventy-two virgins. That seems so hollow compared to what you are telling me."

Jared let out his breath slowly, "Yes Ahmad, that is hollow compared to the free gift of salvation Christ offers to you by faith." Jared carefully drew the little symbol he had been carrying since Christmas. He slowly opened his hand and revealed the old wooden cross. Ahmad's eyes, glassy with tears, fixated upon it. He gently reached over, took it from Jared's open hand, lifted it to his swollen lips, kissed it, and said; "I want this Jesus in my heart, I don't care if they say it is blasphemy!"

Hot tears streamed down Jared's face. He said low and wondering, almost to himself, "Believe on the Lord Jesus Christ and thou shalt be saved."

Ahmad began to pray.

"Lord Jesus, I know I have done wrong against you and now I seek your forgiveness and You are the only One Who can save me, save me in Jesus' name."

Jared began praying a prayer of thanksgiving for opening the eyes of his friend. He knew the prayers for one lost Muslim to be saved were heard and answered thanks to the prayers of the faithful people of Canaan Baptist Church.

"I want to learn more of what your Bible says." Ahmad wiped the tears from his eyes.

"There is much to learn, and I would be honored to share with you what God has taught me." Jared patted him gently on the shoulder. Ahmad winced. "Oh, sorry."

Jared's cell phone rang.

Chapter 40

The Construction Shack

Shirin toggled the talk button. "Mr. Jimbo, do you know where Mr. Jared is? I haven't been able to get him on the walkie-talkie."

A moment of static passed before Jimbo's voice crackled through the speaker. "I've been wondering the same thing. He and Ahmad left a few hours ago to get blanks for the Hilti gun, but they should have been back by now."

Looking at Fatemah, Shirin squeezed the talk button again. "He must be out of range."

"Is there something I can do for you Miss Shirin?"

"No Mr. Jimbo, it's just that—I'm worried."

"Oh? What are you worried about?"

Again static. Shirin waited for it to subside. "Well, you know my brother; he's got a hot temper with a short fuse. I just hope he and Mr. Jared didn't get into an argument over religion."

"That's possible, but they've been getting along fairly well recently." Jimbo said. "What's the other reason?"

"The other reason is that Imam Fahad called an hour ago and scheduled a meeting with Mr. Jared. It's supposed to start in ten minutes, and I'm afraid he might be late."

"Well, we wouldn't want to keep the good Imam waiting, now would we? Have you tried Jared's cell?"

"No, not yet, but I will try now."

"Okay, you let me know if you get a hold of him, I need to talk to him too." Jimbo signed off.

Shirin picked up the phone. "That's funny, there's no dial tone."

Fatemah looked up from her work and reached for her phone.

Nothing.

"I was wondering why it's been so quiet around here. Ever since the Imam called, we've not gotten a call." Fatemah replaced the phone.

Shirin picked up the walkie-talkie. "Mr. Jimbo?"

"Yes." His voice carried an interesting lift.

"Our landline is dead. We can't call out."

"Hmm. Could be anything. I'll be there in a few minutes to check it out. In the meantime can you use your cell phone?"

"Yes."

"Okay, I'll be there as soon as I can."

Shirin began searching in her hand-bag for her cell phone. She found it and pushed the on button, then moaned.

"What's wrong?"

"My cell phone is dead again. I charged it overnight and it did the same thing yesterday."

Fatemah shook her head. "It must be the battery. Here let me try mine."

She dialed the number and waited.

"It's busy."

Chapter 41

The Streets of Stanford

Jared pulled his cell phone from his pocket and looked at the caller ID. He didn't recognize the number. *Who could it be? I hope it's not that mysterious caller from the night Elaine was murdered.* He pushed the speaker phone button.

"Hello?"

A strange voice with a thick accent said, "Don't go near the construction shack, your life is in grave danger."

Then the phone went dead.

Ahmad looked up, startled. For an instant Jared thought he saw recognition in his friend's eyes.

"Uh, oh, we got trouble back at the construction site."

"I heard! What should we do?"

Jared pushed the pre-set number for the office.

"Nothing. That's not good."

Ahmad cocked his head. "Nothing? No dial tone?"

"Nope, we need to get back and warn the ladies. Do you have your cell phone with you?"

"Yes."

"Call Shirin, tell her and Fatemah to get out of the office and make it fast. It's going on noon; hopefully they'll already be out to lunch."

Ahmad wobbled to his feet.

"Are you going to be all right?" Jared watched him with concern.

Ahmad leaned on the concrete tabletop and blinked. "I'll be okay, we must hurry."

They gathered up their stuff and made their way as quickly as possible to the Land Rover. Raleigh, who had been sleeping under the table all through their Bible study, jumped to his feet and caught up in a few bounds.

Jared looked at the phone in his hand, *Should I call the police? And tell them what?* He dismissed the idea and grabbed the handle of the door and yanked it open. Raleigh jumped in.

Ahmad speed dialed his sister's number. "It went to her voice mail, Mr. Jared."

"Okay, we'll just have to hurry."

As they sped through town, Ahmad fingered the Military issued Bible that Jared had handed him. A quizzical look spread across his face.

"How did that hole get into the cover of your Bible?"

Jared took a deep breath, a memory long suppressed, percolated to the surface as fresh as the day it happened. "That's a long story, I'll make it short. The convoy I was leading was caught in an ambush in Mosel. Our lead vehicle hit an IED. It blew the Humvee in the air and it landed upside down. The whole convoy came to a standstill under a classic ambush scenario."

Jared came to a four-way stop. In the distance he saw four disheveled youths walking. It was the same Arab youths from earlier.

He cut his wheels left. "We came under fire from all sides, RPGs and heavy machine-gun fire. We were pinned down. For a while I thought we were all goners. I called in air support. The

Black-hawk gun-ships made it within minutes and reduced the enemy to a few stragglers, but not before my partner was hit."

"Who was your partner?" Ahmad's eyebrows arched.

Jared bit back the rising guilt. Reaching over, he rubbed Raleigh's furry neck.

"My partner was a German shepherd named EJ short for Iwo Jima. She was named after one of the toughest islands in the Pacific that the Marines ever took." He sighed heavily."

Ahmad's shoulders slumped, his swollen face creased. "Now I understand your love for Raleigh."

Raleigh cocked his head with a whine deep in his throat.

"She was badly wounded. I was dragging her to safety when a round hit me in the chest . . . knocked me on my backside. For a minute, I thought I was dead. It took the wind right out of me and my chest burned like fire. One of my buddies grabbed me and EJ and dragged us out of harm's way. The round hit me right between my body armor, in the left pocket where I kept this little Bible. Had I not had it there, I would have been killed. This Bible has saved my life two ways; my body and my heart, spiritually and physically."

Ahmad lifted the worn Bible and inspected it closer. "I am beginning to love this Bible more and more, it not only saved your life but now it has saved mine." He said, suppressing a second round of tears.

Jared allowed a moment to pass without speaking. *Lord, thank you for saving my life and Ahmad's soul. Protect us*. He checked his watch. It was exactly noon. His wheels hit the gravel road leading to the parking lot.

The ground shook and the impact of an explosion rocked the Land Rover. Jared's heart pounded in his chest as he watched a thick cloud of smoke ascend. He caught movement to his left, it was Jimbo running.

Chapter 42

The Construction Shack

"Busy," Fatemah said, looking at the clock on the wall, it said 11:59. Ending the call, she sighed. "I was hoping to talk Mr. Jared into bringing us lunch. I'm starved."

Her cell phone rang causing Fatemah to jump. "That was quick, maybe there's time for him to pick up lunch after all.

"Hello?"

Shirin watched the color drain from her face.

"Get out of there or you will die."

Fatemah screamed, dropped the phone on the desk, grabbed her laptop and ran for the back door. "Run."

Shirin followed her, without unplugging her laptop from the wall. She was out the back door in a flash. A moment later the house exploded sending them sprawling. Brick, glass, shingles, and wood flew past them like small missiles. The shed groaned and collapsed upon them.

Then silence.

Fatemah awoke and tried to make sense of what happened. *Where am I? Where's Shirin?*

She tried to move but she was covered in debris. *I can't breathe. Lord, help me.*

One hand moved, and blindly searched for Shirin. She found her hand, wet and sticky. Fatemah wasn't sure if it was her blood or Shirin's. Feeling for a pulse . . . she found none.

Fatemah lay still for a moment. Then she struggled for a deep breath, and tried to move again, but something heavy lay on her legs. She had precious few minutes to save Shirin's life. With a gigantic heave, her back popping painfully, she fought her way closer to Shirin. Her face was buried in the mud, and a piece of metal protruded from her back. Carefully Fatemah rolled her over, and saw the look of death written on her friend's beautiful, dirty face. *Lord! Oh no. Please spare her!*

It's so beautiful, Shirin thought to herself. *What is that white light?* Hovering over her broken body was a shimmering, radiant form. She saw her hands stretching out, fingers separated, as if to catch a basketball. The closer she came, the more the light eluded her. Her hands flailed in a futile, wild attempt to catch it. It was further away. She tried to move her feet but nothing happened. They were mired in clay. She yearned to be free but fear held her back. She heard herself call, out but the shimmering light dimmed, fading. *"Oh God, help me."*

The nebulous form gathered into the shape of an angel. It drew near. The Spirit looked down at Shirin's hands. They were stained with something dark. It carried with it a spirit of sorrow, and shook its head. *"No, wait. Don't leave me. What have I done to have offended you?"*

The hovering Spirit pointed from her hands to her heart. Shirin knew in her heart what He meant. Fatemah had been sharing the gospel with her. She had refused to surrender out of fear of what Ahmad would say or what the Imam would do. She did not trust Him to protect her.

"I'm sorry that I grieved you Lord—what must I do . . . What can I do to please You?" Again the Spirit pulled away. "Nooo!"

Fatemah leaned over Shirin's lifeless body. Her prayer echoed through the halls of Heaven and throne of God. *"Lord, give her more time! Please, she cannot go yet—and You are not willing that any be lost, You love her more than I. Please . . . But You know our hearts . . . "*

Shirin's eyes fluttered. Fatemah knew she'd heard her—and God had answered.

Shirin blinked, her eyes glazed. She moaned coughed, blood dribbled from her mouth. Fatemah squeezed her hand. At least one lung was punctured, and she was probably injured internally, but she was conscience. Hope sprang up in her heart, but faded when Fatemah slid an arm under her and felt the blood oozing from the wound in her back.

"Fatemah, I heard you praying for me," Shirin's voice was weak.

"Shhh, you must rest, don't speak, help is coming."

Shirin smiled through the pain lines gathering around her mouth, "No, I told Him I was sorry. I need to believe Him before I die."

"No," Fatemah said, shaking her head, not willing to accept death's appointment. "You are not going to die—I won't let you. God won't either, until you have heard the truth of Who He is."

Shirin shook her head. "No, I have heard enough. You told me what to do." Her voice trailed off.

Warmth streaked down Fatemah's cheeks, sorrow and joy mingling, in one river.

"Shirin, just trust Him alone to forgive your sins and clean you in His blood, and He will do it."

Shirin closed her eyes and with a weak voice, prayed. "Dear Jesus, I believe you are the Son of God, I ask You to save me."

The Spirit of God moved closer, Shirin reached out—and they became one. When she opened her eyes, she was looking into the gentle face of Jesus.

Chapter 43

The Construction Shack

A pile of smoking debris stopped Jimbo as he neared the construction shack. Looking through the haze, all he saw was the collapsed building. The smell of burning wood and roofing tile assaulted his nose, causing his eyes to flood. What wasn't destroyed in the blast was burning.

Wheels crunched the gravel as a vehicle skidded to a stop. Jared jumped out of his Land Rover, with Raleigh beside him.

"Everything is a total loss," Jimbo said, shaking his head in disbelief.

Ahmad came around the truck. His clothes torn, dried blood stained his shirt. "Shirin, where is Shirin?" he demanded and began a frantic search of the area. He lifted a large piece of sheetrock and tossed it aside.

Jared held his hand up as other men assembled. "Listen! Everybody be quiet."

Dead silence settled over the debris like fog.

"Listen." Ahmad cupped his hand over his ear. "I think I hear something."

Someone hollered. "I hear someone crying." An uneasy silence settled over the scene as acrid smoke wafted through the air.

Jared walked toward the shed, a jumble of twisted sheet metal and pulled it back. Men raced to help. His knees buckled. He fell beside Fatemah and lifted her head. She was holding Shirin's limp hand. "Jared—she's gone."

Jared leaned close, he felt no breath on his cheek, no beat in her wrist.

He closed his eyes and sagged forward. "I am so sorry," he breathed. "I tried to come as quick as I could." He looked down on Shirin's face. It held peace, and a trace of pain, but no fear, no dread.

Ahmad rushed to her side and cupped her face in his hands. "Shirin!"

"She's gone, Ahmad," Jared wrapped his arm around him.

"No! She can't be—I just talked with her an hour ago."

Jared's heart broke to see his friend and brother so crushed. He sought for the right words but all he could eke out was, "I'm so sorry, Ahmad." He knew what it was like. Memories long banished forced their way back into his mind. "Oh God, help us!"

Ahmad sat, rocking his sister, muttering her name. Jared kept his hand on his back.

Jimbo placed an arm under Fatemah and helped her up. Her knees buckled, but he caught her. Smoke swirled around them partially shielding them from the others.

"Let me help you to that tree until the ambulance arrives."

"Thank you, Jimbo," she said, barely above a whisper. "I can't believe this happened. Shirin's dead."

Jimbo's voice grew husky. "I'm sorry, Miss Fatemah" He got her settled, then knelt next to her. "Do you know what happened?"

Fatemah shook her head, still dazed. "I don't know, the place just exploded."

Jimbo looked over his shoulder at the burning piles. "You could have been killed. How did you know to get out of there?" He turned back to face her.

She closed her eyes and leaned her head against the tree. "I got a call. Someone said get outta there or we'd die. I screamed, and we ran. We made it to the shed before everything blew up."

Jimbo wiped sweat from his brow. "Well, that rules out a gas leak."

"I feel so responsible," she said, then buried her face in her hands and sobbed.

"Look, Miss Fatemah, whoever did this is responsible. It sure enough wasn't your fault."

Jared walked over and brushed some dirt from Fatemah's face.

"I heard you say you got a call. So did I. We tried to call you and warn you but all we got was a busy signal. Ahmad called Shirin's cell, and it went into her voicemail."

Fatemah lifted her gaze, her eyes bore the pain of her loss. "That's because our phones were out and Shirin's phone was..."

"Dead?" Jared finished her statement.

She nodded.

She cocked her head. "Jared, did you know you had an appointment with the Imam at noon today?"

Jared looked at Jimbo. He shrugged.

"No, when did that happen?"

Fatemah's forehead wrinkled. "He called about eleven o'clock. Said he wanted to meet with you at noon. After that the phones stopped working."

Jimbo scanned the crowd of stunned men, some poking through the mess, others gathered around Ahmad, screening them from casual onlookers beginning to gather. "I haven't seen hide nor hair of that man's skinny self."

"It's clear *someone* knew a bomb was planted in the house, and that it would blow exactly at noon." Jared eyed Jimbo.

Jimbo inhaled sharply. "A bomb? How do you know it was a bomb?"

Jared studied his face. For a moment, their eyes locked. "What else would cause such an explosion? It was probably some of the left-over dynamite."

"But who would have wanted to kill you, for crying out loud?"

A cloud of smoke from the burning timber wafted around them. Ahmad rocked back and forth over his fallen sister.

Jared lifted his chin. "For a while, I thought you did. I got a note on the seat of my Land Rover back before Thanksgiving saying 'One Day' and it was smeared with blood. The next day, I found another one saying, 'Watch your back.'"

Fatemah cupped her hand over her mouth, eyes darting between them.

Jimbo raised his hands as if in surrender. "It wasn't me boss, that's not my style, you should know that," he muttered.

The ambulance wailed into the lot. Jared rose. "Well, someone wants me dead, and this project stopped. Ahmad and I got into a big fight with some punks back at the hardware store a little over an hour ago. Had that not happened, we might have been killed, too."

Jimbo stroked his chin. "How did they get in and set the bomb?"

Shaking his head, Jared's shoulders slumped. "It could have been anyone at any time. They could have gotten in through the outside entrance, perhaps," he said without conviction. Scanning a cluster of men, he saw some of them with their fists clenched; others were deep in animated discussions. "Either way, that's for the professionals to figure out. Now we have a hurting brother and a bunch of angry Muslims to deal with."

The police chief approached him, and Jimbo went to the work crew. His call was quiet and strong. "All right men, why don't we call it a day? Take tomorrow off. We'll see to it you get paid. Come back Monday." He did not ask for permission from Imam Fahad. He was nowhere to be found.

The workers looked at each other. One of them said, "I want to say for the record, we are not responsible for this act of violence. This was the hand of an infidel, not a Muslim."

The rest took up the chant. "Not a Muslim!"

Jared laid his hand on Fatemah's shoulder. "I'm afraid this could get ugly."

One of the police officers stepped to the back of his cruiser and pulled a bullhorn from his truck, "Okay, that's enough. Why don't you boys go on home for the day and let us sort all this out?"

The men quietly scattered.

Chapter 44

Michigan's 42nd Circuit Court

Don Gibson's morning began early. He and Pastor Carlson drove to Midland County. Having won the first court round in the 36th District Court, he was headed to Michigan's 42nd Circuit Court to try to put a stop to the madness.

"Rather than fighting a bunch of small fires popping up," he explained to the pastor as they sped along US Highway 10, "I might as well put out the whole forest fire in one fell-swoop."

Pastor Carlson flipped through the stack of briefs and interrogatories on his lap, Gibson rattled on.

"I have submitted a bill to the state legislature. If it passes, it will prohibit judges from considering Islamic law when deciding cases in Michigan. That way, when any appeals go up through the courts, they will have the state constitution behind them."

The pastor looked somewhat overwhelmed, "I can't say it enough. I really appreciate what you and your firm are doing."

Don fingered the leather steering wheel, and looked straight ahead. "Don't thank me too soon. We still have a long road ahead of us. But I'm glad to have you with me. I hope you're prayed up." He gave the pastor a sideways grin.

"Oh yes. That's been well covered.

Gibson continued, "The issue at root is, should Michigan courts be restricted to making decisions based solely on state and federal law? Or can they consider international law, or the Islamic law, for final rulings?"

Pastor Carlson nodded. Don tried to explain his next move.

"I feel we have a lot of backing statewide, but the Organization for Islamic Development is well funded and well organized. They've poured tons of money into the lobbying effort already," he admitted candidly.

"Where's the money coming from to support our effort?"

"You'd be surprised, Pastor. My colleagues are getting checks from the Knights of Columbus, the VFW, and conservative groups such as the Tea Party. There are all sorts of rich fat-cats who are interested in upholding the state and federal constitutions."

Pastor Carlson let out his breath slowly. "Politics has many bed-fellows, doesn't it?"

Don shook his head. "It's a crazy thing, but you're right. Folks who don't normally agree with each other find they can work for the common good when their freedoms and liberties are threatened."

"When the Nazis came for the Jews, no one said anything. When they came for Poland, no one said a word. Then when they came for me, there was no one left to speak out. It's like that," the pastor said.

"They say lawyers are good story tellers, but I think I met my match on that one, Pastor." The two men laughed together and pulled into the parking deck of the court house.

They exited the elevator, and Don turned to the pastor before entering the court room.

"I believe we have a good shot at getting the matter resolved on the grounds that it is a free-speech issue, protected under the US Constitution. Plus as a Separation of Church and

State issue, the State, or in this case the city, has no business making laws that control the affairs of the Church, at least as far as what was said from the pulpit."

"You've sold me, now sell it to the judge." The pastor patted Don on the back and they stepped into a packed court.

The bailiff announced the judge. "All rise. The Michigan 42nd Circuit Court is now in session."

The room held an uncomfortable silence. Judge Hawthorn, a stately, gaunt man with a probing gaze, stepped out of his chamber. He took his seat and gruffly laid out the ground rules for his courtroom. "Ladies and gentlemen, this is my court. I will not put up with any foolishness." Using his glasses to point at the bailiff and other officers stationed around the court, he said, "Remember what the good books says, 'they bear not the sword in vein." He sat back and gave a wry smile at the pastor. "Now let's get started."

The bailiff looked at a clipboard, "The court calls Don Gibson."

Don Gibson rose to his feet and stepped around the dark brown mahogany table. He took his time as he strode to the well of the courtroom, turned, cleared his throat and addressed the audience. His resonant voice was clear and commanding.

"Where was the outcry when a noted TV preacher made inflammatory statements about our country from the pulpit? Yet when a humble pastor stands and preaches to a small group of people from the Bible, he is censured and driven from the public forum. What's wrong with this picture? Where were the ACLU guys? Where was the outcry from the OID? Aren't they for tolerance? Where is the tolerance when it comes to opposing views? Did anybody say anything to the Reverend when he defamed America? If we can't speak about God, then we might as well burn our dollar bills, because the last time I checked," he held a one dollar bill up high over his head, "It says, 'In God We Trust.' If we can't speak about the Ten Commandments, then we might as well tear down this very courthouse."

Someone hollered, 'No!'

"If we can't mention God in the public main, then we should arrest everyone at the next baseball game or football game, as they sing the national anthem."

Another voice cried, 'No!'

Don smiled. He was on a roll.

"If we can't hold a Bible and swear by the God of that Bible that we will tell the truth, the whole truth and nothing but the truth, then we might as well close up shop here, Your Honor, because we can't trust what anybody says from the witness stand."

"No!" shouted one man, followed by another and another. "That is not our America!"

Judge Hawthorn brought the gavel down several times on the wooden plate, and Pastor Carlson jumped.

"Order in the court," he said, his voice echoed off the paneled walls. "You may continue council."

Gibson turned to his notes. "I submit to the court that if we prohibit this pastor," he pointed at Pastor Carlson, "or any pastor from speaking the truth of God's Word, which I may add, is the very foundation of this constitutional republic if they can't tell us, 'thus saith the Lord', then this nation is doomed. Our country, as we know it, will collapse under the weight of its own sin. We will be relegated to the trash-heap of history with the USSR, Nazi Germany, Rome and all the nations that have forgotten God. Is that what we want for our children . . . to grow up and not know God? What will we say to your forefathers who fought . . . who bled . . . and who died for the freedom to speak . . . to speak about God?" His voice rose. "What will we tell those brave Pilgrims, or those who starved to death in Williamsburg, or those courageous men who froze to death in Valley Forge? I appeal to you, Your Honor, by the very Bible on your desk, give this man his liberty, or give me death."

The courtroom burst into cheers. Don Gibson took his seat.

The judge gaveled the room into submission.

"Does the attorney for the state have an opening statement?"

"Yes, Your Honor. Yes, we do," Attorney Abdullah Teriek Rahim paced forward, lithe and lean and hungry.

Gibson leaned over, "Pastor Carlson, this guy is one of the best. He's already represented the OID in many cases involving state encroachment upon Muslim rights, anti-defamation and Muslim divorce. You can bet he's loaded for bear. I wouldn't be surprised if he's not one of the strategists behind the growth of the radical Muslim movement in the first place."

Rahim stood and addressed the courtroom.

"The state asked these questions of the appellate, Reverend Carlson. Is it tolerance to sit back and listen to Allah being dishonored by a man who says his God is a God of love? Where is the love of God when he says that all Muslims are going to Hell? Where is the tolerance of God when he says there is just one way to Heaven? Don't we as American Muslims have the right to preach our book of truth . . . the Qur'an?"

"No!" voice sounded from the back of the room.

Rahim continued. "Does the Qur'an not contain truth equal to that of your Bible? Is not Allah the same as the God of the Bible . . . the God of the Jews and Gentiles alike? Why can't we exercise the liberties afforded us, yea, demanded of us, by Allah?"

"Boo!" the court rustled, and the first hum of refusal was joined by others, a spreading plague.

Judge Hawthorn lifted his gavel and slammed it down. "Order in the court or I will empty this court room."

"That's fine, we've heard enough," said a guy in the back. He moved to leave, and others joined him until the room was empty.

The judge gaveled the emptiness to order.

"I declare a recess until tomorrow morning. We will reconvene at ten o'clock; councilors have your submissions ready for discovery. I will swear you in on this Bible." He lifted it high. His gavel fell; he stood and retired to his chamber.

The bailiff said, "All rise."

Don breathed a sigh. "That is the first of many battles. I think I made some valid points. I just hope the judge will remember them when he makes his determination."

Pastor Carlson nodded. "Look Don, I'm about to split a gasket if I don't get to a rest room."

A wry smile tugged at Don's lips. "Too much coffee huh?"

"Yes, I guess so."

"Tell you what, I'll get the car and come around and pick you up in front. How about that?"

"Great, I'll see you in a minute."

Don made his way to his car in the lower parking deck, got in and turned the ignition key. The explosion ripped through the parking deck. Shards of metal and flaming debris screamed in every direction. The sprinkler system suppressed the burning car, but not before Don Gibson found himself before the judge of the Universe.

The call to the fire department came in at twelve noon.

Pastor Carlson's cell phone rang.

"Hello?"

"Oh honey. I have the most terrible news."

Chapter 45

The Construction Shack

Within minutes the police and fire units arrived and began putting out the fire. An ambulance backed to where Fatemah lay and two paramedics grabbed their medical kits and rushed to her.

"Is that all you can remember, Miss Bashera?" The chief of police jotted down her last statement.

Fatemah gulped back a sob and took a ragged breath. "It all happened so fast, but that's all I can remember." She buried her face in her hands.

Sheriff Lawson gave her a minute, tapping his pencil on the edge of his notepad, waiting. He had a job to do and he didn't like being dragged into an intra-Muslim conflict. Muslims killing Americans was one thing. Muslims killing other Muslims was another.

He gave Fatemah a condescending smile, reached into his uniform pocket and pulled out his card with his contact information. "If you think of anything else, don't hesitate to call me."

It took all the intestinal fortitude Jared could muster not to lash out at Sheriff Lawson. His cold aloofness was a stark contrast to men like his pastor. He wished Pastor Carlson was there, he needed someone. Instead, Pastor Carlson was in Midland at the Circuit Court with his attorney, fighting the good fight.

Jared stepped closer to the sheriff. "Sir, my name is Jared Russell, I represent—"

"I know who you are," the sheriff cut him off with a wave. "And I know who you work for. I just wonder whose side you're on?"

He'd just lost one of his secretaries for crying out loud, and nearly lost another. Didn't this guy have a heart? Jared crossed his arms, and glared back at him. "Can the paramedics examine her now?"

The police chief stared back stoically. He clearly didn't like being pushed. "Sure guys, go ahead."

While the medics attended to Fatemah, Jared went to Ahmad gave him a manly hug.

"Ahmad, would you allow me to pray for God to help us get through this?"

"Oh, Mr. Jared," he said, his voice thick and raw. "I would like that."

Jared did his best to pray, but he felt his prayer was bland, passionless, so devoid of feeling. Nevertheless an overwhelming sense of God's presence came over them.

Ahmad was crying silently. "I never let Shirin learn the truth." He whispered. "I treated her so harshly when she was reading your literature. I refused to allow her to read it, and now she is gone—lost forever." His voice broke and he leaned into Jared's shoulder, sobbing uncontrollably.

With Jimbo's, help, Fatemah hobbled over to where they stood, huddled beside Shirin. Fatemah slipped her arm around Ahmad. "I know you loved your sister."

He nodded, unable to speak.

"You may get angry, but I have to tell you, just before she died, Shirin asked Jesus to save her. She *is* with God."

Ahmad leveled his gaze. "Are you saying Shirin went to Heaven, to live with—Jesus?"

Fatemah's knees buckled and Jared caught her. She lifted her chin. "Yes."

Taking her by the hands, he pulled them close his chest.

Hand to her mouth, Fatemah sucked in a sharp breath.

He smiled through his tears. "Mr. Jared, thirty minutes ago you told me how my sins could be forgiven. Now that I am a believer, I will see her again, I know will." Ahmad choked back a sob "Before today neither of us had any hope of going to Heaven, but now that bright place is real to me. I want to live my life for our true, merciful Lord, Jesus Christ, and honor Shirin."

Fighting back tears, Jared was taken aback at Ahmad's strength and the grace of his words. A wall of emotion, which had been pent up for years, finally broke and he gave into the moment. Together the three of them wept tears of sorrow and joy.

Finally, after a few minutes, Ahmad gathered himself. "Now, if you will excuse me, I need to go. Even though I follow Him, I do not think He will mind our custom. She must be buried before the sun goes down. There is an Islamic funeral director in town. He will make all the necessary arrangements. I must attend to this matter."

Jared patted his shoulder and let him go with a heartfelt nod. Sheriff Lawson was taking Jimbo's statement.

"Sheriff Lawson—"

"Son, we got us a problem." The sheriff pulled his belt back up over his belly.

"There are a bunch of folks who don't want you, or this building project around."

Jared stiffened his back. "Look Sheriff, I'm just here to do a job. I'm not here to take sides on the Muslim versus American issue. Heck, most of the guys working here are naturalized or natural born."

The sheriff eyed him suspiciously, "Yeah, well, most of their papers have been blown to smithereens."

Jared pointed at the smoldering frame of the construction shack. "I sure hope not, all the important paperwork was filed in heavy-duty, fire-proof filing cabinets. They probably survived. Plus, I noticed the ladies grabbed their laptops as they ran out. If the computers survived we may be able to retrieve a lot."

He paused before making his next point. "By the way, that reminds me, Muslim's have a custom of burying their dead before the sun goes down. Could yoask the coroner to release her body to Ahmad Hassani, her brother for burial?"

"I'm well aware of Muslim customs and I sure as ..." he looked down at Fatemah. "I don't need *you* to tell me how to run an investigation. Frankly, I'm sick and tired of all this Shari'ah law stuff." He peered over his glasses, looking for the coroner. "Warren, can you release the body?"

The coroner opened his mouth, shut it, and nodded slowly. "Sure, we can arrange that." He marched toward what was left of the construction shack.

Jimbo eased up next to Jared. "I don't envy you, buddy."

Jared let his head fall forward, a knot formed in his stomach. He wiped his face with his sleeve. "Yeah, now I get to call the home office."

Chapter 46

Mayor Talibani's Office

Imam Ahem Mohamed Fahad slipped through the back entrance of the city hall unnoticed. A light tap on the mayor's private door gained the Imam access to the inner sanctum. Mayor Talibani fingered a sheet of paper lying on his desk. There was a slight tremble in his greeting. He hoped he didn't notice.

Finally, after adjusting his tunic, meticulously, the religious cleric spoke. "I thought by now you would have gotten control of the *situation.*" His tone was malevolent; the pupils of his eyes like an owl, stared at him, unblinking.

A cold chill ran the length of Talibani's spine, and he shrank back. Cotton mouthed he began a litany of well-rehearsed excuses. "My Father, who could have known that Jared would be . . . *delayed?"*

"Had it not been for those goons of yours getting into a brawl with Mr. Russell and that Hassani guy, they would have been where they were supposed to have been." The Imam stated. Noticeable bitterness escaped his stretched lips.

The mayor sat up straight. "How was I to know you had, uh, other plans? By the way, were you aware of the fact that

Ahmad is Shaquille's nephew? That he's in charge of the unskilled—"

"I couldn't care less about what he does, he's a Hassani. I have sworn to wipe Sirus Hassani's children off the face of the earth." The sinews of his neck bulged.

"My Father, surely you wouldn't carry out this vendetta against his children."

Fahad's eyes spoke fire. "I hold Sirus responsible for the death of my child, and I will not rest until I have wiped his seed from the earth."

Talibani shifted under his uncle's evil gaze. "That's not what I heard." His comments made Fahad's jaw drop.

"What have you heard?" he shot back. this time it was his uncle's turn to squirm. He shrugged his shoulders. "Only that your precious little girl was suffering from wounds inflicted *before* the accident occurred." He said in a snide tone.

The Imam leveled his gaze. "Wherever did you get such drivel?"

The mayor knew he'd hit a nerve. "I have my sources."

They locked eyes. "You wouldn't be trying to blackmail me now would you?" The words came from deep within the Imam's chest.

The mayor's pulse quickened. The thought crossed his mind, but he also knew how dangerous the Imam was when he was cornered. "No uncle," he lied. "Your secret is safe with me. We all have our skeletons in the closet, don't we?"

"Enough talk about skeletons, the question is, what are *you* going to do about the investigation? Can you slow it down…hold them off until our big announcement?"

Talibani leaned forward, his elbows on the desk. "I don't know. Interfering with an on-going investigation is risky."

Fahad templed his fingers. "You have two men on the police force who are members of my congregation. Put them on the case. Once they are in place, I will instruct them to dispose of any incriminating evidence which might surface and point to us or Ameer Abu el Telami."

The mayor sat straight, "Why do I not want to know who that is?"

The Imam smirked. "Let's just say he is very good at what he does."

"You know uncle, simply because Gibson is gone, the case will still move forward." Talibani lit a cigar. The smoke curled up in ever increasing circles above his head.

He nodded and followed the blue haze with his eyes. "Yes but I feel confident that our attorney is well equipped to take on this Tate guy. He is much less articulate. Rahim will eat him alive."

The mayor savored the thought of seeing the man he defeated in the election swallowed by a giant tiger. "I can do nothing about the state investigation uncle."

"That is true, but there is no way they can tie the two ... *events* ... together."

"Oh? I think they can."

"How so?"

"Are you forgetting that both took place exactly at noon on the same day?"

Fahad waved the comment to the side. "Pure coincidence. Once your guys remove the key pieces of evidence the whole thing will collapse like a house of cards."

Talabani took another drag of his cigar, let it out slowly. He doubted his uncle's confidence. "By the way, what is this *big announcement* you spoke of?"

Imam Fahad stood, smoothed out his rumpled tunic, placed his hands behind his back and began to pace. "Our Mosque is within six months of completion. Once it is complete, I will announce the coming of Al Mahdi, the twelfth Imam."

With his mouth gaped open, Talabani couldn't hide his shock. He knew the Mahdi was coming. He believed in him. He prayed for his return but in his lifetime? *No, it couldn't be.* All at once, all bets were off. Whatever he could do, however humble the task, no matter the danger to his reputation or life, he was willing to do it.

Talibani rose to his feet, came to the front of his desk and prostrated himself before Imam Fahad, the one who would proclaim the coming of the great one.

Fahad slipped out of the mayor's office without a sound.

Sitting in the office outside of the mayor's suite sat Mrs. Kasha. The small device in her ear went unnoticed under her head covering. As the mayor's newly hired personal secretary, she was both competent and discrete. She listened intently to the Imam spawning plan after plan. Her identity, her portfolio, everything about her was a fabrication except for one thing; she was a Sunni Muslim, brought up in a strict Sunni home. From her earliest memory, she was taught that the Muhammad Al Mahdi was coming. But her father's interpretation of such prophecy was far different from that of the Imam's. She believed he was coming, and coming soon. But the difference was that when he came, he would rid the world of such vermin as the Iranian Shias."

Mrs. Kasha excused herself and nodded to the other secretaries. "Please cover my calls while I take a break." She passed through the secretarial office and made a beeline for the Ladies Room, checking the stalls for any occupants. She pulled out her cell phone and dialed a number she'd committed to memory.

"Sir, I have information, I think we need to move quickly."

Chapter 47

Jimbo's Apartment

By the time he returned to his apartment, Jimbo was spent. Never in his years of service had he seen such wanton destruction. A perfectly innocent human being was killed and for what, to stop something that couldn't be stopped? It was like throwing stones at a locomotive. *This Muslim train was out of control and no one, not even a bomber was going to derail it.* He wasn't sure if it was an act of anti-Muslim violence or Sunni against Shia. Nor did he care. All he knew was that Shirin was gone, and it hurt him.

He plopped heavily at the kitchen table and pulled out his cell phone.

"Shoo, I need a shower," he told himself.

He mindlessly pushed buttons one after the other. It rang and the voice on the other end sounded as worn as the numbers on his phone.

"Sir, things are getting out of hand."

"You're telling me, Jim. We got a report earlier today that the lawyer representing that church in town was killed at noon in a car bomb."

"What?" Jimbo blurted.

His handler continued giving the gory details but his mind was locked on one thing—noon.

"Sir, did you say it happened at noon?"

He heard papers rattling. "Yes, at twelve noon. That is confirmed."

"Sir, I think we have a connection between the Imam and the two bombings."

"Oh? Please elucidate."

Jimbo, not being used to such large words, let it out in a huff. "You mean you want me to *edumacate* you?"

"Yeah sure Jim, please do," said the voice with a chuckle.

"I have it on good authority that Jared was supposed to have met with Imam Fahad at exactly twelve noon. He never showed up. Instead a bomb went off."

"Hmm, is that so. That being the case, we have a connection between the Imam and the bombing, the Imam and the mayor. All we need now is to connect the dots between the Imam and the killing of the mayor's secretary and that lawyer guy, and we can sew this case up."

Jimbo heard muffled voices and wondered what he was missing.

"Look Jim, I just received a preliminary report that the explosive device used in the car bombing was a couple of sticks of dynamite. Do you think you could check it out and see if they came from your work site?"

Jimbo let out a low whistle. "No can do boss."

"Why's that?

"Because all the dynamite we had kept down in the basement of the construction shack, in the event we needed to do anymore blasting. That must have been used to make both bombs."

"How much was left down there?"

"Oh, about a half of a case . . . maybe twenty."

"Well it sure as heck didn't take twenty sticks to blow up the car or the construction shack. That means someone has about a dozen of those things that could make a satchel bomb or vest bomb, anything."

Jimbo pushed his hat back and rubbed his forehead. "Then we can't move on the Imam, not until we find out who the bomber is and neutralize him."

"Jim, I gotta go, I have an incoming call from another operative. I'll call you back."

Jimbo showered, dressed and waited for the call. He picked it up after the first ring.

"Jim, I just got off the phone with an asset we placed in the mayor's office, and she overheard a very interesting conversation between the mayor and the Imam."

Chapter 48

Canaan Baptist Church

It was a somber day when Jared entered the newly renovated warehouse where Canaan Baptist Church met for worship. After the rioting, which had left their down town church in shambles, Jared arranged for his company warehouse to be used until a more permanent solution could be found.

He stepped into the cavernous building and was greeted with a warm handshake from Fred Dunlop. "I'm sorry to hear of your loss, my friend."

Jared tried to smile but couldn't. His eyes searched the floor. "Yes, thank you Fred, and I'd appreciate your prayers."

"I guess you heard about Don Gibson?" Mr. Dunlop asked, as he guided Jared to a gathering of his friends.

Jared stood with his hands in his pockets. He looked into the faces of men who not long ago opposed him, even tried to vote him out of the church. All that had changed in an instant. His act of valor in the face of personal danger won them.

"Yes, I did. It appears to me that the two explosions were timed in an attempt to take both of us out."

Fred placed a firm hand on one slumped shoulder. "Jared my friend, the battle is the Lord's. Lift up the hands that hang down and be encouraged. I don't know why the Lord allowed this to happen, but I have an idea that He's about to do something big. We need to be ready when He does."

The men nodded in support of Fred's statements.

Pastor Carlson stepped into the middle of the circle. "Bother Jared, let me say again how deeply saddened we were to hear of Shirin's passing."

A cloud passed over his tired features. "Thank you Pastor. I am still shaken up about how close you came to being killed as well."

Releasing a heavy sigh, he added. "We can thank the good Lord for his protection and mercy."

"Speaking of God's mercy, I haven't had a chance to tell you about this. Just before she died, Shirin asked the Lord into her heart."

A ripple of joy spread throughout the assembly. Older women stopped talking, children gathered close to their parents and the circle tightened around Jared.

"I didn't know it, but Fatemah, my other secretary is a believer, and she had been witnessing to Shirin since we started the Open Hands, Open Hearts Ministry. Remember when they came by Pastor? You kinda got into it with Ahmad? Well, Shirin took some literature and because of that, Fatemah had an opportunity to share Christ with her."

Pastor Carlson crossed his arms and raised a finger. "How is Ahmad handling all of this?"

Jared rocked back. "Oh brother, I haven't told you the best part. The same day of the bombing, he and I were out running errands when he got caught in a fight and was pretty badly beaten."

"No, I hadn't heard, go on," the pastor said.

"I got there before they killed him. But because of that, he opened up and asked me to tell him about my faith. Before you knew it, I was sharing the gospel with him, and he received Christ as his Lord and Savior."

The effect of his statements was immediate. The church broke out in applause, rose to their feet and began to sing, *Praise God from Whom All Blessings Flow.* Jared and Fred stood arm in arm smiling and rejoicing.

Chapter 49

The Construction Office

The crunch of tires on gravel announced the approach of a taxi. As it passed the charred ground where the old construction shack once stood, Fatemah pinched her eyes shut, not wanting to see how close she came to death, or to see the place where Shirin died. The stench of burnt wood, and shingles still lingered in the air even after ten days. The memories were as fresh as the day it happened.

Still too battered to walk the distance Fatemah waited for the taxi to come to a halt in front of the new modular unit. With great care, she eased out, paid the driver and hobbled up the ramp. It was much easier than steps. The smell of new carpet, coffee and the hum of a copy machine greeted her as she stepped inside. Jared turned from a stack of papers and gave her a wide smile.

"Welcome back, stranger," Jared said, and he stepped across the spacious office and to give her a soft embrace. "I didn't hurt you, did I?"

Fatemah shook her head. "No, I'm beginning to learn to live with pain."

Jared looked down at the brace on her leg and the crutch. "Are you sure you're up to this? You could take another week, if you need to."

"If I didn't get out of my house, they'd have to medicate me for depression and claustrophobia. I'm already on something for infection, insomnia, pain and a few other things, I'd like not to mention."

Jared motioned to a chair. "Here, take a seat. Let me get you situated." He doted over her like a well-trained butler.

Fatemah let her eyes wander around the office. It was brightly lit and the feel of the new carpet under her feet was a welcome relief to the musty construction shack.

"I appreciate all the visits, and flowers you and your church brought me in the hospital. After five days in a hospital room, and five more at home though, I was ready to get out."

"Yeah, there's nothing like sleeping in your own bed to make you feel like a new man."

"Uh, or a new woman. Oh and by the way, I need to get a thank-you note to send to the person or persons who cleaned my house. When I got home, it smelled like someone used bleach on everything."

Jared's face widened into a grin. "You mean to say that's not how you clean a house?"

Fatemah cupped her hand to her mouth. "Don't make me laugh." She wrapped her arm around her ribs and winced. "Don't tell me it was you."

He looked down and scuffed the floor. "Well, me and a few others. At least it's clean. That is, according to Marine standards."

The sound of heel clicking on the tile floor interrupted her laughter.

"Oh hi, I'm Sonja. Sonja Davis the new secretary. Jared's told me so much about you." She stretched out a soft white hand.

"It's nice to make your acquaintance, Sonja. "I hope you don't mind working for a slave driver." Fatemah cut her eyes in Jared's direction. An impish grin played on her lips.

"I was just saying how you and, uh," he paused. "How you and Shirin got along so well and kept the construction office running like a well-oiled machine." His voice thickened as the last word escaped his throat. "I hope you're not planning to work a full day today or even this week. I want you to take it easy."

"Now you're sounding like my doctor rather than my boss." She gave him a salute. "Or my Drill Sergeant."

Jared smiled, picked up her handbag and carried it to her workstation as the front door swung open.

"What do you think of our new construction shack?" Jared asked.

As she answered, Jimbo stepped inside. "Only it ain't no shack no more," his stomach giggled with a chuckle.

Fatemah eased to the edge of her chair. "Jimbo," she held her arms out and gave him a warm embrace.

"Enjoy it buddy, that's more than I got." Jared said. His laughter was contagious.

The telephone rang, and Sonja stopped laughing long enough to answer in a professional tone.

While she talked, Jimbo filled his mug with fresh coffee and headed to the blueprint room. "I see Xavier got the plans here pretty quick."

"Yep, he sent them by FedEx overnight."

Jimbo looked over the rim of his mug. "I like the new office. We should have had this in the first place."

"You know ol' Xavier. Always looking to save a company dollar."

Jimbo leaned over the blueprint and took a measurement. "Just as I thought. I'd better get back to work or those..." he paused a moment. "...before those guys put a wall in the wrong place." He pivoted. "Oh, by the way. Ahmad said he'll be a few minutes late for our staff meeting tomorrow, something about a dentist appointment."

Jared took a final sip of coffee and nodded. "Good to know, that way I'll have time to swing by Fatemah's house and pick her up."

"I heard that," she called from the other room. Jared followed Jimbo out of the blueprint room. Fatemah sat looking confused. "Mr. Jared, you don't have to pick me up, because you feel sorry for me."

With one hand in his pocket, he shifted his weight from one foot to the other. "Good, that takes a load off my mind. I'll just pick you up because I want to then."

Jimbo smirked and went back to work.

Chapter 50

Stanford, Michigan Police Department, Detective Division

The rhythmic tapping of fingernails on a computer keyboard stopped long enough for Nora Peterson to answer the phone.

"Chief Lawson's office," the police chief's secretary said.

"Is the chief in?" asked the caller.

"Oh, hello Mr. Mayor. Yes, he is, but he is in a meeting. Could I have him call you back?"

"No, interrupt the meeting, NOW! I need to speak to him."

"All I'm saying is the blast signature and the powder residue have the same markings," said Detective Ashby, a ten year seasoned veteran and lead investigator.

"Do you have—,"

"Sheriff Lawson, I have the Mayor on line one."

The sheriff cursed under his breath. "Right on time, that guy has been on my case for the last ten days bugging me about the investigation."

Ashby stroked his chin. "Politicians, they're all the same. He wants something to brag about on the news."

"Well fortunately for him, we have a scrap of information he can feed to the press."

"Hey, it might work out for our benefit after all."

"Why's that?"

Ashby shrugged. "Well for one thing, we've hit a brick wall. At present, it isn't going anywhere."

Sheriff Lawson grimaced and picked up the phone. "Hello, Mr. Mayor, I just said to my lead detective that I was expecting your call. How can I help you?"

"You can start by telling me you found something significant. The press is all over me like a pack of wolves, and I gotta have some tid-bits to throw them."

Lawson smiled at the phone. *I guess you got more than you bargained for when you won the election, welcome to politics.* He took a sip of water from a plastic bottle and set it down. The mayor could wait.

"You can relax, Mr. Mayor. Today I have a scrap of news you can wave in front of your media buddies."

"Oh?" his voice brightened. "And what would that be?"

"I've got forensic evidence matching the explosives used to blow up the construction house on the Mosque property and the car bomb."

The phone fell silent and Lawson wondered if the connection was lost. "You there?"

"Yes, I'm there, uh, here. I was surprised. Do you have any finger prints?"

Lawson chuckled. *You are desperate for news aren't you?* "No sir, that I can't give you."

The mayor cleared his throat. "Well, good work Lawson. Oh, and by the way. I'm assigning two more officers from Traffic to beef up your team. We need a suspect, and fast."

Since when did you care about the Detective Department and take it upon yourself to start assigning officers.

"Thanks, I just hope they don't get in the way. I have enough ineptitude around here without a couple of bumbling traffic cops stepping on the evidence."

"Oh, they will keep out of your way. I've instructed them to stay in the background and help out."

A long sigh, "Well, send them along. I'll put them to work doing something," the chief said, and slammed the phone down.

Detective Ashby shook his head and rose to leave, "I hope it's not those two Arab goons. I wouldn't trust them to guard a milk truck."

Chapter 51

Michigan's 42nd Circuit Court

Judge Hawthorn gaveled the 42nd Circuit Court to order. A silence settled like the moment before a great battle.

"Ladies and gentlemen, I will not tolerate outbursts like those of ten days ago. Anyone voicing their opinion will be summarily arrested for contempt of court and held without bail, until I get good and ready to hear their plea. Do I make myself clear?"

Silence.

"I take that as a yes. Let's have the briefs, and then we will entertain the oral arguments."

Pastor Carlson sat through the day's proceedings. He hoped that his sermons weren't as boring. The crack of Judge Hawthorn's gavel on the wooden plate brought him out of his reverie.

"Let's have a fifteen-minute recess while I consider the issue and make my determination."

Crack! His gavel struck again. The room emptied with reporters heading to a quiet corner to report in and the rest of the attendees making a bee-line to the lavatories.

Fifteen minutes later Pastor Carlson and his attorney took their seat and waited for the judge to settle in and read his decision.

The pastor wiped his palms on his pant legs. "My stomach is in knots," he whispered. "I feel like the proverbial cat in a room full of rocking chairs."

Keeping his voice down, Tate said, "Don't worry. This is all part of the game. Remember, he is as much a politician as any. Plus, he's up for reelection next year."

The judge shifted in his seat. His summation was a study in needle threading. A dour look drifted over his face.

"Though I agree with the main premise of the appellate, I am inclined to rule on the side of the State—"

A murmur spread like leaves kicked up by the wind. Hawthorn looked up, and everyone fell as silent as the dead.

"—since at this time it is the law of this city and county." He paused to let the reporters snap a few pictures.

"Now if you are obliged to appeal my decision, as I believe you will—you might have a different rendering, especially if you wait until after November 6th." He looked over his glasses at Mr. Tate.

"If the ballot initiative passes, I have the distinct impression it will, then the law of the State will over-rule the laws of this city and county. Once that is signed into law, Mr. Rahim, you will have an up-hill climb to sway the next court. I will, however, uphold the right of Pastor Carlson to continue preaching as he pleases." He slammed down his gavel and dismissed the cheering courtroom.

Mr. Tate sat behind his desk and waited for his morning coffee and newspaper. It was November 7th. He expected the headlines to read INIATIVE PASSED.

A light tap on his door caught his attention. "Come in."

Mrs. Bowen, his secretary of thirty years, waddled in with his coffee and the paper. "Good news sire."

Tate couldn't keep himself from breaking a big grin. "That good, hmm?"

"It was a landslide." She laid the paper down and he skimmed the details.

"Just as I expected, the voters of Michigan have spoken, and very loudly. I hope the Muslim community listens. We don't want any part of foreign law, especially Shari'ah law infringing on our rights as free Americans."

"That sounds like a good opening line for the Appellate court."

Tate stood and walked to the window, then took a sip of coffee. "Yes, it is. I just wish it was Don making the speech."

"The victory certainly came at a high price," Mrs. Bowen said, her face darkening.

"Yes, it is bitter sweet."

Mrs. Bowen looked up, tears in her eyes. "It's too bad ol' Don isn't here to enjoy it."

"I'm pretty sure he's up there looking out of the portals of Heaven cheering us on."

She nodded and wiped her cheeks. "Speaking of Heaven, don't you think you should call the preacher and let him know?"

He gave a quick nod. "He's probably dancing down the aisle as we speak."

Chapter 52

The Construction Office

Jared brought his Land Rover to a stop in front of Fatemah's house and honked the horn. He jumped out as she closed the door, threw the dead bolt and rattled the handle.

Jared followed her every move. "You sure it's battened down enough?"

She inspected the doorknob and turned. "Hey, a girl can't be too careful."

"Maybe you need to get a dog if you're that edgy."

With narrowed eyes, she asked, "Who said anything about being edgy." She lingered, fidgeting with her keys. "I'm just . . . cautious. That's all."

Taking her by the arm, Jared guided her toward his vehicle.

"By the way, you didn't have to honk." The corners of her lips curled into a smile.

"What, you don't want the neighbors to know you have a chivalrous boss?"

A light breeze blew a wisp of black hair across her face. She nonchalantly brushed it behind her ear, revealing a dainty earring. A beam of light danced off the diamond surface.

"Those are nice, a gift from an admirer?"

She smiled. "You finally noticed. I wore them all day yesterday."

Jared shrugged. "Sorry, I guess the light wasn't right."

He looked down at Raleigh, who watched the exchange. "What, you noticed?" Raleigh shook his head and barked twice.

"Just so you know, I don't come running every time someone honks their horn. A girl has her standards." Her voice danced in his ears like a whirling Dervish.

Palms raised in surrender, "I wanted you to know I was on time."

"Don't worry, I saw you when you pulled up in a cloud of dust. Your timing was impeccable."

As he helped her into the Land Rover, he caught a whiff of perfume. Jared stood by the open door until she eased in and fastened her seatbelt. Her light fragrance wafted around him, enveloping him in a warm embrace of vanilla and spice. He savored it a moment and closed the door. A few miles later, Jared's mind cleared enough to think of a question.

"What do you think of the modular unit?"

Fatemah deliberated. "It's not the same. I mean, I like the new building and all, but …"

"But what? You miss Shirin?"

Her face clouded; she sniffled. "Don't get me wrong, I like Sonja well enough. But she's not Shirin." Her voice trailed off. "She'll take some getting used to. I've caught myself calling her Shirin."

Jared's throat constricted. "I hired her the first of last week, and if I've called her Shirin once, I've called her that a dozen times. But she's a good sport. Sonja lost her husband to cancer a year or so ago. She knows what we're going through."

"Yes I know, she told me over lunch. How did you find her?"

"Someone at church recommended her. I think she'll work out in the long run."

Fatemah's voice grew distant. "What did Mr. Xavier say when you called him?"

"I was a little concerned how he would respond to Shirin's death. Even so, he was remarkably moved. He sent a large bouquet of flowers to her graveside and offered to pay for the entire funeral."

Fatemah forced a smile. "That was kind of him. Did Ahmad accept the offer?"

Jared shook his head. "No actually, there was such an outpouring of love from the guys on the work site, all the expenses were paid for. I've never seen such love and kindness than at that funeral service."

Her eyes widened. "You actually went to the funeral?"

Jared watched the road, not blinking. "You were so out of it for the first couple of days I didn't mention it to you, but yes. Ahmad insisted I come and pray before they lowered her body in the ground."

With her hand to her mouth, Fatemah said "I can't believe it. They let you pray in the name of Jesus at a Muslim funeral?"

Jared's shoulders rose and fell. "Well actually, *they* didn't. Ahmad was amazing. The grace of God was all over him and at the end after the Imam finished his spiel and dismissed everyone, Ahmad asked me to come and say a few words and close in prayer. It was a sweet time."

For the rest of the journey, Fatemah stared out the passenger window. As Jared brought his vehicle to a gentle stop, she blinked.

"Oh, we're here, so soon?"

Jared reached over and gave her shoulder a light squeeze. "You must have drifted off for a moment."

He released his seatbelt, climbed out and ran around to her side. After helping her inside, he poured her a cup of coffee and set it down on her desk. "Can I bring you anything before I head out to the construction site?"

Fatemah scanned the new filing cabinets and office equipment. "You know, I think I could get used to working here. It's a lot brighter, and I won't have to go down those rickety stairs to that musty old basement." An impish smile played on her lips.

In mock surrender, Jared held up his hands, "Hey, Jimbo and I worked on those stairs. They were as solid as Jacob's ladder."

She shared a smile with Sonja, who'd been watching the two banter back and forth. "If it was as solid as Jacob's ladder, then why did I nearly fall and break my neck going down them? I think I'll take the heavenly escalator." Fatemah's pithy comment made Jared crack a grin. His shoulders slumped and he feigned defeat.

"Guess I'd better get to work. Come on Raleigh, let's see if we can find us a ladder to work on."

Chapter 53

The Stanford Police Department Evidence Room

The wind howled outside as an unexpected cold front battered the old police station. Officer Duncan stared mindlessly at the magazine he'd brought to work and listened to the incessant banging of a loose piece of metal against the building. He was assigned to the Evidence Room. Nothing was happening; neither was anything going to happen. *How could the weatherman get it so wrong?* Duncan drummed his fingers on the desk and looked at the clock.

His reverie was interrupted by footsteps on the tile floor leading to the window. He peered out of his little world.

"Good evening, Duncan," greeted Officer Mohan Amin.

"Evening Mohan, what do *you* and your *sidekick* want down here?" His greeting barely masked the distain he and the other officers had for them.

"Chief wanted us to check out the evidence surrounding the mosque and car bombings. The mayor is putting pressure on him to come up with some results."

"And you two rookies think you are going to see something trained eyes overlooked?" Duncan's voice was tinged with sarcasm.

Mohan narrowed his eyes but never blinked.

"Okay, okay, I was just saying." Duncan held up his hands in mock surrender. He pushed the button, and a soft snap sounded. Mohan pulled the door handle and the two slipped in without another word.

They paced the aisles of shelves looking for the box marked Mosque Bombing. Exactly five minutes later, they found their query and pulled it out. For the most part, the box was empty.

"There sure isn't much to go on," Mohan lifted a stack of forensic reports.

"Nope, just this," his partner held up a plastic bag containing scraps of paper, which once encircled the sticks of dynamite.

Mohan nodded. "Good, that's what we're looking for," he whispered. He pulled out an empty bag which looked like the one Mubarak held. Taking out a sharpie, he scribbled the date and time exactly as they appeared on the other bag, and laid it in the box.

"That should slow things down even more. Now put that bag in any box you can find while I replace this one. Then let's get out of here."

The two acted quickly and soon returned to the front desk to sign out. Officer Duncan picked up the clipboard, checked the names and hung it back in its place, as the two men disappeared around the corner.

"Do you think he noticed?" asked Mubarak.

"Doesn't matter."

"Doesn't matter? Why'd you say that?"

"I signed in for both of us but rather than using our names, I used Richardson's and Steven's names and badge numbers."

Mubarak stopped, laid a hand on Mohan's forearm. "Do you know how much trouble we'll get in when they find out you not only tampered with evidence, but you falsified the log book?"

"You obviously don't know what's going on here, do you? That little bit of bravado put on by Duncan? It was all for show," Mohan smirked.

"I don't get it,"

Mohan shook his head in disbelief. "With what Duncan was getting paid under the table for that little act he could retire and move to Hollywood."

The elevator doors closed. Mrs. Kasha emerged from around the corner. She'd followed them down to the Evidence Department and recorded their last conversation. *The noose is tightening.*

Chapter 54

The Construction Office

"Fatemah, it is so refreshing to have someone to talk with about spiritual things," Jared said. He finished signing a purchase order handed it back and allowed his fingers to brush against her hand. *What are you doing, you jerk? Talking spiritual and invading her personal space.*

He stepped back. A soft smile parted her lips. "It is so good to be able to speak freely about the Lord. I've been so afraid Imam Fahad will connect me with my father. If he ever found out I'm a believer, he will have me killed."

"I've got the feeling he has everyone in fear, the men, you, and the whole community."

Nodding, Fatemah took a deep breath. "Did you know that it is a capital crime for someone to leave Islam and become a Christian?" she turned her warm brown eyes toward Jared.

Jared's heart did a somersault, but he controlled his voice. "Yes, I learned that by reading the Qur'an and the newspaper a few weeks ago. This guy is serious about pushing Islam on America, isn't he?"

"Yes, I'm afraid so."

Jared glanced in the direction of the work site. "That means Ahmad's life is in danger, yet he knew that before he made his decision to trust Christ."

An uncomfortable silence filled the next moment. Fatemah spoke first.

"I shudder to think what might happen if Imam Fahad decided to enforce Shari'ah Law to the max."

Jared ran his hand across the back of his neck and began to pace. "I hope the lawsuit ends this nightmare before it comes to that."

Fatemah fidgeted with the papers in her hands, then took a seat. Her face clouded.

It was hard not to stare at her. "What's wrong, are you not feeling well?"

She shook her head. "It's not that, I feel fine. Well, maybe not that good. I have a confession to make." Then she dropped her chin and let her hair fall forward.

Eyebrows knit, he waited.

Finally, she looked up. "You know the person who called the day of the explosion?" she asked without taking her eyes off Jared. "That was my younger brother, Kaleel," her voice faded.

Jared stood staring straight ahead. "Kaleel? He's your brother?" he repeated and stepped back.

She nodded gently, as if she would break if she shook harder. "Yes, my younger brother. He is a general laborer here on site. He also is a believer."

Jared inhaled and let it out slowly. "I had no idea. With so many men, day laborers, skilled and unskilled, many having the same last name, it never dawned on me." He plopped down on one of the couches.

"Well, it was something we agreed not to publicize for obvious reasons."

Jared rubbed his forehead. "Does Ahmad know?"

"Yes, he does now."

"Somehow I didn't get the connection. Did you tell the police it was your brother who called?" he asked as he stood and began to pace the floor.

Shaking her head, "No, I fear if the Imam finds out it was him, he wouldn't last a day," Fatemah turned her attention to the window, biting her lip.

With his hip perched on the corner of the desk, he thought about her last statement. "Why did you say the Imam? Do you think he's behind these bombings?" he pressed with growing concern.

Fatemah looked at Jared. Her shoulders rose and fell slightly. "I don't know what to think, but we must be very careful."

Again, a pregnant pause filled the room until Sonja came in with the day's mail. A cool breeze swept in behind her, and she quickly pulled the door shut. "I knew I should have worn a wrap, just the short distance to the mail box gave me a chill."

She looked up from the stack of letters and did a double take. Her eyes shifted from Jared to Fatemah. "Am I interrupting something? I can go back out to the mail box."

Jared smiled. "No Sonja, you don't have to do anything like that. Fatemah was just explaining that she has a brother working here on site.

"Oh, you mean Kaleel? I thought you knew. They practically look like twins."

Unable to hide his chagrin, Jared offered no defense.

Laughter broke the guilty silence as Ahmad and Kaleel burst through the door.

"Hello, Fatemah," Kaleel said in a cheerful voice. "Why the worried look?"

She shook her head. "I always worry when it comes to you, my brother, and now I have two brothers to worry about," looking at Ahmad.

The two young men smiled sheepishly and glanced at each other. "Well, don't worry too much, Fatemah. I wouldn't want your beautiful black hair to go prematurely gray over us. We can take care of ourselves, right Ahmad?" Ahmad's head bobbed.

He turned to Jared. "Uh, Mr. Jared? Kaleel and I have been thinking."

Jared crossed his arms and stroked his chin. "Uh oh, that could be dangerous."

Undaunted by Jared's wry smile, Ahmad continued. "We would like to have a Bible study, where we could learn more about God." He could hardly contain his enthusiasm.

Jared ran his hand across the back of his neck and considered the request. "I don't know about that, not here at least."

"No, not here," Ahmad said. "Why not meet at your house, Mr. Jared? You have plenty of room," he continued with an impish grin on his face.

Pacing the floor, he considered his options, "Tell ya what, let's have it on Friday night at Fatemah's house." He cast his eyes in her direction, hoping for a positive look, a sign, anything to indicate she liked the idea.

Fatemah's gaze met his.

"That's such a great idea," Sonja threw herself into the conversation. "On the Muslim day of worship it shouldn't raise suspicions."

Half smiling, Fatemah narrowed her eyes. "Nice of you to invite a crowd to my house without a warning. I'm still convalescing you know," she said with feigned impatience.

Jared scrambled to recover from her piercing gaze. "Maybe I could talk my pastor into coming and teaching us the Bible." he blurted.

Fatemah leaned back in her chair while all eyes were on her. The air scintillated with anticipation. "You'd better call the pastor before you dig yourself into a hole you can't get out of."

Jared's hand was already pulling his phone from his pocket.

"Hello, Pastor?"

Fatemah sat and began scribbling down the plan as Jared unfolded it.

"Okay, the Bible study is set for this Friday at six o'clock. Nothing fancy, we'll all pitch in and bring something."

Fatemah wobbled to her feet and held her hands up. "Stop the presses. I know what three bachelors will bring to a party. A bag of potato chips, a box of donuts, and a pizza."

Three pairs of eyes stared back at her as if she were speaking in a foreign language. "If you're coming to my house on Friday night, come hungry because I'm planning on serving a traditional Islamic meal. Of course, I'll need to leave a smidge early to stop by the grocery store and pick up a few things," she said with feigned innocence.

A feather could have knocked Jared over. He was surprised and pleased at how quickly Fatemah got the vision, his vision . . . now, her vision.

Chapter 55

The Mosque Minaret

The snoring within Jimbo's truck resonated like a bear in hibernation. He'd been ordered to keep a watch for the wily cleric, but as the vigil extended into the small hours, he drifted. His sleep ended abruptly as a loud call emanated from one of the ninety-foot tall minarets on either side of the nearly completed Mosque. Jimbo jolted to life, unfolded himself from behind the steering wheel, stood and stretched. In the side-view mirror, he caught a glimpse of his face. His eyes were red. He had a blotch on his cheek from where his hand had been and his mouth felt like gravel. He hitched up his sagging britches and waddled toward the Mosque in search of the source of that annoying voice.

He followed a group of men as they gathered in the open court yard and faced east. Avoiding the temptation to get too close, he worked his way around to the side door leading to the top of one of the minarets. Curiosity drove him to grab the handle and pull. To his surprise, it opened. He slipped in and began the long climb.

Ever since the incident between him and Imam Fahad, the Imam did his best to avoid contact with him. The daily prayers called over the loudspeaker system from the minarets went on with regularity, but Jimbo couldn't help but notice the men as they dutifully assembled. They were like mind-numbed robots going through the motions, as if forced to comply under duress.

Half-way up the narrow staircase, Jimbo stopped to catch his breath. His heart was nearly beating out of his chest. Great rings of sweat formed around his armpits despite the fact it was early November. Cold air whistled through the upright tunnel like a freight train. After a brief respite, he resumed, trudging slower the higher he got. Finally reaching the top, he was met by a steel-reinforced door and the rustling of someone on the other side.

The prayer time ended, sending the men scurrying back to their respective tasks. It would only be a moment before the door swung open, and he would find himself in a very awkward, untenable position. Jimbo did the only thing left for him to do. He squeezed against the wall, hoping when the door opened he would be blocked.

Nothing. He waited another five minutes. No more voices, no movement, just the rhythmic pounding of his heart. In those moments, he got his breathing under control. After wiping his slick hand on his shirt, he reached for the doorknob.

It turned.

He pulled. The door eased open enough for him to peek inside. Imam Fahad sat, with his back to the door. Above him, a ledge held a bank of computers and a radio transmitter. Lights blinked wildly, and the low hum of the radio created enough white noise that the Imam didn't hear Jimbo pull the door closed again. *What was the Imam doing with a radio transmitter? All he needed was a speaker system for the daily prayers. I'm going to come back after the old man leaves and get a closer look at it, he thought. In the meantime, I'd better get the heck out of here before my luck changes.*

Mid-way down, Jimbo heard footsteps behind him and the hairs on the back of his neck stood at attention. With only seconds to spare, he doubled his pace. To his surprise, he no sooner rounded the corner of the Mosque than the elderly cleric stepped out. He looked around, scurried to the nearest entrance, and disappeared. This was Jimbo's chance. He had several hours before the next call to prayer, but his legs felt as if they would collapse. He dreaded the climb, yet duty came before glory.

He began the long ascension, this time with an even pace. He stopped at the door, wiped the sweat from his brow, and knelt to inspect the lock. He fished a pocketknife out and pulled out the screwdriver blade. Within seconds, the door swung open, and he ambled in. Closing the door he went to work on the computer. He prided himself for being a reformed hacker and guessed at the password. 'Qur'an' failed, 'Mecca' failed, 'Allah' . . . bingo, he was in. *Now to the main files*, he thought. Jimbo scrolled through the membership files. *Nothing appreciable.* He opened Accounts Payable. The columns of numbers meant nothing to him. Next, he tried Accounts Receivable...*Pay dirt,* he thought. *If only I had a printer.* He pulled his cell phone, hoping his battery was charged.

It was.

He focused the lens and snapped picture after picture of names and sources of the money that funded their activities. Yemen, Iran, leaders of the Islamic Brotherhood. It was all there. The case against the Fahad was building, and Jimbo needed to act fast.

A little voice inside his head told him to open one file marked, Things to Do. *Interesting,* he thought. *The file name seems benign enough. I think I'll click on it anyway.*

The screen flashed Password, and he knew he needed to keep digging. 'Qur'an' failed as well as 'Mecca' and 'Allah'. Jimbo scratched his forehead. *That's it, why didn't I think of it first?* His fingers flew over the keys spelling *'Muhammad'.* The screen flashed, and he was staring at—

Crack!

Sudden pain shot through his skull. The butt of a handgun came down in a glancing blow. He turned to see the Imam's goons. His eyes full of fury, the veins of his neck bulging. The man pulled his arm back to strike again.

For a large man, Jimbo's reflexes were surprisingly quick, quicker than his attacker expected. Before he could retract, Jimbo rammed a screwdriver into his midsection. Blood spurted. The man grimaced and pivoted, striking Jimbo in the jaw with his elbow. His head jerked to the side, and he tasted blood. Jimbo slashed again, this time missing only by an inch. He tumbled forward, losing his balance and struck his head on the counter. His attacker lunged for him, but Jimbo rolled to the side. The man landed hard against the counter and cursed.

Your training, remember your training, Jimbo's mind screamed. He made a sweeping action and caught his attacker in the gut with a side kick. The man groaned and fell. Before Jimbo regained his footing, the man raised the gun and fired. The shot zinged past Jimbo's head and struck the overhead light sending sparks flying.

Jimbo's ears rang with the near impact. He shifted his weight and kicked the man's hand. The weapon clattered to the side, and both men dove for it. They tumbled on the floor struggling with the gun. The man kneed him in the groin, Jimbo saw stars. A moment later he heard the click of the trigger. The weapon jammed. *Do something.* Desperate, Jimbo brought the screwdriver up and caught him under the sternum. The man's black eyes widened, his head rolled back, and he slumped to the floor. A pool of blood formed around his body.

"Man I hate that. Look at what you've gone and done," He said, staring at the dead man and breathing hard. "You shot up the light fixture and then bled all over the place. Now I've got to clean up this mess and get you out of here before the next prayer."

Jimbo pocketed his knife, the man's phone and gun, then did his best to mop up the blood. The light fixture was hopeless there was no time to undo what was done. He was about to hoist the dead man to his shoulder when the radio came alive.

Apparently this was why the guy came up here. The voice spoke in Farsi as far as he could tell, then switched over to broken English.

"Abull, come in, over?"

"Well, at least I know your name," Jimbo looked down at the dead man.

Using his best Farsi accent, he toggled the microphone. "This is Barrack, Abull couldn't make it. Over."

A sickening pause filled the air.

"We await the Imam's orders. Over."

"Praise be to Allah. You are a good Muslim. Allah will reward you. Come to the Mosque headquarters at midnight and wait for further instructions. Over."

Another pause. Jimbo's stomach churned. How was he going to explain the blood on his clothes? He looked at his watch. If he didn't get out, he would meet the Imam coming up.

"It is arranged," thick accent interrupted.

"Very good, we will await your arrival. Over and out."

Jimbo retraced his steps, making sure he cleared the area unobserved. Disposing the body in one of the drainage ditches, he hiked to his truck and found another shirt. He placed a call.

"Yes sir, I'm e-mailing the pictures from my phone." His boss gave the special encoding protocols. "Yes, I got them. I'll send them now."

"By the way, have you been keeping an eye out for the Imam? What is his status?"

"Today was the first I've seen him in weeks. The man keeps a low profile." Jimbo added.

"What do you think that call was all about?" his handler inquired.

"I can't prove it, but I think the old man is recruiting young men to join the Jihad and smuggling in weapons. I inspected the gun of the guy who whacked me. It was foreign made."

"That doesn't mean a thing."

"No, but that he even had a gun is significant. I'll bet you if we searched the facility, we would find a cache of weapons."

"How do you suppose they're getting them in?"

"Probably bringing them in as spare parts, or he has individuals buy them for him. When you nab those guys tonight, you watch, they'll be armed to the teeth."

"All right, watch your back."

"That's your job, boss."

His boss laughed, and Jimbo ended the call.

He punched in the ten digit sequence. A high-pitched scream was followed by three clicks. He was into the mainframe. He forwarded the pictures and waited until he got confirmation. Then he closed his phone and slumped in his seat. "Man, I need a nap."

Chapter 56

The Construction Office

"Are you ready, Miss Fatemah? Jared twirled his keys around his index finger.

"Is it time to leave already? It's only four-thirty," she eyed the clock.

"I thought you wanted to stop by the store and pick up a few items before the Bible study." Jared reached for her coat.

"Oh yes, I nearly forgot. She stood and supported herself against the desk. "Still a bit wobbly."

Jared held her elbow while she crutched her way toward the door.

"Sonja, as soon as you finish up, why don't you take off too?" He called over his shoulder.

"That's okay, I still have a few more things to do. Don't worry, I'll kill the lights when I'm finished."

Raleigh awoke from an afternoon nap and pawed the door. He was ready to leave as well. Smiling, Jared pulled it open and Raleigh bounded out.

"Go gettem' boy, make sure there is no bomb under the car," he said with a widening grin, shooting a look at Fatemah.

She shook her head. "That's not even funny."

Jared cut his eyes over to Sonja. "Don't look at me. You're on your own there, she said."

His smile faded like a forgotten dream. "Sorry," he said, lowering his eyes.

As he pulled onto the main road, he met a line of traffic. Raleigh pranced from side to side impatiently and stared out the window.

"Relax Raleigh, we'll get there when we get there."

Looking in his rearview mirror, Jared reached up, adjusting it slightly. The pickup truck four cars back, was the same one he'd seen following him every day the past week. Traffic began to move, and Jared shifted lanes. For a few miles, he'd thought it was his imagination playing tricks on him. When he exited the main thoroughfare to a side street, there it was…again.

Jared cut the wheel so suddenly that Raleigh skidded across the back seat and slammed against the other side.

"What are you doing?" Fatemah asked, gripping the handle. "Sorry, I think someone is following us, and I thought I'd throw him a curve.

"Well you certainly threw us a curve. You nearly lost me for a second."

Jared checked the rearview mirror. "I really am sorry. I should have warned you."

Fatemah shifted in her seat and looked through the back window. "That's okay. Do you think you lost them?"

Shrugging his shoulders, he let out an impatient breath. "I don't know, but we'll need to be very careful."

He reached under his sports coat and fingered the butt of the Glock, if he had to, he'd use it.

All the time she was in the store, Jared kept near the window watching the parking lot. He counted on his fingers as the same pick-up truck passed by several times. A single street light gave enough illumination for him to see the driver; a rather large man with a hat pulled low, scanning the area. In the dim light, it was impossible to make out any features.

Jared waited until the man drove out of sight before dashing to his vehicle. He skidded on an icy patch and nearly fell. Regaining his equilibrium, he reached his vehicle and he and Raleigh jumped in. He watched from an unlit section of the lot as Fatemah stepped from the store. Her body language begged the question, *Where is Jared?*

"Psst, over here," Jared waved.

Eyes wide, Fatemah pushed the grocery cart in his direction. "Why the cloak and dagger?"

"I saw the pick-up truck cruising around the shopping center. I think he's looking for me. I hid my truck here in the shadow, and I've been watching for him."

"What do you think he wants?"

"I don't know. Maybe he's just trying to rattle me."

"Or worse."

Jared patted the bulge under his arm. "Well, I'm ready if he tries anything." He looked at Raleigh. "Right Raleigh?" Raleigh put his front feet on the dashboard and gave two sharp barks.

Chapter 57

Fatemah's House

After three weeks of intensive Bible Study, Ahmad and Kaleel were baptized at Canaan Baptist Church. They came faithfully to every service. One evening, they brought Sumatra Adeeb as their guest. Being from Turkey, Adeeb was very open to the gospel.

"Pastor Carlson, when is God going to write a second book?"

For a moment, the pastor stared back at his young student, wondering what he meant. "Ah, I know what you mean. Sumatra, the Bible is God's complete revelation of Himself. I don't think God will write another." His eyes twinkled, delighted in the young man's interest.

Kaleel's cousin Ghazi adjusted his rimless glasses. "We were taught that the Bible has been contaminated by the Jewish scholars, is that true?"

Pastor Carlson flipped through the pages of his worn Bible. "Think about it a moment. If you were writing a book about Islam, would you include all the bad things some of your key leaders have done?"

Ghazi blinked, then shook his head. "No, I would only say the good things. Why do you ask?"

The pastor shifted forward and leaned on his elbows. "This is just one of many proofs that the Bible is infallible, because it tells us the truth about ourselves. It tells of mankind's fall, of Moses committing murder, of Israel's rebellion, of King David's sin. No other book is like the Bible. Believe me, it is God's word.

Rashed, the newest member of the Bible study group sat quietly, then raised his hand. "Why would the God tell all the bad things about his chosen people? I mean, wouldn't that be even more reason to reject the teachings of...," he paused not ready to say the name.

"Of Jesus," Ahmad said.

He lowered his eyes. "Yes."

Pastor Carlson sat back, amazed. Ahmad carried the conversation forward. "Jesus is the light of the world, he came unto his own people and preached against the hypocrisy of his day. The religious leaders hated him because he told them like it was. But he called sin, sin."

Rashed swallowed hard, and struggled to make sense of it. "Is that why they killed him?"

Ahmad didn't miss a beat. "Well, yes and no. You see, Jesus came to die for those sins. It was all part of God's master plan. They didn't take his life, he freely laid it down. He said, no man takes my life, I will lay it down that I may take it up again." I learned that reading the book of the Gospel of Saint John."

"His zeal for the Lord is contagious, Jared. It puts me to shame," Pastor Carlson said under his breath while the conversation bounced around the room.

Jared crossed his legs, balancing a plate. The smiling, joyful faces of his friends and brothers in Christ warmed him. "Yes, the way they pray, their fervency and faith amazes me. Seeing their enthusiasm for the Word has renewed my hunger for it too."

"I understand their boldness has grown."

Jared swallowed his last morsel of food and washed it down with luke-warm coffee. "Yes, I've heard they are even handing out literature to their coworkers."

"Oh? And how are they responding?"

"The results aren't in yet, but some of them are fit to be tied. On the other hand, there are others, like most non-religious people, who just ignore them."

Kaleel sat next to Pastor Carlson and looked at him with pleading eyes. "We need to share this exciting truth with our brothers who are still blinded in the Muslim faith. But our attempts so far have been in vain."

The pastor's forehead creased. "You must be careful, not everyone is as open to the gospel as you two."

"Well I sure wasn't open to the gospel," admitted Ahmad, joining Kaleel. "I was downright antagonistic. I hated Jared for two reasons. He was an American and he believed in Jesus."

He looked at Jared and his face grew somber. "Mr. Jared, it was me who put the message on the seat of your Land Rover, threatening you. I hoped you would get frightened and leave." His shoulders slumped and he bowed his head expecting a strong rebuke from his boss.

Jared stared into his empty coffee cup and let out a slow breath. "Well, I thought about it, but decided if I could face danger in Iraq and Afghanistan, I could face it here."

Pastor Carlson shifted his mug from one hand to the other. "Well I, for one, am glad you stayed."

Ahmad, who'd been looking down, raised his head. "I am especially glad you did."

"I can think of several good things that came out of those threats." He looked at the sleeping Raleigh.

"What would they be, Mr. Jared?" asked Kaleel.

"For starters I prayed a lot more. Second, I got Raleigh." Upon hearing his name, Raleigh came to his feet and pranced to Jared. "And who could resist these big brown eyes," Jared said as he roughed up Raleigh's head and ears.

"Hey, watch the tail." The pastor said, as Raleigh's tail swept across his face. "Speaking of tails, I understand you've had someone tailing you. Is it still happening?"

Jared rested his elbows on his knees. "Yes, they even followed me here."

"Then that means our little Bible study is probably known by whoever's been following you."

All at once, everyone's eyes were on Jared. "I never thought about that, I guess it's too late now. We'll just have to deal with the consequences."

Kaleel's face was tense. "Surely they wouldn't think of coming here and arresting us, would they?"

Standing and glancing through the curtains, Ahmad stared out into the darkness. "Let 'em come, I'm not afraid."

"Afraid of what?"

Ahmad jumped as if touched by a bare electrical wire. "Oh Fatemah," he said, holding his chest. "Don't sneak up on people like that."

She gaped at him. "Well, maybe I should just keep these cookies for myself," she said with a coy smile, then turned.

"Not so fast." Jared reached out, "We may need those to keep up our strength."

By then, the aroma filled the sitting room and other anxious hands grabbed the freshly baked goodies.

Ahmad slunk to his seat. "I guess I'm a little jumpy."

"A little? I thought I was going to have to peel you off the ceiling." Fatemah giggled.

The mood lightened as the four men passed around a plate of Fatemah's cookies, fresh from the oven.

"Mm-um-um! Are these delicious or what?" commented Jared and reached for another.

Kaleel shook his head vigorously. "My sister is the best of cooks. I would put her up against anyone." He attempted to fake the accent of a French maître d, his chest swelled.

Jared and the others rolled with laughter.

"Getting back to what we were discussing—. "If I were you, I'd prayerfully approach someone who is not so hard lined, someone who will listen. Start by asking them if they would like to talk about God," Jared said.

"Yes," Kaleel interjected. "Muslims always like to talk about God in a general way." He scanned the faces of his friends. "If you bring up the name of Jesus, that's when they get antagonistic."

"You may have to do as I did with Ahmad, show them that you love them. Tell them about God's love and forgiveness. Go slow, and let the Holy Spirit do the work." Jared reached over and gave Ahmad a gentle hug. "You might even try saving their life from a falling scaffolding to get their attention."

Pastor Carlson stood to count heads. "It looks like if this group grows any larger we'll need to meet someplace larger."

"Since most of us are already coming, why not meet at the church, and make this group a Sunday School class?" Jared asked.

"That sounds like a good idea. But do you think the church family will go along with it?" concern etched Fatemah's voice.

The eyes of everyone in the room focused on the pastor. His face brightened and spread into a grin. "Don't worry about that. I'll just tell Fred that it was Jared's idea and he'll be all for it."

Chapter 58

Jared's Office

At his desk, Jared bit his thumb nail to a nub and spit it out. He'd watched the little flock of Muslim believers grow. His mind wandered, and he was struck with the sudden realization that something else was growing. His appreciation of Fatemah had grown beyond a passing interest in her as a fellow believer. And it wasn't only her fine cooking skills. Somewhere along the way he noticed how beautiful and intelligent she was. He found it hard to concentrate on the blueprints when she was in the modular. It was even more difficult when he was out on the construction site. With anticipation, he looked forward to Friday and then to Sunday.

Lord, I've got to keep my focus, but at times I even question my motives. Why am I going to church, to worship you or to spend time with Fatemah?

Jared paced the floor, trying to generate enough courage to ask Fatemah out for dinner. *It's amazing, I can face Al Qaeda insurgents armed to the teeth with weapons of mass destruction and I chicken out at the thought of asking a helpless young lady out to dinner. Well, here goes....*

Stepping from his office, he sneaked a look in Sonja's direction. *Good, she's out getting the mail.* He casually walked up to her desk. Fatemah was working on a stack of papers. He cleared his dry throat.

With as much confidence as he could muster, he asked, "Fatemah, if you don't have any plans for dinner, would you like to join me?"

She eyed him warily. "Oh I don't know, my schedule is kinda full these days, what with the Bible study and all."

She is playing hard to get.

He straightened as if to walk away, "Okay, I guess I'll just have to eat alone . . . again." A grin tugged at the corners of his mouth.

Fatemah cocked her head. A few strands of black hair fell across her face. "Well, hold on a minute big boy, let me check my date book."

Jared's stomach knotted while she rooted through her purse.

She scanned her itinerary, lifted her eyes with a playful glance. "I see here that I have a few openings, what night did you have in mind?" Her eyes twinkled.

Jared held his breath to slow his throbbing heart. He leaned over to peer at her calendar. "I know it's short notice, but would tonight be open?"

A bright smile lit up her face. "Why yes. I don't have any plans, at least nothing that can't be changed. I was going to do some shopping and grab a bite to eat while I was out."

"Well how about I come by at seven p.m.? We can go to dinner and a show, or wherever you like." His face had the look of a child asking for permission to go out for recess.

Fatemah furrowed her eyebrows, "That only gives me a couple of hours to get ready, but if I leave a tad bit early, I think it could work out. Maybe over dinner we could talk about Thanksgiving, since you aren't going home this year."

Sonja stepped back inside, and the spell was broken. A flicker of interest lit her eyes. "Do I need to step out . . . again?"

Jared straightened. "No, that won't be necessary, we were just, uh"

"We were planning our Thanksgiving dinner," Fatemah said smoothly. "Why don't we plan to have it at *your* house, Mr. Jared?"

Feeling the pressure, he nodded and went along. "Yes, and we can invite Jimbo, Sonja, Ahmad and all the rest. They are all welcome."

"Count me in," Sonja said with a knowing look in her eyes.

Jared pulled up at Fatemah's house at seven p.m. sharp and got out to escort her. Fatemah answered the doorbell and greeted him with a pepsodent smile.

"Where would you like to go? I'm open to suggestions."

Fatemah pursed her lips in thought, "How about Japanese? I love to watch those chefs cook the meal. That way we'll know it is fresh."

"That sounds great; there are two on this side of town. Do you have a preference?" he asked and started the engine.

"Either one is fine by me, I've eaten at both," she admitted, checking her lipstick in the mirror. Her lips glistened like a freshly polished apple.

Jared nearly drove off the edge of the pavement as he caught her actions in the corner of his eye. Rather than risk any further embarrassment, he wisely chose the nearest restaurant.

The dinner crowd had thinned just enough for them to get an eight seat table all to themselves. The special of the night was a combo meal of steak, chicken, and shrimp for two.

Fatemah's eyes danced in the flame when the grill flared.

A piece of grilled shrimp flew in Jared's direction as the chef flipped it with his ladle. "Watch it," he said.

With cat-like agility, Jared caught it in his mouth.

They sat mesmerized with the skill of their chef. He went through his well-worn routine of tapping, juggling and cooking. In between bites, Jared and Fatemah took turns quizzing each other on a wide array of subjects.

"Okay, besides Japanese, what's your favorite food?" she asked.

Jared washed down the last bite and dabbed his lips. "You haven't eaten until you have set your feet under my momma's table and tasted her chicken and dumplins'."

"Are they coming to Stanford this year?"

"No, dad's decided to oversee the painting of the house, and they can't get away."

"You should have told me, I love to paint."

"Oh? You like to paint houses or the rooms inside?"

"Actually, neither, I love to paint flowers," she said with a distant, rather forlorn look. "I have to confess, I dream of setting up an art studio and gallery to display my work."

"So you're an artist, not a house painter."

"Yep, I've even sold some of my paintings on eBay and to three or four local gift shops. People seem to like my painting. Maybe someday I'll get discovered."

Jared took his credit card from his wallet and paid the bill, then helped her into her jacket. A pained look creased her eyes. "Still tender?"

Fatemah nodded, "Yes, but my shoulder is improving. Another week of therapy and they say I'll be good as new. I can't wait to get back to painting."

"I'd love to see your work."

"Do you remember that large painting in my dining room?" she asked.

For a moment, Jared scanned the room with his mind's eye. Then his face brightened. "Why, yes. You did that?"

Fatemah nodded.

The scene with flowers, set in vivid colors flashed before his eyes. "I'm impressed."

They stepped outside, and Fatemah shivered and rubbed her hands up and down her arms. "Is it my imagination, or is it getting colder?"

Jared inhaled and let out a column of condensation. "I think you're right, it must have dropped ten degrees."

He glanced in her direction. Although she wasn't that much shorter than he was, it always seemed that he towered over her. "Do you want to take in a movie or go to one of the local art museums?"

The soft glow in her face was worth the price of dinner.

"I'd love to go to an art museum."

"An art museum?" his voice lacked enthusiasm.

"Yes, and I know of just the one. It closes at ten on Tuesdays so we have plenty of time." Her voice rose with excitement.

Like the art connoisseur that she was, Fatemah guided Jared from one painting to the next. "Oh, look Jared, this is new to the gallery. It's a Berthe Morisot, an Impressionist of the 1800's. His pastoral scenes of quiet, everyday rural life are displayed in almost all of the Impressionist exhibitions. My personal favorite is this one called *Henri de Toulouse-Lautrec*, or the girl in a boat with geese. It was prominently displayed in the gallery and it was for sale, Jared noticed. He made a mental note.

The curator cleared his throat and looked at his watch.

"Oh my word, it's nearly ten fifteen. We should be going," Jared was exhausted. After a long day at work, and after being pulled from one wall of pictures to another, his feet and back ached, but he smiled and tried to ignore the pain.

"Could I interest you in a cup of coffee?" he asked hoping for a yes so he could rest his feet and still spend time with Fatemah.

She glanced at her watch. "Okay, but just one, I don't want it to keep me up all night."

By eleven, Jared's ears rang pleasantly with her laughter, but he knew the evening had to end.

"Wow. Will you look at the time? I'll never get up for work tomorrow. We had better be going or my secretary will be wondering where I am when she shows up for work and doesn't see me."

"Yes, well, I sure hope my boss doesn't get too upset if I show up just a tad bit late." Her voice curled into a giggle.

He looked over at her and smiled, "Oh, I think he'll understand. If he says anything, send him to me and I will straighten him out." Fatemah broke into laughter that made her eyes sparkle and Jared's heart pound.

After dropping her off, Jared padded back to his vehicle. He pulled out into the night, and a set of headlights flickered in the distance, and began to follow him.

Chapter 59

The 6th District Court of Appeals

The courtroom fell in silence as Judge Fulsome, a balding man with a thin ring of hair encircling his head like a Franciscan monk, strode in and took his seat. He read the newspapers and listened to the talk shows, and had an uncanny ability of knowing which way the political winds would be blowing before they blew.

He gaveled the room to order. "I appreciate the extra security provided by the members of the State Department of Corrections and the State Patrol. Ladies and gentlemen, if anyone so much as hic-ups without my permission, I will have you hauled out and charged with disorderly conduct."

He peered over his desk at Mr. Rahim and Mr. Tate, like a principal looking down at two unruly fifth graders. "I see you have brought your share of trouble makers, uh, protesters who have gathered outside of my courthouse. I trust you have instructed them to remain peaceful. If not, I will hold you both in contempt of court."

Tate swallowed and nodded. Rahim stared at him unblinking.

"After hearing the thoughtful and impassioned pleas from both sides, I feel it only fitting that this case be heard in Michigan's Supreme Court. Had this been an issue over anti-defamation, I would have ruled for the defendant, but since this involves a much larger issue, and encompasses the concepts of international law, I feel it only fair to both sides to have our highest court hear it, and so I am ruling for the state."

His gavel smacked, and he dismissed the proceeding. The courtroom emptied as reporters ran to file the latest installment to their news outlets.

"How long will it take for the State Supreme Court to get it on the docket and hear it?" Pastor Carlson asked while he, and Attorney Tate walked to their cars.

The attorney slowed to face him. "I don't know, if they fast track it maybe—three months. I'll petition the court for a writ of certiorari, which is an official request for the Supreme Court to review the case in a timely manner. They are not required to hear the case but because this issue is related to how the State Constitution is interpreted, they will probably want to hear it maybe as soon as February next year."

The pastor nodded, "Tomorrow is not soon enough as far as I am concerned."

Tate jammed his hands in his pockets and looked stoic, "Be careful what you pray for, my friend...it just may come to pass."

Chapter 60

Canaan Baptist Church

"Why is there such a discrepancy between what some Christians say they believe and how they live?" asked Ali, a Muslim friend of Kaleel. "My neighbors go to church nearly every Sunday, but all week long they are fighting with their kids, and all sorts of stuff goes on. Why?"

Pastor Carlson acknowledged the question, pondering his answer. Nadine, Ali's girlfriend, said, "Yeah, you don't see that kind of hypocrisy among the faithful Muslims." She looked around for support.

No one moved. The air crackled with tension.

"It's like this," the pastor said gently. "As long as we are still living in these carnal bodies, we as believers still have to decide *daily,* " he emphasized, "to deny sin and put it behind us or to give in. It's that simple. Sometimes we are better at it, and sometimes we fail. Our goal should be to walk by means of the Holy Spirit then we will not fulfill the desires of the flesh," he explained with warmth in his voice.

"Yeah, well we, as faithful Muslims, don't have to deal with that. We just have to obey the words of Allah and his prophet Muhammad, and we will be fine. All you are doing is trying to confuse us." Nadine's words cut through the air like bullets.

An uncomfortable stir wafted through the congregation, and he could see that the group didn't like her line of questioning.

"You are right," he said.

She blinked. "I am?"

"Yes, young lady you are, and here's why. The Qur'an teaches a doctrine of works. You must constantly be doing something to please him, and then you never know if you have. But could I ask you a simple question?"

Nadine shrank in her seat. "Yes." Her answer was weak and foreboding.

"How many works must you do before you are guaranteed a place in Paradise?"

She paused and rubbed her forehead in thought. "We can never know for sure that we will be allowed into Paradise. Maybe if we follow Jihad, but even then, we can't be sure. It is all up to Allah."

Pastor Carlson's voice dropped a notch and sadness notched his eyes. "That is unfortunate, to have lived your life for a cause that at the end holds no hope. God's word, on the other hand, tells us that salvation is not by works of righteousness, which we have done, but according to *His* mercy, He saves by the "washing of regeneration and the renewing of the Spirit" of God. You are saved by grace, not of works, it is the gift of God, and we have no room for boasting."

Nadine stood and grabbed Ali by the arm, "Come on Ali, I've heard enough. Let's get out of here."

"No. I haven't. I want to know more," he pleaded.

"Suit yourself, but I'm not converting. What do you think the Imam will do if I tell him you are?"

Ali dropped his head. Nadine looked triumphant.

"Then God's grace will see him through," interrupted Ahmad. "You can't frighten us with threats. God has not given us a spirit of fear, but of a sound mind. If you want to leave, then go but don't force Ali to go if he doesn't want to."

The auditorium broke out in applause as Nadine stomped out."

Pastor Carlson allowed the applause to subside then dismissed the service.

"Man, am I glad that's over," said Jared, as he and the pastor headed for the coffee. You know we have a special birthday get-together planned for Fatemah, don't you?"

"Yes, but I was willing to spend as much time as necessary to point Nadine to Christ."

"You're right. I guess I got my priorities out of whack."

Pastor Carlson poured Jared and himself a cup. "That's okay. I was beginning to wonder how long it was going to be before she stomped out. I was so proud of Ahmad. He really knows his Bible, doesn't he?"

"He sure does."

Jared excused himself, and while Fatemah wasn't looking, he unveiled the portrait from the gallery that he'd purchased earlier in the week. Fatemah turned and faced the painting. Her look was priceless. The room filled with cheers and laughter.

Chapter 61

Stanford, Police Precinct

Rashad Abdul Rehman, one of the new converts to Christianity quietly stepped up behind Jared after the Bible study and asked to speak with him. He scoffed at the floor gathering the courage.

"Mr. Jared, since I trusted Jesus as my Savior, I have been thinking about a very important decision I must make," he said in broken English.

Jared's eyebrows rose. "What is that, Rashad? How can I help you?"

Rashad's voice grew husky, and he dropped his head again.

"Mr. Jared, I know who blew up the construction shack. He's the same guy who killed the attorney. I am afraid of what might happen to me if I say anything."

The memories of that day collided with bone-jarring force. The thought of Shirin and Mr. Gibson's deaths—the pain caused by such senseless acts.

He took Rashad gently by the arm, led him to a quiet corner, and spoke in low tones. "Rashad, I know this is difficult to hear, but you must tell the authorities. They will protect you, and it will help bring justice to the ones who killed Shirin."

Rashad nodded, not convinced. "I fear less for my safety now that my eternal destiny is settled, but I fear for my community and the reaction against the Muslim people. Americans already hate us, what will they do to us when they find out that there was a bomber living among them, and they didn't even know about it?" He looked about as if an unseen enemy hunted him.

Jared moved closer. "All the more reason we need him arrested, before he does any more damage. You must speak up!"

Rashad squirmed. "Would you make the call?"

Taking a quick glance at his watch, Jared noted the time. It was 9:30 in the evening. He hoped the police chief was on duty. He pulled his phone out and dialed the station.

"Sheriff Lawson please." As he waited, Jared sent up a prayer for wisdom.

Sheriff Lawson flipped through a stack of reports and cursed. *Nothing, absolutely. This investigation is going nowhere.* It was getting late, and his shift was nearing its end but he dreaded leaving as a new weather front moved in. It would be another long night for his deputies.

Not even the one-hundred thousand dollar reward has brought forth anyone with a scrap of information leading to the arrest of the bomber. That is amazing! And strange.

The phone rang, jolting him forward in his seat.

"This is Sheriff Lawson."

"Sheriff Lawson, this is Jared Russell. I am standing here at church with a young man who has some information for you, can we come by now and let him tell you what he knows?"

The chief leaned back in his chair and looked at his watch. It was nearing time for him to leave. But it might be about the case.

"Yes, I was just leaving, but I'll wait. You get here as fast as you can."

Without saying good-bye, Jared and Rashad slipped out into the night and loaded into Jared's Land Rover. They got to the station just before nine-thirty. Sheriff Lawson greeted the pair and ushered them into one of the interrogation rooms.

Looking at Jared's friend, Lawson pointed to a chair. "Sorry I can't be more accommodating son, but this is all we have. Can I get you something to drink?"

"No sir, I'm fine, I just want to get this over with." Rashad said. The room was empty. Sweat beaded on his forehead.

The sheriff pulled out a small tape recorder and set it on the table, then paused. "Son, do you mind if I record this conversation, just for the record?"

Rashad blinked a few times. "No sir, that would be fine."

Sheriff Lawson pushed start. He cleared his throat. "Okay, now son, state your full name and then tell me what you know."

Rashad leaned forward. "My name is Rashad Abdul Rehman . . . I know who set those bombs that killed Miss Shirin and that lawyer guy . . . I saw him do it, at least some of it."

Sheriff Lawson, sitting back on the rear legs of his chair, rocking, his arms crossed, fell to the floor with a screeching crash. His mouth gaped open. He gulped in some oxygen. "Okay . . . what did you see and when did you see it?" he probed.

Rashad's chair squeaked when he shifted. "It was the day of the bombing. I saw Ameer Abu el Telami, he's one of Imam Fahad's men, coming out from under the construction shack. He was carrying a tool bag and acted suspicious."

"What do you mean, 'acted suspicious?'" the chief pressed.

"I don't know, I mean he kept looking around to see if anyone was watching."

The chief leaned his elbows on the table and looked Rashad straight in the eyes. "Now I gotta ask you this, 'cause I know the Feds will be asking. Where were you and why were you there?"

A sheepish look drifted over Rashad's face like a cloud. "Miss Shirin . . . I liked her very much, and during her lunch break I would go and hide behind the out building and watch her and Fatemah when they sat outside and ate their lunch. I feared to talk to Ahmad about her because I am a poor Arab with no money."

Jared leaned on the table into the light of the overhead. "Were you the one who called the ladies and told them to get out?"

He shook his head violently, "No, I was afraid, and so I went and told Fatemah's brother, Kaleel. He called just in time or they both would have been killed. Rumor had it that you were supposed to have been back by then," he said looking sideways to Jared.

Jared nodded. "I would have been had I not gotten into a brawl with that gang of thugs at the hardware store. God was watching out for me that day."

The chief turned to him.

"Do you have any idea where this Ameer guy lives?"

Jared pursed his lips. "Yes I do, I have his application and his address in my files at the office. They survived the explosion."

"Can you get them now?"

Jared looked at his watch. "Yes sir, I'll go now, if you'll watch Rashad."

"I'll have one of my officers take you. They can use their lights and siren and get you there and back in short order." He buzzed the duty officer and made the arrangements.

Less than thirty minutes later, Jared and the officer returned with the application and Ameer's address.

"Do you think he still lives there?" inquired the sheriff.

Jared shrugged. "Can't say for sure. What about you Rashad? Do you know if he's moved?"

Rashad glanced down at the document. "I think that's right."

The sheriff rose to his feet. "Then I need to get a warrant for his arrest and another one to search his house for evidence. In the meantime, I need to place Mr. Rehman in protective custody."

Rashad bolted from his chair. It skittered on the floor. "Am I being arrested?"

The sheriff held out his hands apologetically. "No, no Rashad, we're not arresting you, but if these guys will kill once, they will kill again. You need to wait here while I get this started."

He left the door standing open.

Rashad filled out a few official papers giving the police department permission to enter him into protective custody. As he finished, he looked up. Two burly police officers were entering the precinct, dragging Ameer.

"Quick, close the door Mr. Jared!" Rashad whispered harshly. Ameer turned. His eyes locked on Rashad's. Jared swung it closed as fast as he could.

"He saw me."

"Rashad, you can't be sure."

"No, I saw the look on his face. He saw me. He knows who I am. He will not sleep until he gets revenge."

"I demand my right to a phone call," Ameer Telami spat the words, the veins of his forehead pulsing.

Sheriff Lawson leaned on the table. "And who would you be calling at this hour? Your lawyer friend, what's his name, Rahim?"

"It's none of your business, now do I get to make a call or don't I?"

"Yeah, you can make your call, but I wonder if Shari'ah Law affords a man one phone call?" The sheriff quipped.

Ameer struggled against the fast-ties. "One day soon you will find out."

Chapter 62

Imam Fahad's Headquarters

Imam Fahad's headquarters was buried deep beneath the superstructure of the mosque. His lair provided little by way of amenities, but it was here he spent most of his time planning his next move, plotting how he could carry out his 'blood curse' against Ahmad Hassani, and how he could spread Islam. He knew his movements were being watched.

A phone call broke the silence of the night.

"What do you mean, they arrested you?" he waited. Ameer related the news. "And you saw who, at the police station?" he paused and scribbled a note. "I'll take care of everything."

He hung up and dialed Officer Mohan Amin's cell phone. "I need some trash picked up . . . "

Within minutes, a van driven by Amin and Mubarak left the back of the property of the Islamic Training Center and wove through the slick streets of Stanford.

"Look Mubarak, we've got one shot at this guy. So here's how we're gonna play it . . . "

Rashad counted the twelve by twelve-inch squares of tile as he paced over them. He'd already drunk his fill of coffee, and he and Jared had used up most of the small talk he could think of.

Jared stepped from the interview room and called Fatemah, "I'm sorry about having to leave the party so quickly. Rashad had information that needed to be brought to the sheriff's attention."

Fatemah sighed into the phone. "Do you know how much longer you'll be?" she asked.

"I don't know. This is going to take a while. The Sheriff is tied up interrogating Telami and going through the evidence. Enough about me, how are you doing?"

She lowered her voice, "I made it home safely after cleaning up, but I missed saying good-bye to you."

Jared closed his eyes and imagined her face. "I'm sorry about that; I'll try to make it up to you."

When he opened his eyes, he noticed Rashad trying to get his attention. "Well it looks like they need me again. I'll call you as soon as I can. Stay safe."

Jared went into the interrogation room.

"Mr. Jared, I don't like the idea of…what did he call it . . . protective custody? Maybe I should go back to my country and hide there," he eyed the door.

Jared shook his head. "No, Rashad, that's not a good idea. They will just hunt you down and kill you. You are safer here under protective custody than any other place."

Rashad pulled out the metal chair and retook his seat. "I wish it was all over." Crossing his arms, he buried his head. "It is hard to admit, but I am afraid."

Jared sighed heavily. "I can't blame you. This waiting has got me rattled. I wonder why it's taking so long."

Rashad looked up. "Do you think it would be all right if I walk around outside and get a breath of fresh air? This room is closing in on me."

Jared rose to his feet and peered out of the interrogation room. Seeing no one but a couple of janitors, he nodded. "Well, I guess, but don't go outside. And think about this verse of scripture,

'God has not given us the spirit of fear; but of power, and of love, and of a sound mind.'"

Rashad stepped out and began wandering the halls. Without warning, the two janitors he'd passed struck him on the head and stuffed him in the four-wheeled trash bin they were pushing.

A moment later, they were gone.

"Why don't you go home, there is no reason for you to stay up and wait for word from Jared." Pastor Carlson told his wife following the church service.

"I hate leaving you here."

"I can't leave, the guys are still praying, and I was hoping to be here when Jared and Rashed got back, that's all."

It had been a long day, and the pastor could see the worry in her eyes. "Look, we'll wait another hour, if we hear nothing, I'll send them home and close up. Don't wait up for me, I'll be okay."

She reached out her arms and gave him a reassuring hug. He knew she would stay up. She would do as she always did. *She'll be sitting in her chair, looking out the picture window, watching and praying for me. My faithful wife. You give me such great comfort.*

In an hour, the only call he'd received was from Jared, informing him nothing had changed.

"Okay guys, I think we might as well call it a night."

Ahmad drummed his fingers on the back of the pew. "I guess you're right. Sitting up won't bring them here any faster. Let's go guys, I'll drop you off."

Ten minutes later, Pastor Carlson adjusted the thermostat, flipped off the lights, and stepped out into the night. He threw the deadbolt and turned, two hooded men faced him. Guns drawn. They forced a hood over his head, and threw him into a van. The van drove into the night.

Chapter 63

Ameer Abu el Telami's apartment

Crack!

The door to Ameer Telami's apartment flew open, and a team of S.W.A.T. members rushed in. Their infrared laser beams cut razor thin lines across the rumbled furniture.

"Clear!" hollered the lead officer. Everyone relaxed slightly as Fred Camperson flipped the lights on.

A hand-full of detectives wearing gloves stepped in and began snapping pictures and gathering evidence.

"There certainly was a lot there," Chief Lawson muttered to his counterpart in the FBI. "That tip was all we needed to break this case wide open."

Agent Fred Camperson crossed his arms. "Yeah, we found schematics for making bombs, bomb-making material, and a bomb vest complete with dynamite left over from the construction site."

"Detective Ashby, be sure to get all this evidence properly marked and brought to the Evidence room pronto."

"Wait one minute." Camperson put his hands on his hips and glared. "This is my jurisdiction now, and I'll be taking those boxes with me."

Ashby headed for the door, box in hand.

"Hold it Ashby. This is still my investigation," Lawson barked. "They haven't crossed any state lines. All you want is something to crow about tomorrow."

Camperson froze. "And you don't?"

Lawson squared himself. "I already have evidence linking the two bombings, if you fight me on this, I'll bury you in paperwork, and you'll never see a shred of it."

They stared at each other for longer than either would admit. Finally, Camperson blinked.

"You'll be hearing from my office in the morning." Then turned on his heels and stomped off.

Detective Ashby slammed the door to Ameer's apartment. "There were the addresses of the court house, the pastor's house, and dates indicating when he planned to do the bombings. It looks like we have a high-value suspect in custody."

"Yes and we'd better move him to a more secure location. These guys will stop at nothing to keep him from ever seeing the inside of a court room."

Chief Lawson agreed.

"Yes. Thankfully, we just might have an open and closed case against this guy if he makes it to trial." Detective Ashby observed as he got into the chief's car.

"Yeah, and that's a big if . . . " Chief Lawson's statement was interrupted by his phone. He gave it an annoyed look and answered.

Ashby waited as his chief held the phone close to his ear.

"You have what?" He waited. "I'll be there in five minutes." Slamming the cell shut, he let out a string of expletives.

"What's up?" Ashby asked.

"We just got word. Someone abducted Rashad and is making demands."

"Demands? What kind of demands?"

"They said, 'we've got twenty-four hours to release Telami, or they'll kill Rashad.'"

While the sheriff conducted the house search, Jared fought to stay awake. What might be happening at Ameer's held small interest at the moment. The clock on the wall marked the beginning of a new day. It also measured how long it had been since Rashad disappeared. Jared's heart sank further. *Had he run? Surely not.*

He got up and walked to the dispatcher, who was reading a book. "Did you call the sheriff and tell him about Rashad?"

"Yes, just as soon as we realized he'd disappeared," he said, still staring at his book.

"Since there is nothing more I can do here, I might as well go home and try to sleep."

The police sergeant looked up. "Yeah, you probably should, you look beat. We'll let you know if we hear anything."

Jared drove the dark streets leading home, one hand on Raleigh's warm head. He glanced in his rearview mirror. *There they are again, the same tail that's been following me for weeks. I'd sure like to know who it is. But it's late, and I don't want to worry about it now. I just need to get home and get some rest.*

His cell phone rang, and hope sprang up at the caller ID.

"Sheriff, what's up? Got any news about Rashad?" he glanced in his rearview mirror again.

A moment of static and then, "Yeah I just did, Rashad didn't run like you thought. They got him." his voice was cold and hard.

Jared swerved around a corner and made a U-turn, tires squealing. "Who got him? How did ya find that out?"

"I just got a call from the dispatcher. He told me after you left, that he received a call from the people who snatched Rashad. They are demanding the immediate release of Ameer Abu el Telami or Rashad will die. They gave us a twenty-four hour window."

"Twenty-four hours?" Jared repeated.

"That's right. These people mean business."

Jared's cell beeped. "Sheriff, I'll call you back, someone beeping in."

"Hello?"

"Jared, have you heard from my husband, it's been hours, and he hasn't come home." Mrs. Carlson's voice was tinged with concern.

Chapter 64

The Construction Office

The telephone rang, Fatemah jumped. "Oh shoot, I'm a nervous wreck."

"Fatemah, you must be calm." Sonja said, her voice tight with anxiety.

"Every time the phone rings, I jump. I've been waiting all day for some news about Pastor Carlson and Rashad. This time I knocked over my cup of tea and spilled it on my best burka."

She walked to the coffee station and pulled off several sheets of paper to clean up the mess.

"It's only Monday, at this rate, you're not going to make it through the week."

Fatemah finished dabbing up the puddles of spilt tea and plopped in her seat. "I know, but I'm so worried."

Jared walked out of his office with a stack of purchase orders. "Fatemah, you look like you are a nervous wreck. After work, would you mind if I drove you home?"

Fatemah leaned back in her chair, her hand to her throat. "Oh Jared, that is so nice. I don't think I could drive home alone."

Sonja watched the way Jared looked at Fatemah. It wasn't like so many men who were filled with lust. It was a look of concern and appreciation, and maybe more. Jared returned to his office, and Sonja drew close to Fatemah. "I think he likes you."

"You noticed?"

"Even the Blind Sheikh could see that," she said with a crooked smile. "I see another thing too."

"Oh? And that is . . . "

"You have feelings for him, too."

"It's that obvious?"

"Yep, you haven't heard? That's all the guys out there on the job are talking about. They are even betting on when you two will make it official."

Fatemah began fanning herself. "I had no idea we were the talk of the town."

"Well, maybe not the talk of the town, but you are the talk of the job site."

Fatemah let a chuckle escape. "Knowing Ahmad and his friends, I'm pretty sure it's the talk of the church folks, too.

A knowing look covered her face. "Believe me...it's true."

The day dragged to a close and Jared, feeling the effects of a short night, stepped out of his office. In one hand he held a stack of papers; in the other, his briefcase. "Come Raleigh. Let's go make our final rounds." He looked over at Fatemah, "I'll be back in about thirty minutes, will you be ready by then?"

Her face brightened. "Oh yes, I'll be so ready."

The phone rang, and Fatemah jumped again.

When Jared returned from his rounds, he found Fatemah in the cab of his Land Rover. She had been crying.

"I'm sorry Jared, I'm just so worried," she said between sniffles.

Raleigh laid his head in her lap and looked up with a soulful gaze. Jared gave her shoulder a gentle squeeze. "We'll get through this. Pastor said it might get rough before it's over."

"Yes, but I doubt he thought of being abducted."

Jared let her comment pass and drove in silence. He rounded the corner and came to a gentle stop in front of Fatemah's house. He guided her to her door, cleared his throat. "Fatemah...I would just like to say how special you—" His phone rang.

"Excuse me, it might be the sheriff." Turning to the side, he answered it quickly. "Hello?"

"Jared, are you near a television?" asked Sheriff Lawson.

"Yes, I'm at Fatemah's house, what's up?"

"Go and turn it on, you gotta see this." He hung up.

Fatemah took a hard swallow. "What's wrong?"

Jared's stomach knotted. "I don't know, Sheriff Lawson said to turn on the television. Do you mind if I come in and look?"

Fatemah wrapped her arms around her waist, motioned him in, and looked carefully from side to side before closing the door. Jared slipped passed her, found the remote and flipped on the television. It flickered for a moment, and then cleared. His knees refused to hold his weight. He stared at Pastor Carlson's face on the screen. He didn't notice Fatemah as she slipped next to him and took his hand. All he could see was his pastor. He'd been beaten, his shirt torn and bloody. He read from a sheet of paper. "...release Ameer Abu el Telami within the next twenty-four hours or they will kill me." Behind him two men armed with AK 47's sporting black hoods.

"What's he saying?" asked Fatemah.

"I didn't catch the first part, but the news will repeat in a moment."

Fatemah and Jared sat quiet and still for fear of missing anything. As if waking from a sleep, Jared felt Fatemah slip her arm around his waist. She gave him a gentle squeeze, and he drew strength from it.

"I can't believe what's happening. You've got to do something. What can we do—what can I do?" her horrified eyes did not leave the screen.

Jared flipped the channel. The same images played.

"I wonder where they are holding him?"

"I don't know, Fatemah, but the authorities are doing everything that can be done."

She pulled away. "I feel so helpless." Pain etched her voice.

Jared forced his mind to slow down and focus. He needed time to think, to pray. He needed God in a big way.

"Fatemah, we can pray. We can claim the promise of God that all things work together for good to them that love God, to them who are the called according to His purpose."

"I wish there was something more. Isn't there anything I could do?"

Jared thought a moment, "Yes, there is. I know we just got here, but why don't I take you back to the office, you get your car and I'll follow you to Pastor Carlson's house. After all they've done for us, it's the least we can do to stay with Cynthia."

"That's a great idea. She must be worried sick." her face beamed.

"Well, with you being there, I'm sure it will be a big help. God has not given us the spirit of fear; but of power, and of love, and of a sound mind."

Fatemah zipped her coat and slipped on a pair of gloves. "You're right, Jared."

Every time she said his name it was like an arrow hit his heart. He held out his arms and wrapped them around Fatemah, enveloping her. "Lord you know where Rashad and Pastor Carlson are and I pray that you would put your strong arms around them and protect them from harm. If it is your will, please God, bring them back to us unharmed. In Jesus' name, amen."

Fatemah pulled out a Kleenex and blew her nose. "Thank you."

Jared felt the warmth of her body through his shirt. After a moment, he released his hold and looked into her eyes. "Now I know what it was like for my parents when they prayed for me when I was in Afghanistan."

Fatemah dabbed her eyes. "They must have prayed for you all the time."

"Them and a whole lot of people."

"Are you going to stay at the Carlson's? She asked, hoping to spend more time with him.

He let his arms drop and shook his head. "No, after I follow you over to the Carlson's house, I'm heading over to the project . . . uh . . . precinct. I have a hunch . . . " Jared said and walked her back out to his truck, Raleigh at his heels.

Chapter 65

The Pastor's House

Fatemah eased up on the gas and brought her car to a halt in the middle of the street. *Where am I going to park? It looks like the entire church is here.*

The street was lined with cars. She got out and walked back to where Jared waited. "I'm going to have to park way back along the side of the road."

"Well, all right, but at least let me get you a little closer to the house."

She nodded. "I'll just be a minute." After parking on the shoulder of the road, she got out, locked her doors and slid in next to Raleigh.

"Excuse me, Raleigh."

Raleigh nudged her with his nose as if to say, 'that's my seat.' He yielded when Jared said sternly, "Raleigh."

"Do I detect a twinge of jealousy in you, Raleigh?" Fatemah stroked his head.

He yawned and shook vigorously, tongue lolling.

"What's that mean, Jared?" she looked around his thick, furry neck.

Jared stopped in front of the Carlson's house and glanced down at Raleigh. "I think he didn't like you taking his warm spot, let me say that."

She cupped Raleigh's head in her hands and wrinkled her forehead. "I'm sorry. I'm getting out now, so you can have it back."

Raleigh pranced on his back paws, his front paws drumming on the seat.

"After that reception, I don't think you'll be going on a date with me." Fatemah said, looking into the eyes of her furry friend.

Raleigh whined and looked forlorn, his ears dipping.

Jared didn't miss a beat. "That's okay. I'll take you out with or without Raleigh."

Fatemah tucked a few strands of hair behind her ear and allowed her smile to push its way forward. "On second thought," she said, looking at Raleigh, "I would be delighted to go on a date with you, as long as you bring your boss with you." With a wave, she got out and walked up the driveway.

Jared waited until she made it safely inside the Carlson's house before pulling away.

As Fatemah approached the front door, she noticed that nearly every light on the house was lit. She stepped into what appeared to her as a party atmosphere.

"Oh Fatemah, it is so kind of you to stop by. You really shouldn't have," Cynthia Carlson extended her arms and gave her an affirming hug.

"It's the least I could do. When I saw—your husband—on the news, it struck me how alone you must feel."

She shook her head in a lady-like fashion, "No Fatemah, I'm not alone as you can see. I have a house full of friends from church and the neighborhood. And I've felt the presence of the

Lord all through this ordeal. Now with you here, it is just one more of His blessings." She held the hand Fatemah gave her tight.

"I have decided if it's all right with you, to stay with you until he comes home, even if it means staying all night."

A tear leaked out of the corner of Cynthia's eyes. "Oh Fatemah, I think I'd like that very much."

"Well then, it's settled. Later, after the crowd thins, I'll just run home and get some things. It will only take a few minutes."

Cynthia steadied herself, "it was so frightening, seeing my husband beaten, hurt, reading some statement for men he never harmed. It is like watching the world news from Lebanon or Iran. I never thought I'd see the day . . . here" Her voice trailed off.

Fatemah stepped close. "I know, who would have ever thought it would come to this: not in America. All the time our soldiers were fighting to give these Muslim countries their freedom, they were sending over clerics like Imam Fahad, with the goal of bringing us into bondage."

"It's ironic, isn't it, bondage for freedom?"

Moments passed in which each struggled to make sense of it all.

Cynthia dropped her voice. "Where's Jared?"

Fatemah's brow wrinkled. "Oh, he followed me here, said he had a hunch about something, and headed to the police department. After that I'm not sure."

"He certainly is a nice man." Cynthia said with a dreamy look in her eyes as she led Fatemah into the kitchen.

Fatemah, sensing a speech coming on, smiled..."Look Mrs. Carlson, he's my boss and a friend. Yes, we've been out on a dinner date, and yes he bought me that incredible portrait but right now, that's as far as it goes."

Cynthia loaded a tray of cookies and cupcakes and handed it to her.

"I see the way he looks at you. It's the way James looked at me when we were dating."

"Oh, Mrs. Carlson, aren't you stretching things a bit?" she sputtered.

She scrutinized Fatemah for a moment. "You're not getting any younger, and neither is he. Maybe you should, uh, encourage him. You know, in subtle ways."

Fatemah cupped her hand over her mouth to keep from laughing out loud.

Their laughter was cut short with the entrance of Mrs. Dunlop. "Cynthia, they are showing your husband again. I think he looks worse than the last time."

Fatemah clasped her hand. "You don't have to look."

Cynthia took a step in the direction of the sitting room and paused. She looked over her shoulder at Fatemah and Thelma. "My place is at my husband's side. Even if it means standing beside that television." She steadied herself against the door frame, took a deep breath and stepped through.

"I hate leaving the Carlson's, but I need to get to the police station. Lord protect us, protect them until I get back. There's a lot of people there, and they are safer with You, without me." Jared muttered.

Raleigh barked sharply as if to say, "Amen to that. Let's go."

Rubbing his velvety ear, he smiled, "Always ready for action, right Raleigh?"

The dog put a paw on Jared's leg nudging him, looking up into his face.

"Looks like we might see some tonight, ol' buddy."

Jared left the Carlson's heading in the direction of the police station. His phone rang again. He looked at the caller ID.

"Hello?"

"Jared, are you alone?"

"Yes, why?"

Jared listened and waited. "Well, I didn't tell you much the last time we talked for fear of upsetting Fatemah, but there was a box along with the video—with Rashad's head in it. These people are dangerous."

Jared slammed his hand against the steering wheel. Raleigh jumped to his feet and gave a sharp bark. A moment later, Jared pulled his truck to the shoulder of the road. His breathing shallowed, his head was spinning. *I lost another man. He was under my care, and I lost him.* Jared curved his arm on the steering wheel, buried his head and sobbed. A wave of anger, hatred, grief and guilt formed in the pit of his stomach. *Oh, God why? I don't understand. I am supposed to love my enemies, but right now, I don't feel very loving.* The tender voice of God's Spirit echoed through in his ears, "Father, forgive them, for they know not what they do."

As if a cool breeze blew through the car of his vehicle, Jared felt the grace of God and the peace that passes understanding stir.

"Sheriff, I'm on my way."

Chapter 66

The City of Stanford

Jared looked in his mirror. "Looks like we've got company."

Raleigh sensed it too and pranced from one side to the other.

He took the Land Rover around a corner, and the headlights drew up to one car length behind. He could feel the hair on the back of his neck rising. His skin crawled like it did when he was in Afghanistan before an IED exploded. He fingered the butt of his Glock and flipped off the safety.

"Five minutes...just five more minutes."

The road widened. His time was up. The vehicle made its move.

Wham!

Metal scraped and squealed. Jared's truck careened out of control. He gripped the wheel in an attempt to stop his truck's spin. It was too late. Tires screeched on pavement; he smelled burnt rubber. The Rover slammed against the guard rail, throwing Raleigh to the floor, facing the opposite direction. Jared released his belt, and drew his weapon. Raleigh found his legs and jumped back on the seat, snarling. "Hold on, Raleigh." Jared panted. His tires spun as he tried to coax the Rover forward. Two headlights bore down on them. A moment later his windshield exploded as shots rang out from behind the blinding lights. Jared ducked and pointed his gun through the shattered window. *Aim for the headlights.* He squeezed off three quick rounds knocking out the beams, and then fired again, striking the center of the cab.

Raleigh poised to jump. "Stay." Jared commanded.

More shots came from his unknown assailant.

He fired again.

Movement caught his attention. More lights, another vehicle approached. *I hope whoever it is has the sense enough to stay out of the crossfire.*

The oncoming vehicle neared, and skidded to a stop. An instant later, the flash of a discharged weapon broke the darkness. Instinctively, Jared ducked thinking they were shooting at him. The dashboard provided little shelter. He lifted his head enough to see the angle of the flash... *Whoever it is, isn't shooting me.*

Glancing up, Jared saw in the headlight, the dark van that tagged him. It wasn't a pickup as he'd first thought. Again, guns barked orange fire. He emptied a clip reloaded and kept firing. The opposing fire thinned. Jared jumped from his Rover and fired. Raleigh crept out in front growling, ears pinned back. The van cut its wheels, gunned the engine, fishtailed and raced away, throwing rocks and debris in the night air.

Jared emptied his magazine, striking the fleeing van in the rear panels. The strange car on the other side of the road also poured fire into the retreating van. Jared stayed low until the firing stopped. He stood and kicked the front tire as he watched his attackers get away. The thought of giving chase crossed his mind, but with limited ammunition and the condition his vehicle was in, he rejected the idea.

Grateful for the assistance, Jared took a step in the direction of the car. The driver dimmed his lights and backed out of sight. Silence reclaimed the night, he looked at his watch. The whole thing took less than three minutes. Leaning against the hood of his Rover, he allowed his muscles to relax and for his heart to slow, breathing in the cold night air. *Thank you, Lord for your protection,* he prayed, then climbed shakily back into the Land Rover.

Two minutes later he came screeching to a halt in the police station parking lot. Adrenaline still coursed through his veins. He jumped out and ran toward the station. Raleigh beat him to the door and waited, panting.

Jared grabbed the handle, pulled it open and rushed into the police chief's office.

The sheriff looked up from a stack of papers. "What happened to you? You're covered in glass."

"I'm surprised you didn't hear it, a few miles from here, someone tagged me, spun me around, and shot at me."

Lawson sat up and leaned his elbows on his desk. "Did you get a good look at them?"

"No, but the funny thing is, someone pulled up and began firing on the guys shooting at me. It was enough to scare them off."

"Was anyone injured?"

"I can't say for sure, it was dark."

The sheriff stiffened. "You don't sound very confident."

Jared, still breathing hard said, "Like I told ya, it was dark, but I think I hit someone from the way the van moved."

"I'd better notify the hospitals to keep an eye out for a shooting victim."

Jared flopped into a chair. "That will work if they go to a hospital, but put out an APB on a dark van with a lot of bullet holes, too."

Lawson rubbed his forehead. "Yeah, that too," he buzzed the dispatcher and relayed the information.

Jared stepped out and headed to the men's room to clean up. When he returned, the sheriff stood pacing.

"I'd like a closer look at that video," Jared said.

"Sure, follow me."

They stepped into a room with a big-screen television, the police chief shoved the video cartridge in and the screen came to life.

Jared crossed his arms, and absorbed every detail. He noticed the position of Pastor Carlson, watched the hooded men for any telltale signs. He looked at the paper the pastor was holding and then scanned the background. Then he blinked.

"Thank you Sheriff, once you've seen one of these video clips you've see them all. Any idea where they may have recorded it?" he kept his voice even with an effort.

Lawson shook his head. "Nope, not a clue, but I've given a copy of it to the FBI. They are going to analyze it. We don't have much to work with."

"Well thanks again. I gotta go."

"Where?"

Not wanting to lie to the sheriff, Jared looked away. "Can't say for sure, but I have a hunch."

Chapter 67

The Mayor's Office

Mrs. Kasha, the mayor's secretary, forced her way passed a wall of news trucks, lights and nosey reporters in order to enter city hall. Slipping through the security detail, she made her way to the mayor's office. This Monday night, city hall was a blaze with the pastor's abduction and the terrorist's demands. The mayor had called an emergency meeting with his staff and city councilmen in thirty minutes.

She entered the executive suite. Angry voices echoed from the mayor's office. She stepped closer to the door. She recognized the mayor's voice, but the other was unfamiliar. Things were spinning out of control, and she knew it.

The door burst open, and two dark skinned, middle-eastern police officers emerged. One was badly wounded, holding his stomach, as blood seeped between his fingers. For a moment, the three stood, their eyes locked.

"Officer Mubarak, not that way, go out the back entrance," the mayor said sharply.

The door closed.

Mrs. Kasha crept closer and pressed her ear against it. It felt cold and hard to her touch yet she lingered and tried to hear every word.

"Mubarak, take him out."

"Out, sir?"

"Yes, out. Kill him. Dispose of his body in the landfill. I'll make up the paperwork assigning you to another department, and that will be the end of it. Now go."

She heard the wounded man groan in protest as Mubarak dragged him out. A door closed, and she backed away from the mayor's office. She barely had time to take her seat before the mayor stepped out of his office.

"Tell the committee to assemble in the conference room. I'll be there in fifteen minutes. In the meantime, I have a job for you ..."

She stood a moment, unsure, then stepped into his office.

A trail of blood tracked across the carpet from his door to the private exit, several footprints in it.

"Get a bucket of cold water and see if you can get this mess cleaned up. I don't want anyone to know."

Mrs. Kasha sweated. *Here is evidence of a cover-up, and I am about to become an accomplice. If I do what he says, who's to say that I won't be the next victim?* Her chin came up. "You go and have your meeting. I'll stay and clean up. When you're finished, don't come back here. I'll make it look like you are having your office redecorated or something. Now go Insha'Allah."

Mayor Talibani grunted, grabbed a file folder from his desk and went out. She wished she could have seen what was in it, but that would have to wait. She had more pressing business.

She pulled out her cell phone. Snap, flash, snap, flash. Then she forwarded the pictures. Her phone vibrated.

"Yes?" she waited.

"What the heck are those pictures you just sent me?" an impatient voice questioned.

"It's blood stains from one of the mayor's hand-selected officers. The ones he assigned to the detective division."

"How did that happen?"

"I don't know how. Here's what I have. The mayor ordered Officer Mubarak to kill the other guy and bury his body in the city landfill. If you'll hurry, you can probably catch him red handed. You'd better get down here quick. This thing is about to blow."

A foot scuffed the over carpet, and she whirled around. Mayor Talibani and Officer Mubarak stood in the door.

She kept the phone to her ear. "Uh oh,"

"Is it someone I should know?" The mayor's voice was guttural with malice. "Give me that phone."

In one move, Mubarak grabbed the phone from her hand and tossed it to the mayor.

"I'm very disappointed in you, Mrs. Kasha. I was beginning to think you, and I would have a long and productive career. But alas, you're just going to have to settle for a short and unsuccessful one. Get her out of here," he said, with the wave of his hand.

Mubarak covered her mouth with his hand. The smell and taste of blood was fresh on his flesh. The more she struggled, the tighter his grip became until she felt her body go limp.

Chapter 68

The City Landfill

The silence of the night shattered. A van sped through an unlit alley. Wheels screeching, it rounded a corner. It burst through the intersection, nearly hitting Jimbo's pickup truck. He slammed on his brakes and skidded to a stop inches before hitting it. He smacked the steering wheel and cursed, then cursed his aching hand. After the report about Pastor Carlson's abduction, he had prowled the streets around the city hall in hopes of catching a glimpse of Imam Fahad. He'd had no luck. This bozo would do. What a way to drive on a night like this, where nightmare and dream fought for life. He tromped on the gas pedal and sped after it.

With his headlights off, it was difficult to see, but he stayed with them. The van swerved wildly through the back streets until it reached Main Street. It turned right and sped toward the city limit, at times exceeding sixty miles an hour. Jimbo kept his distance as the van led him out of town. The scenery changed from urban to country, and Jimbo had an idea where they were headed.

The van slowed and turned down a narrow dirt road. Jimbo stayed back. Once inside the landfill, the driver brought the van to a halt and ran to the rear doors. A thin cloud skittered passed the moon. From Jimbo's vantage point, he saw the man was a police officer. But he was alone, and the van was unmarked. Jimbo got out and crept closer, his gun drawn. The police officer dragged a limp body out of the back and dropped it. Then he reached in and pulled out a woman. She was kicking and struggling, her hands secured behind her.

An angry voice broke the silence of the night. "Shut up! Don't make this any harder than it has to be," Mubarak said and back-handed her.

The man lying on the ground tried to move, groaning, but the police officer pulled his service revolver smoothly, leveled it and shot him. He then turned his weapon on the woman.

"Hold it right there." Jimbo called.

The officer spun around but did not see him.

"I've got you for one count of murder. Do you want to die with two people's blood on your hands?"

The officer fired wildly in the dark.

Jimbo held his position and squeezed off two rounds. The officer collapsed, a dark pool of blood forming around him.

A moment later, Jimbo emerged from the shadows. "Are you all right?" He knelt and fished the handcuff key from the dead man's pocket.

"I'm fine, I'm fine, just get me out of these." Mrs. Kasha turned around for Jimbo to unfasten the cuffs. She rubbed her wrists, breathing fast and sharp, her body trembling. "Thank you, Thank you. I thought I was next."

He shifted nervously as he glanced at her shaded face. "You would have been. This guy nearly ran me off the road when he came out of a dark alley with his headlights off. He—well, I was so mad, I decided to chase him down." He smiled and chuckled. "Call it road rage."

Mrs. Kasha leaned against the van to steady herself. "It's a good thing you did. By the way, my name is Camilla Kasha." She stuck out her hand. "Thanks for saving my life."

Jimbo took hers, "I'm Jim, don't I know you from somewhere?"

"Yes, I think we've met, but I'm not sure where." Her glance took him in.

Jimbo looked down and tugged at his shirt, wishing he'd worn something looser, or cleaner. "Why did he want to kill you, anyway?"

She reached down and picked up the officer's weapon. "Can't say, or I'd have to shoot you."

"That serious, hmm"

"Yep."

"Can I take you someplace? Obviously not to the police, seeing they were the ones who abducted you."

"Right, not to the police department, take me to city hall. I've got a meeting with Mayor Talibani."

"Oh? Is he expecting you?"

"No."

Chapter 69

The Conference Room

Mayor Talibani adjusted his cufflinks, smoothed his suit and strode into the conference room. He was a man with a mission. He stepped to the head of the table, and he scanned the anxious faces of his inner circle.

Sheriff Lawson sat, arms crossed ... not happy at being summonsed, interrupted in the middle of an interrogation.

Talibani's lead attorney shuffled and fidgeted, while his press secretary mopped his brow.

"Ladies and gentlemen, it is at times like this, we see the best and the worst in people. As you know, the pastor of Canaan Baptist Church has been abducted by a group of radical Muslim terrorists. Their demands are well reported. I want to get out in front of the situation by releasing my statement to the press condemning their actions. He gave a quick nod to his chief of staff, who stood and handed out a copy of his notes.

He cleared his throat, "As a moderate, peace-loving, Arab-American, I condemn the actions of these Arab terrorists. I am calling upon all people to reject the actions of a few. Our heart goes out to the family of Pastor Carlson, and we pray to Allah for his quick and safe return."

A dozen hands shot into the air. Talibani chose the one closest to him.

"But sir, are you serious? You can't defy the orders of the Imam. That would be suicide."

Talibani touched the tips of his fingers together. "Of course I'm not defying the Imam, or rejecting Jihad."

"But sir, you just finished saying the opposite—"

He dismissed the question with the wave of his hand.

"That's because you heard what you wanted to hear. I said, quote, 'As a moderate, peace-loving Arab-American.' For one thing, I am neither a moderate nor am I a peace-loving Arab-American." His voice rose.

"But sir, what are you going to do about public opinion. This whole debacle is going to make the Muslim community look bad. It will make it even harder to win the anti-defamation case against that preacher."

"Not to worry, there is a reasonable explanation for this mess."

A committee member stood. "Who, Mr. Mayor? Who could you possibly blame this on?"

Talibani began a slow, measured pace around the table, scanning each of the men and women sitting before him. He came to the one standing and placed his hand on his shoulder.

"Please sit. I am not without my powers. I have it on good authority that my secretary, Mrs. Kasha, and one of Stanford's finest have been working behind my back, undermining the investigation, stealing key evidence and wreaking havoc among the non-Muslim community. They inspired that poor, deluded Ameer what's-his-name, to commit that heinous crime. It was they who abducted the preacher and forced him to make those threatening demands." He paused, and the members of the committee bristled.

"To prove my assertion, I have dispatched Officer Mubarak to go to the city landfill where Officer Amin and Mrs. Kasha have been meeting to swap information. I am waiting even now for a call informing me that they have been arrested and are being brought in for questioning."

Lawson leaned forward and placed his elbows on the shiny mahogany table. "Mr. Mayor, I don't have to remind you that you assigned those men to my detective department. How do you explain that?

The mayor put his hands on his hips, held his breath, and let it out slowly. "Sir, I didn't assign them to the detective department. You kept asking for more officers to help your investigation, which, I might remind you, was flagging. They were on loan for a few days."

Lawson shifted in his seat. "What are you going to tell the press about my key witness being snatched out from under our noses?"

Talibani crossed his arms and stared at him. "Sheriff Lawson, I have been concerned for quite some time about the lax way you run your department. I suggest you prepare your own statement explaining how *you* let a couple of thugs into *your* police department and steal *your* key witness right out from under your nose."

His lawyer looked up from his stack of papers. "Mr. Talibani, do you have any idea about the whereabouts of our witness?"

"No Uzi, I don't, but I'm sure the Sheriff is doing everything in his power to bring him back. Isn't that correct, Sheriff?"

Lawson's face had paled, and he looked like he was going to be sick, but he nodded.

Another hand got the mayor's attention. "Sir, two against one, won't Officer Mubarak need a back-up?"

"No, he is a skilled professional, and I have issued him orders to use deadly force if they resist."

The door burst open and a dozen FBI agents stormed into the room shouting, "Everyone freeze," their weapons at the ready.

The mayor turned to run when a shot rang out. The bullet struck the doorframe above him. He froze.

The wide eyed assembly sat like manikins around the table. No one breathed.

"Good evening, Mr. Mayor, going someplace?" Mrs. Kasha stood in the entrance, hands on her hips.

The mayor slowly turned, his face ashen.

She pushed passed the wall of agents with their weapons drawn and pointed at the frightened council members.

"Do you mind explaining how you came into possession of this?" she tossed the bag containing the ballistics report on to the table, it slid across the smooth surface and landed in the sheriff's lap.

"Or this, she held up her cell phone and displayed the pictures of bloodstains on his carpet.

She closed the distance and waved it in the air.

"I can explain," he said. In a flash, he grabbing her and began to back away.

The room erupted in screams as women and men alike watched in horror. In the mayhem, Camilla squirmed and stomped on the mayor's foot. He loosened his grip on her enough for her to break free. In a desperate and foolish move, the mayor reached inside his coat.

"Gun!" Agent Camperson cried.

A hail of shots rang out and Mayor Talibani fell backward against the wall. His lifeless body slumped to the floor.

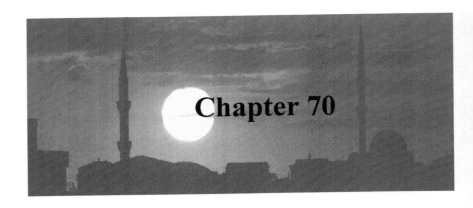

Chapter 70

Jared's house...

A shadow moved.

Raleigh alerted, his ears back, head low.

"That's okay boy, it's just a limb," Jared said in an assuring tone. Raleigh growled as he rubbed his neck. "Good boy, watch my back."

Jared, dressed in black, closed the door of his house and padded to his vehicle. Bullet holes dotted the hood and side panels, and shards of glass hung from the corners of the windshield. He brushed the debris aside and placed his gear in the back seat. The illuminated hands of his watch showed two o'clock Tuesday.

"It's been a long day, and a longer night," he said to Raleigh, who sidled close and looked up at him as if to say, "Wherever you go . . . I go."

Having been up awake nearly twenty-four hours, he was running on nervous energy, adrenalin and black coffee, most of the preceding day. He would rather have been in bed than to go on a wild goose chase. Instead, he took his seat behind the steering wheel, started the engine and drove into the night.

The street lights glowed orange through a light rain that fell. With one headlight, visibility was difficult. He glanced into his rearview mirror, and a cautious sigh escaped his throat. "Good, no one is following us." Raleigh stood on the seat and watched the blackness behind them.

Occasionally, a lone figure crossed the street, but Jared gave it little thought. At last, he pulled off the rain slick road, and headed to the Center for Islamic Studies.

In the gravel driveway, he flicked off his headlight and pulled to a stop. With no moon and low cloud-cover, the view outside of his vehicle was black as ink. He slipped on his night-vision goggles and eased open the door, Raleigh jumped out and began to search the area. Jared called him and with a measured pace started toward the mosque, his eyes stabbing the darkness on all directions.

Raleigh took up a position in front, just as he was trained. They made their way around the first of two buildings—nothing! As Raleigh made his way to the library building, he saw a shadow move, and stopped, nose pointing.

Jared raised his gun.

"Don't shoot, Mr. Jared! It's me, Ahmad."

Jared froze and held his position. The greenish figure emerged and approached with caution.

Raleigh closed the distance and sniffed, and whined.

"Ahmad, what are you doing here?" Jared whispered, his voice laced with surprise and frustration.

Keeping his voice low, he said, "Fatemah told me about the video and figured you might be coming here."

"Yeah, I kinda let it slip." He holstered his weapon. "Look Ahmad, this is a dangerous operation; you are unarmed and could get hurt." Jared said not hiding the tension in his voice.

Ahmad looked over his shoulder, then back to Jared. "I have a gun, I know how to use it, and I am not leaving your side."

Knowing Ahmad as he did, Jared figured he would never persuade his friend to turn back ... not once he'd made his mind up.

Jared looked down at Raleigh, "What do you think? Should we include him?"

Raleigh shook his head and nudged Ahmad forward.

"Looks like you're in." He adjusted his goggles. "In an odd sort of way, I'm sorta glad to have someone else with me. The thought of going into that underground maze alone was fearful."

Ahmad eyed the NVG's. "I have been down there so many times I could get around without those."

Jared nodded. "Yeah, me too, these are for seeing the unexpected. Now, if you're ready, let's go, but stay behind me," he cautioned. "And *don't* shoot me in the backside on accident.

Ahmad grinned, "Yes sir, Mr. Jared."

The three of them made their way to the outer perimeter of the Mosque. Every fifty yards was an entrance to the lower level. No sign of the pastor.

Jared had borrowed a shirt belonging to Pastor Carlson. He let Raleigh sniff it and get familiar with his scent.

They approached another entrance, and Raleigh alerted.

Jared knelt and used a pen-light to inspect the ground.

"By the looks of it, someone pulled up to the doorway and dragged a body from the vehicle into the lower level."

Raleigh whined again.

"Mr. Jared, I think Raleigh found something else.

Jared came to where Raleigh stood, reached down and picked up one of the pastor's shoes.

"He is here, all right, hidden somewhere in one of those anterooms or chambers. It will be a nightmare to go in and not have backup. How do you suppose we get in without setting off the alarm?" he asked Ahmad.

Ahmad leaned close. "Don't worry, it hasn't been activated yet. We were working on it, but the fire marshal hasn't given the final okay," he whispered and brushed some dirt from his knees.

"Good, I have the master keys to the entire complex. Let's see if I can find the right one in the dark."

He withdrew the wad of keys from a pocket, and flipped through them.

"There, that's the one," barely above a whisper, "Before we go in, I'd better call the sheriff and let him know where we are and where we believe they are holding the pastor." As he spoke, he pulled out his phone and dialed Lawson's personal cell.

"Hello, Sheriff Lawson?"

"Jared, is that you?"

"Yes, what's all that commotion? It sounds like you're in a zoo."

"No, I'm not in a zoo. It's more like a mad-house."

"Oh really, you gotta tell me about it sometime. Look, I'm out here at the Mosque and found something you might be interested in." His breath formed light puffs of condensation, which disappeared in the cold morning air.

"Okay, you have my attention. What is it?"

"It's a shoe, Pastor Carlson's shoe."

"Jared, this thing is unraveling fast. There is corruption from the mayor's office all the way to the Mosque. I know you want to find your preacher and all, but you need to sit tight and let me handle it."

A clap of thunder rolled over head, and Raleigh growled.

"Okay, if you say so. But hurry, the clock is ticking." As he spoke a loud hiss filled his ear and the phone went dead.

"What did he say?" Ahmad asked, concern filling his voice.

Jared pulled off his NVG's and looked at Ahmad. "The sheriff said to wait until he can send back-up."

Ahmad shook his head, "I don't think we should wait long. Things could get out of hand real fast for Rashad and Pastor Carlson."

"Look Ahmad, I know how much you hate the Imam and all, but once we get down there you can't let that be your driving force. Our main mission is to find and rescue." He paused as Ahmad held up his hands in surrender.

"Don't worry, Mr. Jared. You have taught me well. Love your enemies, pray for those who despitefully use you. I have already forgiven him. He's in God's hands now."

His words struck Jared in the heart like an arrow. He had some serious praying to do before he entered the Mosque.

Chapter 71

The Police Department

Sheriff Lawson's squad-room was a bevy of activity. Agent Camperson and his men processed their detainees and filled out their reports.

"Come to find out, the mayor didn't have a gun after all. He was reaching for his cell phone." Camperson said.

The sheriff inhaled sharply, and looked at his hands, "They call that Police Suicide. He knew what he was doing. I think he didn't want to face the public humiliation of being arrested. Maybe he thought going out like a martyr would gain him favor with Allah."

Camperson shook his head. "Well, I don't know about that, but it saved the state a boat-load of money. Is his lawyer saying anything?"

"Nope, just that he wants to talk with *his* lawyer."

Camilla Kasha stepped into the sheriff's office and sat with her legs crossed. "Looks like we've got our moles, and the guys who grabbed Rashad."

Sheriff Lawson cocked his head, "Oh? Is that so."

"Yes sir, I've been following them around ever since the mayor assigned them to the detective department. You'll be happy to know that you won't have to pay Officer Mubarak, and Officer Amin overtime for their services." Camilla managed to keep a straight face until the sheriff figured out what she meant.

His weak chuckle was interrupted by the dispatcher. "Sir, you've got a call holding on line one, it's that Jared Russell guy. Said he's at the Mosque."

Jimbo stepped into the crowded office as the sheriff picked up the phone. He listened without comment.

"Look Jared, I don't think it's a good idea for you to go poking around down there, not with what's been going on down at the city hall."

Detective Ashby squeezed into the office and dropped an arm load of warrants on the sheriff's already cluttered desk. The sheriff nodded and began signing them as he spoke.

The phone crackled as a clap of thunder sounded overhead. For a moment the sheriff thought he'd lost the connection.

"I want you to stay put until I show up. Don't do anything and especially don't go getting yourself shot at again."

He waited, but static filled the line before it went dead.

Jimbo stood and pushed his back in place, then slipped out. He had work to do.

Chapter 72

The Institute for Islamic Studies

"2:30," Jared sighed.

Ahmad placed his hand on his forearm. "Mr. Jared, we have waited long enough. If we wait any longer there is no telling what might happen to Rashad and the pastor."

Jared bit back the temptation to tell his friend about Rashad. If they were going to survive, he needed Ahmad to stay focused, stay calm.

Ahmad's voice penetrated his thoughts. "If the police show up with their lights and sirens, they will spook them. I know some of those people, they are zealots, killers. The Imam may not even wait the remaining hours, he might kill him out right. We need to go in."

Jared considered their options. The pastor's chances of survival were slim to none. Ahmad was right. He had to do something, at the risk of losing it all. They'd already killed Rashad, and they could easily kill again. "You're right, but we must be very careful. So here is what we're doing . . . "

He gave Raleigh a hand signal, and he began a measured pace toward the door. Jared put his finger to his lips as he leaned against the basement door—nothing. Holding his breath, he gently slipped the key into the slot and turned it. There was a soft click, and the door eased open. Breathing again, he signaled to Raleigh and he slinked inside ahead of Jared and Ahmad. The door closed quietly behind them.

Jared looked around, allowing his eyes to adjust to the dim light.

Good . . . no alarm. Let's just hope no one steps into the hall. If so we have no place to hide. Jared said as he lowered himself to a prone position.

Ahmad nodded. his jaw set.

"Okay Raleigh, which way?" Jared whispered.

Raleigh looked up at Jared knowingly and began to follow an unseen trail.

At each corner, Jared used a mirror to check the next hall before proceeding. Each time the coast was clear. He drew his weapon, charged it and released the safety. Ahmad did the same to his.

They had passed several recessed doors, Raleigh ignored them. A door behind them opened and a shaft of yellow light cut through the darkness. Laughter spilled out into the hall. A man wearing a tunic stepped out.

Jared and Raleigh leaped into one of the recessed doorways. Ahmad jumped into another. As the man walked by, Jared stepped out behind him and slugged him with the butt of his gun. The man fell with a sickening thud, his weapon clattering to the floor. Jared dragged him into the doorway where he'd hidden. He waited for his pulse to slow. After months of hammering, and sawing, the silence of the building was eerie. In the dim light, the hall looked like it descended to hell.

After a few minutes, he nodded to Ahmad. They stood and continued down the corridor. A minute later gunfire erupted. Flashes from the unknown shooters illuminated their angry faces.

Jared and Ahmad were caught in the open with no place to hide.

"Run!" Jared fired and plunged down the dim hall. Bullets whizzed past them and ricocheted off the walls. Raleigh stood snarling at the attackers as Jared, and Ahmad hunkered down and pumped more rounds into the dark.

Without warning a hulking figure emerged from a door firing wildly. Raleigh lunged at him. He threw his hands up to fend off the vicious attack, but Raleigh was an unrelenting whirl of slashing teeth. The man fell backward against the wall. Jared stood and raced to Raleigh's aid, but the man took aim on Jared.

"Nooooo!"

In one sweeping motion, Raleigh leaped at the outstretched arm. The gunshot exploded, and Raleigh sprawled to the floor. He let out a sharp yelp and tried to stand, but his back legs refused to move. A pool of blood spread around him. Jared squeezed off two rounds, and the man fell limp, then he knelt and reached down, lifting Raleigh's head.

Raleigh looked up as if to ask, 'Are you all right?'

Jared cradled his friend. "Yes Raleigh, I'm safe, thanks to you."

Raleigh attempted to stand, and his body shuddered. "No boy, you lie still." Jared inspected the exit wound. He knew it would only be a few moments before he died. "Good dog, you saved my life."

All at once, shots rang out pinning Jared to the floor. He fired. Someone groaned and fell. He scooped Raleigh in his arms. "Hang in there, Raleigh, I'm going to take care of you," he dashed for the corner. He rounded it, and more bullets followed him. One struck him in the arm spinning him around. He fell hard against the wall and slid to the cold tile floor. Raleigh winched in pain as Jared tried to lay him down.

"Sorry buddy, looks like we're both pretty badly shot up." His dog licked his hand and let out a gurgled whimper and laid his head on Jared's lap. "I love you Raleigh, you have been a good dog and a good friend." As he spoke he stroked his thick coat, letting his soft fur slide between his fingers. Jared cupped his head in his hands and kissed the dimple between his eyes. Raleigh roused, then took one last breath and let it out. The light in his eyes faded, and Jared knew he was gone. At that moment, time stood still, Jared sat, rocking his companion.

As the reality and danger penetrated his mind, so did the shock of being hit with a bullet. Pain shot up his arm causing his head to swim. He groaned, then everything grew distant, he couldn't focus—couldn't move—couldn't breathe.

More rounds hit around him ricocheting off the walls.

With great effort, he willed himself back to reality and dragged himself around the corner. He lifted his head and saw Ahmad standing over him, firing wildly. He emptied one clip, reloaded and continued firing until it was empty, then picked up the weapon from the other man and opened fire. The shooters in front of him fell one by one. Then, in the dimness, gunfire erupted from the opposite direction.

"Mr. Jared, they're coming from both sides."

The men down the corridor jockeyed for position. Hazy figures moved through the noxious mixture of stale air and gun smoke.

Ahmad crouched next to Jared, "Mr. Jared, you're losing a lot of blood."

Jared tore off a piece of his shirt and wrapped it around his arm and tied it tight. "That will have to do until we get out of here," Ahmad said, his face calm. "Can you walk?"

Jared roused and tried to roll over. Raleigh lay next to him.

"Yeah, I think I can, but I don't know about Raleigh."

"He's dead?"

"Yes."

Another blast of shells echoed off the walls.

"How about I cover you, and you make it back down the hall to the next entry way."

"How much ammo do you have?"

Ahmad paused and felt in his pocket, "I got one more clip."

Jared nodded, "Take mine and use it too. I think I can make it."

Standing, Jared lifted Raleigh's limp body over his shoulders. His hair rubbed against his neck. A dozen memories flooded his mind. Memories of wrestling with him for hours, waking up with him at his side, and even sharing a part of his dinner with him flooded Jared's mind. He choked back his emotions. This was not the time to grieve that would be later. For now, he needed to focus, to fight and to live. All at once, Fatemah's soft brown eyes jumped into his mind. He had to make it out of there, if only to tell her how he really felt He leaned against the wall for a moment, then took a deep breath. "I'll go on three."

On the count of three, Ahmad stepped out into the corridor and began squeezing off rounds systematically, one every second. Jared began racing down the hall, carrying Raleigh and clutching his arm. Ahmad followed, but kept firing.

In a heartbeat, the floor vibrated as an automatic weapon unleashed a barrage. Bullets whiffled through Jared's shirt barely missing him. Ahmad grabbed his chest, shoved forward in a rush, and collapsed on Jared inside the next entryway.

"I'm okay, I just got the wind knocked out of me." Ahmad lifted his hand, it was covered in blood.

Jared lay disoriented under the weight of his fallen comrade. The stench of sulfur, sweat, and burnt flesh filled the air. Jared pulled himself up enough to see the life fading out of his eyes.

"Ahmad," he yelled over the gunfire and men's voices.

He lifted his head. A weak smile crossed his face. "Are you safe?"

Jared nodded. "Yes my friend, you saved my life."

"Then I have paid my debt to you and I am glad." He coughed; blood formed in the corner of his mouth. "You have been good to me, you told me about Jesus, it's . . . " he coughed again, "it's the least I could do."

With care, he lifted him and held him close, "Ahmad, I love you as a brother, now don't go dying on me, I need you around here."

Ahmad reached up with his bloody and squeezed Jared's. "I'll see you in Heaven, my brother," his eyes closed.

"No!" Jared cried even as he held Ahmad's limp fingers. The grief of having lost two of his closest friends was palpable. Warmth streamed down his cheeks as a concoction of grief, guilt, and anger washed over him. He struggled to free his hand and swiped his sleeve across his face. He needed to focus, to think, he needed to figure out a way to make these guys pay.

A moment later another wall of bullets ripped through the air. He ducked. The hair on the back of his neck began to crawl at the pounding of feet. He picked up his gun with his left hand. It wobbled crazily. He couldn't tell who it was, but in the blue/gray smoke a ghastly figure approached, firing wildly.

"Don't shoot," a voice called.

"Sheriff, is that you?"

The figure lumbered forward, panting. "No, it's me, Jimbo, don't shoot, I'm coming in."

"You're already in."

He fired a few covering rounds around the corner. "Yeah, I guess I am," he gasped. In a futile attempt to squeeze into the recessed door, he hugged the wall. His gut hung out like Alfred Hitchcock's. Jared winced at the thought of getting hit there.

"Where did you come from?"

Jimbo's face wrinkled into a grin. "I was in the neighborhood and thought I'd do some target practicing . . . you?"

The pain in his arm made every muscle in his body quiver. He gritted his teeth. "Raleigh and I are following up on a hunch."

"Yeah, well, it looks like that hunch of yours got Ahmad and Raleigh killed," Jimbo said. Pain marked his face.

Another burst of gunfire erupted, Jimbo squeezed off a few rounds. Someone groaned and fell.

"Really Jimbo, how did you get in here? It's not your fight."

"The same way you did, you nut." They both ducked as rounds flew over his head.

"I have every key you do, and besides, I've been following you around for the last six months keeping an eye on you. Now you go and get yourself in this mess, and you dragged me in. You owe me big time," he said with a wry smile.

Gunfire exploded and they ducked their heads. Again Jimbo fired, another body fell.

"I think I got another one," Jimbo muttered as he re-loaded.

"I knew someone was following me, but you?"

"Oh they didn't tell you in one of your weekly briefs?" he chuckled.

"I'm with the CIA, and I've been tracking Imam Fahad for months. We lost him and had no idea where he was until he showed up here. I couldn't arrest him, because the time wasn't right. And now it may be too late . . . too late for us and him."

He reached out and fired a few more times. Someone let out a groan and fell.

"Look, we gotta get you out of here or we'll be shooting it out all night. Can you walk?"

"I think I can, but I can't leave Ahmad and Raleigh here." He reached out and tried to pick up Ahmad's body.

Jimbo grabbed him and yanked him back just as another burst of gunfire ripped through the air. "Look, Jared, you're in no condition to carry Ahmad outta here. You'll get us both killed."

Jared's eyes flashed, "I left my wounded driver in a firefight and swore I'd never leave a comrade again, now let go of me." He pulled away and grabbed Ahmad's arm and slung him over his shoulder.

"What about your preacher? Wasn't he why you came here in the first place?"

Jared wobbled under Ahmad's weight. "With all this shooting, he's probably dead too. We got to save ourselves. Now grab Raleigh and move." He ordered then fired down the hall.

Reaching out Jimbo took Raleigh by the collar hoisted him up and backed away.

They rounded the last corner and Jimbo turned and peered back. "You keep going. They don't know I'm down here so I'm going to hide here and nail then as they come by," he said, still breathing hard.

Jared nodded and kept walking. Jimbo turned a corner and shot out the overhead light. As the shooters crept past the intersection, he stepped out behind them. Three quick shots and all the shooters were lying dead on the floor.

After reloading, Jimbo did a quick triage on Jared.

"Jared, if there is a chance your preacher is still alive, I want to try and find him. Can you hang on just a little longer while I check?"

He nodded and fingered his gun.

"Good, you stay here. I'll be back in a minute." Then he crouched low and disappeared in the haze.

Searching the remaining halls and anterooms, he stumbled upon a storage room. His heart jackhammered as he assessed the stockpile of weapons from AK-47's to handguns, ammunition and a couple of bomb vests. Noticing the packaging on the floor, he felt his skin crawl. *This doesn't look good,* Jimbo said to himself. *Somebody may be a walking bomb, and we don't have a clue who it is.*

Retracing his steps, he noticed a light coming out from under a door. He tried the doorknob . . . it turned. The door opened quietly; he peered into an empty room. Only a single chair occupied the room and ropes hung loosely from its arms. As he scanned the room, he noticed something else . . . blood, lots of it. He followed the trail and jolted when he stumbled over Rashad's headless body. It lay crumpled on the floor; hands bound behind his back. Jimbo caught his breath and tried to calm his racing heart. He felt sick. *Where is Pastor Carlson?*

Chapter 73

Outside the Center for Islamic Studies

A dozen police officers and SWAT team members huddled in the rain like Michigan State linemen on their twenty-yard line; a column of condensation billowed upwards. To the man, each one was willing to go into the labyrinth alone. Together they were a force to be reckoned with. They made the final adjustments to their body armor and facemasks. Then, without warning, the door swung open. Jimbo and Jared emerged carrying their buddies over their shoulders.

"Drop your weapons—get on the ground...now!" Sheriff Lawson's voice crackled through the morning air.

Jared and Jimbo stood like wooden Indians in the glaring lights.

"Wait a minute guys. Hold on before you go tearing up a perfectly good door," Jimbo cried. Then he eased Ahmad to the rain-soaked ground, tossed his gun out in front of him and knelt with his hands raised. Jared did the same.

Sheriff Lawson stepped from behind a spotlight and walked to Jimbo. "Where'd you guys come from?"

Jimbo squinted up into the lights, "From the belly of the beast. Can't you tell?"

"I told Jared to wait 'till back-up arrived. We had a little mess to clean up down at city hall, or we would have gotten here sooner."

Standing, Jimbo helped Jared to his feet.

"Back-up for me came in the form of Jimbo. If it weren't for him, I'd be dead," Jared said leaning heavily on Jimbo's round shoulder.

"By the looks of you, they nearly succeeded; let's get you to the ambulance." The sheriff paused and looked at Ahmad and Raleigh. "Had you waited, they might still be alive."

Jared bit back the tears as the reality of what happened collided with bone-jarring force. "We waited as long as we could. We feared the pastor's life was in immediate danger, and we had to do something." He looked into the eyes of the sheriff and saw . . . sorrow.

Sheriff Lawson's shoulders slumped and he shook his head slowly. "You were probably right, going against my judgment. They would have killed him, had we showed up in force. I'm truly sorry for your loss though."

"I didn't think you cared a whit about Ahmad," Jared said, jaw tight.

Releasing a heavy sigh, the sheriff continued. "Yeah, well, I knew you two were close. I know what it's like to lose a friend; it hurts. I'm sorry about your dog. I know how you loved him."

Jared nodded as the memory of losing his first dog flooded his mind and scraped off a long forgotten scab. "That's the second dog that's given his life for me," his throat closed.

He looked down at the leash he'd taken from Raleigh's neck.

For a moment, the passage of time no longer mattered as the three men stood in the pre-dawn darkness. The silence was intensified as Jimbo reached into his pocket, pulled out the small cross and opened his hand. "I think Ahmad would have wanted you to have this."

An explosion of joy and sorrow reverberated deep within Jared's heart. His eyes misted. Slowly, he lifted a trembling hand and closed his fingers around it. "Thanks Jimbo, I think you're right."

Finally, Sheriff Lawson broke the moment. "You'd be happy to know we found your pastor, or rather he found us."

"You did? Where?"

"Yep, he's over there in the ambulance." The police chief nodded in his direction.

"How'd that happen?"

When we approached the library building, Pastor Carlson stuck his head out from around the corner . . . said he heard a lot of shooting down in the lower level, and his captors ran out to see what was going on. He broke free and got outta there."

"Good, I've got something for him."

"What's that?" The sheriff asked.

"His shoe." Jared walked over and picked it up. "We found it over there." He pointed to a set of tire tracks. "He must have lost it when they dragged him down stairs. I figured if we found him alive, he might need it."

As Jared neared the ambulance, he caught a glimpse of Pastor Carlson. He'd been through a lot.

Pastor Carlson lifted his head from the gurney when Jared stepped closer. "Hello Jared. I understand you've been looking for me."

Jared handed him his shoe. "You lost this, thought you might want it next Sunday."

The pastor smiled. "Your arm looks pretty bad. Are you going to be okay?

"I've been shot up worse, I'll make it," Jared said with a nod.

As the EMTs began to strip away his jacket and shirt, one of them placed his arm on Jared's back and said, "Sir, we need you to lie down."

Jared looked at his wound. "Looks like it was a clean shot."

The EMT helped him to the gurney and rolled him on his side. "It sure is, the bullet missed the artery and bone and passed through the muscle; a lot of bleeding, no permanent damage. You're a pretty lucky guy."

Jared shook his head. "I'm grateful to God for sparing my life."

The EMT wrapped the wound and immobilized his arm, and placed cold packs around it to keep down the swelling. "That will get you to the hospital. Now let's get you hydrated." He handed Jared a bottle of water while he hooked up an IV drip.

Pastor Carlson pulled himself up and leaned on an elbow. "How'd you know where to look?"

"I had a hunch that you were being held down there," he looked over at the Mosque.

"What made you think that?"

"Well after watching the video several times, I noticed in the upper right hand corner of the screen something that looked like a Persian rug. That could only mean one thing—you were being held in one of the rooms beneath the Mosque. I thought it would be Raleigh, and I hunting for you, but as it turned out, Ahmad found out and insisted he back me up. We were coming around a corner when they opened fire. Raleigh got hit and died in my arms. I took this," he indicated his bandaged arm. "Then everything went black, I woke up and found Ahmad protecting me. As we tried to get out, a couple of rounds struck him in the chest; he gave his life for me, Pastor." He choked back a sob.

Out of the darkness came four men with two sheet covered gurneys. They stopped just short of the ambulance. Jared stood and walked to the gurney. He lifted the sheet covering Raleigh, his eyes closed as if he was sleeping. He felt at any moment he would jump to his feet and prance at the door ready to follow him wherever he went. Jared carefully lifted his head and rubbed the soft fur behind his ear for a last time.

"I'm gonna miss you buddy. You were a good dog. You saved my life more times than I can count." He cradled him close, he was still warm. Steadying himself, he placed a kiss between his eyes and gently laid his head back down. "I'll see you in Heaven, ol' buddy." Then he turned away to hide the tears that threatened to come.

Pastor Carlson rose from the gurney and placed a hand on his shoulder. It was warm and tender, and Jared took strength from his touch.

Jimbo, who'd been standing to the side, stepped close and put his arm around Jared's shoulders. "I'm really sorry about Ahmad and Raleigh. I wish I'd gotten there sooner."

The silence became intense . . . no one spoke . . . no one needed too.

The paramedics had tucked the sheet around Raleigh and guided the gurney to another ambulance. Jared jammed his hand in his pocket and rocked back on his heels.

"You remember Jimbo, don't you, Pastor?"

They shook hands. "Yes I remember you. Didn't you visit us at church a few times?"

Jimbo reddened. "Yes, but it was a while back."

"Were it not for him, I'd be dead. After Ahmad fell, I was virtually helpless. He showed up in the nick of time.

Jimbo scuffed the ground. "Well like I said, I was in the area." A sheepish smile parted his lips.

"Come to find out, it was he who'd been following me all these months." Jared ran his hand across his face and looked at Jimbo. "Was that you who showed up when the van pulled a PIT maneuver on me?"

The wrinkles around Jimbo's formed. "I don't know about them pulling a turn-around on you, but yeah, I caught them in the cross-fire." He paused and pushed his hat back. "I followed that same van after it came out of a dark alley behind the city hall. It nearly ran me down."

"You did, where'd it lead you?" Jared asked.

The ambulance driver stepped up. "Guys, I hate to break this up, but we need to get moving."

"Hold on one minute, sir," Jimbo said, hand extended.

"Tell you what, I'll fill you in on all the details later, but I gotta ask you, Pastor, did you see Imam Fahad at all while you were down there?"

The Pastor nodded slightly, "Yeah, he was there all right. He stood in the background and watched his lieutenant rough me up. Then they made me make a video. After that, I just sat there listening as the man ranted and raved about the coming Al Mahdi. When the shooting started, he tucked tail and ran."

"I wonder where he was going?" Jimbo shifted his weight from one foot to the other.

"I think I can answer that," the sheriff said as he stepped up and put his hand on Jimbo's shoulder, his eyes on Jared. "We just got a call from the Imam, he's holding Fatemah hostage."

"That spells big trouble," Jimbo straightened.

"How so?"

"I noticed a bomb vest missing from their cache. Fahad must have taken it"

"How do you figure that?"

"Because I counted four boxes where they kept the bullet proof vests and one was empty."

Jared, clutched his arm, yanked the IV needle out, rolled off the gurney and began hobbling in the direction of his truck.

"Hey, wait a minute," called the paramedic. "You're in no condition to go traipsing off."

"I gotta go," he yelled over his shoulder.

Jimbo did a double take. "Where are you going?"

"To Fatemah's house."

"Not without me you're not," Jimbo pushed away from the ambulance.

Jared waited for Jimbo to climb in, jammed the truck into gear, and spun out of the parking lot, a rooster tail of mud, stones and dirt rising in his wake. Too many had died at the hands of Imam Fahad. It would not happen again. Not this time; not to Fatemah. He skidded around a corner and sped through the lonely streets. Without thinking, he let his hand slip from its sling and reach into the space where Raleigh once sat—nothing. Guilt and anger clouded his mind. *"Oh God, I know I shouldn't hate this man, but he has caused me so much pain."* He gritted his teeth. The weight pressing in on his heart made it difficult to breathe. He struggled to form a cogent thought. He needed to pray for his enemy, but whenever Imam Fahad's thin face came to mind, all he felt was rage. *Lord, You know I was just as big a sinner as the Imam when You saved me ....*

The gentle voice of Jesus echoed from Heaven and spoke as if He were in the cab. I died for sinners just like you, Jimbo, and the Imam. Jared looked to his side, Jimbo sat staring forward. "Did you say something?"

Jimbo lifted an eyebrow. "Who me? No."

Chapter 74

Fatemah's House

Like a rat jumping from a sinking ship, Imam Fahad slipped out of the lower level of the Mosque, just after the shooting started. He placed the extra bomb vest on the rider's seat, climbed into the shot-up van and picked his way to Fatemah's house. All was dark except for one light in the kitchen.

He pulled his vehicle around back and got out.

I wonder where she is. I'd love to get my hands on her, I still have a score to settle with the Bashera family.

Being a resourceful man, Fahad was used to getting what he wanted. If he couldn't use men to accomplish his means, he'd use a woman. *If killing Rashad didn't work and if killing the pastor didn't work...then maybe settling an old score with Ibrahim Bashera's daughter would get their attention.* He sneered at the thought of seeing her squirm.

"I'll wait," he said to himself.

Fatemah sat, sipping coffee from a large mug. "Mrs. Carlson, I think the crowd has thinned enough by now. Why don't I run back to my house and get a few things."

"Oh Fatemah, are you sure? It's awfully late, and you look exhausted."

"No more tired than you. And I promised you I'd stay until your husband comes home." Her voice, though weary from talking, carried a tone of resolution.

"It's beginning to rain, and I know how you hate driving at night in the first place."

"That's all right." Looking at her watch, she saw that it was going on two-thirty a.m. "I should be back in, let's say thirty minutes, max, and I'll be extra careful," Fatemah said, with as much courage as she could muster.

Mrs. Carlson fidgeted with the hem of her sweater. "Are you sure I can't go with you. This is not the kind of night to be out by yourself," she pleaded.

Fatemah shook off the thought. "No, I'll be okay, it's not that far, and as I said, I'll be very careful."

She pulled on her heavy coat and stepped out as a gust of artic air mixed with rain pelted her face. It felt like a thousand tiny pin-pricks against her exposed cheeks. She braced herself and plunged into the night.

The roads glistened; a grimy streetlight lost some definition in the cold drizzle. The windshield wipers swished back and forth keeping rhythm with her heart. By the time she got to her house, her hands were trembling. Hoping she could hold them steady enough to slip the key into the lock, she brought her car to a stop, took a gulp of air, and ran. The naked limbs scraped against the house like someone sharpening a knife. The single porch light offered little comfort.

As she dashed across the soggy lawn, a shadow moved, a hand stretched out from behind a tree and grabbed her. The sudden stop knocked her legs out from under her, and she fell, landing on her back. She struck her head on a root outcropping and saw stars.

An instant later, the shadow pounced on her. She fought to pull the pepper spray from her pocket, but a bony hand held her in place while the other covered her mouth, suffocating her. The weight of the person holding her down was too much for Fatemah to fight off. Everything grew dark as reality faded into a bad dream.

Fahad, though small for his size, was in excellent physical condition. He hoisted Fatemah over his shoulder and carried her to the house. With one powerful kick, the door splintered, he stepped in and slammed it shut. Like a sack of potatoes, he dropped Fatemah on the couch, and began tying her hands. Then he dragged her to the kitchen, found a chair, lifted her onto it and strapped the bomb vest on her.

Fatemah's eyes fluttered open and she realized her life was in danger. Her struggle against the fast-ties only resulted in more damage to her hands.

"Sorry I didn't have the time to get a more form fitting one—we just stock the one-size-fits-all variety, I hope you won't mind," the Imam said, his vile breath enveloping her, causing her to recoil.

"Let me go. Why are you doing this to me? What have I ever done?" She demanded as she twisted her wrists until the flesh became raw.

The Imam stepped back and admired his work. "Struggle all you want, but remember, I'm holding the remote. Even if you were to escape, I'd blow you to pieces before you got to the end of the street. Just think of all the innocent people you would endanger if you did such a foolish thing. Now relax and pray that Allah will be merciful."

Fatemah's eyes flashed with defiance. "Allah is not merciful. He doesn't even exist. I believe in Jesus, He is the God of mercy. If Allah did exist he would be the most merciless, cruel, mean-spirited person in the whole world."

Stepping back, Fahad glowered at her. With a quick move, he raised his hand and slapped her across the face. Fatemah's head jerked to the side, her cheek burned like fire, and the irony taste of blood assaulted her mouth.

"Allah will not be kind to you for saying such blasphemous things about him."

She glared at him. "If I am going to die, then at least you'll know where I stand." Fatemah couldn't believe the boldness that came over her. "Just so you know; I believe Jesus Christ is God's Son, and that He died for the sins of the whole world—including your sins. If you'll repent and believe in Jesus as your Savior, He will save you too, Imam Fahad."

No one had ever spoken so boldly about Jesus in his presence. They rightfully feared to do so, knowing the consequences of such an act.

Smack!

The room spun out of control.

"Don't you speak to me about the name of the man who is responsible for all the wars and heartache in the world. Remember, the Christians invaded *our* land during the Crusades. They tried to drive us out of Palestine. It is the Christians even now who occupy *our* lands and are desecrating *our* Holy sites. Who is it that has built military bases in Turkey, Saudi Arabia, Kuwait, Iraq, and even Afghanistan? It is America, the Great Satan backed by the little Satan, the Zionists, spreading their lies; their propaganda, their Christianity. You ask me what you have done? I'll tell you what you have done—you have become one of *them*. Now, with the coming of Al Mahdi, Allah will take vengeance upon you and your infidel country."

Chapter 75

Outside of Fatemah's house

Jared crouched beneath the window, listening to the Imam's hate.

"I know what you're thinking Jared, and you don't have a chance," Jimbo whispered as he came up behind him.

Jared looked over his shoulder. "What was I thinking?"

"You were thinking about going in, guns blazing."

Jared shook his head. "Nope, I was thinking about negotiating with him, you know, talk him down."

Jimbo's face contorted. "That ain't going to happen. This guy is a radical of radicals. He won't be talked down no matter how long you spout hot air." He peeked over the window and dropped back down on one knee. "It's as I suspected. He has that bomb vest strapped on Fatemah, and he's holding the remote. If he relaxes the pressure off the triggering mechanism for any reason, bang, your girlfriend is a goner."

Jared's head snapped up, "My girlfriend?"

"Yeah your girlfriend. Remember, I've been following you for six months. I've seen the way you look at her. I just hope she lives long enough for you to finish that sentence you started twelve hours ago."

Jared narrowed his eyes. "Has it only been twelve hours? It seems a lifetime."

"You said it. It feels like I've been at this forever," Jimbo observed.

A moment passed as each man thought on the consequences a rash move would have.

Finally, in the dark, Jared looked up. "What statement didn't I finish?

Jimbo smirked. "You know, the one about *'your feelings.'*"

Mid-sentence Sheriff Lawson and his team arrived. Jared watched as the sheriff crouched low and scurried to where they knelt.

"What's the status, Jared?" the sheriff asked.

"The Imam has a bomb vest strapped on Fatemah and is holding the detonator in his right hand," Jared whispered. "For the time being, he is just letting off a lot of steam."

"Has he called the television or radio station and made any demands?" Sheriff Lawson asked, his no-nonsense demeanor cutting through the emotion of the moment.

Jared shook his head. "He hasn't called anyone since we got here. What do you think he wants?"

The sheriff lowered the volume on his walkie-talkie. "He probably wants us to release Ameer. I guess it's all or nothing with this guy,"

"I'm just glad we got here before the media hears about a hostage situation," Jared said.

"It won't be long," observed the police chief. "When we tried to arrest the mayor for conspiracy to commit murder and evidence tampering, he made a move like he was reaching for a gun, and we opened fire. He's dead and now the media will be on this like white on rice."

Jared's head whipped around. He leaned against the wall. His knees complained. "Then we don't have a lot of time before this turns into a media circus. What do you want me to do?"

The sheriff looked at his watch. "We've got a universal jamming device that will render the bomb trigger useless." He glanced at the house across the street. "And right about now the sharp-shooter should be ready, waiting for an all-clear. All I need to do is to give him the word."

Imam Fahad paced across the room. "Only when we are rid of the Zionists with their vague claims to Palestine and Christianity, the scourge of the earth, we'll be able to establish a righteous caliphate under the Al Mahdi. This country of yours is corrupt. You haven't even been true to your own claims. You have sold your souls to the goddess of commercialism and have worshiped at the altar of greed and lust. Money is your god, and your sacrament is the flesh of your children and the wine of pleasure. You have no right to call yourselves a Christian nation. America is weak, ripe for the picking, and I will strike the first blow against her. She will fall like a house of cards, and you my pretty will feel the wrath of Allah. Now beg for his mercy."

"No Fahad, I will never deny my Lord. Killing me will only further divide this community, this country. It will turn all Americans, even Muslim-Americans against you and your radical beliefs.

"Shut up, woman." He shouted

Smack!

Blood oozed from her swollen and lacerated lips, yet the love of Jesus for his lost soul urged her forward. *Oh, Lord, what can I say to get through to him?* Her mind cleared. "For God so loved the world that He gave His only begotten Son, that whosoever believeth on Him, would not perish, but have everlasting life."

His arms flailed wildly as he cursed everything that was holy.

Jared heard every word the Imam said, his abusive language, his blasphemy, his hatred for his Lord. Fatemah was suffering for the cause of Christ, and it was all he could do to keep from charging through the door.

"He's got to know we're out here. Maybe he's trying to draw you in and give him cause to pull the trigger."

Jared bit his lip in pain. "I'd do it in a heart-beat, if I thought for one minute, it would do any good."

Lawson took a peek over the ledge. "He's making it difficult to get a clear shot at him because he keeps on moving."

Jimbo's face tightened. "Maybe I should call him. If he stops long enough to answer the phone, your sharp-shooter can pick him off," he whispered.

"What about the triggering device?" Jared asked.

"Oh, we've already disarmed it. That thing in his hand is totally useless," The sheriff's tone rang with pride.

"Then maybe I should call him and ask to speak with Fatemah. When he hears it's me, it just might stall him long enough to get a clean shot," Jared said.

"Sounds like a plan," Lawson said, "let's make it happen."

He toggled the walkie-talkie, "Okay everybody, here's how we're going to play this . . . "

Jared put in the call.

Imam Fahad looked at Fatemah, "Expecting a call?"

She looked at the caller ID, "Yes, it's Jared Russell, my . . . "

"I know who he is, let him rot in hell."

"If I don't answer it, he'll think something's wrong and come over here. That could be trouble for you."

"The trouble would be all his," Fahad picked up the receiver.

"He's all yours, take your best shot," came the voice in the sharpshooter's earpiece.

He never missed a shot and wouldn't miss this time. In a millisecond, the sharpshooter performed a myriad of very precise calculations; the wind, the light rain, the distance, even the barometric pressure. He adjusted his scope and inhaled. *I have one shot, make it count, go for a chest shot.* He flicked off the safety and let out his breath slowly.

Fahad paused just long enough and the sharpshooter squeezed the trigger. An instant later, the bullet exploded from the muzzle of his rifle, ripped through the air at 2,850 feet per second and slammed into the center of Imam Fahad's back. His spine split, freezing his hand as it gripped the detonator; he was dead before he hit the floor.

The SWAT team rushed, in followed by Jared.

Lawson grabbed the triggering mechanism. "Get it off of her," he ordered, looking over his shoulder.

Jared, looking confused, obeyed his command.

"Sorry to be so rough, honey."

"I'm just so glad to see you. I thought he was going to kill me, and I'd never see you again." She reached out and embraced him.

Jimbo glanced over at Jared. "See, I told you so."

With a blank look, Jared asked, "What?"

"I told you she was your girlfriend." Jimbo grinned.

Fatemah disregarded Jared's bloody, sweaty shirt and hugged him tighter. Her breathing quickened. She laid her head on his shoulder and felt his heart beating against hers. *Girlfriend? That's so junior-high, I think we're past that point. By the way he looked at me, the way he risked his life for me. We're way past that.* She felt Jared's good arm around her waist, it was strong and steady, like the man she loved.

Another police officer grabbed the bomb vest and rushed it to a waiting bomb squad vehicle. A moment later the ground shook as the vest was safely detonated.

Jared stood wide-eyed. "I thought the triggering mechanism was rendered useless?"

Lawson stepped back into the house. "Yeah, well so did I until I remembered that we don't have all the international frequencies. This thing was made in Russia or somewhere."

Jared plopped down on a chair and stared back at Lawson. "Now you tell me."

Chapter 76

Canaan Baptist Church

A long black limousine followed by a dark van pulled to a stop in front of the warehouse. Four men in dark suits stepped out and surveyed the area. Seeing no one, they entered the building used by Canaan Baptist Church. They found Pastor Carlson, who was still recovering from his ordeal in the Mosque, ready with a smile and warm handshake.

"Gentlemen, come in," he said. "It's brutal out there," referring to the arctic blast that moved in to Michigan overnight. "Let's set-up down front," he pointed to the open area where they could place the flowers and the casket containing Ahmad's body.

"I have never seen such an outpouring of love in my life." The pastor observed as they began unloading the bouquets. The aromatic fragrance soon filled the room, but as many times as Pastor Carlson smelled it, it always brought him a sense of loss.

"Yes sir," said the funeral home director. "We've gotten flowers from as far away as Seattle and New York City, and one from Daphne, Alabama. There is even one from the commandant from Fort Lawson."

"I hope we have enough room for everyone," Pastor Carlson said.

"Guess we'll find out in about an hour."

Pastor Carlson stepped out of the way and let the men finish, returning to his office to skim through his notes and to pray. By the time he reentered the auditorium, it was at near capacity. He saw people he'd never seen, friends, Muslim and non-Muslim, city fathers and government officials, all coming to pay their respects to Ahmad.

The soft organ music lowered as the pastor led Ahmad's family and close associates down the aisle. Behind him, followed Uncle Shaquille and his wife, then Jared, Fatemah and Jimbo following the casket. Out of respect, the entire congregation rose to their feet as the processional passed by.

"Please, be seated," the funeral director said in a low tone.

The pastor, sided by Jared, took their seats on the platform. Pastor Carlson was the first to address the crowd. After reading the twenty-third psalm, he read Ahmad's obituary.

"Ahmad was preceded in death by his parents Sirus Rashed Hassani, his mother Aisha Hassani, and his sister Shirin. He is survived by his uncle Shaquille Hassani and his wife, along with many, many friends, most of whom are seated before me. Today, we are here to celebrate the home-going of a warrior of Christ.

One of my favorite lines from the book, *The Last of the Mohicans* by James Fenimore Cooper, 'A warrior goes to you swift and straight as an arrow shot into the sun. Welcome him and let him take his place at the council fire of my people.'

Three days ago Ahmad Hassani heard the tender voice of his Lord and Savior, Jesus Christ say, 'Welcome home my child, you have fought a good fight, you have kept the faith, henceforth there is laid up for you a crown of righteousness, which the Lord, the righteous judge will give.'"

The pastor paused to wipe the tears from his eyes, cleared his throat, and pushed ahead.

"The reason I can say with confidence that our friend Ahmad Hassani is in the very presence of Jesus is because several months ago he placed his faith in the finished work of Christ on the cross. I have observed the drastic change which took place in Ahmad's life. He turned from a Christ-hater to a Christ-lover, from hating Christ to loving Him. He passed from death unto life and the giver of eternal life took up his abode in our friend's heart. Many of you can testify to the changes in his life. And I implore you to make the same preparations that Ahmad did."

The pastor concluded and turned the platform over to Jared.

Jared, in full military uniform, strode to the pulpit and stood at attention. He slipped a single sheet of paper from his pocket and slowly unfolded it. Looking down, he read, "Greater love hath no man than this that a man lay down his life for his friends."

He lifted his eyes from his notes and glanced at Shaquille, then at Mr. Xavier who gave him a quick nod. Mr. Tate smiled, and Jimbo lifted his thumb.

Jared's heart ratcheted up a notch; he inhaled and held it hoping to reign in his emotions, then wiped the sweat from his upper lip.

"I declare to everyone within the sound of my voice, that the highest compliment I could give to Ahmad Hassani is to say we were friends." He chuckled nervously, bit back the tears which formed just beneath the surface, and forged ahead. "As many of you know, we didn't start out friends. As a matter of fact, we started out, not liking each other. But that all changed because of a serendipitous encounter with a teetering scaffold. You might call that a 'God thing.' I shoved him out of the way, and it was that act of kindness which led us to become the deepest of friends. He told me he would spend the rest of his life repaying me for saving his life. I didn't ask him to do that, but he did it in obedience to his law, then in gratitude to me." He again paused to collect his thoughts.

"In a greater way, I want to publicly say in gratitude to what my Lord has done for me, I want to live my life in service to him who died for me."

He glanced down at Fatemah; tears streamed down her cheeks.

Jared willed his mind to focus, then straightened.

"Ladies and gentlemen, please rise as we post our colors and honor another fallen comrade and friend."

The congregation rose, not knowing what was to follow. Heads turned as four uniformed soldiers lead by Captain Kelly carried a small casket, draped with an American flag down the aisle. They stopped directly in front of Jared. His right arm, though still in a sling, slowly rose to a crisp salute. He held it while the soldiers carefully and with great respect, smoothed out any wrinkles. Warmth streaked down Jared's cheeks and he realized that his heart was breaking. He'd lost a dear friend—Raleigh.

"Thank you, you may be seated," his voice raspy and thick.

Jared placed his good arm on the casket to steady himself.

"It has been said that a dog is man's best friend. I have been privileged to have had two such friends. The first, EJ, died at the hands of Afghani insurgents; I never had an opportunity to thank or honor her passing. The second is Raleigh, a recognized war veteran and decorated hero from the Middle-east conflict. We were the best of friends and I will miss him deeply. Thank you Raleigh, I will never forget you," his voice broke.

Following the service, a mile long procession snaked through the streets of Stanford from Canaan Baptist Church all the way to The Center for Islamic Studies.

"This is the first time this many non-Muslims have been here," Jimbo said as he, Fatemah and Jared came to a stop in front of the Mosque.

Jared nodded. "Yes, were it not for the insistence of the new head of the Muslim Institute, we wouldn't be here."

"That's a real shock and honor," Fatemah said as she gathered close to Jared. Hand in hand they walked from the car to a green awning over two newly prepared grave plots.

Six of Ahmad's closest friends assembled at the rear of the hearse, while Captain Kelly, flanked by four others gathered behind the vehicle carrying the casket of Raleigh. With great care each team of pallbearers moved into position.

Pastor Carlson read, "I am the resurrection and the life; he that believeth in me, though he were dead, yet shall he live. Lord, into your hands we commit the spirit of our friend, Ahmad. Give his body a resting place at the council fire of thy people until you sound the trumpet and the dead in Christ rise and we who are alive and remain slip these mortal shores to meet you in the air. So shall we ever be with you Lord."

Jared approached the casket bearing Ahmad's body, he laid his hand it. The smooth mahogany wood felt like silk. Then with great care, his pulled the cross from his pocket and placed it on the top of it. "This cross has made all the difference in our lives, I'll see you soon, my brother."

He retook his seat next to Fatemah. She slipped her hand into his and gave it a gentle squeeze.

Then the four uniformed men stepped apart, took the corners of the American flag and snapped it from its resting place. They stepped to the side and followed the military tradition of folding the flag into a triangle.

Jared rose to his feet and stood rock solid while the men in uniform finished their routine. Captain Kelly stepped in front of Jared. The two men locked eyes as each lifted their arms to salute each other. They held their position, then slowly brought their arms to the side.

"On behalf of a grateful nation, please accept our condolences and this flag."

Jared placed a hand beneath and on top of the folded flag and clutched it to his chest. "Thank you," his throat closed with emotion.

Captain Kelly saluted again and joined the formation. They did a crisp about-face and marched to the side.

Above them, fighter jets approached leaving five pure white contrails. As they neared, one jet veered sharply upward toward the sky. The impact of the moment was palpable.

The command was given and three riflemen raised their weapons to their shoulders and fired seven times. As the last shot echoed off the surrounding buildings, a distant trumpeter lifted his instrument to his lips and began to play *Taps*.

The last tone faded, and Jared felt a peace wash over him like he'd never felt before. He honored his fallen friends from war and peace-time. He'd finally laid to rest all the guilt, the pain and the bitter memories which haunted him. He'd never need to take the medication for post traumatic distress syndrome again.

Chapter 77

Seattle, Washington

It was Christmas Eve at Raymond Russell's house in Seattle. Jared sat across from Fatemah at dinner, watching the candlelight dance in her eyes. As much as he enjoyed eating his mother's food, looking at Fatemah's graceful movements was even better.

"Oh, Mrs. Russell, that was a wonderful dinner," Fatemah said, dabbing the corners of her mouth lightly. "Can I help you clean up?"

"You certainly may," Mrs. Russell corrected subtly. "Oh, and just so you know, you may call me Flora," her voice was kind and tender.

Jared and Fatemah had flown to Seattle in order for his parents to meet her. They welcomed Fatemah into their home and into their hearts.

"We are so glad to have you and Jared here safe and sound. That's the best Christmas gift I could ask for," Flora said as she snuffed out the candles. "Those were Jared's idea," she chuckled. "They added a nice romantic touch, don't you think?"

Fatemah nodded. "Oh absolutely, I could see the way Raymond looked at you."

Flora feigned embarrassment. "Phooey, don't let him fool ya, he looks at me that way with or without candles. He's such a romantic at heart."

"Then I guess Jared gets it good and honest."

"Oh?" Flora's voice rose an octave. "How so?"

Fatemah, knowing she was expecting some big announcement, smiled and brushed a few strands of hair behind her ear. "Didn't he tell you about the portrait he bought me for my birthday?"

"Oh yes," she was nonplussed. "He did mention that. I hope you liked it."

"Liked it? I love it. I could stand and stare at it for hours."

She paused and reflected as Flora continued talking. Her mind fluttered like a moth around a streetlight as the memory of the night Jared unveiled the portrait replayed again; her squeal of joy, the laughter of her church family, the grin on Jared's face.

Then her thoughts darkened, *those next forty-eight hours were a living hell*. She wished she could hit the DELETE button, and they'd be gone. She bit back her anger at the Imam, at Islam, at God. *Oh God, why did you let Rashad, Ahmad and Raleigh die...I just don't understand. What good could come from their deaths?* She caught her breath and prayed that she would have more faith, faith to believe, faith to see beyond her pain.

In the distance, she heard her name. She blinked, "You two have certainly been through a lot in the last few months, but I can see God's hand in it. It's like the Bible says, God does all things well."

Fatemah's heart smote her like the crashing of surf against a sea-wall, and the wall gave way. A flood of salty tears streaked her cheeks.

"You poor child, whatever has come over you?"

Fatemah took a ragged breath, and held it. She let it out slowly and confessed, "I've been so angry at God for letting all the senseless killing take place. Oh yes, I put on a good front, but deep inside, I've been questioning His wisdom, His plan."

Flora's expression softened, "Oh honey, we have all questioned God at times, but remember this, never doubt in the night what God has promised in the light." She closed her eyes and read from the pages of her memory. *"For I know the thoughts that I think toward you, saith the LORD, thoughts of peace, and not of evil, to give you an expected end."*

She opened her eyes and patted Fatemah softly on the arm, "All things do work out for good to those who are called for *His* purposes." Her smile melted Fatemah's heart like a flame under wax.

"Thank you for sharing that. I'm so blessed to be here. I thought I wouldn't see another Christmas when Imam Fahad strapped that bomb vest on me, Mrs. Russell, uh Flora."

The conversation followed them from the dining room to the kitchen and back again. "Coffee, or tea?"

"Coffee, with cream and sugar."

Flora poured two mugs and handed one to Fatemah. They returned to the table. "Weren't you afraid . . . I mean of dying and all," her face possessed an interest that came from deep within.

Fatemah allowed the scene to replay in her mind. "You know Flora, it was amazing, the peace God gave me that day. Can you believe it? I actually witnessed to Imam Fahad. No one has ever done that," she added with a bright smile.

"Well at least he heard it once before he died." Coldness shrouded her voice.

"Sadly, he made his choice a long time ago, I'm afraid, Mrs. Russell."

Flora didn't correct her.

"He and the other Imams and Islamic clerics have taught their people to hate the cross. They don't even let an airplane fly over many of their countries for fear the shadow will form a cross. Even the telephone poles are made of one single pole, with no cross bars, for fear of someone thinking it was a cross."

"That reminds me, Fatemah," Flora said as she stirred her coffee

"Reminds you of what?"

"It reminds me of a gift that Jared received last Christmas. A little hand carved cross. He spoke of it often as we talked throughout the year. Do you know anything about it?"

An impish look formed in Fatemah's eyes. "Well yes, Flora, yes I do." She took a sip of coffee and reflected. "I have to admit, I gave it to Jared. It was my grandfather's."

"Oh really, you must tell me about it."

Fatemah smiled at the memory of how she waited until Jared stepped out to make his rounds. She and Shirin had kept the secret all day and were absolutely giddy with excitement over the idea of leaving him the gift.

"We waited all day. I thought he'd never leave. Finally, he claimed he had a headache and was going to make one last inspection before leaving for the Christmas weekend. No sooner had he left than I crept into his office and placed the box on his desk. I nearly knocked that poor Christmas Tree over in the process."

"Flora clasp her hands together excited as a child amidst a bedtime story. "What happened next?"

"Well I straightened the tree as good as I could and got out of there. Then we turned off all the lights except for his, and left before he returned.

"I wish I were a fly on the wall when he saw the gift." Flora's eyes danced.

"We did better than that. Shirin nearly froze to death, but we wanted to see what he did, so we came around to his window and peered in. He was so cute, like a child at Christmas."

"Did you say your grandfather carved it?"

Fatemah took a sip and bobbed her head. "Yes, he carved it and gave it to me as one of his last living acts. My grandfather, on my mother's side, was a devout Christian and often spoke openly about his faith. He lived in a little village called Brummana, Lebanon."

"So you are from Lebanon?" Flora asked.

"Well actually I'm a first-generation immigrant. My parents were from Lebanon; I was raised in Michigan. I visited him once after I turned nineteen. That was before the radical Muslims took over and ran all the Christians out.

"Was your father a Christian?"

Fatemah lowered her eyes, her voice softened. "No Flora, my father was not a believer. He was an Islamic evangelist and traveled throughout the middle-east preaching. But that's all I remember about him before we left the old country, I was rather young."

Taking her by the hand, Flora gave it a gentle squeeze. She let a few minutes pass without speaking.

Fatemah shook her head, and a soft smile pushed past her grief. "I was so ashamed for the way Shirin and Ahmad had spoken to Jared that day he brought in the Christmas tree. I waited and when no one was looking, I pulled off a small branch and laid it on my desk. I could see how confused Jared was when he noticed it. Shirin and I had been playing hop-scotch throughout that week. We were just so excited about Christmas, we couldn't hold still.

"What did Shirin think about the tree branch?"

"She never said, but I think secretly she yearned to be a Christian, but she was afraid."

Flora folded her hands in front of her and listened as Fatemah spoke. "What was she afraid of?"

Surprised registered on Fatemah's face. "Persecution."

Flora sat motionless, trying to make sense of it. "Persecution? In America?"

"Yes Flora, in America. Not all Muslims are so anti-Christian. There are many Muslims who believe in Jesus, but they pay an awful price for their faith," she paused. "I should know. I too was persecuted mercilessly, before I ran away from home."

"Oh, you poor child. I had no idea."

Nodding Fatemah continued, "Had I not done so, my father would have killed me. My story is not that much different from many others."

Flora's features gave way to sadness as the impact of Fatemah's testimony struck home.

"In a small way, I think I can empathize with you. As a black woman being raised in the Deep South, I am no stranger to violence or abuse."

For a moment, she let her mind wander back to her childhood days in Selma, Alabama, during the dark days of the Civil Rights struggle. Then in the background she heard Fatemah say her name.

"That's terrible, Mrs. Russell, I had no idea."

Flora shook off the memory with a sigh. "May I offer you a slice of pecan pie while we talk?" her movement indicated that 'no' was not an option. After serving her an ample slice, she sat back and waited for her to take a bite.

"Umm, this is delicious; I've got to get your recipe for this pie." She eyed a second piece.

"Oh honey, that recipe is locked away up here," she pointed to her head, "but I'll see what I can do."

The two ladies sat in silence with their own thoughts for several minutes.

Laughter interrupted their reverie as Jared, and his father came in looking for the source of the aroma from the pecan pies.

"I'm so sorry that we didn't get a chance to meet your brother Kaleel. Jared has spoken so much about him." Raymond said, slicing himself and Jared a huge piece of pie.

She smiled at the thought of her brother, "Kaleel would have liked to have met you, but he was so looking forward to spending his first real Christmas with Pastor Carlson, and he had a part in the Christmas play."

"Oh? And what part did he play?" Raymond asked.

A smile lit up Fatemah's face. "He played the part of Joseph. He was so excited he could hardly contain himself."

"I'll bet he did great." Flora mused.

"He did have a little trouble memorizing his lines."

"Yeah, and it didn't help that he had a crush on the girl who played Mary," Jared said as he cut another piece of pie.

"The change that Christ has made in his life is dynamic. He tells everyone, Muslim and non-Muslim, about the Lord. I think that God is calling him to be a missionary to the Muslim people." Jared continued.

"You tell him if he feels that is what God wants him to do, then we will pay for his college training—all of it," Raymond said with a broad grin.

"Jared, I love your family."

Jared sidled up next to Fatemah, wrapped his good arm around her shoulders and squeezed lightly. "Does that include me?" he said with a sheepish grin.

A few strands of hair fell across her face as she reached into her pocket. Her movement went unnoticed by all until she brought her hand to the table, and laid it upon his.

"This ring on my finger should be answer enough for you, lover-boy."

Flora clasped her hands together, and stood to wrap her arms around Fatemah. "Welcome to the family."

Fatemah smiled. "I can hardly wait to become the next Mrs. Russell."

Chapter 78

Michigan's Supreme Court

The morning of February twenty-first broke bright and clear as Attorneys Bill Tate and Jack Sutterfield, flanked by an army of police officers, approached the lower level of the Michigan Supreme Court building.

They went through the usual security checkpoint and received their clearance badges. From there they made their way to the waiting area where they would spend the next few hours making final preparations before addressing seven justices.

"Well, this is it ol' buddy, we finally made it to the big league. You feel we've got a strong enough opening statement?" asked Jack Sutterfield, an old veteran at verbal gamesmanship.

Tate cocked his head, "You know, as many times as I've done this, I still get butterflies."

"If you didn't, you wouldn't be human," his partner jested.

"Well, Don's opening comments were so strong, I thought I'd take what he said, and build on it. That opening statement he made convinced me, and I was already on his side."

"Yes," Jack said ruefully, "Don was one of the best." They waited in silence for the elevator to arrive.

The clock on the outside of the courtroom struck twice and the bailiff took center stage and cried, "All rise, the Supreme Court of the great state of Michigan is now in session. The Honorable Chief Justice Theodore S. Stoner, presiding."

Jared and a host of people from Stanford packing the courtroom rose as the five men and two women in black robes took their seats. Chief Justice Stoner gaveled the court to order as they settled.

"Mr. Tate, I understand you have submitted an addendum to your plea."

Tate stood, "Yes, your honors, may we have a side-bar?"

Attorney Rahim stood, "I object."

Chief Justice Stoner looked over his glasses, "On what basis, Mr. Rahim?"

"On the basis that Mr. Tate is seeking to circumvent the will of the people with the spurious claim of nepotism."

Stoner straightened and leaned forward. "If you are referring to the fact that Talibani and Imam Fahad were related and in cahoots, I've read the FBI report. It's pretty clear to me that they were."

"But your honor—" One look and he was cut off.

"Gentlemen, yes, you may approach the bench."

Jared leaned over to his pastor, "What are the chances of it getting thrown out?"

"I talked with Bill and that is exactly what he's talking to the justices about now, since this whole case was predicated on a false premise."

Movement caught Jared's eye as the two attorneys returned to their respective tables.

"I would like to hear each attorney's opening statements, and then we will go from there," said Chief Justice Stoner.

Attorney Rahim was the first to address the court. "Your honors, we are pleased to speak to you on behalf of all Muslim-

Americans. I know you are well acquainted with the issues that are being weighed before you: Issues that will govern the affairs of this nation for generations. Issues that will determine whether we as a people will truly live up to our potential.

The Constitution...this Constitution," he held a copy up for all to see, waving it like a flag, "the authors wrote this over two hundred years ago. They could never imagine the complex society we live in today. We must look at the Constitution as a living, breathing document and interpret it using the wisdom and experience over these last two hundred plus years. When Thomas Jefferson and the others wrote about free speech, they never thought about the danger of one man hollering 'fire' in a crowded restaurant. Today we don't have total freedom of speech nor should we. We need limits and restraints put on us so that we don't destroy ourselves."

Bill looked over at Jack and wondered where Rahim was going with this line of discourse.

"Objection your honor. Where is this leading?" Mr. Tate complained.

"Mr. Rahim, could you get to your point?"

"Yes, your Honor, I submit to you my honorable justices, that Pastor Carlson does not have the right to defame the Islamic people or their religion simply because we are a minority, or because we are different, or because of some radicals in some other countries. No, Pastor Carlson must play by the same rules that everyone else is required to play by. He should not be allowed to decry and besmirch the name of Allah, whom we say is great. The name we pray to five times a day. His law is called the 'path'. It is the way we Muslims govern the affairs of our lives. No one objects when rabbinical statutes are used to ensure that orphaned Jewish children receive a kosher upbringing. No one objected to the Roman Catholics adhering to 'Canon Law', which is frequently cited in divorce cases. Why can't we Muslims choose to live under our Law . . . Shari'ah Law?"

Jared clenched his fists. "Why doesn't Tate object or say something?" he whispered to Fatemah.

She leaned close. "It's just the opening statements; I don't think you can object yet."

He nodded, not speaking.

Rahim paced from one side of the gallery to the other as if he were an evangelist. He ended with a final charge.

"Even our president's legal adviser for the State Department says, and I quote, 'there's nothing wrong with Shari'ah Law; that judges should interpret the Constitution according to other nation's legal norms' unquote. To further underscore the importance of limiting inflammatory rhetoric, allow me to quote from a speech made before the United Nations by our president. "The future must not belong to those who slander the prophet of Islam.

"I don't have to remind the court that the equal protections clause of the US Constitution guarantees the right of practitioners of Islam to invoke Shari'ah law in legal matters involving American Muslims.

Such is the case we are considering today, and I know that you, in all of your wisdom will render a just decision." Attorney Rahim concluded his opening statements and casually took his seat.

A stir rippled throughout the room, which was gaveled into silence.

"The court calls for the opening statements of the appellate." Attorney Bill Tate stood and stepped into the well of the courtroom. He cleared his throat.

"Honorable justices, we have heard my esteemed colleague raise many very important questions, thought provoking questions, questions that have been asked before and have been answered by the blood of our forefathers, on the battlefields of Gettysburg, Vicksburg and in the fields around Atlanta, Georgia." He paused.

Jared shifted his weight and whispered in Fatemah's ear. "Now we're getting somewhere."

She smiled when his breath tickled her ear. Bill Tate droned on, she let her mind wander. She glanced down and fingered her engagement ring. Jared noticed and gave her hand a gentle squeeze.

In the background, Bill made his final statement. "I appeal to the honorable Chief Justice by the very Bible that sits on your desk, give back to this man, his God given right. His God ordained responsibility, to speak the truth without fear or favor."

"Objection, your honor," Rahim said.

"Overruled." The judge stated flatly.

"I don't have to remind the court of the inflammatory statements made by The Reverend Wright, the president's pastor for over twenty years. Now *his* statements were inflammatory and defamatory. Did anybody say anything to *him* about defaming America? Where were the ACLU guys when he said, 'God blank America, not God Bless America, God blank America'? Where was the outcry from the OID? Aren't they for tolerance?"

"Objection, your honor," again attorney Rahim said, in an attempt to slow Tate's momentum.

"Overruled," Judge Stoner reiterated.

Tate nodded at the judge "Thank you, Judge," he took a sip of water, then continued. "Where is the tolerance when it comes to opposing views? If we can't speak about God, then we might as well burn our dollar bills, because the last time I checked, it says, 'In God We Trust.' If we can't speak about the Ten Commandments, then we might as well tear down this courthouse because the last time I checked, they were etched on the walls of this very building. Even the second verse of our national anthem says, 'For this be our motto, In God is our trust'. If I can't hold a Bible and swear by the God of that Bible that I will tell the truth, the whole truth and nothing but the truth, then we might as well close up shop here because we can't trust what anybody says from the witness stand. I submit to the court that if we prohibit this pastor, or any pastor, from speaking the truth of God's Word, which I might add, is the very foundation of this republic, if they can't tell us 'thus saith the Lord', then this nation is doomed, my friends. We are doomed to be relegated to the trash-heap of history along with the USSR, Nazi Germany, Rome and all the other nations that have forgotten God. But let me quote what the Muslim Brotherhood of 1991 says, and I quote, 'Shari'ah law is a totalitarian set of laws that contradicts the U.S. Constitution and the vision of the Founding Fathers. America is now becoming a victim of radical Islam."

"Chief Justice, I must object in the strongest of terms. Why are you allowing this man to besmirch our religion? He is insulting us right before our faces."

Chief Justice Stoner glared over his glasses. "Mr. Rahim, if you don't stop interrupting this man, I will have you ushered from this court room and charged with contempt. Now sit down and listen, you might learn something."

Attorney Tate nodded and continued without losing any steam. "The cultural jihad is a monster that's absorbing whatever it can with this Jihadist indoctrination. It seeks to eliminate Western civilization from within and 'sabotaging' its miserable house by their hands and the hands of the believers so that it is eliminated, and Allah's religion is made victorious over all other religions,' unquote."

"Is that what we want for our children and our grandchildren . . . to grow up not knowing God or being allowed to speak the name of Jesus Christ? I think not! What would our founders say? What will we say to our forefathers who fought . . . bled . . . and died for the freedom to speak . . . to speak about God? And let me say this, the God of the Bible, as I understand it, is not . . . . could not . . . cannot be the same as Allah. Their natures are diametrically opposed. Now if by saying that, I am defaming Allah, so be it. But let us not be confused. We are talking about two different entities.

What will we tell those brave Pilgrims who braved the chilly waters of the deep in search of a place where they could exercise their God-given right to worship as they pleased? Or those poor souls who starved to death in Williamsburg, or who froze to death in Valley Forge in the fight to be free?"

Bill Tate finished his impassioned statements and took his seat.

For the next three days, Jared and the others listened as the attorneys bickered over the details of the Constitution. Both were pummeled with questions of religious nature.

Pastor Carlson stood chatting with his attorney during one of the breaks. "I've heard more Scripture quoted and expounded upon than at a fundamentalist preacher's convention."

Tate nodded. "Yes, it was my goal to lay the Constitution and Law of Christ side by side with Shari'ah Law and let the justices see the contrasts. Is that what we want for this country?"

"You convinced me," Jared rocked on his heels.

"The million dollar question is, did I convince the majority of the justices?"

Their voices were gaveled into submission as the five men and two women reentered the court room. Jared's shoulders tensed as he looked at the taught faces of the seven justices, the people who would decide the fate of Michigan and possibly the direction of the country.

Chief Justice Stoner cleared his throat and adjusted his glasses. "In the case of Canaan Baptist Church verses the state of Michigan, it is the opinion of the majority of the court that the State, has no grounds for its appeal. I therefore rule on the side of the defendant and further declare, for the record, that all judicial decisions will be based upon the Constitution of the state of Michigan and backed by the US Constitution, foreign law, notwithstanding." A wave of excitement wafted throughout the room.

Stoner glanced up quelling the excitement. "I therefore declare the caliphate of none effect, the newly instituted anti-defamation laws null and void, and Shari'ah Law banned from use in any city, town, or municipality within the state of Michigan." His gavel smacked crisply on its wooden plate, sending reporters and witnesses flooding from the court room.

Chapter 79

Outside of Michigan's Supreme Court

"Now that Imam Fahad is out of the picture, are you going back to CIA headquarters Jimbo?" Jared asked. He and the others descended the steps leading from the court house.

Jimbo looked down the street, "Yeah, it looks like my job is finished here. Your company only agreed to hire me until we apprehended or eliminated Fahad."

Jared slowed his pace, "How did they know that Fahad would show up at this Mosque project anyway?"

"We'd been monitoring his activities and contacts. It all pointed to him coming to America. By building one of the largest mosques in the country, we figured it would draw him in." He shook his head and rubbed the back of his neck. "Heck, we even let him slip across our border. We were betting he'd show up, and he did. That day he showed up was a bit of a surprise. Fahad looked a lot older than he did in the picture I had. After our confrontation, I was nervous that he might go back into hiding, and we'd lose him again. That stunt you pulled with requiring the work crews to compensate their prayer time with coming to work earlier threw the Imam a curve. I think he stayed around just to get revenge on you."

"Well, I didn't know who I was dealing with either." Jared confessed. "Had I known, I might not have been so bold." He hailed a cab.

"I did enjoy working with you guys. My only regret is that I couldn't save Shirin. That move to blow you up got past me. I'd been spending so much time keeping up appearances, working with the men and tailing you, that at times I literally fell asleep on the job. I'm really sorry about that."

Fatemah reached up and patted him on the shoulder. "Well, the good thing that came out of that situation was that I had an opportunity to speak with Shirin about the Lord before she died."

Jared squinted at his supervisor, "Wait a minute, what happened to your Alabama accent and double negatives?"

Jimbo jammed his hands into his pockets and chuckled. "I'm not from Alabama. I'm from Atlanta, Georgia and as far as my drinking is concerned, well, that too was just for show. I needed a convincing cover and Jimbo from Daphne, Alabama was the perfect character."

"Well you sure had us all fooled," Fatemah said.

"Not everyone."

Jared cocked his head, "Oh? Who knew?"

Jimbo pulled a handkerchief from his pocket and wiped his brow. "Elaine Rakestraw. I didn't think of it at first, but it was her, all right. She must have pegged me right off the bat."

Fatemah's forehead wrinkled. "How did she do that?"

Jimbo's face took on a distant look. "She was a student of mine."

"In high school?" Jared asked.

Jimbo rocked on his heels. "No, at the farm, the CIA's training school."

Jared's eyes bulged.

Jimbo brightened, "Look, after I finish my report at CIA, I plan to come back to Stanford. I'd like to say good-bye to some of the workers. I'd gotten to know them pretty well, and you know." He paused and swallowed. "Then I'll head on out."

"You sure you're not stopping for one more visit with Miss Camilla Kasha?"

Jimbo straightened, "Whatever could you mean?" his unusually clean diction betrayed him.

Fatemah smiled at Jared, and they stepped into the taxi.

Jimbo knelt down by the open door. "Hold on just another minute. Before you go, let me make a recommendation."

"Okay, shoot, not literally," Jared smiled

"I think that Kaleel would make a great supervisor. He has shown strong leadership skills, he knows OHSA's rules and regulations, and the men respect him. You should think about promoting him to my position."

"That's a fine idea Jimbo, I think the suits back in Seattle will jump at the chance to build a stronger relationship with the Muslim community and that would be a great start."

Jimbo stretched out a fat hand and shook Jared's. "Great, I hope that works out." He pushed the door shut, then leaned in the open window. "Well it was a privilege to work with you. The next time you get in a gunfight, I would count it an honor to stand by your side."

Chapter 80

Stanford, Michigan

The city of Stanford was abuzz with activity as the first signs of spring appeared.

Jared pulled to a stop in front of Fatemah's house and dashed up the walk, slipping on a latent patch of ice and nearly falling into the shrubbery. He recovered and rang her doorbell.

"Sorry I'm late. You ready?"

"Yep, what kept you?"

"Traffic, I've not seen so many cars since before all the trouble began. I think the city of Stanford is making a come-back. Business in the shopping district is thriving. Soccer moms are out in droves. It's unbelievable."

Fatemah grabbed her purse and sweater and closed the door. "I'm so excited. This is unreal. The new Imam asked us to teach a Comparative Religion Course on Saturdays.

He opened the car door for her. "I still can't believe it. Abu Hanifa is very conservative in his views of other religions. He and I were talking the other day, and he said, 'We conservative Muslims must reclaim the discourse from the hands of the extremists who benefit from hatred and violence.' He was quoting his friend Imam Rauf. He went on to say 'that ninety-five percent of the people in the world who want peace are in the stands watching the extremists battle it out in the arena. We must enter the arena and retake control of this important global discussion.'"

"It sure sounds like he's open to letting us come and hold group discussions with his Muslim students and to teach the truth about Christianity." Fatemah said as she let the wind from the open window blow her hair.

Jared cocked his head and looked at Fatemah. "Yeah, I think, after Pastor Carlson gets finished with our pre-marital counseling session, I'll invite him to come and listen to my talk with the students."

"Do you think he'll have time, what with the church growing like it is?"

"Yeah, you're right. I still can't get over the OID letting Canaan purchase the old Mosque property and renovate it."

They arrived at the new church facility and walked into the auditorium. "This is great, just look at this place."

Jared stood next to her and scanned the area. All of the Islamic icons were gone, a new paint job covered the pro-Islamic murals and portraits embedded in the ceramic tiles. Hundreds of chairs stood in the open cathedral where once countless numbers of Muslim worshipers gathered.

"We can seat scores of people here." Fatemah spread her arms wide and swung in a circle.

Jared stood back and smiled. "It's a great place to have a wedding too."

She let out a squeal of laughter.

A door opened. "I thout that was you." Pastor set his hands on hips and looked at the ornate ceiling. "This place must have cost millions to construct."

Jared nodded. "Yes, and there is more where that came from. I gotta say one thing about the giving habits of Muslims.

When it comes to funding their agenda, they put their money where their mouth is."

The pastor smiled. "God was very gracious in letting us purchase it on His terms though, and I'm glad for that. Let's come in and get started."

He opened their counseling session with prayer and leaned back in his chair. He'd made a complete recovery and was anxious to begin preparing them for marriage.

"I am so excited over the prospect of marrying you and Fatemah here in this new facility. Do you realize you will be the first non-Muslim couple to be married in this place?" He waved his arm at the resplendent charm the building held. "What a change God has made in this community all because you had the courage to step out and follow God."

Jared reflected on that day in the airport when he questioned God and wrestled with the whole idea of a Christian building a Mosque.

"You know Pastor, if I'd known, then what I know now," he stopped short. "If it weren't for me being obedient, I'd never have led Ahmad to the Lord, neither would I have met Fatemah." He smiled and gave her hand a gentle squeeze.

"Not to mention all the open doors God is providing for you to speak," the Pastor added.

Fatemah glance around. "I see God's hand in this from start to finish. From Jared hiring me, to me meeting Shirin and sharing my testimony with her, and through the bad things that happened, God was at work. And I'm seeing my goal of the American dream expanding to the whitened fields of the Muslim people."

"That's right, Pastor, as we study the Bible, our goal of buying into the American Dream is fading. In its place, God is birthing a passion for finding and doing His will whether it is handing out water and literature at the 'Open Hearts, Open Hands ministry or serving across the ocean."

Pastor Carlson crossed his arms and leaned his elbows on the desk in front of him. "I've been watching your love for each other grow alongside your love for the Muslim people. You need to keep in mind that your relationship must be based on agape love. The kind of love described in I Corinthians 13. Couple that with submission, honor and mutual respect for each other, and you have the foundation for a successful home."

"Thank you pastor, that's a powerful statement," Jared said.

Pastor Carlson turned a few pages in his tattered Bible. "Allow me to read from Mark 10:45, 'For even the Son of Man did not come to be served, but to serve and to give His life a ransom for many.'" He lifted his eyes and looked at Jared and Fatemah. "The Son of God didn't come in all of His regal splendor. Rather, he came as a humble servant to seek and save his fallen creation. It behooves you and me to follow his example and to serve through sacrifice." He closed his Bible, and folded his hands. "Never lose your sense of humor and adventure, as you grow old together, because in this life, there is enough sorrow around to knock you off your feet. You will need to learn to laugh and cry together, work and play together and especially learn to pray together," he counseled them.

Jared leaned forward and laced his fingers. "Pastor, we want you to help us pray for the Lord to lead us to a place where we can make the greatest impact for the kingdom of God."

The pastor's eyes danced with an inner joy. "With a heart like that, God can and will move in a powerful way. But His will might not always look big."

"Well, it's no secret," Jared said looking at Fatemah then back to him. "Because of our growing burden for the Islamic people, we thought that combining our honeymoon with a short-term mission trip would be a great opportunity."

The pastor shifted in his chair. "Where might you be thinking of going, if I may ask?"

Fatemah smiled, her eyes glassing over. "God has laid the country of Lebanon upon our hearts."

"Lebanon? Why there?"

Jared looked at Fatemah and gave her a nod. "Lebanon is the country from where Fatemah's father immigrated, where most of her family lives. It's a beautiful country, rich in culture and history."

"Yes, and a country torn with civil unrest and war."

"That's correct, Pastor, but there are over four million Muslims divided between the Sunnis, and Shi'a, who need to know the Lord."

Pastor Carlson stood and came around to the front of his desk. Looking down he said, "It sounds like your hearts are already pointed in that direction, if you ask me."

Jared nodded, "You're probably right."

A bright smile lit the pastor's face. "Well if that's so, then you can count on our church to be behind you one hundred percent."

Taking Fatemah by the hand, Jared stood, a look of steel determination burned in his eyes. "Then let the adventure begin ..."

Epilogue

The winds of change shifted in America; the collision course she was on was averted. It has been said, all it takes for evil to triumph is for good men to do nothing. Pastor Carlson and Jared took their stand and altered the course of history. Jared and Fatemah are ready to launch out on a new venture, one that will stretch their faith to the limit and beyond. They plan to spend the first days of their married lives in Lebanon—and possibly their last.

Author's Note

I am often asked the question "Is it true? Can America really be being taken over by Shari'ah Law? My answer? A resounding *yes!* It's happening in Michigan and in other states.

So how are we to relate to the changing culture around us?

Not all of us can start an "Open Hands, Open Hearts" ministry, but we can follow Pastor Carlson's timely advice and seek ways to love our neighbors. Not just the immediate next door neighbors, but, as our Lord pointed out, our neighbor is that one whom God brings across our path in His divinely appointed time.

Part of my story was affected profoundly by one such encounter. I'd stopped at a gas station to get a ginger ale for my wife, when a man wearing traditional Islamic garments approached me. He needed a few dollars to pay a locksmith to open his door. After making his request known, he added, "I did not ask an Indian or a Catholic for money because they worship many gods. There are only three religions who worship one God; the Jews, the Christians and Islam." He held up three fingers as he spoke.

Since he brought up the subject of religion, I was impressed to pull a five dollar bill from my wallet, with these words. "That is true, but only one of those religions worships a risen Savior and in the name of Jesus Christ I give you this." Then I handed him the money.

The man blinked, speechless. The love of God, struck him with full force.

I never saw that man again, but from time to time, as I pass that gas station, I pray for him and trust that, that brief exchange will bring him to the light of the glorious gospel. That's how we win the culture war, by loving them to Jesus, as Pastor Carlson admonished.

But we don't need a cultural war to reveal the hidden man of the heart. Jared dealt with racial bias, his motives were questioned, his character maligned. Not to mention his own demons of doubt, guilt, hatred for those who hurt him. All too often I find myself in exactly the same place as Jared, and I find my way out the same way he did. "Love your enemies, pray for those who despitefully use you."

I hope you enjoyed the journey as much as I did, and I trust that the metamorphous that Jared and I have undergone, you too experienced. God bless you. I hope you will join me on my next journey as Jared and Fatemah get caught in a wave of international intrigue of global proportions which threatens to tear the world apart and tests the very fabric of their marriage, in Power Play.

"LIKE" me on Facebook at www.facebook.com/brryanmpowell
Follow my Blog/Website at
www.authorbryanpowell.wordpress.com
View more books at www.thehirambookstore.alibrisstore.com

Reflection Questions

1. Which conflict affected Jared in a greater way? His conflict with forgiveness or with the people who opposed him?

2. How do you deal with these conflicts in your personal life?

3. Was Pastor Carlson's approach to winning Muslims effective? Why?

4. Which character did you most identify with?

5. Was there any redeeming quality demonstrated by Imam Fahad?

6. What human weaknesses did Jared demonstrate?

7. Was Shirin's fear of getting saved justified?

8. Do you think that Fatemah did the right thing by running away from home?

9. Who demonstrated the most change throughout the story? List the ways in which they changed?

10. List the ways God worked throughout the story to bring about His will?

Power Play – book two in The Jared Russell Series is now available and begin watching for book three – The Final Countdown.

Jared and Fatemah Russell move to Beirut, Lebanon and open the Harbor House, a safe house for converted Muslims. They hire as their housekeeper the fifteen year old daughter of the prime minister. Little did they know she is desperately trying to escape an arranged marriage. She meets Habib Hadif, a young college student with a shaded past and sparks fly. Soon they find themselves caught in the middle of political intrigue, personal crisis, and the chaos of war.

Anita overhears her father's plans to draw Israel into war, but before she can expose the plot, she is kidnapped and taken deep into Hezbollah held Syria. Meanwhile, Anita's two brothers come to America bent on stealing our nuclear codes and attacking our icons of freedom. With the world on the brink of war, Habib and Jared, set out to rescue Anita and stop her madman father before it's too late, in *Power Play*.

Made in the USA
Charleston, SC
14 February 2017